Apache Gold

A Classic Old West Story of The Strange Southwest

By Joseph A. Altsheler

PANTIANOS
CLASSICS

Published by Pantianos Classics

ISBN-13: 978-1-78987-014-5

First published in 1913

Contents

Chapter One - The Station...4

Chapter Two - The Start 12

Chapter Three - In the Desert.. 22

Chapter Four - The Lost Village 30

Chapter Five - Making A Home 38

Chapter Six - Marooned 51

Chapter Seven - Among the Stars 67

Chapter Eight - A Sudden Encounter.. 76

Chapter Nine - New Resources 83

Chapter Ten - The Lost Herd 89

Chapter Eleven - The Ancient Tower 102

Chapter Twelve - The Community House......................................113

Chapter Thirteen - The Grip of The Shaman 125

Chapter Fourteen - The Witless Dance..132

Chapter Fifteen - The Shot of Shots 139

Chapter Sixteen - "Behind the Veil" 144

Chapter Seventeen - Winter in The Canyon 152

Chapter Eighteen - Gray Wolf's Coming......................................160

Chapter Nineteen - The Mighty Defender....................................169

Chapter Twenty - The Departure..176

Chapter Twenty-One - On the Hot Sand.......................................184

Chapter Twenty-Two - The Desert Battle 193

Chapter Twenty-Three - The Last Fight..201

Chapter One - The Station

The young agent, a boy only, but large and strong beyond his years, sat at the door of the station, and he was alone in his world—he was nearly always alone. Two parallel lines of shining steel stretched away to the east, across the hot sand, and two other parallel lines stretched away to the west, also across the hot sand. On the crest of a low hill a giant and malformed cactus stood out against the burning blue sky, in the rude simile of a gallows. At times, especially in the twilight, when the resemblance increased, it seemed to offer the lad an invitation to come and make use of it.

Far in the northwest showed the dim, blue line of mountains, and Charles longed to be there among the forests on the slopes, rambling as he chose, but he took his gaze away from the temptation, and brought it back to his prison, the little railroad station, where he was agent and telegrapher, for the meager salary that he needed. Jefferson, although it had hopes, was not a large place, consisting of two buildings, the station of corrugated tin, with a glittering red roof, and the water tank. At normal periods it had a population of two, but Dick Anthony, the assistant, was off duty for a few hours—he had gone down the line on a visit to Madison, a magnificent metropolis of at least fifty people.

The boy was terribly lonely, and, as he sat in the doorway at an angle that protected him from the fiery sun, he looked around at his world, merely a circle in the desert, dotted at the center with the station and the water tank. About these two structures empty tin cans flashed in the sunlight, but beyond this area the desert showed only dead grays and browns. It was absolutely silent, seeming to have been so for thousands of years, and ready to remain so for eternity. Charles looked at his watch. The 'Frisco express, that ray out of the live world, coming and going like a spark, was not due for three hours, and he wondered how he could ever pass the time. Far to the south two or three "dust devils" rose, and danced across the desert. He watched them eagerly, not because they were a novelty, nor because anything would come of them, but because they represented motion, and, when they sank away in the sands, he sighed. The diversion was over.

He looked up at the sky. Perhaps a bird would be flying across it somewhere, but the blue was unmarred by a single dot. He groaned, and let his hands fall helplessly to his side. "How long! Oh, how long!" he repeated. Thus he sat, an athletic lad, in shapeless clothes of dark brown canvas, and lamented, because he had reason for lamentation. He remained awhile, motionless, a yellow straw hat, with a wide brim drawn down over his eyes. At last he took a novel, with paper covers, from a shelf in the corner of the room and tried to read, but it failed to interest him, and he threw it abruptly on the floor.

Charles Wayne was often rebellious, as any other youth would have been thus cast away, but his mood was stronger than ever that afternoon, and when he walked about outside, in search of distraction, he found none better than to kick savagely at the empty tin cans. They only flashed the sunlight back at him in the same brilliant, monotonous fashion.

He returned to the station, and presently the telegraph key began to chatter. It was merely the agent at Madison saying that the 'Frisco express was on time, and would take water at the Jefferson tank.

The sun was going down the slope, but the intense burning heat still hung over the earth. All things were parched and lifeless, there were no more "dust devils," but after a while, as the sun sank lower, gray shadows came out of the east, and a sudden coolness swept down from the north. Then the shining rails began to hum, and the red eye of the train looked over a bare hill.

When the express stopped and the connection was made with the water tank, Charles strolled along beside it, speaking with the engineer and brakemen, who were his messengers from the real world outside.

"Things lively in Jefferson?" asked the engineer.

"Fairly," replied Charles. "A cowboy from the Mexican border looked in about ten days ago."

"That so? You can't down Jefferson!"

The passengers, cramped by the long journey, alighted from the train, and walked up and down in the twilight, which was now full of chill. Among them was a large elderly man, with a heavy, red mustache, and a pompous arrogant manner, accompanied by a tall, slender boy about the age of the young agent.

The two walked side by side, and Charles noticed the lad particularly. He had fair hair and a fine face, but he saw that he was not used to wild life. His face and hands were untouched by tan, but he wore a suit of the finest khaki, obviously cut by a high-priced tailor, and once he looked at a beautiful, jeweled gold watch that he drew from his belt.

"A mollycoddle! only a mollycoddle!" murmured Charles. He felt for the moment a bitter pang of resentment, because the lad was so obviously favored by fortune, while the same fickle dame had resolutely turned her back upon him.

He glanced again at the man, and he thought that he had never seen a face more repellent. The narrow, heavy-lidded eyes had the look of a vulture's, and the folds beneath them continued the simile. He spoke sharply to his companion, and the boy's fair face flushed. Charles dismissed his resentment in an instant. His nature was too high to cherish such thoughts, and his sympathy was with the lad who apparently had received an unjust rebuke about something. He heard the man call him Herbert, and once he would have

5

laughed at the name. He had classed Herbert with Percy, and thought both effeminate, but now it made little impression upon him. His sympathies were still with the fair youth.

The two did not notice him, and they walked on, the man speaking contemptuously of Arizona to the boy. The conductor of the train appeared on the steps, and Charles, indicating the couple, asked him if he knew how far they were going.

"Only to Phoenix," was the reply; "but they've come through from New York. That's Mr. George Carleton, and the boy is a cousin of his, I think. I don't know who Mr. Carleton is, but whatever he is, he doesn't let you forget it."

Charles slipped away from the light and bustle of the train, which he had been awaiting so anxiously, and withdrew into the station. He was just as eager now for the train to go on, and leave him alone in his desert. The sight of the other lad had only made him unhappy. But a clamor arose, and there was the sound of a blow and protesting cries. He went out again—it was quite dark now—because something had happened; nothing had ever happened before in Jefferson, and this could not be missed.

There was a ring of people on the sand, and a commotion at the center of it. Wayne pressed into the crowd, and saw on the ground a dark figure, shapeless and repellent. He was not sure what it was, but the other form, bending over it was certainly that of a man, Jim Grimes, a brakeman on the express.

"Now you clear out o' this!" said Grimes, kicking the bundle, which groaned, and resolved itself into the shape of a tramp.

Herbert Carleton saw the rough act and became indignant.

"Why do you do such a thing? It's a shame!" he exclaimed, his fair face flushing with anger—Charles liked him better than ever now.

"Excuse me, me bold young champion," replied Grimes, ironically raising his cap. "You wouldn't say that if you had to travel through these parts and learn the tribe to which this scamp belongs. They are murderers, when they're brave enough, an' sneak thieves when they ain't. I found him ridin' on the brake beam, an' he couldn't have stood it much longer. I've saved him from sudden death, by pitchin' him off here in the sand."

Grimes grinned a little. A life of constant motion had not taken all his sense of humor. The man on the ground stirred and groaned again.

"Playin' 'possum," said the brakeman scornfully.

"All aboard!" shouted the conductor, and the train bell began to ring. Most of the passengers hurried up the steps, but Mr. Carleton, refusing to relax his dignity, would not hurry, austerely following his young relative.

Charles stood farther back in the shadow, and gazed at the lithe figure of the lad, as he stood at the car entrance, watching the tramp who still lay motionless in the sand. He plainly saw pity in his eyes, and his own sense of loneliness suddenly became overwhelming. "I, too, ought to be pitied!" was his angry thought. The engine whistled, and the train shot away into the dark. "Gone forever, like all the rest," murmured Charles, as he saw the rear light die in the desert. Again he was alone in the silence.

Charles Wayne had felt the spur of ambition already, and longed for a great place in the world, but as he had not a single relative who was able to help him, it seemed very far from the little station in the sand to any higher step on the ladder. Young as he was he had been fortunate to get even so small a position.

He returned to the station, and, lighting a train lantern, put it upon his telegraph desk. He was touching the depths of despair. The space between what he was and what he wanted to be was as wide as the world, and he felt it in its full measure. The apparition of the other boy, in his fine clothes, passing gayly from one great city to another, deepened his loneliness and desolation fourfold.

"Jim Grimes was right," he said to himself, "this life in the desert is different, and it makes people act differently."

The thought took him back to the tramp. The fellow, whom he knew to be shamming, might prove dangerous. Courage was instinctive with the boy, but having no mind to run foolish risks, he took a loaded revolver from his desk, and went into the dark. He expected to be met by an able-bodied man with a request for food, and incidentally for drink, but the tramp was still lying in the sand. Wayne saw that his eyes were fitful and uncertain, and he was struck with pity.

"Poor devil!" he murmured. "This is no make-believe."

The face that looked up at him belonged to an old man. It was seamed and wasted by the winds and heat of the desert, by want and suffering. Gaunt and hollow, it was stamped deep with the marks of decay. He was not pretty to look upon, and the boy had a sense of repulsion, but his feeling of pity was stronger.

"Do you want something to eat?" he asked, bending down.

Fear leaped into the man's eyes, as he saw the face approaching his own, and he shrank away.

"He's been running a gantlet somewhere," thought Charles, who knew much of life in a wild region, but he said aloud:

"I'm a friend, and I want to help you."

The man looked at him in wonder, and then shook his head slowly, as if he could not understand. Charles, perplexed, gazed down at his recumbent form. Here was one who was either sick or out of his head or both, and what was he to do with him? It was brutal of the railroad to throw him off there. The other boy was right.

The moon was rising slowly over the desolate plains. From the far mountains came a chill wind. Charles shivered. The stranger began to mumble something.

"What is that?" asked the boy.

The man raised his voice and said in a kind of chant:

"O'er the measureless range where rarely change
The swart gray plains so weird and strange!"
"Well, what of it?" asked the boy in anger, because the words struck upon his own mood. "They won't change for you, nor for me, nor for anybody else. We can't expect that."

But the man was not disturbed by the comment of his critic. He merely crooned on:

"O'er the measureless range where rarely change
The swart gray plains so weird and strange,
Treeless and streamless and wondrous still."
"Stop it!" cried Charles impatiently. "Tell me who you are, and how you came to be hanging under that train!"

He felt chilled and afraid, not of any real danger, but just of the world and the dark. Out on the plain the wind was moaning, and the night was growing more chill.

"Who am I, who am I?" replied the man in a high sing-song tone. "I'm nobody but Ananias Brown, nobody but just poor old Ananias Brown."

Charles was inclined to smile, but he did not do so; instead his feeling of pity deepened.

"Well, Mr. Ananias Brown," he said, "you may deserve your name or you may not, but one thing is certain, you need help."

He stooped down, lifted the man in his arms—he was very powerful for one so young, and the tramp was astonishingly light—and carried him into the station, where he put him on a bench.

"Now, Mr. Brown," he said, "we'll see if something can't be done for you. Unless I miss my guess, you've been rather short on food and water for more days than are good for anybody."

Quick and skillful, he hastened with his task. He gave him a stimulant from a flask, and then, lighting a little oil stove, he cooked eggs and strips of ham. A pleasant odor filled the room, and the stove threw out a grateful heat. Charles enjoyed the service that he was rendering; it was a break in the terrible monotony of his life, and he was helping a fellow creature.

"All ready in a minute," he said cheerfully. "I'm not such a bad cook, either, as you'll soon discover."

But his attention was called presently by the hard breathing of Mr. Brown, and his alarm increased when he looked at his face, which had assumed a grayish pallor. The wanderer was gasping and his eyes roved wildly. He muttered his western verse unceasingly, but now he never got farther than the first line:

"O'er the measureless range where rarely change—"
He began to move nervously on the bench, and threw up his hands, as if warding off a danger. Then Charles saw something that made his blood turn cold. Each palm was blackened and seared.

"I will not! I will not tell! You cannot make me!" he muttered, stubborn defiance thrilling through words of pain, while the hands moved fretfully like those of a sick man.

The boy walked to the window and looked out. The mighty desert, lying there under the darkness, had new aspects of awe and terror. Somewhere in its immensity a man had been put to the last test of cruelty.

He came back to the patient, who was growing more quiet, and offered him food, but Brown could take nothing. Charles felt his pulse and saw that it was weaker. He was assailed by a fear that the man was going to die, and he was now sorry that he had offered to do his assistant's work for a few extra hours. Dick Anthony should be there with him. He did not like to be alone in the presence of the dead. But his annoyance was driven away by the wave of pity which always returned at regular intervals.

And beneath this flood of sympathy there was an undertow of curiosity. What was Brown's story? What was it that had happened to him out there in the immensity of the desert? But he clearly saw that the man was sinking. In all likelihood he would die by daylight, and his secrets would die with him. Merely another insignificant human being lost in the vastness of the desert!

Charles went to the key, and telegraphed Madison that a man was dying in the station. Could they send a doctor down on the freight due at 12:30? One would come, was the answer. Dick Anthony, too, would return on the same train.

He went back to the man, who had neither moved nor made any sound. His features were gray and sunken, and he seemed to be asleep. Charles sat beside him a full hour before he opened his eyes. His look then was weak, but it was that of one whose mind was clear, for the moment at least.

"Do you think you could take a little food now, Mr. Brown?" asked Charles.

The man laughed a husky laugh that ended in a gasp.

"No more bills of fare for me," he said, his words coming hard. "I don't need 'em. What's your name?"

"Charles Wayne."

"Well, Charles Wayne, I'm goin' out on the great trip. It's a wonder I lasted long enough to get here. There's none of my blood, an' I leave it all to you, because there's nobody else to leave it to. I guess I owe you somethin', anyway."

He laughed weakly, and again the laugh ended in a gasp. His manner was unreal and weird, and Charles was chilled.

"Brace up, old man," he said, "you've got many years yet before you."

"I know! I tell you I know!" said the man with some irritation. "You don't understand all that I've been through! I'm goin' out, I say, an' I leave it all to you! There will be enough for you, yes, for twenty, a hundred men!"

The wild light appeared in his eyes again, and his breath became shorter. The ashy gray of his face deepened. Charles knew that the doctor, due at 12:30, would be too late. The man's fingers were fluttering. He began to

9

speak, but in such low tones that Charles could not understand without bending down.

"Enough for a hundred! Enough for a hundred!" he murmured. "I leave it all to you! Beyond the base of Old Thundergust! In the ravine with the dwarfed pines! Up and down! Up and down!"

He paused, his breath exhausted and Charles wondered what tricks of fancy, what delusions were leading him on.

"Behind the veil! Behind the veil! All yours! I give it to you!" murmured the man. He did not speak again, but, in a minute or two, raised his head slightly, and when it sank back again, the assertion of Mr. Brown that he was about to take the great trip came true.

Charles, young and healthy, felt all a boy's awe of death, but he decently covered the poor, worn body with a cloth, and then sat in silence, wishing for the coming of the 12:30 freight as he had never wished before.

The desert was quiet. Around him was nothing but empty space and the darkness. He was alone with the dead on an island in the sand. "Behind the veil! Behind the veil?" he murmured to himself after a while. "I wonder what he meant by that? What could have been in his mind then? Do those about to die indeed see behind the veil?" He tried to turn his thoughts elsewhere, but his mind came back incessantly to the words of the dying man. Moreover, Brown had left to him all that he had, whatever it was, and wherever it might be. An inheritance of air castles that he was not likely ever to find or claim.

The long hours dragged on. Sometimes the telegraph key chattered a little, but it said nothing of importance, and Charles stared vaguely at the figure of the dead man, shapeless in the dusk. "Behind the veil, and he left it all to me! Well, of all the queer bequests!" he repeated.

His mind was in a greater ferment than he knew. The impact of this tragic event upon the long days of loneliness and despair had caused a mighty stir. He was approaching the stage, at which one takes chances that, under favorable conditions, he would shun like death. He rose, and looked at his world, the bare little room with the circling rim of darkness and sand, and, once again, he was appalled by the loneliness and desolation. Then he reverted to Brown's last words—they had burned a place in his mind.

The crisis in life often comes without warning; there are no preliminary shadows and clouds, no prophetic voices, but Charles had looked upon two faces within a few hours, and each had stirred him deeply, one a boy's and the other a dead man's.

The long whistle of a train rose in the black night; it was the 12:30, and the freight was approaching. It was like a ship coming to his island in the sand, and, taking his lantern, he welcomed it. Dick Anthony, his assistant, a youth with irresponsible eyes and large teeth, sprang off, and the train doctor followed, with more deliberation and dignity.

"Is it a bad case?" he asked.

"Not now, Dr. Wharton," replied Charles gravely.

"Then it's a pretty quick recovery, and a wasted trip for me."

"The man died two hours ago."

"Ah!" exclaimed the doctor. "But it's as well that I came. I can make out the regular death return."

They went into the station, and Anthony, a voluble youth, with a head as light as a feather, was awed into silence by the sight of the still form on the bench. But the doctor uncovered the face, and looked at it long.

"The man died of exhaustion, caused by lack of food and general hardship," he said. "That is quite evident I have seldom seen a form more wasted. See the thinness of his hands."

He lifted one of the cold hands, and then he uttered a slight exclamation as he pointed to the seared and blackened palm.

"I noticed it," said Charles. "The other palm is the same way."

"The cause of it?" said Dr. Wharton.

"There is nothing to indicate," replied Charles with gravity.

The doctor shook his head.

"Nobody knows how these tramps drift out of the world," he said. "And, I presume, nobody misses them. I cannot see that there is anything to do but to bury him. You'd better put the body on a freight to-morrow, and send it down to Madison."

"If there is no objection, doctor, I should like to bury it here," said Charles. "I was with him when he died."

The doctor turned a swift, searching glance upon him.

"That is a bit of sentimentality, my boy," he said, "but it does you credit. Bury him here yourself. Of course there is no objection."

Dick Anthony did not fancy the proposition; he did not like to have the body there so long, and he said angrily to himself that he was no gravedigger. But he stood in unusual awe of his superior, who was no older than himself, and he did not venture to remonstrate aloud.

The doctor departed in an hour or two on another freight train, and Charles sat up all night with the dead man. When he saw the sun come out of the sand, and gild the bare plains with a purple and rosy light he took a shovel and dug a grave near the station, under the branches of an Australian eucalyptus, brusquely declining Anthony's feeble offer to help. Then he made a coffin out of an old pine box, and buried Ananias Brown.

After he had filled in the grave again, he put a board at the head, and proceeded to cut upon it the proper inscription. But he hesitated at the name "Ananias." "That couldn't have been his real name," he thought. "Every man is named when he is a baby, and nobody would burden a baby with such a thing as that. I think I'd better call him John Henry."

So he cut upon the board "John Henry Brown, Departed This Life in the Desert," and then he gave the date.

After that he felt better. In fact, Charles Wayne was stirred by an unusual exhilaration, and it was all because he had made a resolve. He went back to the station and Dick Anthony, who had been leisurely watching him from the doorway, asked:

"All through now, Charlie?"

"Yes; except one thing. I've got to send a message to the division superintendent at Phoenix."

"Is the old man kicking?"

"Not at all. I merely want to give him my resignation."

Dick Anthony stared at his young chief.

"Now you know you're joking," he said. "You can't get another job."

"I don't want another, and I'm not joking. Here goes my message, and I'm only hoping that the superintendent will make you chief here in my place."

He sent the resignation, and in an hour the request came from the superintendent that he call, as soon as he could, at his office in Phoenix. Another man would be sent to Jefferson in the afternoon, and, confirming the request of Wayne, Dick Anthony would be made chief there.

"It's all right, Dick," he said. "You are to succeed me."

But Dick Anthony was not overjoyed. Perhaps the slight awe that he felt of Charles increased his attachment to him, and he did not like to be left with a new man.

"It's going to be lonesome without you, Charlie," he said.

"It has been lonesome with me," said Charles, looking out at the gray desert.

He packed his small baggage, putting his money carefully in the inside pocket of his waistcoat, and, after a good-by to Dick Anthony, took the train in the afternoon for Phoenix. The last thing that he saw in Jefferson was the new head board of the grave under the eucalyptus.

Chapter Two - The Start

Phoenix is a city literally created out of the desert by the hand of man, who has known how to draw the life-giving waters, and spread them where he would, and, like any other oasis, it shines and attracts by contrast with the sands. The burning sunlight of the afternoon had just begun to soften when Charles Wayne approached, and the sight of green grass, fresh foliage, and trees hanging with fruit was like a vision of delight to him. The effect of everything was heightened. How very green the green was! The water in the irrigation ditches actually seemed to him to sparkle in silver, and such oranges as those on the trees never grew before. He sighed in deep content. Phoenix was coming into fame, and to Charles it was all that it had promised.

He went at once to the office of Mr. Gray, the Division Superintendent. Mr. Gray was sorry to lose so capable a lad, and asked him to reconsider; he thought that they could give him a better office in a few months, and while promotion was slow, yet, in a case like his, it was sure. Charles shook his head.

"I thank you, Mr. Gray," he said; "but I've decided to try something else."

Mr. Gray's curiosity was aroused, but he would not ask any questions.

"This, you understand, is the middle of the month?" he said.

"I know," replied Charles, "and I should leave at the end of the month; I don't ask any salary for the two weeks."

"I think we will pay you for the full month," said the Superintendent. "It is not usual in the case of a sudden resignation, but we shall make an exception with you. I hope that the money won't trouble you."

The boy was moved by this liberality, and he replied frankly that it would be welcome.

"Do you go east or west?" asked Mr. Gray.

"I think I shall stay in Phoenix a little while."

"Then come in and see me again, and, if you should change your mind, and wish to return to our service, don't hesitate to say so."

When Charles left the office the sun was just sinking in the plain. The great splash of rainbow lights that marked its going lingered for a few moments, and then came the dark. The electric lights flamed out, and the vivid night life of the little city began. The awful feeling of loneliness and desolation swept over Charles again, because he knew no one there, or at least no one to whom he wished to speak just then.

He strolled a little in the streets, keeping as well as he could in the shadow, and he came at last to a hotel with a wide piazza, where people from the east, travelers of wealth and leisure, sat in the evening and talked of wonders, some of those that they were seeing in the west, and others of those that they were leaving in the east.

The group upon the piazza was larger than usual this evening, the last limited having brought many who wished to stop in Phoenix.

Charles saw Herbert Carleton and the elderly cousin among them. Both were in evening dress—the boy wearing a dinner jacket—as were other eastern people. Charles felt again the pang of envy that he sought so quickly to stifle. Everything for the other boy, nothing for him! But he did not succeed in crushing the feeling, and then he felt a little pity, too. This other boy was not in good hands. Charles had lived a rough life long enough to read the human countenance, and he knew that George Carleton was a bad man.

He stood in the grounds awhile and then turned away to seek the obscure little hotel at which he was staying, and to sleep, but when he had gone a hundred yards a small man, with a large head, wonderful white teeth, and a pair of beautiful gold glasses astride his nose, put his hand upon his shoulder.

"Pardon me," said the stranger in a well-modulated voice, "but can you direct me to the Pacific Hotel?"

"It's but a short distance," replied Charles, with the ready comradeship of the border, "but I will not give you any directions. As that is my own destination we can go together."

The little man, without a word, turned and beckoned violently. A figure of great height, crowned by a small round head, the chief feature of which was a nose of alarming length and thinness, emerged from the dusk, and stood waiting.

"My follower, assistant and friend, Mr. Jedediah Simpson of Lexin'ton, K—y," said the little man. "Do not say Lexington, Kentucky, but Lexin'ton, K—y, which he thinks is always sufficient."

The tall fellow grinned good-naturedly, and, when he grinned, his face was cleft from side to side.

"You are very kind," said the little man trotting by Wayne's side, while Jedediah Simpson of Lexin'ton, K-y, followed on behind, "but I find most people in the southwest obliging, when you don't try to mind their business."

Charles glanced at him again. He wore a hideous pith helmet, like those of the English in India. From one pocket of his gray Norfolk jacket protruded the head of a little hammer.

"You look at me inquiringly, and I suppose you can guess my occupation from this hammer," said the little man merrily.

He took it from his pocket and twirled it deftly as a drum major does his baton. Then he laughed again.

"I use this, not for cracking heads, but for cracking rock," he said, and Wayne almost fancied that he could see his eyes twinkling behind the big glasses. "I am a scientist, a geologist, an archæologist, and several other things. I am Professor Erasmus Darwin Longworth, at your service. I am from the University of—Sh! but I won't tell you what university it is; that must remain a secret."

"Why?" asked Charles, amused at the stranger's air of importance and intense earnestness.

"Because another man has come to the southwest for the purpose of anticipating me in the discoveries that I hope to make," replied Professor Longworth venomously, "and I do not wish it to be known yet that my university is represented here."

Jedediah Simpson of Lexin'ton, K-y, nodded his head violently as if he fully shared the Professor's feelings.

"Do you mind telling the name of the other man?" asked Charles, still amused. "It may enable me some time or other to give you warning of his coming."

"He is Professor Nicholas Humboldt Cruikshank. We are rivals. Mr.—Mr.——"

"Wayne—Charles Wayne."

"Mr. Wayne. No, Charles, I'll call you; you're too young to be Mr. Never believe a word that man says! He is no geologist! He is a fraud! I've never heard

14

of his boasted books nor of his honorary degrees! He is certainly a beginner, and he is merely following me now for the sake of profiting by the discoveries that I am going to make!"

"I am sure of it, Professor," said Charles soothingly. "Such conduct is low and base to the last degree."

"I expect to prove," continued Professor Longworth, "that Northern Arizona is now the oldest land above water. It is generally thought that the Laurentian Mountains in Canada have that honor, but I assure you, my dear boy, it is a mistake, a terrible mistake. I will prove it by means of geological specimens, but, as surely as I do so, that scoundrel Cruikshank will step in and claim that he, too, has the proof, and that he got it first."

Jedediah Simpson again nodded his head violently.

"I think not, Professor, I think not," replied Charles.

These complimentary remarks soothed Professor Longworth, and he gave way to no more outbursts until they reached the hotel. But there, when they entered the lobby, his face turned purple, and he struggled with an inarticulate cry of rage.

Leaning against the clerk's desk was a tall, thin man, clad just like Professor Longworth; the same enormous pith helmet, the same heavy glasses, and the same Norfolk jacket. Also from the pocket of the Norfolk jacket protruded a little hammer.

"Cruikshank! Cruikshank!" Professor Longworth at last ejaculated.

Walking up to the long man he shook his fist in his face and exclaimed:

"Cruikshank, you have followed me here to profit by my discoveries! I have said to others that you are a fraud, and now I say it to you!"

"Longworth, I should strike you if we did not both wear glasses," said the thin man. "And your accusation, sir, is as false as your reputation for learning. It is you who have followed me. Keep away, sir! I want no trouble with a man of your caliber, or, rather, lack of it."

Professor Longworth grew purple again and Jedediah Simpson drew near the threatened conflict, but Charles interfered between the rival scientists.

"Come, come, Professor!" he said to his new friend, "it's too late to quarrel. Let's talk."

Professor Longworth allowed himself to be persuaded, and went with Wayne to the lobby, followed as always by Jedediah Simpson, while Professor Cruikshank remained, leaning scornfully against the desk. They did not stop in the lobby, but passed to a little piazza, where the three sat down, Jedediah Simpson keeping a little in the rear.

"I shall ask your pardon, my lad, for showing passion before you," said the Professor with much dignity; "but we scientists and students of old things are sometimes stirred deeply by matters which seem trifles to other people, but which, nevertheless, are important to us. It is not alone the rivalry which this man Cruikshank offers, but I have never been able to place him. I thought

I knew, by reputation, all the very learned men in America, but he is new to me, and the fact annoys me."

"Jest say the word, Purfessor, an' I'll go in an' thrash him," spoke up Jedediah Simpson.

"Good gracious, no, Jedediah!" said the little Professor hastily. "We don't do things that way in the world of learning. You'll overlook Jedediah's violent and primitive ways, Charles. It's true he was born in Lexin'ton, K—y, but his parents were mountaineers, and he has inherited their instincts."

"But I was shore born in Lexin'ton, K—y," said Jedediah Simpson with unction, "an' nothin' can take that honor from me. An' as fur violence, Purfessor, you didn't mind it that time in the South Seas when I h'isted right overboard the chief who wanted to whack you on the head with his club."

"No, Jedediah, I didn't. You saved my life, and I'm grateful. You've saved it more than once, and you're likely to save it again. Although Jedediah has his faults, Charles, he also has his virtues, and he is a wonderfully handy man. He has a delusion, however. He thinks he was born to be a great musician, and that chance or fate has defrauded him."

"Wouldn't you like to hear me sing 'Poor Nelly Gray' and play it on the accordion?" asked Jedediah Simpson proudly.

"Not now, Jedediah! Not now!" said the Professor in great haste. "Spare our young friend."

"All right," replied Jed, calmly. "Mebbe he ain't used to music, an' it has to be broke to him gradual. But when I get rich I'm goin' to have in my house every kind o' musical instrument thar is. Mebbe I won't play 'em all, but they'll be thar, an' I'll know they'll be thar, even while I'm asleep."

"But it isn't so easy to get rich," said Charles.

"There ain't no tellin'," said Jed with cheerful philosophy. "They say the mountains up in these parts are chuck-full o' gold, and mebbe me an' the Purfessor will strike a mine when we are lookin' fur funny rocks."

"As I said," remarked the Professor, "Jedediah has his virtues, and one of them is an unfailing optimism—a great, a most precious quality."

They talked a while longer, and Charles felt a strong liking for both. Eccentric they certainly were, but they seemed to him interesting and sincere.

"You'll beat Mr. Cruikshank, Professor, you'll beat him. I have no fear of the result," said Charles at last. "And now I'll tell you and Mr. Simpson good night."

He passed through the lobby on his way to his room, and he noticed Professor Cruikshank still there, his attitude unchanged. Evidently he was watching his rival. Charles smiled, despite himself. "It ought to be a pretty fight between them," he thought.

He had checked his valise on his arrival, and now it was taken up to his room by the Mexican servant. The apartment was small and bare, a fact that did not trouble him, as he was used to the border, and was thoroughly tired.

"Where put him, boss?" asked the Mexican who brought the valise.

"Oh, anywhere," replied Charles; "and that will do. I don't want anything more."

The Mexican put the valise down near the door, and went out, Charles put himself in bed and went to sleep. Then he had a succession of dreams flitting after one another; one was of a lad whom he had envied, sitting on a piazza in the dusk of a semitropical evening, another was of himself lost among high mountains, and a third was of a swarthy man like a Mexican, who entered his room and made a minute search through his clothing and valise.

The last dream was so vivid that Charles awoke and sat up. He seemed to hear the sound of a faint footfall and of something closing softly, and, after that, the intense silence of a house asleep.

He took his revolver from the pillow under his head, stepped out of bed, and lighted the lamp. There was no one in the room, and the door, which in his haste for sleep he had left unlocked, was closed. But when his eyes fell upon his valise he started. The valise was open.

The boy quickly examined the contents. Nothing was missing, although all the articles seemed to have been moved about. Then he looked at his clothing, and he was confident that not all the garments were lying where he had left them before going to bed. But everything was there, even to the gold watch and loose chain in the waistcoat.

Charles was puzzled. He was sure that someone had been in the room, but nothing was taken, although there was enough to tempt any sneak thief. "Who was he, and what could he have wanted?" was his unspoken query. But he now locked the door with care, and, being too young and healthy to be bothered long by mysteries, was soon asleep again.

He rose early and ate breakfast, but when he came from the dining-room the thin, long figure of Professor Nicholas Humboldt Cruikshank presented itself in his path.

"Young Mr. Wayne, I believe?" said the Professor in nasal tones.

"Correct," replied Charles. "I am happy to meet you, Professor Cruik-shank."

"Pardon me for intruding or interfering at all in what is your business, but I wish to give you a warning, a warning that you will do well to heed. I saw you in close converse last night with that arrant humbug, Longworth. Have nothing further to do with him, sir. The man is a pretense and a mockery, a gross fraud. He has not really earned a single one of his degrees. He is always stealing from me. He has, in fact, stolen enough from me to make a reputation for himself."

"But, Professor," said Charles, "I am sure that, even after those unfair losses, you have sufficient left to make a great reputation for yourself."

"You are a clever lad," said Professor Cruikshank, obviously pleased. "Do you do anything in geology yourself? I am going forth presently on an expedition to prove that the oldest ground now above water is not the Laurentian Chain in Canada, as is generally supposed, but Northern Arizona."

"Now here, indeed, is a pretty fight," thought Charles, for the second time, but he said aloud:

"It is an arduous quest that you are undertaking, Professor. Arizona is large, and there are deserts and mountains in plenty."

"I am glad of it," said Professor Cruikshank triumphantly. "They do not daunt me, but they will keep back that rascal, Longworth. If you are not employed, may I suggest that you go with me? I can pay well, you are young, but you seem very strong, and you can be of valuable assistance, in a material way, while I attend to those finer, I may say, almost spiritual, things pertaining to science."

"I thank you very much, Professor," replied Charles hastily, "but I cannot do it, as I am thinking of going to 'Frisco in two or three days."

The professor expressed his regret, and Charles, with a word of adieu, left him. He did not like Professor Cruikshank, while he had liked Professor Longworth. In neither case could he give the precise reason why.

He spent the day in preparation for a long journey, and made his purchases with the greatest care—a horse and a pack mule, warranted strong and faithful, a collapsible tent, two breech-loading rifles of the finest make, a large supply of cartridges to fit the rifles, another revolver to match the one that he already had, a compass and blanket, some mining tools and canned and dried food that would give the largest possible amount of nutriment in the smallest possible space.

The boy had many errands, but, as he was swift and skillful, it did not take him long to do them, and, by the middle of the afternoon, he was back at his hotel with his goods around him. Here he read some important items of information in his evening paper. The first stated that Mr. George Carleton and his young cousin and ward, Herbert Carleton, rich and conspicuous New Yorkers, were in the city, and would shortly go northward to look after valuable copper mining properties.

The second paragraph chronicled the arrival in Phoenix of two distinguished scientists, Professor Erasmus Darwin Longworth and Professor Nicholas Humboldt Cruikshank. They were about to conduct investigations, the paper said, which would give Arizona a place in the world, even more conspicuous than that which she now enjoyed.

A third item stated that two ranchmen had been wantonly slain by Earp's band of outlaws in the northern part of the territory, and that pursuit seemed to be hopeless, the trail having been lost among wild and inaccessible mountains. A fourth stated that Apaches in the tangle of peaks and ridges to the north had become troublesome.

Charles was very thoughtful after reading these paragraphs, and he decided to hasten his departure, going at night, instead of waiting until the next day. Prospectors, tourists, health seekers and others were continually leaving Phoenix by horse and mule, and his own obscure exit would not be likely to attract much attention, but he was not willing that it should have any at all.

He had left his horse and mule at the stable, from which he bought them, and his other supplies, by his orders, being sent there, nothing was left for him to do but to pay his bill and leave the hotel, which he did unobtrusively just after dinner at the twilight hour.

As he turned away from the clerk's desk the thin, long figure of Professor Cruikshank presented itself, and stretched out a hand.

"Good-by, my boy," said the geologist; "I wish you luck, but I am still sorry that you could not accept my invitation and go with me."

"Why do you assume that I am about to leave?" asked Wayne in some surprise.

"I saw you putting change in your pocket, and I knew that you must have paid your bill, which we are not in the habit of doing at a hotel until we are ready to go. Ah, my boy, we scientists are much cleverer and much more observant than you think we are."

Charles smiled at his rather childish pride, but did not see fit to make any comment.

"Good-by, Professor," he said. "I sincerely hope that we shall meet again in the west."

The Professor returned his good-by, and gave him a grip of amazing power for a thin man.

"I suppose that comes of wielding a geologist's hammer for twenty-five or thirty years," thought Charles, as he slipped away quietly in the dim street. Everything was waiting for him at the stable, and, quickly saddling his horse, he loaded the supplies on the mule, riding away through the streets, past the irrigation canals, and on into the bare country, beyond the habitations of men. He would have liked to tell Professor Longworth and Jedediah Simpson good-by, but he thought it best not to look for them.

The night was good. Clear stars swam in a vast blue sky, and the air, though chill, was full of freshness and vigor. The boy, inured to the border, thrilled with a sense of freedom and hope. He was released from the monotonous round at Jefferson that was dwarfing him, mind and soul, and he was his own man. His was truly a quest in the dark, with only the slender guidance of a few scattered words, but young blood flushed his veins and told him not to despair. The desert, so lonely and terrible to him at Jefferson, was neither lonely nor terrible now; he was a part of it, a sharer in its immensity and majesty; he did not feel the want of either guidance or companionship.

He rode on steadily for hours, and the mule, with the stores, followed faithfully. The night grew more chill, and then he walked for a while beside the horse until the circulation was restored. Occasionally he repeated the cabalistic words: "Beyond the base of Old Thundergust! In the ravine with the dwarfed pines! Up and down! Up and down! Behind the veil! Behind the veil!" and then came the grim refrain:

"O'er the measureless range where rarely change
The swart gray plains, so weird and strange,

Treeless and streamless and wondrous still."

With that echo in his ear the old feeling of awe that the mighty desert gave him came back, although it could not endure long in the face of his new hope.

Toward morning he slept a while on the plain, and then resumed his journey under a blazing sun, in a measureless sea of sand. All day he traveled, his eyes dim with the heat and glare, and his tongue parching in his mouth. But when the sun, burning into red and gold, sank in the western desert and the twilight drew a great cool canopy between the earth and the molten sky, the last of the dancing "dust devils" passed out of sight. From the far mountains a gentle breeze stole down, and wandered over the sandy wastes. Charles felt its pleasant breath upon his face, and his tired brain grew strong and fresh again. His eyes were soothed, as if a soft wet cloth were pressed upon them, and his whole frame vibrated with thankfulness.

Nor was fortune unkind. Just after the sun had gone he came to a kind of dip or valley, between high hills, where underground water, seeping down, rose to the surface and formed an oasis. In a fresh, green country it might not have seemed much of a place, but, compared with the sands of the desert that stretched away on every side, it was a little Eden. The horse, as they rose upon the last sandy ridge, scented the water, and, raising his head, uttered a neigh of thankfulness that the mule echoed as best he could. They went down the slope at a swifter pace, and Charles uttered a little cry of joy of his own at the sight that rose before him.

In the shade of some green trees a tiny fountain bubbled from the earth, ran away a distance of fifty yards over hard sand, in a stream two feet wide and three inches deep, and then sank into the earth, whence it had come. But there were trees, bushes and grass on either side, filling all the space of the little valley. Water and green, the most blessed of all things to the eyes, soothed the vision and, as he rode into the grass, birds rose and whirred away in fright.

He and the animals drank deep at the little stream and then he turned the horse and mule loose. No need to tether them! They would never wander from the green oasis and the water into the brown sands. Then with a desire for company—the household flames are company—Charles built a fire of fallen brushwood, and, sitting before it, ate his supper of crackers and dried beef.

The little oasis, the fire, and the boy sitting beside it were but a pin point in the desert. The sandy swells, rising on all sides, would have hidden the flames from anybody only a few hundred yards away, but Charles, in all the immensity of the desolation, did not feel lonely. At the telegraph station, bending over the monotonous telegraph instrument, he had been sick of the desert, and pining for the haunts of men, but now a great peace and calm came over him, and his mind was soothed and at rest. He was free; in a way the world was his; he was on a quest, but at the moment he felt no anxiety about it; he might or might not find the gold, but in either event he should feel glad that he had come. The mighty wilderness, the desert and the silence suddenly made a new and wholly different appeal to him. They were not lone and bare, but were clothed in a majesty that was suffused with kindness. Over him curved the twilight heavens, protecting and good.

Darkness flowed steadily out of the east; in the west, the last spark from the sunken sun died, and gave way in its turn to darkness. Into the blue sky the stars came one by one, and twinkled down kindly on the single human figure, sitting in the vast desert before the fire. The boy ate a little, and then drew closer to the flames, because the night wind had begun now to grow chill, and the desert that burned a few hours before with fiery rays was touched with an icy breath. Presently he built the fire a little higher, and also wrapped himself in a blanket The animals, tired of cropping the green grass, came nearer to the flames and warmth, and stood, looking contentedly at their master.

Never was one more absolutely alone than this boy, without kin or friends or acquaintances. He still sat by his little fire, but all the while the peace that lay over him was deepening. Old instincts, hidden in his nature, which, without the magic, awakening touch, might have lain forever dormant, were stirring within him. He was beginning to give to the wilderness not only his friendliness, but his love as well. The spell lay upon him.

From a point far out on the desert came a weird, plaintive cry, but the boy did not stir. He knew that it was only the howl of a lone coyote, and such things now troubled him not at all. The coyote came nearer, lay at the edge of one of the sandy swells, and gazed, with red eyes, at the formidable human figure beside the fire. Then his heart filled with fear, and he crept away over the desert.

Charles rose after a while, walked to the crest of the enclosing sandy swell, and looked to the north. Always to the north! No other point attracted him now. He fancied that he could see vast dim mountains through the loom of the darkness, and they beckoned him on. He stood there a full half hour, gazing in the direction in which his quest led him, and then he turned back, walking slowly to the fire. He chose a smooth place, and, wrapping the blanket about himself, prepared to lie down. He hesitated, and then he did something that he had not done since he was a little lad. He knelt upon the grass and prayed, prayed to a vast, infallible Presence, not a God of fear, nor a God of revenge, but to a great merciful Deity who knows our weakness and temptations, and who will forgive. Then he lay down and slept at once.

The night thickened, but the boy lay, a shapeless object before his fire. The fire itself soon died, and all the oasis was in darkness. The full moon came out, and, as the heavens turned to a sheet of silver, the night grew lighter. But the boy still slept and stirred not. The birds, that his coming had disturbed, came back, and settled on the branches of the trees. They were not afraid. All the desert was at peace, and the hours passed one by one.

Chapter Three - In the Desert

The lad slept long. He had been keyed to high tension, both physical and mental, and nature now demanded the price of many hours from youth and health. The night sank away, and the day flooded the earth with a great light of white and yellow, in which the yellow gradually gained upon the white. The sun, in time, turned to glowing brass, and the desert quivered under the hot and pitiless glare. A single vulture of the southwest wheeled slowly in the blue.

Charles Wayne awoke at last, and found, to his surprise, that the noon hour had passed. Yet he was not sorry, knowing that, in his case at least, the maxim of more haste less speed was true. Moreover, he had all the time there was.

He rebuilt his fire, ate a little dinner, and again he was ready for the trail, but he advanced slowly, resolving that he would do most of his traveling by night, and rest in the day to escape the heat and glare.

He came after a while to the bed of a creek in which flowed a slender rill, and he followed it steadily to the north. By and by the bed of the creek widened out, the living stream disappeared, but here and there were tiny pools of surface water, with green grass around them, a fortunate thing for the animals, and better than he had hoped. He arrived at a pool larger than the rest, and in its muddy edge he distinctly saw the traces of horses' feet. How many had passed he could not tell, but he reckoned at least six or eight, and the fact set him to wondering. Who were they? He followed the traces to the hard plain, but there, being no experienced trailer, he quickly lost them. He concluded, however, that they were only cowboys, not worth the trouble of another thought, and he went on.

Weird night came again, black and vast, enfolding the earth. Charles still clung to the friendly creek bed, for the sake of the water to be found there, and continued his course. He did not stop until nearly midnight, and, once more, fell asleep, as soon as his preparations for bed were complete. But his slumber that night was troubled. He dreamed again the bad dream that he had dreamed at Phoenix. Someone, whose face he could not see, was in the tent, searching minutely through all his belongings. He saw the man dimly, from eyes heavy with slumber, which at last overpowered him, and he did not awaken until the day. Then he remembered his dream, and again he found evidences of another presence than his own. His goods were moved about, but, as before, nothing was missing.

In the sand of the creek bed in front of his tent he saw traces of footsteps, evidently those of only one man. The horse and the mule had not been disturbed. The boy, western born and bred, was not superstitious, but he felt a chill. If he had seen the stranger twice, in what then looked like a dream, how often had the man come when he was not seen at all? What did he want?

That was the strangest part of it. This constant search, and the taking away of nothing was beyond explanation.

But with his breakfast before him, Charles forced himself to believe that it was, after all, a dream, and that the footsteps in the sand had been made by some wandering cowboy. He drew comfort, too, from the fact that he was always left unharmed, if it should prove to be other than a dream. Nevertheless, the circumstance induced him to hasten, and, after eating, he left the bed of the creek and struck out across the desert.

Now he was amid the desolation of sand and cactus, a burned, dreary, God-forsaken land, hot sand under a hotter sky, in which every scanty little shrub seemed to say wearily, "I thirst." Now and then a "dust devil" whirled on the horizon, but nothing else that moved met his eyes. Once he passed bleaching bones, but he would not stop to see whether they were those of man or beast, and rode on, not looking back.

The dust, picked up by stray gusts of wind, powdered the boy and his beasts until they were a ghastly whitish-gray. Fine and stinging, it crept, too, into his eyes and ears and down his back. But he pushed steadily on. His lips parched, and his throat grew hot and husky. He moistened both with a little water from the Indian bottles that he carried—how cool and glorious it was to the taste!—and he craved more, but he resisted the temptation; he knew how precious water might become.

Charles had only a general idea of the country, but he believed that he could pass this portion of the desert before nightfall, and he was both brave and hardy. In fact, he felt less fear for himself than for his animals, which were very necessary to him.

Toward noon he stopped once on the crest of a bare hill and examining all the horizon still saw nothing but desolation. The desert stretched away on every side, bare and endless. He was gripped for the first time by a sudden fear. How could he, a mere dot in the wilderness, succeed in such a quest as his?

He crushed down the fear and rode on, not so fast as before, but with a strong heart. The sun passed the zenith, but was hotter than ever. He felt himself grow dizzy in the fiery rays and the desert danced before him. Blue peaks, with green slopes beneath, rose out of the sand, but he knew that it was only a trick of his heated fancy, and he permitted himself no such false cheer. Again he spared a little of the water, and poured a portion of it down the throats of the animals at the imminent risk of losing it all, and then went doggedly on. The wind rose and clouds of dust and alkali swept over him, filling eyes and nostrils, and scorching like hot ashes. The horse neighed wearily, but the mule plodded along with his head down. The sun shone through the haze like a great globe of molten fire.

The horse began to stumble and at last Charles got down and walked, finding some relief in the physical exertion. He sought vainly through the clouds of dust for the blue of the mountains, but he refused to despair. He was well aware that his life was in danger, although he resolutely shoved the fact aside, drawing instead upon those deep wells of tenacity that were in his nature. He had the invaluable quality that causes one to grip all the harder when defeat seems certain, and with head bent and hat well down over his eyes, he plodded resolutely forward in the way that his compass told him to go.

The afternoon touched the zenith of glare and heat, and then began to decline. The sun faded into the west and night came, where the burning day had been. The dark and the coolness were grateful, but the boy was still on the sands, where naught lived but the cactus. The water in the bottles was low, none to spare for the beasts now, although they neighed pathetically, and he slept at last, wrapped in his blanket.

He rose in the morning, with a clearer and stronger head, but with a dry throat and aching limbs, and resumed his flight over the gray desert. Presently the sun shot high again, and glowed with living fire, but from the deeps of Charles Wayne's tenacity fresh courage rose. The spirit of combat flamed out, he would match himself against the desert, and he would conquer, his victory all the greater because of his foe's greatness. He knew that he was lost, but he was resolved to find himself.

The hours passed and the little dot that was a human being still struggled over the immensity of the plain, the head bent lower perhaps, and the steps somewhat slower, but the spirit as firm and high as ever. Behind followed the two animals, the horse first, and then the mule.

Noon came and passed, and again the heat and glare were at the extreme point. Charles once more saw a mirage, a mountain slope with pine trees on the side and the hope of green grass and water. But when he rubbed the sand from his eyes, he knew that it was reality and no false hope; the mountains were there, they refused to move away, but stood immovable, awaiting his coming. The animals raised their heads and hastened their steps, and if he had doubted himself, here was the proof of keener instincts than his own.

Charles felt all the joy of victory, all the surge of a strong spirit that has triumphed over a great enemy, and new strength created itself in him. To his sanguine courage it was also an omen of other and greater success yet to come.

Although he increased his speed the mountains did not seem to come nearer, they were before him, solid and blue, a fortress, but the thin, clear air was deceptive, and he knew that where one mile seemed to be, there were ten. The ground grew rougher, running away in waves, and his feet sank in the sand. He shifted his stores to the horse, and tried riding the surer-footed mule, but the animal, exhausted by the heat and lack of water, stumbled so badly that he dismounted and took his place again at the head of the dusty and weary little procession. Then as the sun began to wane, a storm of dust and sand came out of the south, and clothed him about in darkness and suffocation. He struggled through it a long time, fiercely resolving that he would not yield, but staggering more and more, and beating the air with his hands like a blind man. His senses wavered. Again and again, with the force of his will, he called them back to their duty, but at last they wandered away into infinity, and he fell unconscious upon the earth.

When Charles returned from the vague country to which he had gone so suddenly, he was lying comfortably upon his back, with his head upon something soft, and he looked up at a clear sky, in which a peaceful moon and peaceful stars swam in the same old placid way.

"Ha! our young friend is taking notice at last!" said a jerky, merry voice. "That canteen again, if you please, Jedediah, and we'll see how he likes a draught of the pure and beautiful. This is not the vintage of Flora, 'cooled in the deep-delved earth,' but it is something a good deal better for you, namely, fresh water."

The boy sat up abruptly. Before him was the short figure of Professor Longworth, merry and perky, beneath his huge helmet, the canteen of water in his outstretched right hand, and the long figure of Jedediah Simpson just behind him.

"You may drink deep, my son," said the Professor, "because as you have already imbibed while in your unconscious condition the stage of approach has been passed."

Charles needed no urging, but promptly drank deep, and the fire of life coursed anew through his veins.

"It was a lucky thing for you," said the Professor, "that my scientific investigations led me in this direction. You fell almost in sight of the promised land, scarcely a mile from trees and water. In fact, the instinct of your two animals caused them to continue, and when we brought you here, we found them drinking peacefully along the slope, not fifty feet from where you are now lying."

"Professor," said Charles gratefully, "you have saved my life, and, of course, I can never repay you, unless I find a chance to save yours."

The Professor chuckled merrily.

"Say no more about it," he said; "but it proves that we scientists are sometimes better plainsmen than you who do nothing but roam the plains. Exact knowledge, founded upon mathematics and an observation of nature's processes for thousands of years, is not to be beaten."

"I yield, Professor," said Charles humbly.

Professor Longworth, M.A., Ph.D., etc., sat down upon a fallen pine stem, adjusted his glasses, and regarded the boy critically.

"It strikes me, my young friend," he said, "that you have not taken the direct route to San Francisco, where you told me you were going. There is a railroad from Phoenix to that city, but the way that you have chosen is long, hot, tedious, and, as you now know, not without dangers."

Charles flushed. He was truthful, not liking to tell even an innocent falsehood under the stress of circumstances, and liking still less, if he should have to tell one, to be caught in it. He hesitated a little, and then he decided that it would be best to come somewhere near the truth.

"I fibbed a little there, Professor," he said, "As a matter of fact, having a great deal of time and very little of anything else, I decided to prospect a while through the mountains. Whenever a fellow does that he grows secretive, with or without reason, and here I am. That's all there is to it."

"It's enough," said the Professor with irony. "I was young once myself, but young men remain a cause of wonder. You risk your life in a search for what you have not one chance in a thousand to find. Moreover, it would be a bald, uninteresting accident if you found it, while I am armed with knowledge and all the exactitude of science, which, with mathematical and absolute certainty, is bound to lead to a result; the only doubt is about the nature of that result, and in that very doubt lie the charm and mystery of my expedition."

"Again I yield, Professor," said Charles humbly.

Professor Longworth glowered at him for a few moments through his great glasses, and then resumed cheerfully:

"At any rate, we are here. The desert is passed, there is water for drinking, game may be found in the mountains, and life should not be wholly unpleasant. Let that suffice for the present. Now, as the night is young, if you will eat a little of the food that Jedediah has ready for you, and then go to sleep, you will find profit in it."

This seemed to Charles good advice, and he was ready to take it, while he lazily watched the Professor pottering about on various little offices. He was lying on soft pine boughs and his head reposed on a pillow made of his own saddle with a blanket spread over it. The Professor's party consisted only of himself and Jedediah Simpson, but they had several animals. Various articles scattered about indicated thorough equipment, and Charles was bound to confess that the scientist, indeed, had shown more prevision than himself, who, presumably, knew something of wild life.

The boy's confession brought no sting to him now. He felt a most singular comfort, both of the mind and the body. He was on the slope of the mountain, and he lay in a pine forest. Below him and far out glimmered the gray desert, which still threatened, but now in vain. Grass grew here and there, grass thick and rich by contrast with the bare plain, and as he lay he heard at last that most wonderful of all sounds in a parched land, the trickle of running water.

The moonlight brightened and then he saw it, a baby waterfall, a stream that he could step over, falling down a mighty precipice almost a foot high. But it glittered bravely in the rays of the silver moon, and to the worn eyes of the desert traveler it looked like the stream of life. And such it was!

Charles, despite his willingness, could not go to sleep just yet. He was deeply grateful to the Professor, and he did not rest easy under a sense of obligation. Yet he did not see how he could repay him, except in one way. He could confide to him the object of his search, take him as a partner, and then they might push on together. But he hesitated, the Professor's mind seemed to be on other things, and his proposal might not be taken at its full value. He concluded that, on the whole, it was better to wait.

His sense of peace and ease increased. Far up the mountain side he heard the wind among the pines, and its tone was like music to him. The fire near him burned red and cast out a glowing heat. The great stems of the pines began to waver at last, and then the boy hastened away to the land of dreamless sleep.

When he awoke in the morning the fire was burning more merrily than ever, and there was a most persuasive odor of cooking food. He sprang to his feet, a little ashamed of himself. He was not willing to let others serve him, and he so young and strong.

He drank at the little waterfall that he had admired so much by night, and he admired it not less by day. All his supplies he found in a pack, neatly arranged for him.

"I had Jedediah clean out the dust and the alkali," said Professor Longworth. "You would have found them very annoying."

"Jest you set still," said Jedediah Simpson, "it ain't no use to fuss yourself up, when the best cook this side o' Lexin'ton, K—y, is gettin' breakfast an' is enjoyin' his task."

"Better do as he says," said Professor Longworth. "Jedediah is a really wonderful cook, and he does not like to be interfered with."

The coolness of the early dawn was still in the air, and a singularly pleasant aroma was arising from strips of bacon that Jedediah was frying over some coals. A few moments later another aroma, that of glorious coffee, arose and mingled with the first. Then Jed sliced bread that he took from a box, and set out three tin plates.

"Ef you can find a better meal in Arizony than this is," said he to Charles, "I'd like for you to show it to me. Me an' the Purfessor have traveled in strange lands an' we have hobnobbed with strange people, but wherever we have gone, I've hung on to this here old dishpan, this an' my accordion that's packed on one o' the mules. Ef you want me to, I'll git down that accordion after breakfast, an' play you 'My Old Kentucky Home.' It's a pow'ful movin' tune."

"Never mind about the tune, Jed," said the Professor hastily. "This is wild country and Apaches might hear it."

"What ef they do? 'Music hath charms to soothe the savage breast' is an old proverb, an' I guess it would work here."

Nevertheless he refrained from taking out the accordion, and the three sat down on the grass to the finest breakfast that Charles whose appetite was of the keenest had ever eaten. The boy's heart warmed to the two men, and he was sorely tempted to mention his quest, but after all they were little more than strangers. The Professor spoke.

"Charles, how old are you?" he suddenly asked.

"Nearly eighteen."

"Hum! Well, you are large for your age, and your birth and life in wild sur-roundings have made you courageous and resourceful, but you are neverthe-less young to be so deep in the wilderness alone. Yours is bound to be a very dangerous quest."

"With nobody to cook your victuals," said Jed.

Charles was moved again to confide in them, but again he refrained.

"I must go on, Professor," he said.

A shade of sadness passed over Professor Longworth's face, but he said no more on the subject. Presently the shade of sadness was replaced by an un-mistakable look of anger.

"I made a terrible discovery a little while ago," said the Professor in omi-nous tones. "The worst that I feared has happened."

His countenance bore out fully the import of his words, and, Charles, in silence and apprehension, awaited his further explanation.

"Jedediah and I have found the trail of footsteps," said the Professor, "and I am sure that the rascal and fraud, Cruikshank, is in these mountains near us. He is spying upon me. He wishes to reap the reward of my labors, to profit by an intelligence that he knows to be vastly superior to his own. We must evade him!"

Charles wondered at the bitterness of this rivalry, but he reflected that science was everything in the world to these men, and hence there might be cause for it. It was not for him, whose mind was on other things, to criticize them.

Jed packed quickly under the directions of Professor Longworth, whose manner became abrupt and decisive. Charles was in a quandary, not seeing his own way clear, but the Professor promptly solved it for him.

"We leave you, my young friend," he said. "Although you had a bad time of it in the desert, you know how to take care of yourself. This duel is none of yours, and it would not be fair to drag you into it. It must be fought to the bitter end by Cruikshank and myself. I wish you success in your search, as I know you wish me success in mine, and I hope that we shall meet well, suc-cessful and happy in Phoenix, say, six months hence."

His animals stood loaded and ready, Jed was waiting, and, springing upon one of the horses, Professor Longworth led the way rapidly. Charles stared after them until they were lost among the pines on the slopes.

"Professors are certainly queer," he said. Then he turned his attention to his own affairs, which now seemed to him to promise well. The sun was again a glittering ball, and the heat entered the pine woods, but he sat by the side of the cool rivulet, and studied the little map of his own making that he had taken from his pocket and that had never left his person night or day.

Somewhere in the vast chain of mountains upon whose fringe he now was, towered Old Thundergust, his white head high among the clouds, and be-yond His Majesty, the peak, the road led, but by the vaguest of directions. The immensity of his task once more was borne upon him, but did not appal him. He calculated that Thundergust was yet at least a hundred miles away, but he could travel nearly all the distance through the vast pine forest which occupies so large a space in Northern Arizona, and whatever happened at the end of it he would have a journey worth remembering.

Despite his absorption of mind and his intense interest in the great quest, he felt lonely now. He missed the Professor and Jed of the musical mind. When he had wondered at the Professor's queer words and abrupt departure, he did not know that they had perhaps been caused by the man's own sorrow at leaving alone in the wilderness a youth whom he had learned to like—perhaps that more than geological rivalry.

He rode steadily for two days in the direction in which he surmised Old Thundergust lay, and now he enjoyed the march, though often the way was rough and not without danger for both man and beast. At the end of the second day he shot a deer, and, as he saw a new stretch of desert ahead, he stopped to dry and cure the meat which he would certainly need.

He made his camp in a little glen, that contained a water hole, and here he luxuriated, feeling how he had grown since he left Phoenix, how his muscles had toughened, and how his self-reliance had increased.

He yet had all the time there was, and knowing it, he let one day slide into another while he lingered. The weather had been misty, as if threatening an unusual rain, but now it cleared until the air became of a transparent brilliancy. Then Charles saw a beautiful white dome showing in the north, and he knew that it was Old Thundergust. He was flushed at once with zeal and enthusiasm, and a half hour later was on the march again.

The new desert was not as bad as the first, and he crossed it in a few hours, riding straight on toward Old Thundergust, who rose before him, grand and white, always growing in size and majesty.

He again reached the foothills, the pine trees and little streams that trickled down the slopes, and now he began the semicircle around Old Thundergust which would take him to the northern side, a task of several days. He explored for two or three days more, and, at last, he came to a deep ravine almost choked with dwarf pines, but leading in a general way toward the north, the bottom of the ravine gradually ascending, but its cliffs rising and falling in height. He felt sure that this was what Ananias Brown had meant by "up and down, up and down," and his heart, suffusing with joy, bounded within him. He had taken the longest of chances, merely an opinion formed from the few vague words of a dying man, but his hope was coming true, at least so far; one link in the chain would lead to others.

It was hard footing in the great ravine for the animals and at one of the widest and smoothest portions Charles stopped to camp, although it was only a little after the noon hour. He had killed small game and he had an abundance of food. At the bottom of the ravine flowed a creek or little river, now narrow and deep, now wide and shallow, and feeling that he lacked nothing he made himself easy.

After dinner, while the animals grazed, he climbed the side of the ravine. It was a hundred feet up, but as the slope was gradual and bushes grew in plenty for support, he was soon at the crest. Here the sweep of his eye took in a vast expanse of broken country, but when he looked again, he saw something that gave him an unpleasant surprise. A thin blue line of smoke to the eastward rose up and lost itself in the bluer sky. Somebody was trespassing upon his domain!

The boy felt all the rage of one whose rightful possession has been assailed by impudent interlopers. The whole country, as far as he could see, was his by right of occupancy! Who were they, and why had they come? But he was a youth of action, and his resolution was quickly taken.

Chapter Four - The Lost Village

Charles descended the bluff to his camp. He had not built a fire, and he had no apprehensions on that point. The horse and the mule would not leave the wide space in which they were now grazing, and there was nothing to hold him back from the expedition that he had planned. He took one of the rifles, a beautiful weapon of high range and power, from his pack and filled his belt with cartridges. Then he started.

He reascended the cliff, and struck off across the broken country toward the blue smoke, which yet lay like a line across the bluer sky. His feeling of jealousy, even rage, against the strangers increased, yet he intended no violence, unless in his own defense, and the necessity of the latter was never improbable in so wild a country. It might be either Professor Longworth or Professor Cruikshank, but he did not consider it likely, as he had thought they would turn much farther to the eastward.

The way was slow, broken by hills, ravines and cliffs, and the sun shone down like fire, but the boy with the rifle and the resolute eyes would not turn back. The wisp of smoke grew larger, and, at last, from the crest of a low hill he looked down upon a camp, and those who had made it.

When Charles gazed into that camp he drew a breath deep and long. Never before in his life had he felt so much surprise. On some pine boughs sat the handsome boy, Herbert Carleton, whom he had seen at Jefferson, and again at Phoenix. He was in a khaki suit as before, but he was much tanned, and the suit showed many signs of wear and travel. He seemed tired and anxious, and Charles felt a thrill of sympathy. The throb of envy did not come now.

Not far away stood Mr. Carleton, sour of countenance. Three or four men, guides or servants, were engaged in various tasks, and animals for riding or the pack, grazed on the thin grass.

Charles' amazement abated when he remembered the story of the copper mines that he had read in the Phoenix newspaper. Doubtless they were prospecting.

He spent a half hour on the hill, and, when he turned away, he was very thoughtful. As he went back to his own ravine, he began to have a fear that not nature alone, but man, too, was in the way.

The animals were still grazing and as Charles prepared for the start, intending to camp further on, he noticed an impression near the edge of the tiny rivulet, where the earth was fairly soft. He was not trailer enough to say decisively, but it seemed to him that it was the outline of a human foot. He stared at it and tried to persuade himself that a mountain lion had made it—which, indeed, seemed likely—but he could not do so. The obsession that man had passed there was upon him, and he was not able to shake it off.

It was about three o'clock in the afternoon when he resumed his march, and he resolved, if the character of the ravine continued the same, to push on far into the night. He did not doubt, as he pondered the last words of Ananias Brown, that he had come to the first part of the trail, but the next steps puzzled him. The words "behind the veil" were mystic, cabalistic; they seemed to bear no relation to the others, yet he was confident that the relation existed. But how was he to connect so meaningless a statement with the surface of a country? He saw nothing to do but to keep on, and to recognize the phenomenon whatever it might be, when he came to it.

The floor of the ravine smoothed out considerably, and also widened, making his travel easier. Down the center of this cut flowed the stream, shallow but clear, and of a coldness that indicated its source far up among the snows on some soaring peak.

The scene now became one of the most solemn loneliness and grandeur. Looking down the gorge he saw range on range of mountains, guarded here and there by mighty peaks like bastions. Often the ranges were bare, vast walls of stone, shot in the sunlight with red and purple and blue turquoise, that shifted and changed as the rays fell. Again, the pines hung in fringes of green on the slopes, and now and then through them came that most grateful of all sights in a dry country, the flash of running water.

Once he heard a quiver among the bushes on the slope of a ravine, and he saw the tawny form of a mountain lion scurrying away. His sporting blood leaped up, and he longed to follow, but his search forbade it. An hour later his animals raised their heads and the horse whinnied uneasily. "Another mountain lion," thought Charles, though he saw nothing, and gave the matter no further attention. Soon darkness came down thicker and heavier than usual, and changing his mind about further travel in the night, he decided to camp where he was beside the stream.

A feeling of uneasiness due, he thought, to the knowledge of the presence of others, in the vast domain that he had taken for his own, kept him from building a fire. He sought to dismiss this foreboding, but it refused to go and lay heavy upon him.

He ate but little, and, tethering the animals, he wrapped himself in a blanket under a pine tree. The night had voices, the moan of the wind among the pines, the rustling of some small animal in the bushes, and the chirp of an insect, but Charles paid small heed to these things. It was his own littleness in the immensity of all this space that made him lonely.

He fell asleep, and then awoke, oppressed by an extraordinary sense of coming evil. He lay with his ear to the earth and, either in reality or in fancy, he heard cautious footsteps. That some one was near he felt with all the power of intuition, and, in that tremendous desolation, he who came at night, treading softly, must be an enemy. Charles always slept with a rifle by his side, and reaching out his hand he grasped it. The feel of the cold steel barrel was to him as the touch of a friend. He heard the animals moving restlessly, and his belief that it was time for him to be wary was confirmed.

It was very dark in the gorge. A good moon rose high in the heavens, but its pale rays did not reach him where he lay, and the trees, the earth and the stream were blended into a black blur. He still listened with his ear to the earth and he was confident that he heard again the soft crush of cautious footsteps.

His blood chilled. A danger that comes in the darkness, and without a name, a danger that may be one part reality and one part fancy, can awe the bravest man, and Charles, who had acute sensibilities, now felt all this mysterious dread. Yet it was not fear, because he was alert and ready to encounter it, if he must. He slipped from the blanket, and, holding the rifle, rolled noiselessly to one side. He had listened to the lore of the frontiersman, and he felt sure that if an enemy were near, the spot where he lay had been marked already by the one who sought him. So he left the blanket there in a dark, long shape, like that of a man, and, when he had gained a few feet by rolling, he rose to his hands and knees and crept cautiously into the bushes. But even his sense of impending evil could not make him forget the indignity of such a position, and he felt a great mental relief when, a rod or two away, he sank on his knees in a clump of bushes, the rifle held firmly in his hands.

Charles was now higher up the slope of the gorge, and, looking down on the place where his blanket lay, he could still see its dark and huddled outline. But nothing stirred. The animals had ceased their uneasy movements. The moonlight filtered in wan rays down the cleft, and the boy, with his hand upon a deadly weapon, ready to use it, began to believe that he had been a prey to the darkness and loneliness, and to nothing else. Yet, with the instinct of caution, he did not move, but crouched lower and lower among the bushes, blending completely with the dark.

The moonlight shifted, and the wan rays fell in a circle about the place where he had slept. Then he thanked God for his premonition of fear, and his quickness to act upon it. Out of the darkness came a face, hideous with the

32

passions of the brute, a face blackened by generations of a burning sun and distorted by equal generations of cruelty, the face of an Apache warrior, the most pitiless of all the Indians. Even at the distance and in the dusk the boy could see the savage gleam in the yellowish eyes.

There was no talk of an Indian uprising, no trouble with the Apaches, but here in these wild mountains who would ever know? Charles again thanked God for his intuition. The hideous face came farther into the moonlight, and after it the creeping body, naked to the waist. The boy knew perfectly well that he was the intended victim, and that the dim shape of his blanket was taken for himself. He filled with horror and repulsion at the sight of the midnight assassin, and his finger crept nervously to the trigger of his rifle. But prudence told him to withhold the bullet, and he waited in silence.

The Apache crawled forward, not making the faintest noise, until he was within a yard of the blanket. Then he evidently saw the fraud, and, swiftly turning about, disappeared in the bushes. Charles could read the savage mind, which at that moment feared an ambush, and he was sure that he was in no farther danger at present. But the hideousness of the dark face remained with him, and the chill was yet in his blood. Factors of a varying nature and of which he had never dreamed were entering into his search, and he must take account of them.

He must warn the Carletons of this danger, and he never hesitated. Careless of his own risk, he hastened down into the ravine and secured his animals which were able to clamber out of the cleft at the most gradual slope.

Charles, as he scaled the cliff, felt a quiver now and then, as if the bullet of the Apache were coming, but he was not attacked. There was no noise, save that made by himself and his two beasts. But when he stood on the crest he felt deep and intense relief. He paused only a moment or two to draw a deep breath, and then, mounting the horse, the mule following, he rode back in the direction in which he believed the Carleton camp to lie. In the distance rose the white dome of Old Thundergust, and, with its guidance, he believed that he would not go astray.

He came out upon what may roughly be called a plain, much broken, however, by swells and corresponding depressions. Here it was lighter, the moon's rays finding no obstruction, and he could see across the sweep of low country to the mountain ranges, with Old Thundergust towering among them like a frosty-headed king.

His was a good and faithful horse, but the way was rough, and he stumbled more than once, until Charles, doing as he had often done before, dismounted and led him. The mule trotted loyally behind, and, if there was any pursuit, the boy knew nothing of it.

The night waned, and he yet saw no sign of the valley in which the Carletons had camped. The day came, and peak and ridge swam in the glittering light. Afar rose the thin blue spire of smoke, and his heart beat joyously.

The spire of smoke broadened, and Charles saw that he was now coming very near. For the first time since the appearance of the Apache he felt embarrassment; in what manner should he approach the Carletons, how tell of his presence and why he had come? He was almost at the crest of the last ridge, enclosing the valley in which the Carleton camp lay, and he paused there a moment to gather his thoughts and consider what was before him. The sun poured down fiery rays and, in their luminous glare, Charles was silhouetted against the rocks, a brown, dusty figure, but instinct with strength and vitality. Far above a wide-winged vulture wheeled in the vault of blue.

The brown and dusty figure suddenly straightened up, as if quickened into new life, stood a moment at deep and surprised attention, and then seized a rifle from his saddle bow. Charles had heard something that turned his blood cold, the sound of a shot, then of another, and then a cry. Weapon in hand he sprang to the edge of the valley.

It was a trim little valley, with pine trees, good grass and running water, the best of places for a camp, but now it was filled with terror and confusion. One man had fallen face downward in the grass, another was clasping his shoulder where the bullet had struck, and even as Charles looked he fell shot through the heart this time. Brown, hideous faces issued from the undergrowth, and Herbert Carleton, impelled by this sudden and awful terror that had come upon them, was fleeing, certainly the wisest thing for him to do. He came straight toward that point in the rim of hills where Charles stood, although he neither saw Charles nor dreamed that he was there.

Charles noticed a savage pursuing, and knelt on the rock, raising his rifle. Never in his life had he taken calmer and steadier aim. It seemed to him that he could see the black spot on the forehead of the warrior where the bullet struck, and, whether he could see it or not, he knew that the Apache would never move again.

Another second, another cartridge shoved in, and another Apache fell, then a third bullet struck among them, and they recoiled from the rim of hills that sheltered such an unexpected and deadly foe. Without rising, Charles shouted to Herbert to come on, that friends were near, and Herbert, obeying the tone of command in the strong voice that bade him hasten, reached the crest of the hill. In an instant Charles dragged him over it.

"Come!" exclaimed Charles to the panting boy. "We must run for it!"

"But the others!" cried Herbert Carleton, his courage rising even in that terrible moment. "We can't leave them!"

Charles cast one swift backward glance at the little valley.

"It's too late to save anybody!" he cried. "It's too late even to try!"

Herbert looked also and shuddered. All were down, and certainly there was no hope for them. Saying no more he ran with this new and resourceful friend until they reached smoother ground, where one mounted the horse and the other the mule.

Charles knew that the Apaches, daunted for the while by his three deadly bullets, would recover soon from their confusion and follow; he knew, too, that the desert had never bred a tribe of men more cruel and tenacious, and in his anxiety he fairly urged the horse and mule into a gallop over the rough and broken ground. He knew that the only chance of escape lay in reaching some corner that they might be able to hold against all who came, and hence he resolved to return to the ravine.

"Sit steady," he said to Herbert, and his tone was firm and encouraging. "If we reach a place I know, we can beat them off."

Then they galloped over the rough ground, Charles explaining who he was, and telling frankly that he was looking for gold, although he said nothing about the secret of Ananias Brown.

"It's certainly been lucky for me that you came wandering through this wilderness," said Herbert. "What an awful thing that was!"

"Brace up!" said Charles, reaching over and tapping him on the shoulder— he knew that Herbert was thinking of Mr. Carleton and the others. "You'll get out of this all right."

The two boys, reared so differently and hitherto treated so differently by fortune, exchanged glances. Suddenly they felt like brothers. A single terrible moment had bound them together.

Charles looked back once or twice, but he did not see the Apaches. He did not expect to see them. The rocks and the mountains burned in the sun; nothing stirred; nothing lived. The stillness of death and desolation seemed to hang over the vast wilderness, and this very quality of it was at this moment the most terrifying.

An hour, two hours passed and they entered the pine forest beside the great gorge. When they were in the darkest shadow of the pines, Charles told Herbert, who was riding the horse, to dismount.

"We are going down into a deep ravine, and the horse might fall with you," he said.

"All right," said Herbert with a little laugh, "you've been a good enough friend for me to trust you."

They dismounted and led the animals. Presently they were at the bottom of the ravine, beside the little stream of water that trickled over the stones. Charles' plan, formed in their hasty flight, was to push on, at their utmost speed, up the canyon, abandoning the animals, if the way should prove too rough for them, until they came to some defensible point, such as was likely amid the rocks; there he would stake all on their ability to hold off the Apaches.

They continued their flight up the ravine, which grew narrower and deeper, with dwarf pines and cedars clinging to the steep slopes, taller trees of the same kind on the crests, shutting out most of the hot sunlight. Thus it was cool and shadowy below.

After many hours they stopped. Both were stiff and tired, and Herbert staggered at first, but walked to a rock, sat down, and smiled faintly.

"What you need now," said Charles, "is food and drink. Food I have in my pack, and water flows in plenty before us."

He spoke with a gayety that was not wholly assumed, and produced crackers, dry venison and a canned vegetable.

"Eat," he said, and Herbert obeyed. They drank out of those curious Indian bottles, which retain water almost at the temperature of ice on the hottest day, and then they replenished them at the brook flowing before them.

Charles was now bright and cheerful, and Herbert, too, showed great relief for a while, but presently his face saddened again, and Charles saw a tear on his cheek. Charles knew of what he was thinking, and he named the many things in their favor. More than ever he felt that this boy whom he had saved was a brother, a younger brother, as it were.

They did not deem it wise to linger, and resumed the journey up the ravine. They were following the stream, and presently the canyon opened out into another and still larger one, down which a creek of considerable size was flowing. As they advanced the walls rose rapidly, towering above them, vast masses of black basalt, sometimes sheer like the side of a house, and then sloping a little. Far overhead showed a dim strip of sky. Charles' eye at last was caught by something in the face of the cliff.

"We'll climb up there," he said.

He sought the easiest way to ascend it, and at the base of the cliff he found a place that looked as if an ancient path, now overgrown with bushes, had been there. It seemed significant to him, but he said nothing of his thoughts to Herbert, and led the climb up the old trail, leaving the animals in the canyon. It was steep, but all along he saw evidences that man had been there, how long ago he could not say, perhaps centuries, but the proof was unmistakable. In one or two places the old path had been cut partially out of the side of the cliff, and it led diagonally across the side of the wall, but always upward, as if to some predestined end.

Far above the stream they came to the object that had caught Charles' eye, and Herbert uttered a little cry of surprise. Half built in the cliff and half cut out of it was the semblance of an ancient dwelling, with a low, arched door, that one could enter only by kneeling. It opened upon a sort of terrace, and farther on were a dozen or more ancient houses just like it.

"What are they?" asked Herbert Carleton in wonder.

"The cliff dwellers have lived here," replied Charles. "These houses may have been cut out a thousand years since, and they may have been abandoned by their builders four or five centuries ago at least. But, in my opinion, somebody else has been here since then. Whether that is true or not, we are in luck—wonderful luck."

"In what way?"

"Cliff dwellers never became such for the love of it, but for the sake of defense. These houses I fancy cannot be approached, except by the path along which we came. Above the terrace the cliff rises almost like a wall to a great height. A vigilant defender ought to keep off many enemies here, and that is exactly what we will do. Just wait a moment, will you; I intend to pay a call in this house."

He knelt down and entered the first of the dwellings, having no fear of anything, except perhaps snakes, which might have made a lodging in the abandoned interior. Once on the inside, he stood up at his full height and listened intently, but heard no rustling nor fluttering to indicate the presence of things that creep or fly. Light entered at one or two apertures, but not enough to illuminate the dusky interior, and, after some hesitation, for fear of a possible accumulation of gases, he struck a match.

He stood in a small, low room, his head almost touching the roof that had been practically carved out of the stone side of the cliff. After his eyes became used to the dark he saw the whole interior. Against a wall leaned a rude ladder of sticks, tied with thongs, at equal distances on a pole. Some fragments of broken pottery lay on the floor, and on a shelf, also cut out of stone, stood two earthenware vessels like water jars, quite sound and whole. The place in a region having so little rain was free from damp or mold.

At the eastern side of the room was another opening, which led to a stone tank or reservoir, cut out of the mountain side. A little canal, to gather the flood rain on the slope higher up, led to it, and the tank was quite full of good water, hundreds of gallons. It was evident to Charles that the water poured down into the tank after a rain, displacing the water already there, thus constantly replenishing and refreshing itself.

The discovery of the tank and the water gave Charles more joy than anything else he had seen, and put the cap on his satisfaction. The tank could be approached only through the house, and the house could be reached only by the path, along which he and Herbert had come. Standing by the side of the tank he looked out upon the great ravine with an exulting eye. "We are masters here," he thought. "Neither Apache nor any other can come without our consent."

He slipped back through the opening, and saw a look of relief on Herbert's face at his return.

"This," he said, putting his hand on the arch over the low opening, "is the Château de Carleton. I name it after you, Herbert. It is dry and comfortable, I assure you. The next good one we'll name after myself, the Castle of Wayne."

"No snakes in there?" said Herbert.

"Not a snake, and as for scorpions and lizards, we can soon set our minds at rest on that point."

He reëntered the room, Herbert going with him, and they poked about in all the corners, among the fragments, and in the little clusters of dead leaves, which, in the course of time, had drifted in at the openings. Again there was no stir of any kind, but, in turning over the leaves, Charles' eye caught an object that had a peculiar dull color. He picked it up and found that it was a coin with the date of the seventeenth century upon it, but not much rusted. He stepped to the light, and examined it minutely. Although he could not read it he knew the inscription to be Spanish or Portuguese, and judged that it was a coin known in that century as a piece-of-eight.

He turned the gold piece thoughtfully in his fingers. Either of two inferences might be drawn from its presence in the abandoned cliff dwelling. Spaniards of the olden time had been there, or Indians who knew Spaniards had brought the coin. It must signify something, and it helped to strengthen a conviction that had long been forming in his mind. Herbert, absorbed in the search for reptiles, had not noticed, and deciding to say nothing about the coin for the present, Charles slipped it into his pocket.

"No scorpions, no snakes, no anything!" exclaimed Herbert. "Perhaps not as well swept and garnished as we could wish, but not to be despised! And we know, too, that the terms will not be high!"

The sun was declining, and glowed redly on the other side, until each bastion and pinnacle of stone stood out in luminous light like carving. The pines and cedars showed deep green in the glorious sunlight. But the side on which they stood was already dusky in the shadows, and the two boys, when they came outside, gazed at the ancient cliff house with a certain awe, a feeling that came from the mystery of it. Those who built the village had been gone for centuries, and no one would ever know who or what they had been.

"We must prepare for camp," said Charles cheerfully, and Herbert nodded in silent assent.

Chapter Five - Making A Home

Charles descended to the floor of the canyon, and removed the packs and all the trappings from the animals, leaving them to wander at will, because for the present they could be of no more use to Herbert and him, and he and Herbert could be of none to them. But he might reclaim them some day, and, patting each in turn on the back, he bade them a regretful farewell, knowing that they would find grass and water in the canyon and would not suffer.

Then he carried the baggage up the path, and laid it in a heap at the door of the house.

"You seem to be preparing for a comfortable stay," Herbert said.

"I like good hotels when I travel," Charles replied, "and if they haven't the proper equipments, why I just help them out."

They put most of the supplies inside and Charles found that Herbert had already been at work, clearing out the leaves and trash, and all the silt of generations. He had raised a great dust, but it was being blown away now by a little wind, and the place would be habitable. Herbert's cheeks had become flushed by his labors, and his eyes sparkled with interest. He had forgotten for the moment the tragedy in the valley. Charles glanced at him with approval. It was apparent that there was good stuff in this eastern boy, whom he had taken to be coddled and dandyish, and west and east were surely going to be great comrades.

Then the two looked again at the tank full of water, and contemplated it with great satisfaction.

"I suppose it was to save those old, old people the trouble of going down into the canyon after it!" Herbert said.

Charles nodded.

The night now rapidly covered the gorge, and pinnacles and bastions of stone faded away in the darkness.

"Supper time," said Charles.

"All right, I'm good and hungry," said Herbert.

"We'll eat it in the open air," said Charles, "and if you'll only wait a moment I'll bring you the menu. Ah, here we are, water fairly cold, biscuits, sardines and dried venison! What more could you ask? And we'll take it cold tonight, too; it's rather late to light a fire; it would consume time, and we are both tired to death and sleepy."

He rattled off the words glibly, especially those about not lighting the fire, and Herbert accepted, without question, the reasons that he gave. The night, as usual, came on full of chill, but Charles had two blankets in his pack, and each wrapped one around his shoulders.

"I think it's time to sleep," said Wayne. "Your lids are drooping, and old Nod wants to claim you."

"I'm about all in," said Herbert with a little laugh; "but I think I'd rather sleep out here in the open air tonight. I should feel as if I were smothering in there."

"All right," said Charles. "It's not a bad idea."

Herbert, wrapped in the blanket, stretched himself luxuriously on the terrace.

"I'm going down the slope a little," Charles said, "and I'll take a rifle. Maybe I'll see a deer coming up the valley in the moonlight, who knows? And there will be fresh meat for us. Be back soon."

He shouldered the rifle and clambered down the path a space, but his thoughts were not on any deer. That for which he looked, and which he feared to see, was altogether different.

A third of the way and he stopped, looking up and down the canyon upon a scene of weird grandeur. The floor of the canyon was invisible in the darkness, and the lofty walls seemed to stand without support. Far away the dim, white head of Old Thundergust lowered through the mists of the night.

The tall youth himself, although he knew it not, was at that moment in unison with the scene. Burned by the sun, leaner and stronger than ever, he bent in the path, the rifle held ready in his hands, keen eyes searching the dusk, and keener ears listening intently for the slightest sound. He was now agitated by the same emotions that had often moved those cliff dwellers, gone long ago. He looked for something which he hoped would not come, but if it should come? His hands moved down the steel barrel of the rifle, and the eyes were stern and menacing. Far away in dim antiquity, the cave-man stood in the way, club in hand, and threatened the foe who sought to invade his home.

The clear stars rose in the sky, and the moonlight silvered the gorge. Crags and pinnacles appeared once more through the luminous haze. The weird majesty of the scene had now a weird beauty, too, but Charles, intent, watchful and menacing, did not notice it. The primitive youth still remained, and the rifle barrel was yet thrust forward in a threatening gesture, ready to drive back the invader. At last, he turned and crept quietly back up the path, half-cut, half-trodden centuries ago by those mysterious people, come out of the dust, to which they had returned.

Herbert awoke at the sound of his footsteps.

"Find that deer?" he called sleepily.

"No," Charles replied, and in a moment Herbert was asleep again.

Charles also wrapped himself in a blanket, and lay down at the edge of the terrace. But he had no intention of sleeping that night. He rolled over presently, and lay with his ear to the stone, trusting now to sound rather than sight. It was the darkness covering so much of evil and evil attempt that he feared most, and, though his senses, dulled and wearied by exertion and intense anxiety, cried out for the opiate of slumber, he steadily refused the boon. He lay there a long time, alive to anything that stirred, his eyes scanning, as far as they could, the dim path which was the only approach to the dead village. He heard nothing but the soft breathing of the wind up the canyon.

Once he rose and going to the head of the path, again tried to probe the dark ravine. But his eyes could not reach the bottom, and he went down the way a few steps. Then he listened, and still heard nothing but the faint wind. He began to hope that his fears were idle, that he watched in vain, but, while hoping, he had no thought of ceasing the watch. Eye and ear were as keen as ever to detect what they might.

But the night passed away without event, and a day of unimagined splendor came. A magnificent sun rose in a sheet of unbroken blue and clothed mountain and valley in the most vivid light, searching out every crevice and cranny on the slopes, and filling the canyon with golden beams.

Charles felt a deep sensation of relief. It would not be easy in all this wonderful light for the Apaches to effect a surprise, and he believed now that they had lost their trail long since on the broken ground. Perhaps they did not know at all of the cliff house in the great canyon! It was very likely, and he began to have a feeling that they were safely hidden from all pursuit. His spirits sprang up.

He walked over, touched Herbert lightly on the shoulder, and in a moment the other boy was awake, a little confused at first, but in a few seconds remembering.

"I've had a fine sleep," he said springing up. "Didn't you have a good one, too, Charlie, old fellow?"

"As good as I wanted, Herbert," replied Charles.

Thus they glided easily into calling each other by their first names, and Herbert did not notice that the rims of Charles' eyes were red from the lack of sleep.

"I'm going to get breakfast," said Herbert. "I'm going to show you that I'm of some use, and that I know a lot about camping."

"All right," said Charles. "Pitch in."

But Herbert first went through the opening to the stone tank filled with water, into which he dipped with a little tin bucket, taken from the pack. Then he dashed the water over his face, and he felt renewed strength and energy. Despite himself, he began to thrill with the feeling of a great adventure.

"After all, the Château de Carleton is not such a bad hotel, is it?" he said gayly.

"Best the country affords," replied Charles in the same tone.

Charles then turned his gaze back upon the path, which he felt that he must yet defend, while Herbert quickly prepared the breakfast, a task light enough in itself, as he had to take only the cold things from the pack. But he craved something warm, and he was glad when Charles said:

"Open that little tin case and you will find an alcohol lamp and alcohol, and there's coffee in the canvas bag; I don't have to say more."

Herbert found a certain pleasure, a sharp relief in doing these tasks; hitherto, he had been passive, a mere looker-on, while his comrade had done everything. He felt that he, too, ought to serve, to have a part in their great work, and now was his first chance.

Despite all dangers, they enjoyed their first breakfast together. Charles still sat in the doorway, rifle in hand—he did not dare to leave it—while Herbert brought to him the food and coffee, the latter steaming, fragrant and very welcome.

"I think that the Château de Carleton is to be congratulated on its cook," he said, "and when the hotels in San Francisco and Denver hear of him, well, salary will be no object."

He kept one eye on his breakfast and another on the trail.

"I want to see the ravine," Herbert said. "How peaceful it looks and how free from the presence of man!"

"Apaches may be there, though I think not. We yet have a long time to watch and wait."

"And I'm going to have my turn at it," Herbert said decidedly. "They could scarcely creep upon us in the daytime without my seeing them, and I mean to take a rifle and keep guard."

Charles saw that Herbert was already developing under stress and danger.

"Are you a good marksman?" he asked.

"I've had training," replied Herbert proudly. "Give me one of the guns and I'll show you—if there's any need to use it."

Charles saw that he could be trusted, and he handed him the rifles and cartridges. Then he confessed that he had not slept at all throughout the preceding night, and Herbert was properly indignant.

"It's time you were asleep," he said.

Charles saw that he must yield, whether he liked it or not, because Herbert told the absolute truth. After the food and coffee he was feeling already a sharp tendency to sleep. His senses were growing heavy, and a thousand little tendrils were pulling down his eyelids. He handed one of the rifles and the cartridges to his comrade.

"Those are yours," he said. "Now watch the path. Danger can come only that way, and if you see anything doubtful call me at once."

Herbert sat in the doorway where he could command the trail, but was well sheltered. Charles lay down on a blanket in the room, but he had put it in a spot from which he could see Herbert, although the boy did not know it. There he lay, and though already numbed with sleep, he did not lose full consciousness for a while. But Herbert's figure became dimmer in time, and he was wafted away on the wings of sleep, still, dreamless and heavenly. When he awoke, Herbert was yet sitting in the entrance, the rifle across his knees, and he seemed not to have changed his position at all.

Charles thought at first that he had slept only a few minutes, but the waning shadow of the sun across the terrace told him that it was late afternoon. He sprang up, amazed and annoyed with himself.

"Say, Herbert, I didn't mean to leave you there all that time," he said; "but—but——"

"But as you were asleep you did not know anything about it and could not help it."

"Why didn't you wake me?" he asked reproachfully.

"Why should I have done so? Besides, I have watched well. Nothing has come up the path."

Charles, from his coign of vantage, examined the ravine and slopes, and could notice no change anywhere, no sign that an enemy was coming. He felt sure now that they were well hidden.

So they relaxed the watch somewhat, and Herbert told Charles how they had come northward to look after the copper mines and then had wandered further in search of gold. Tears again came into his eyes for the cousin who was not a good man, but who had perished so tragically.

The second night in the ancient village came on, dark and close, the skies, for the first time in many months, shot with clouds. Far off toward Old Thundergust were swift bright strokes of lightning which cut for a moment the vapors drifting over the slopes. The air grew thick and heavy.

"If there's a storm," Charles said, "it will be worth seeing, and, in addition, we'll have fresh water in our tank. We must not forget these advantages."

The flashes of lightning ceased for the time, Old Thundergust faded away in the dark, the clouds swung low to meet the rising vapors, and the canyon, and all that it contained, was blotted from their view. But the mountains began to groan, and the ominous sound of wind fighting its way among peaks and through gorges came to them.

The clouds and the vapors parted before a burning stroke of lightning, and thunder rumbled far among the peaks. The clouds grew thicker and heavier, and presently they seemed to open bodily, and let the rain fall out. But the two boys, secure in the old cliff house, watched the storm break and pass. The next morning came and Charles was awake, when the first spears of blazing sunlight shot above the vast ranges of blue mountains in the east. Herbert was still asleep, and, going forth from the low hut that the mysterious cliff dwellers had built centuries ago, he breathed the morning air, sharp with the chill of the peaks. It was yet the misty moment, when the night was gone and the day not yet come. In the east was a suffused luminous glow, but all the rest was in shadow. The great heads of the mountains were still silent in sleep, but the blanket of darkness was being unrolled rapidly. In a moment the mists and vapors were gone, and the golden beams of the sun were reflected from them in a myriad of dazzling rays.

It was wonderful to Charles, this awakening of the wilderness, its sudden emergence from the dusk into a flawless light, so pure that he seemed to see the last little boughs of pine trees growing on slopes miles away.

Crusoe, on his lone island, at first felt despair, but his man Friday did not come until late. Charles had a comrade whom he knew he could trust. He and Herbert were now the lords of all that he could see, and he saw much. The mountains lay before him, coil on coil, peak on peak, but he was on the slope of a mighty summit, and his eye ranged over them, as they rolled away in wave and crest. The vast pine forests showed now blue and now green as the light fell, but above them rose the bare and rocky heights, sculptured into strange shapes by time, and, glittering under the sun, in red and gold and yellow, and all the tints between. Two or three tiny splashes of silver showed through the robe of the forest and Charles knew that deep, cool pools of clear, still water lay there. But beyond and over everything was the peaceful and majestic spirit of the mountains and the wilderness. It seemed to him that, as it was this morning, it always had been, and so it always would be.

He drew a deep breath and turned away. He must come back to earth and his duty. He had noticed the night before an enormous rubbish heap in the dark space, low and angular, at the back of the cliff house, in which they had slept, made by the sloping roof meeting the level shelf on which the house itself stood.

The heap, something like the kitchen-middens of the Old World, was composed of many things, pieces of bone and wood, feathers, fragments of pottery and old woven articles; in truth, of almost everything that the cliff dweller ate, wore or otherwise used, but he had taken most particular notice of some of the bones which he knew to be those of the wild turkey. If the wild turkey existed then in these mountains it should be much more common now, when there were so few to hunt it, and he remembered with pleasure that the wild turkey was very good indeed to eat. Above them hung a fringe of pine forest, and, as he stood looking over the peaks and blue gulfs between, it had seemed to him that a faint gobble came to his ears from the way of the pine forest.

Now he took his rifle from the corner of the hut, and looked carefully to the cartridges. He was a good shot, and luck might help him. Herbert was still asleep, and knowing that he was not yet inured to wild life, Charles let him sleep on.

He turned away, and using the primitive ladder for the first precipitous slope, followed the rough and narrow path. It wound about great rocks, but it led steadily upward, and he knew that he would soon reach the pine forest. He was glad of his strength and agility, because it was no easy journey, the slope being so steep, and he was willing to rest a bit, when at last he reached the first of the pines.

Here he became the hunter, and it was lucky that in his western life he had acquired skill both in marksmanship and in stalking his game. His ear, when he stood on the slope below, had not deceived him, as he soon found a numerous flock of wild turkeys, yet roosting among the pines, the dark, glossy plumage of the gobblers showing like satin in the morning sun. But he chose one of the modest gray hens, because, in this case, while fine feathers might yet make fine birds to look at, plain feathers made those better to eat.

A long and careful aim, steady nerves, a clear eye and the deed was done. The unfortunate hen fell to the ground, her neck severed by a rifle bullet, and the others flew away in terror from the strange, new creature that had invaded their Eden. Charles, carrying his prize in triumph, picked his way down the slope, up which he had come, no easy task, as he was burdened with the rifle and the turkey. But he had a sanguine feeling of achievement, because he had added something of great value to their store.

He found the primitive ladder just as he had left it, and, when he was preparing to descend, he saw Herbert standing on the terrace below, and looking at him inquiringly. Charles raised the turkey, and gave a little shout of triumph.

"Good!" called Herbert, when he saw the prize. "I see a great addition to our larder."

Charles let the turkey drop to the terrace, and then he quickly climbed down with his rifle.

"I heard a shot on the mountainside," Herbert said.

"Weren't you afraid it was an Apache?"

"No; I felt sure that it must be you. And then, when I watched, I saw you coming."

"It was merely a little excursion that I took," Charles said gayly, his spirits bubbling over, "in order to obtain fresh food for our breakfast. I found a merchant with a very large, though somewhat scattered, stock, and, in every case, the price of what he had to sell was a well-directed rifle shot, so I bought this bird that you see at your feet."

Both were in the highest of spirits. Herbert had already lighted a fire, and they began to consider the turkey. Charles had taken forethought. In a number of the houses he had seen great jars, holding several gallons, not very thick, but of such hard earthenware that when he struck them they gave back a fine, clear, ringing tone like that of a bell. They seemed to him almost as strong as iron, and he was quite sure that they would stand the test of fire.

He brought forth one of them, cleaned it thoroughly with water from the reservoir, and then, after filling it from the same source, put it on a fire that he made of Sticks, plentiful about the slopes. In this they scalded the turkey, then they picked it, cleaned it and broiled it over the coals, the two laboring together in a peace and harmony seldom shown by two cooks engaged on the same task. When it was ready, they brought crackers and salt from their store, and drinking water in earthenware cups that they found in the houses. Everything had been left just ready for them, Herbert said.

They will never forget that breakfast. The savor of it was like an incense. They sat on stones, Charles on one side of the fire and Herbert on the other. Neither was lonely or afraid, and neither thought, at that moment, of the past or the future. They were as much lost from the world as if, like Crusoe, they had been cast away on a lonely island in the southern seas, but they were not thinking just then of the way to get back to it. They talked about anything, in the most inconsequential manner.

"That was a fine turkey," said Herbert, looking at the bones. He was a strong, hearty youth, and one's appetite on a mountain is always wonderfully sharp.

"As good as any that ever grew," said Charles. "But I know where we can find others just like it. They roost in the pine grove above us, and fortunately we have many cartridges. Now I suppose we must go to work, although, to tell you the truth, I don't feel like it. Such a day as this is intended for play."

The task was to furnish one of the houses for their occupancy. They brought down fresh pine branches, and spread them in the corners for their beds, covering each with a blanket. In a third corner they put one of the huge earthen jars, and filled it with water. On a stone shelf in the wall they placed vases, jars and bowls, and, by searching carefully through the houses, they found several ancient mats and baskets, which they brought to the new abode. These showed some skill in weaving, being made of yucca, rough grass, willow and little split sticks. They put the baskets by the wall, but spread the mats on the floor.

"We shall be quite spoiled," said Herbert. "We are really arranging too much luxury for ourselves."

"We're lucky to find all these things about," said Charles. "It's my theory that the village was abandoned suddenly under the stress of some great alarm, and that the inhabitants never returned. Still nobody will ever know whether I am right or wrong."

"At any rate, we're in possession," Herbert said. "We have the nine points of the law, and I don't think the original occupants will ever come back with the other point."

"No; that's certain. No cliff dwellers will ever be turning up to call us interlopers. It's a lost world."

"It certainly seems to me to be one in which nobody but ourselves ever comes," Herbert said, looking at the vast maze of mighty mountains and peaks that seemed to spread away to eternity, although both knew that beyond them lay the desert.

"Wandering Apaches may pass through here hunting," Charles said thoughtfully, "and although they are so few, and the country is so large that the chances are about a thousand to one against their seeing us, I think it is best to take precautions. The Apaches are considered the most cruel of human beings. We must always be prepared. Stick this revolver in your pocket. I've another. There are seven cartridges in it, and at any time I can supply you more."

Herbert understood the need, and he put the pistol in his pocket, first patting it tenderly, because it seemed to him a beautiful weapon—and it was so very, very useful.

The touch of the revolver brought to Herbert a feeling of companionship and safety. The wild life was making a strong appeal to him. Without losing any of his fineness, he was becoming primordial in spirit and instinct. He walked to the edge of the shelf, holding his hand lightly upon the revolver that lay in his pocket, and, for the moment, he was afraid of himself. He ought to grieve still for the elderly cousin, selfish though he knew and wicked though he suspected him to be, but he did not.

He looked out over the blue gulf at his feet, and at the mountains beyond, green where the pine forest stretched, and tawny gold on the bare steeps above. Far to the north was the row of dim white crests, the peaks of snow standing like sentinels forever on guard. To the south was the white dome of Old Thundergust. The blood leaped suddenly in his veins. His soul was suffused. The majesty and beauty of the world appealed to every fiber in him.

An old lost chord was touched. Perhaps some ancestor of his ages ago had looked upon such a scene and had felt the same emotions. Even his comrade was forgotten for the moment, and he thought only of the wilderness of which he was the center.

Charles saw and understood. He could feel the same way himself.

"It's our mountains and our wilderness," he said. "It will be a friend to us while we are here."

"It can be a friend and it can be an enemy," Herbert replied. "Do you know I seem to feel, with the actuality of experience, that it can be both a terrible foe and the best of friends."

Then the moment of reincarnation passed, and he laughed a little as he returned to the present. He turned back to the village that hung like a row of bird nests in the face of the cliff.

"Time will not be slow and heavy here," he said. "We must make comforts for ourselves, since we cannot return just yet to civilization."

"That's true," Charles said. "People lived here once, in what must have been to them a fair degree of ease, even luxury, and we, the heirs, take the things they left. Come, suppose we look through the remaining houses and see what we can find."

They were quite modern again as they searched the ancient, abandoned homes, looking with curious eyes into every dark corner. Everywhere they found fragments of pottery, lumps of pigment, from which the pottery was made, ancient arrow heads, various implements of bone, amulets, shells, more jars and bowls, and several pipes of clay, with short stems, the bowls decorated in red.

"The cliff dweller was quite human," said Herbert, picking up one of the ancient pipes. "This is good yet."

"But it would give a fellow an uncanny feeling," Charles said, "to be pulling at a pipe that some other man smoked, maybe a thousand years ago. I don't think I'd do it if I were a smoker."

They found two or three crude knives and chisels, made from the leg bones of the larger animals, and in one of the driest of the rock houses they discovered on a stone shelf a feather blanket in a fine state of preservation. It was made of the fibrils of dry yucca leaves twisted into coarse threads, which were tied together into a kind of net with wide meshes, the whole covered with little tufts of blue-gray feathers, evidently those of the turkey.

Charles took it down, carried it out into the air, and shook the dust away. He expected it to drop to pieces with age and desiccation, but it did not. Instead, as the fine coat of dust, put on it by generations of disuse, fell away it glowed vividly in the brilliant sunshine, and all the delicate colors of the blue feathers came out.

"Why it is almost as good as new, and it is beautiful," said Herbert.

"So it is; and that such an article as this, which must have been very precious to the cliff dweller, should have been left behind reinforces my theory that the village was abandoned in great hurry and alarm, never to be inhabited again. But however that may be, we have a beautiful and warm feather blanket that we may find very serviceable on the cold nights ahead."

They let the blanket hang in the sun the rest of the day, but when evening came it was taken into the house. Meanwhile they looked at the pool from which the reservoir was fed, and Charles noticed with intense satisfaction that the water remained fresh and sweet. Good cause it had to do so, as the great rain had filled it anew, and the tiny rivulet that fed the pool still trickled down between the rocks, the overflow escaping at the far side in another tiny rivulet that fell into the dark-blue gulf below. Charles felt an increase of admiration for these primitive men who had selected such a site in the mighty cliff for their home, and he reflected once more that it must have been a terrible alarm indeed that had sent them scurrying away, never to return.

While Charles was surveying these outward aspects of the village Herbert had gone to their home. "Home," both in word and thought, they called the cliff house that they had selected for their abode, and when Herbert looked at it now, swept and garnished, he felt a queer little thrill of pleasure. The moment of reincarnation returned. For a few pulse beats the blood of some dim cave-ancestor flowed in his being, and the new home seemed good and complete.

He took down the feather blanket and looked at it again. The little blue feathers, restored to their natural hue, after losing the dust of centuries, gave the proper color and tone to the low room. It was all of a piece with the wilderness, and those who belonged there. This house, the village, the mountains, green below and yellow above, and the dark-blue gulfs between, seemed very real and very natural to him, and the great cities and the civilization left behind had faded away in the most sudden and unaccountable manner.

But—and this was the most effective part of it—he did not pause to think over the transition, accepting it, without question, and going, light of heart, about the new tasks imposed upon him by the new life. He plunged into his work. The fire had not been allowed to go out, smoldering under a thick blanket of ashes, and he revived it into a blaze. A part of the turkey was left, and coffee he made from the resources in Charles' pack. This was enough, and when Charles came back down the tree ladder, whence he had gone on a scouting trip, he called to him, announcing that luncheon was ready. While they ate they discussed the possibility of wandering Apaches entering the canyon. But neither really feared on any one of the counts. Food and water they could obtain and, if Apaches came, they were strong, vigilant and well armed.

That evening it was Herbert who stood on the terrace and looked over. The twilight of a wonderful southern night was just coming, and the vast sea of mountains swam in all the glory of a mingled red and yellow glow, fire and gold, each forming a luminous background for the other. The white crests of the long line of silent sentinel peaks to the north were touched with opal dyes, and the great canyons between sank away from blue gulfs into black abysses. The sun, just visible over the last western peak, was a ball of blazing fire, and everywhere silence and the shadow of the coming twilight brooded over a great lone land.

Suddenly the sun dropped behind the last peak, leaving a shower of fire to mark its trail, but the cloud of darkness rose up swiftly and enveloped all the east to the zenith.

The mountains sank fast away. The trail of fire left by the setting sun died like the light of a shooting star, and nothing rose in the dark but the shadowy peaks. Then Herbert went to bed. Charles was already sound asleep.

Left to themselves neither boy would have had a waking moment as long as darkness lasted, but the night was not wholly untroubled. It had come on very black and very still, but after a while a wan moon cast a pale light over the rocks and gorges, and, farther up the mountain, something began to move.

It was a mountain lion, tawny and fierce, his eyes blazing in the darkness. He, too, slipping down a steep path, had found an occasional lair among these strange old homes, and now he was returning, perhaps from some distant excursion of love, war or hunting, to claim a night's lodging. He was one of the largest and strongest of his kind, and he felt no fear as he crept down the steep slope, his red eye sweeping a half circle of darkness ahead.

It may be that long immunity caused him to be less careful than usual, and it may be that, weary with pursuit, he had lost something of his sensitiveness to sight, sound and scent, but the lion was upon the shelf, before the strange and terrible odor of human beings came to his nostrils. He uttered a faint growl of anger and alarm, a deep low roar from his chest that would not have aroused an ordinary man or woman from sleep.

But Herbert Carleton heard. The inherited instinct watched over him while he slumbered, and, in the dark, chilly night, he suddenly threw off his blanket and sat up. A wave of air, rather than a sound, had come to his ears, and his whole being was pervaded by a sense of danger. There was a hostile presence, and it was very near. He could hear his comrade breathing in the other corner of the room, but he did not call to him.

He heard a faint crush, a soft pad as of someone stepping lightly, but he could not tell whether it was made by human footsteps. It might be the dreaded Apaches, but still he was not afraid.

He rose from the bed, still holding the revolver in his hand. The cold touch of the weapon exercised over him a more potent spell than ever. It gave him not only assurance, but also the power and desire of the offensive. The vital spark from the dim ages was in a glow. He was the primitive boy, with the spirit of a man, ready, if need be, to defend his people.

The darkness was almost inky in the cliff house, but he walked with the certainty of absolute memory to the door, making no noise, and then lifted

49

the feather blanket that they had hung there, before lying down. Nothing met his gaze at first save the sheer blackness of the basaltic cliffs, but, as he looked from place to place, he saw at last two points of red fire in the darkness, and then, behind them, rising up gradually, the tawny body of some large wild animal.

Still he felt no tremors, but, holding the revolver in his hand, and with every nerve and muscle taut, he stared into the red eyes of the lion. He could see more clearly now the tawny bulk behind, the ugly muzzle wrinkling away from the cruel teeth, and the switching tail. The beast seemed crouched as if for a spring, but he was still without fear. The old, inherited instinct told him that the lion would not spring, that there was something about him, a human being, that filled this beast's soul with dread. It would not be necessary for him to use the revolver.

The red eyes of the lion were quickly dropped, and their fire was put out, terror entered his being, and took possession. The figure before him, standing at the doorway of the hut, assumed a tremendous aspect. The flame of the bright eyes pierced him like lightning, and he shivered in awe before a power wrapped in mystery and as terrible to him as the thunderbolt to man. Had it moved he might have found it something akin to himself, something to be struck down with his paw, but the figure remained motionless, and the fixed gaze of its eyes still smote him like a spear of light.

The lion gathered a little of his remaining strength, turned, and fled, in abject cowardice, up the steep slope of the black basaltic cliff, rattling pebbles down with his frightened claws, and never daring to look back once at the terrific figure by the doorway. His tawny body blended against the dusk of the mountain and was gone.

Herbert stood a moment longer at the door, then went inside and soon fell asleep again. When he awoke the sunlight of dawn was pouring in at the crevices beside the blanket at the doorway, and Charles was already up. He dressed hastily, and went out into another of the glorious mornings, which now seemed to him to be the only kind of mornings that the Arizona wilderness knew. He saw the same sea of mountains, now purple in the blaze, the pine and cedar forests clinging to the far slopes, and, growing in cosy coigns of the cliffs, crimson cypress and purple larkspur and trees of pink wild plums. The black abyss beyond the shelf had become the blue gulf again, and far down it, where the cleft seemed to narrow to the width of a knife blade, lay a silver thread that was the little river.

They had agreed to take turns at the cooking, and Charles had already prepared breakfast.

It was characteristic of both that they now wasted little time in words. A brief statement was usually sufficient, wherein they were fast returning, under the pressure of situation and necessity, to the habits of their primitive ancestors. So the two sat down and ate and drank with good appetite.

Chapter Six - Marooned

Herbert said nothing of the night's event, of the coming of the lion and of his going, driven by the fear of human kind, but he felt a pride in himself and his primitive qualities were strengthened by the test, through which he had gone with such success. The mountains and the gorgeous sunlight made a more powerful appeal than ever to him, and through every vein he felt flowing a stronger and more sparkling tide of blood than any that had ever throbbed in his body before.

He had been afraid at first that he would show badly under wild and savage conditions, that he might feel fear, or that he might not know what to do. He wanted to appear well in the eyes of this new comrade of his, who was such an expert in the wilderness, and now that he passed the test his joy was great.

"I think I ought to go down and look for the horse—and the mule," Charles said. "They must be somewhere in the canyon, as they would not have wandered far in a day or two, and without them we can never get across the desert. Besides, life will not be always so easy here. Winter will be coming, and it is often very severe on the Arizona mountains."

It seemed impossible to Herbert, with the memory of the hot desert through which they had come, and the knowledge that the heat, too, could gather in the canyon, to associate winter with the serene sunshine of the scene about him, but he said nothing, and when Charles suggested that he stay and guard the house he consented. He also knew a lot of things that he could do while his comrade was gone, and he was quite content to remain.

Charles was not greatly worried about the horse and mule. He might not find them now, but they would certainly remain in the canyon because there alone were grass and water to be found in plenty. Meanwhile he would look for the lost gold, and in good time he would initiate his comrade into the secret. That the gold existed somewhere he did not doubt.

He reached the bottom of the canyon and then glanced upward. On either side the mountains seemed to rise, almost a sheer wall, pathless and grim. The cliff dwellers had chosen well because, from the point at which he stood, their village was almost invisible, and even if the houses were seen it would require more than common boldness to scale the steep cliff in the face of defenders.

But the narrow floor of the canyon itself had a beauty of its own. In the center ran the little stream, clear and cold from the melting snows of the highest mountains, and the pink wild plum trees were numerous. A red tanager now and then darted from bough to bough. Charles thought of trout. They must be found in a mountain river like this, and they would be a delicacy for the table of the two comrades.

Once he came upon traces in the grass which he knew to have been made by hoofs, and he followed them until they stopped at the edge of a wide place in the brook, but he could not find them again. Either the animals had gone a long distance in the stream or had emerged on ground too hard to leave a print visible to his eye.

But he clung to the search, continuing up the canyon until it narrowed perceptibly. The mighty walls moved closer together, sheer cliffs now of black basalt, carved into a thousand fantastic shapes by wind and weather. Charles looked up, and in the light that had grown perceptibly dimmer he saw twisted pine trees, clinging in the crevices of the cliffs, but so far away that they looked like mere bushes. The floor of the canyon, too, was rising, and he surmised that it would soon come to an end, but it went deeper into the mountains than he had supposed. It was a full two hours before he reached the end, where the cliffs came so close together that there was hardly room for the little river, plunging over a fall of two or three hundred feet, to enter it. He might have climbed up beside the fall and have gone deeper among the peaks and ridges, but it was obviously impossible for the horses to have escaped him in such a way, and he had done his full duty so far as that end of the canyon was concerned.

He turned back on his path, and in time passed by the slope that led to the cliff village. He went on down the canyon toward the opening into the desert, and he had no doubt that he should find the horses before he came to the sandy plain. As the great gash in the mountains broadened, and the rays of the sun had a better chance, the heat grew intense. Bushes and trees were thick here, and now and then there were little grassy openings. It was in the latter that he looked for the horses, and at last he caught a glimpse of a dark figure and heard the sound of an animal moving.

He advanced through the bushes, and at that moment the wind shifted a little. The animal threw up his head, he caught the flash of a horn, and then the swift beat of hoofs. A deer! He went on, still intent upon his search, and he became so engrossed in it that he forgot that midday had come. The afternoon advanced and he forgot that, too, but at last he came to the end of the great gorge, and before him stretched the desert, gray and lone, the stretch of it that intervened between these ranges and Old Thundergust. Far out upon it he could see the dancing "dust devils" whirling over the swells and then passing out of sight. But he had not found the horse and mule.

He looked once more at the gray desert, the white gleam of the alkali and the dancing "dust devils" that still troubled the horizon, and then he turned back to the great canyon, and the vast line of purple mountains beyond. How green and fresh the foliage seemed, and how the waters of the stream, when he came once more to it, sparkled in the sunlight! The scene before him, after the scene behind him, invited with all the intimate delight of home. There was majesty in the great line of purple mountains and the dim white crests beyond, but no terror, and he began with ardor the return journey to the safe alcove in the cliff.

He was surprised to see long shadows falling on the slopes. The pine trees burned yellow in the intense gold of the setting sun, and in the far west the dusk was growing. Absorbed in the search, he forgot that he had spent a whole day without food or rest. Herbert would wonder what had become of him; his good comrade might fear that he had fallen a prey to wild beast or savage, and he doubled his speed. But it was long after the moonlight came out when he reached the path leading to the village. Familiar now with all its windings and inequalities, he ran nearly all the way to the ledge, and presently he beheld Herbert standing there, gazing into the vast gulf of the canyon, now black with the darkness. He was not quite sure how his comrade would take the news of the failure to find the animals. Doubtless one reared as softly as Herbert would want to hurry back to civilization, and now he must wait.

"I must tell you," he said when he reached the terrace, "that I have failed to discover the horse and mule. I have searched the canyon from end to end, and they are not here. At the north it is shut in by the peaks, and on the south by the desert. Where those horses have gone I do not know, but I do know that we are shipwrecked, and that, for the present, we cannot escape from our isle."

Herbert actually laughed.

"If we cannot go we must stay, which I think is good logic," he said.

"It certainly is. It would be unwise for us to attempt the trip through the desert on foot. We should almost surely perish, but if we remain here a party seeking you will undoubtedly come in time. When your people are missed the government will send an expedition."

"Then the safest, as well as the easiest, thing for us to do is to wait. I think it is settled, is it not?"

"Those whom it most concerns seem to agree on the subject."

"Then will you come to your supper? It has been long waiting for you, and I'm hungry as a bear."

The two lads went to the place that they had made their dining-room. A cheerful fire was burning, and now that the chill dusk had come its glow was very pleasant. The aroma of cooking food and of good coffee saluted Charles' nostrils, and he began to feel how very hungry he was.

"It's fine to come back to this," he said. "It was a vain journey I took, but at least we know that we did our best."

"That's so," Herbert said, "and don't you think we should now begin to gather supplies? Suppose we try for the wild turkeys again in the morning?"

"It's a good idea," replied Charles. "There's nothing like being forehanded."

Much more they talked as they sat there through the supper, and for a while afterward, and their talk was wholly of the present, never of the past, which seemed to have slid so far away. The fire sank down and only the glowing coals remained. The moonlight had gone and it was dark on the mountains. From the great canyon the blackness seemed to roll up in waves. All the cliff houses had sunk long since into the shadows, and in the thick night showed only a single point of fire, on either side of which sat a human figure. They were lost in the immensity of the black void, and the wind moaned like a dirge among the peaks, but they felt neither despair nor fear.

From a point far above them rose a faint, weird cry, inexpressibly mournful and chilling, as it came in the thick darkness down the great gorge.

"Now, what under the sun was that?" exclaimed Herbert.

"The howl of a wolf," replied Charles.

Then they returned to silence and their steady gazing into the coals, which crumbled and broke apart, and sent up little sparks as they fell. The wind rose and moaned in the canyon, but it conveyed no sense of loneliness or desolation to either. Behind them in the glow of the fire showed faintly the doors of the cliff houses, like openings into the ancient caves of primitive man. On all the continent a more ghostly and uncanny place could scarcely have been found. It was not alone in the wilderness, it was out of the world, mystic and unreal. Here time had not only stood still, the years were rolled back by the tens of thousands. In the sky far above a few stars twinkled, but in the canyon itself there was no ray of light. It was like the vast still world before life came.

As they agreed, the two went early the next morning in search of the wild turkeys, starting when the dawn had not yet fully come on the mountains, and the air was yet chill with the night. In addition to a revolver each carried a rifle.

It was only the trace of a path that led from the village to the summit of the hill, but Charles had marked it well on his former journey, and the two climbed boldly, assisted by jutting rocks and dwarf pines. The chill was still in the air, and the west was yet dusky, but in the east great waves of light were rolling up from the gulf behind the mountains.

They hastened, because the day would soon be fully come, and it was important to find their turkeys, while they were yet in the trees, somewhat stiff with the night's cold. Presently they came out on top of the cliff, and stood there a moment, looking at the mountains, rising terrace on terrace to the north, while, to the south, the earth was lost in a dim gray mist that was the desert. Here as in the gorge there was nothing human but the two lads.

It was a solitary world in the light as well as in the darkness.

"The pine forest in which the turkeys roost is not more than a quarter of a mile ahead," said Charles, "and I feel sure that we shall find them there. My single shot the other day would not be sufficient to frighten them away permanently."

Herbert was stepping very gently, and he began to understand the eagerness of the chase. He was breathing the rarefied air of the mountain crest, and he would justify his comrade's confidence, proving that he could handle a rifle like a veteran.

Before them lay the pine forest, dark green, and yet dusky in the morning shadows, and perched among the branches Charles saw their game, a score or more, their glossy dark blue feathers, showing but faintly among the pines, which looked dark blue, too, in the early half light. He pointed them out to Herbert, and they crept a little nearer.

"Do you think you could hit the fat one in the nearest tree?" he asked.

"I'd like to try," Herbert replied, his eyes sparkling.

Herbert raised his rifle and fired. The bird fell to the ground, and he uttered a little cry of triumph. Charles quickly fired also, and, as the confused turkeys fluttered among the trees, they secured three more. Then they went forward and picked up their prizes, which were more than trophies, being, in truth, a part of the treasure upon which their lives depended.

"Can't I shoot?" asked Herbert triumphantly.

"These turkeys say so," replied Charles.

They were fine, fat birds, and they would last some time. They could dry the meat in the sun, after the manner of jerking buffalo or deer, and add it to their store.

"I think while we're here together we might explore a little," said Charles. "We can hang these turkeys to a bough of a tree with a strip of bark, and they'll be safe until we return."

Herbert agreed with great readiness. The prospect of exploring new country appealed to him, and the scene about them was grand and romantic to the last degree. From the crest, where they were, their canyon was invisible, and the purple mountain beyond seemed but a continuation of that on which they stood. The white peaks, in a line to the north, were clearer and whiter now, and seemed to stand there, solemn and silent, a part of eternity itself. To the south, Thundergust now being to their left, there was nothing, only the gray swells of the desert rolling ceaselessly away, and from the great height on which they stood, hidden mostly in mists. The country around them had all the aspects of an island, surrounded by an ocean, on which no one ever sailed. But they gave no thought to it then, secure in themselves and their strength.

"I'm thinking that the pines stretch away for miles," said Charles. "You know, or you don't know, that the largest forest now standing in the United States is one of pine in Northern Arizona, and we must be in it, or somewhere on the fringe of it."

It was in many respects a beautiful region that they trod. The pines rose before them in endless vistas, often in avenues, as if they had been planted by man. More than once they came to a cool little pool, or a tiny brook that trickled away, to fall down the steep sides of some gorge or canyon. There was little undergrowth, and the soil was dry beneath their feet. As they walked along, they breathed a wonderful perfume of pine and cedar, and it seemed to them that they could feel their strength grow.

"This would have been a splendid site for the village of the people whose houses we inhabit," said Herbert.

"So it would have been," said Charles, "but for one thing, and that was safety—among those old peoples safety came first of all, before comfort, beauty or anything else."

"Yes, I know. I have felt it, too. Beautiful as it is here, I like the cliff best, at least at times."

Charles understood—it was the feeling of security that the cliff gave—but he said nothing, and they continued their pleasant journey among the cathedral pines. The ground began to slope a little, and suddenly Charles stopped, seizing Herbert by the arm.

"Look!" he exclaimed.

The earth had opened at their feet, scarcely a foot before them, cleft to an interminable depth, as if by the slash of a mighty sword blade. Holding to a slender pine that grew at the very brink, they looked down, but the gorge was so narrow that they could see no bottom.

"It cannot be more than fifty feet from cliff to cliff at the top here," said Charles, "but it might as well be a mile. We are absolutely cut off on this side."

"It seems then that this may be a peninsula," said Charles, "which merely heightens the wisdom of the cliff dwellers."

"Yes, they lived in a bird's nest."

They turned to the westward and continued their explorations, both as eager and interested as if they had come into the Arizona mountains for that purpose, and no other. They had gone perhaps two miles when Charles stopped suddenly. Herbert, with marvelous quickness and without awaiting any other signal, did the same. His instinct had taken warning at once from his action, and it was his first belief that Charles had seen some foe, perhaps a wandering Apache who had scaled these heights. But he awaited the result with confidence.

"A deer," whispered Charles. "Lo and behold! Rations on the hoof for many days."

The deer, a fine buck, was standing among the pines some distance away. It was a long shot, but Charles was afraid to risk creeping closer lest the wind should carry the human odor and with it the alarm. But he wanted this deer, foreseeing that they must provide well against a possible lean time. All the primal instincts of precaution were alive in him, too. It seemed to him a matter of course that they should spend months in the canyon, the remainder of the hot season, the winter and whatever followed, and it was their duty to arrange for it. Hence he stole forward with the skill in trailing that he was now rapidly acquiring, and, with a good shot, slew the deer.

They now ceased their explorations in order to dress the body, and both were exultant. Their provisions had experienced a great increase, and since they had found one deer on the mountain they were likely to find more. Here was a splendid source of food supply, and, castaways as they were, they had ample cause for joy.

The day was waning when the task was finished, and then, bearing the body of the deer between them, they returned through the pine woods toward the canyon. It was a matter of extreme difficulty to carry their venison down the steep path to the shelf in the canyon, but Herbert, agile of body and sure of foot, and learning fast, gave much help. At last they reached home in triumph with their great prize. There they hung it securely to a bough of one of the trees that grew in the clefts, and then they lighted their fire, happy in the day's good work.

That night the mountain lion, drawn by a tempting odor, that tickled his nostrils and that made him terribly hungry, again crept down the mountainside to the cliff dwellings. There he saw the rich food hanging from the tree, but that other and strange odor, the odor of human beings that he dreaded, came to his nostrils also, and, with longing looks backward at the body of the deer, he retreated once more from the shelf, climbing to the plateau and hiding himself in the pine forest. A troublesome equation had come lately into the life of this mountain lion who had long made free of an entire village, and he felt a puzzled sense of injustice. But the new occupants of the village slept peacefully. Affairs were going well with them. Now came days of work and absorption, work to develop their home, and absorption in the details. Herbert, the eastern lad, continually found new resources within himself. His mind became more acute, and his fingers understood how to achieve. He learned in a few hours to do physical tasks of which he had not thought himself capable, and he found every day a fresh interest and zest in the singular life that he and his comrade were leading. His very youth was in a way a help to him, as it made him forget. The dreadful scene in the valley was fading fast from his mind. George Carleton had been a harsh and unloved relative, and the pain of his death could not endure.

One day while his comrade was down in the canyon it occurred to Herbert to climb the plateau in search of wild turkeys. The turkey, whether wild or domestic, had been an important factor in the life of the cliff dweller, and in a wild state this great bird was now of equal value to them.

Herbert ascended the path now become familiar to the top of the cliff, and stood once more at the edge, where he could look upon the vast panorama of mountain, forest and turquoise sky, with the gray mist of the desert, hanging like a threat, low down on the horizon in the south. He had become very strong and very agile, but after the climb he was shorter of breath than usual, and he remained for a while at the crest, taking deep inhalations. He did not know that his weariness was due chiefly to an increasing warmth, of a close, suffocating quality that made the air lay very heavy upon the lungs. Yet there was a conspiracy against him, a conspiracy of mountains and sky and the spirit of the wilderness, and it was already at work. Far down the gray desert, so lone and bare, waves of burning air were rolling northward against the black basaltic wall of the mountain. Some broke there, but others surmounted the heights, to roll on over the plateau against the line of white peaks farther to the north where the cold air and the hot air met. Amid the deepest of the gorges and canyons a little wind was making a faint moan, but it did not reach the ears of the lad, whose mind was set only upon the task for which he had come.

Herbert entered the pine forest, but the turkeys were gone from the cluster of trees in which they were in the habit of taking their rest, frightened at last perhaps by the ravages of the marksmen, and he went on farther and farther in search of them. He was chagrined that his search had been fruitless; it hurt his pride to return empty-handed, and he persevered: Absorbed thus in the chase he did not notice that he had gone a long distance upon the plateau, leaving all landmarks behind, and coming into strange, new, broken country, covered with a tangled growth of dwarfed bushes. Here he paused, and for the first time began to look about him with some apprehension. There was a distinctly alien feeling in the atmosphere. The restless winds, which blew usually among the pine trees and the bushes, were quiet on the mountains. The hot, close air enveloped him, and there was a tinge of duskiness in the skies.

The spirit of the wilderness was abroad in a new phase. The conspiracy of earth, air and sky against him was well developed, and he was to be subjected to the last test. The moan of the wind among the far northern gorges grew, and rose now and then to a whistle, the hot air from the desert still rose up in waves, and met the chill air from the white peaks, great clouds formed and floated back from the peaks over the plateau.

But the winds that moaned in the gorges did not yet reach the summit, upon which Herbert stood. The bushes and scant grass were still lifeless, the heavy air remained breathless and still. He was stricken with an impending sense of danger. The primal instincts which had served to strengthen him also served now to warn him. For a moment or two he shivered instinctively with dread. The spirit of the wilderness, with its silence, its growing darkness and its hot, vaporous breath, like a dragon's, made a formidable threat which he understood. The conspiracy against him was well advanced.

He looked about with a full apprehension of his peril, and while the primal instinct that gave warning remained, the primal strength that would defend was there, too.

The voices of the wilderness now began to speak aloud and to menace him. The wind in the canyon and the gorges rose to a shriek, and it kept up, too, a weird moaning among the pine woods. Down from the north came the low, sullen mutter of distant thunder. Flickering lightning played over the pines and cedars, and tinged them, for the moment, with a weird, ghostly whiteness. But when the lightning was not present the whole world was in a brown shadow, which made all things ugly and repellent.

Inherited instincts now peopled the pine forest with vague, terrible forms, huge beasts of the early day that sought him, but he strengthened his will and refused to be afraid. The hot air suddenly gave way to the chill atmosphere, driven southward by the cold waves from the white peaks. Blast after blast was blown across the forest, and the boughs of the pines and cedars were whirled before them. Now and then a tree went down with a great crash, the lightning blazed in stroke after stroke, so vivid that Herbert, with involuntary motion, shielded his eyes with his hands. The thunder maintained an unceasing roar, and the canyons and the gorges took up its echoes.

Herbert, in all his life, had never conceived anything so terrifying. Nature was turned loose upon him, and he was the very center of its most powerful manifestation. He trudged on through the alternate light and darkness, and presently he noticed that the flashes of lightning came farther apart, and that the thunder began to sink. Then the clouds opened and let fall a deluge.

He was afraid that he would be swept away, he seemed to be immersed in a sea, and he heard the water roaring in torrents down the little ravine on the plateau. He stopped running, and, seizing some of the short bushes, clung to them, as one would clutch a rock to fight a sweeping tide. He was wet and cold, but he was conscious of a great pride in his strength and endurance. The storm could not beat him down. He clung to his bushes, and now he was neither weak nor afraid.

Far to the north the elements which had made this scene were now working to drive it away. The torrents of cold air ceased to blow down from the peaks, and the peaks themselves, white, calm and majestic, emerged from the clouds and mists. The shrieking in the canyons and gorges turned to a moan, and from a moan to a whisper. The clouds, empty now, floated away, mere mist and vapor, to be lost over the burning desert. Broad bands of light appeared at the zenith, and the world came out of the darkness and gloom. Earth, mountains and sky were now wholly propitious.

Herbert took it as a personal triumph and calmly traced his way back to the cliff village, the sun drying his clothes as he went. He found Charles in a state of great alarm about him, but Herbert dismissed the affair as nothing. He had passed a severe test, and he felt now that he was a genuine son of the wilderness.

The two together made another search of the ravine for the horse and mule, but discovered no trace of them. It was Charles' opinion that they had wandered into some smaller ravine, opening into the great one, and would reappear later on. He knew too much about their habits to believe that they were gone permanently.

Meanwhile he and Herbert continued the equipment of their house. They shot more of the wild turkeys and dried their flesh in the sun. They saved the feathers also, thinking they would find some future use for them, and on the plateau above the village they shot two more deer. They dried the meat and they tanned the skins also, rather crudely, it is true, but in a way that was satisfactory to both. Charles foresaw a time when they might need deerskin for clothing.

They had just finished the task of tanning the last deerskin, and were sitting luxuriously on the terrace. The chill of evening was coming on, and the fire had been lighted—they were still doing their cooking out of doors. The great canyon was turning from blue to black as the dusk filled it.

Charles leaned back and drew a long sigh of content. Then he said to his partner:

"Herbert, old fellow, you've never asked me what I'm doing up here."

"I think you said once that you were looking for gold."

"But I don't seem to be looking very much, do I?"

Herbert smiled.

"You saved my life," he said. "What right have I to be prying into your business?"

"Well, I am looking for gold, but not just in the way you think. Rather, I should say, we are looking for it. You're my partner—oh, yes you are! I ought to have had one in the beginning. I was foolish to come out alone, and I've been luckier than I deserved. We're looking for gold, not for a mine, but for a lost treasure."

"A lost treasure!" exclaimed Herbert, his eyes opening wide in interest and excitement.

"Yes, a lost treasure, an old Spanish treasure. As we're to be partners in this, half and half, share and share alike, you ought to know everything that I know about it, which is none too much."

Then he told the story of Ananias Brown and his last words. Herbert listened eagerly, his eyes shining at the words "gold," "Old Thundergust" and "behind the veil." His was a romantic soul, and it appealed to him.

"Of course, it's true!" he exclaimed. "There is a lost treasure, and it's somewhere hereabouts. The big white-headed mountain down there is Old Thundergust, that's sure. Now we're bound to stay here until we find that treasure, Charlie, and I want to help in the hunt. I don't care anything about the gold. You can take it all."

Charles smiled tolerantly.

"What kind of a partner would I be," he said, "to let you share the work and then for me to take all the gold for myself? No, sir, it's share and share alike. That's agreed."

"All right, partner, if you want it that way," said Herbert.

Herbert did not sleep well that night. He dreamed repeatedly about a great store of gold, and a man, with black scars in his palms, who beckoned him on. But he concealed his impatience the next morning, because his comrade thought they should continue to stock themselves up with food and other supplies for the coming winter.

Charles himself decided to catch some trout. The little river, probably never fished in before by a white man, furnished an unusually fine variety, and whenever they wanted an especial delicacy for their table they resorted to it. He had put reel, lines and hooks in his pack for such needs, and now he went down to the river, fully equipped.

He strolled along the bank toward the fall, looking down into the clear rushing water. It was a beautiful, cold stream, coming down from mountain snows, and he could see the trout of a delicate golden tint, darting here and there. But further up was a deep pool between steep rocky sides, where the bigger fish were likely to lie, and he would not drop his line until he reached it, because he wanted the best.

The pool was wide and on the shady side, where he thought the fish were likely now to be, the cliff rose steep and high. But he believed that he could climb down it, along the rugged side, at least halfway, and then throw in the hook.

At the second step on the slippery stone face of the cliff Charles slipped. He dropped his fishing tackle, which struck with a splash in the water below, and grasped at a jutting crag. He seized the crag, but his head struck another spur of the rock with force, and stars twinkled before his eyes. He was almost stunned, and the strength was driven out of him for the time being. Yet he hung to the crag, although he knew that he was growing weaker, and must soon drop down below to drown. His eyes were dim, and the terrible thought that he was about to leave the bright world overwhelmed him.

"Jest you sink your fingers into that stun for a spell, my boy, an' we'll save you!" said a voice, and a long, tanned face looked over the cliff's rim.

"Only hold on a half minute longer and you'll be out of danger," said another voice, and a second face, beside the first, looked over the cliff's rim. It was a large head and face, but mostly hidden by an enormous pith helmet, and a pair of huge gold glasses.

The two voices and the two faces pulled Charles Wayne back to earth. His hands closed more tightly on the stony crag, and then something whirred over his head. He felt a light loose coil drop down around his shoulders and suddenly tighten.

"Right and tight she is," sung out the first voice, "an' there's no fall fur you, my boy. Now, Purfessor, a long pull an' a strong pull all together. Yo-ho, yo-ho an' Nancy Lee the sailor's wife is she!"

Charles was lifted bodily into the air. His head was still ringing, and the darkness was yet before him, but as he swung outward from the cliff he felt that he was in powerful and friendly hands. Upward he went slowly but steadily, and then he was drawn over the edge of the cliff and to safety.

"Now, Jedediah, lift up his head while I pour a little of this whisky into him! And it's our young friend, Mr. Charles Wayne! Well! Well! Well! What an odd meeting! And what a lucky one for you! You've got a bad bruise on the head, but there's no damage done. Ah, that's good! Color coming back and strength with it. Yes, it's your humble servant, Erasmus Darwin Longworth, and Jedediah Simpson, who is not humble at all."

"Jedediah Simpson o' Lexin'ton, K—y, an' terrible glad to see you."

Charles opened his eyes and sat up. The little man and the long man were looking at him anxiously and kindly, and he joyfully seized a hand of each.

"How did you come here?" he exclaimed.

"How did we come here?" replied Jed mournfully. "We came here a-whoopin' an a-humpin' at the head o' a lot o' Apaches, an' it wa'n't no church procession, either, I can tell you! It drove all the music quite out o' my breast!"

Despite himself Charles laughed at Jed's lugubrious countenance.

"We were in the edge of the desert," added Professor Longworth, "when we were attacked by Apaches. Fortunately they were on foot, while we were mounted and we managed to shake them off, but we lost ourselves in the mountains, and we've been wandering around for days. We heard you cry out, an involuntary cry, when you fell, and here we are."

"Luckily for me," said Charles gratefully, "because you've saved my life a second time, Professor, and now I must take you up to the house of myself and my partner, Herbert Carleton."

"You live here!" exclaimed the Professor in surprise.

"Oh, yes," replied Charles, who was delighted at meeting Jed and Professor Longworth again, "I'm gold prospecting, and my partner and I have an excellent stone house. We live in a village only a short distance away. It is true that the village was built a thousand years or more ago, but the architects and workmen were so good that it serves well now."

The Professor's eyes snapped.

"Ah, I know," he exclaimed, "it's one of the villages of the lost cliff dwellers."

"Just so," said Charles, "and I should like for you and Jed to be the guests of my partner and myself there at once."

"In a house of your own, built by somebody one or two thousand years ago," said Jedediah Simpson. "Now, that is mighty cur'ous an' interestin'. I 'low I want to see it."

"And so do I," said the Professor.

"You are both very welcome," said Charles earnestly. Even if they had not come at that most opportune of all moments, the moment to save his life, he would have been glad to see them. He had begun to have a feeling that Herbert and he might be threatened at any time by great dangers, and that they needed more strength.

"This way," he said to the Professor and Jed, and he led the way down the ravine. First they looked for his fishing tackle, which was of all the greater value because it could not be replaced, and were lucky enough to find it at the edge of the stream, caught on an overhanging bush. Then they went to the terrace, and, as they ascended the path worn out by the old cliff dwellers, Jed spoke up with admiration:

"Now, this is mighty cur'ous an' interestin'," he said, using his favorite expression. "Me an' the Purfessor have been in a heap o' strange places, but this does beat all. 'Pears to me like we were stuck on top o' a mountainous islan' and were kings o' everything. 'From the center all around to the sea you are lord o' the fowl an' the brute,' only I don't see no fowl, though brutes there are I know."

"And fowls, too," said Charles. "Plenty of them on top of the mountain. Wild turkeys, big, fat, fine fellows, Jed, and, oh, so tender and juicy!"

"Um! um!" said Jed appreciatively. "This does grow mighty cur'ous an' interestin'. Certain! Shore!"

The Professor stopped, when near the terrace and looked out over the vast expanse of mountain and forest, wonderfully vivid in the limpid, golden sunshine.

"One of the earth's wonder regions," he said—"this huge plateau of the southwest. I have traveled in many lands, and it is a great joy to me to have come here."

Charles could see his eyes shining behind his great glasses, and he himself felt the exultation of the moment. They were four now instead of two, and he was sure that they would be equal to any task.

"Where did you leave your animals, Professor?" he asked.

"They are tethered in the ravine. They will be safe until we return."

Charles intended to give Herbert a surprise, and he said to Jedediah Simpson:

"Jed, can you sing 'Home, Sweet Home'?"

"Me?" exclaimed Jed eagerly, "I sing it most beautiful, and I'll sing it fur you right now ef you'll make the Purfessor promise not to pull a gun."

"It's for a special reason," said Charles, turning to the Professor. "I want to give my partner a surprise."

"Then I'll promise not to shoot," said the Professor, sighing.

Jedediah Simpson lifted up a baritone voice, not really bad, but wholly uncultivated, and began to sing the old, old song. At the second line Charles joined in with his own youthful baritone, and the canyon gave back the two voices in a mellow echo. Charles led the way, and as his head rose over the terrace he saw an amazed figure coming forward to meet them. It was Herbert, rifle in hand.

"Don't shoot, Herbert, we're doing our best," he called. "The Professor has already promised not to do so, and it would be a great breach of hospitality for you to send a bullet at us. These good friends of mine are merely helping me to celebrate my return home."

Herbert's eyes opened wider and wider, as he saw the long figure of Jedediah Simpson and then the little one of Professor Erasmus Darwin Longworth, surmounted by an enormous head, the head in turn surmounted by a pith helmet, yet more enormous.

"Before us, gentlemen," said Charles, "lies the Château de Carleton, the Castle of Wayne, and other splendid châteaux and castles. All are at your service. Herbert, these are some old friends of mine, come to pay us a visit at our summer residence. Mr. Herbert Carleton, Professor Erasmus Darwin Longworth of everywhere and Mr. Jedediah Simpson of Lexin'ton, K—y. Herbert, is luncheon ready? I hope that the ortolan and the humming-bird tongues are just right, because Mr. Simpson is very particular about his diet, not to say being a bit of an epicure."

"Me!" said Jed. "I don't know what ortylans are, an' I never heard o' anybody eatin' hummin'-birds. I ain't finicky at all! I could eat the toughest steak that wuz ever carried about on four feet by a twenty-year-old steer an' never whimper."

"Right you are, Jed," said Charles, laughing. In fact, he was in such high spirits that he had to bubble over.

The Professor stepped forward and shook hands heartily with Herbert, his keen eyes behind his huge glasses taking him in to the last detail. He knew instantly that here was one who had been, until a few weeks ago, a tenderfoot, but who was now one no more. And he welcomed the second boy as he had welcomed the first, to his good graces. Jed and Herbert also shook hands with ready comradeship.

"We particularly pride ourselves on the view from the front lawn of our summer residence," continued Charles. "We may have rivals, Professor, but I really don't believe that anybody could beat it."

Jedediah Simpson o' Lexin'ton, K—y, looked outward, then downward, then upward.

"No, they can't," he said with emphasis. "Me an' the Purfessor have been in many strange lands an' we have laid our eyes on many strange scenes, but this I think is the beatin'est o' them all. It seems to me, Charlie, that you do have air in plenty, an' the neighbors ain't crowdin' you."

The Professor was looking about him with eyes that sparkled behind his great glasses.

"An exceedingly interesting place," he said. "Ideal for the cliff dwellers who probably lived here a thousand years, and who might be here to-day had not raging Apaches or Utes discovered them, and driven them out. You young gentlemen were very lucky indeed to have found this village."

"So we think, Professor," said Charles earnestly.

"Because, being gold prospectors, as you told me," continued the Professor, "you are, of course, up here for a long stay, and, when winter comes, immense snows fall in these high mountains, and lie long."

"We'll defy them," said Herbert.

Then the two lads led the way to their house, and proudly showed the interior to the Professor and Jed, who made many favorable comments. After that they gave them venison and wild turkey on the terrace, which both ate heartily.

"How is the great search coming on, Professor?" asked Charles. "Have you yet been able to prove that the mountains of Northern Arizona are the oldest land above ground?"

The Professor shook his head sadly.

"The question remains in abeyance, not to say in doubt," he replied. "I was on the trail of rock formation that might have settled it one way or the other forever, when our own trail was discovered by the Apaches. It was then a question of saving our scalps."

Jed felt of his long thick locks.

"An' me with the finest head o' hair that was ever growed in Lexin'ton, K—y! To think o' its hangin' inside the dirty lodge o' some dirty Apache, a-smokin' an' a-dryin'. Me an' the Purfessor couldn't bear the thought o' it. So we just hopped onto our mules an' skedaddled, leavin' them rock formations to rest in peace for a few more million years."

"Why not stay with us a while," said Charles earnestly. "In union there is strength. That's the motto of your State, Jed, and it's a good one. This village, Professor, affords a great subject for your investigations, and I know that Jed needs rest."

Charles had already said a few words aside to Herbert about his plan, and Herbert thoroughly approved.

"And you two lads can really endure us, that is, we will not be in your way?" asked the Professor.

"We'll be glad to have you," said Charles, and Herbert nodded his head emphatically.

"Then we'll stay," said the Professor. "As you say, in union there is strength, and while you are of great service to us, we may also be of some help to you. The Apaches may come into this canyon at any time, and if there should be a fight four are better than two."

That had been Charles' own thought, and he added: "We must stick together."

After the refreshments, the four went down in the canyon to the alcove, in which the animals were tethered. The Professor had four mules, two horses and a splendid lot of supplies, including compressed food, canned goods, great quantities of cartridges, blankets, medicines, fine scientific instruments, a pair of powerful field glasses and many other things, the nature of which he did not disclose at the time. It took several trips to carry all these articles to the lost village, but when it was done they turned the animals loose. The Professor was sure, as Charles had been about his own, that they never could wander from the canyon, and, when they really needed them, they would find all in one herd. Everything was not completed until the next day, when a second house was swept and cleaned for the Professor and

Jedediah Simpson o' Lexin'ton, K—y. Then Charles told the story of Ananias Brown.

"Now, Professor," he said, "will you and Jed join us in this search? There is likely to be great danger, and while four of us may find the gold and get out with it I don't think two ever could. You see, Professor, we need you and Jed."

"I am a scientific man," said the Professor, "and this appeals to me as a sporting proposition. I've never bothered about wealth, although I inherited enough to enable me to follow unprofitable, but highly interesting and important, pursuits. Speaking for myself, and because I think we really can be of service, I shall join you, although I do not undertake to compel Jed here."

"Me!" exclaimed Jed. "Me need compellin'! An' me from Lexin'ton, K—y, an' me not a sport! Well, I guess yes! I'm signin' up with you, Charlie an' Herb, right away, an' I see myself a mighty rich man inside o' six months. Then I'm goin' to move over to the swell side o' Lexin'ton, K—y, right in the middle o' the big bugs an' the blue-bloods. I know a place on the outskirts that I want, big, red brick house with three hundred acres o' the finest blue grass, runnin' back from it into the country. An' when I go up into the middle o' the town I won't walk neither, nor take no street car neither, I'll drive behind two bays o' the finest blood, in one o' them high-seated vehicles, an' that thar vehicle will be painted red, not any o' your shy, retreatin' reds that ain't quite a red, but a gorgeous, dazzlin' red, a red that'll make the sun wink an' blink, all except the wheels, which I think I'll have bright yellow or gold like the gold I'm goin' to find, or mebbe green. Say, Herb, would you have them wheels yellow or green?"

"Yellow by all means," replied Herbert. "I think red and yellow go better together than red and green."

"She's settled!" exclaimed Jed enthusiastically. "Yellow them wheels will shorely be, because Herb here is an eddicated boy o' taste! Me! I see myself already the bright partic'lar ornament to Lexin'ton, K—y. Some long breaths will be drawed when I drive up the middle o' the town!"

Professor Erasmus Darwin Longworth took off his glasses, and his nearsighted blue eyes were sparkling.

"I find myself sharing Jedediah's enthusiasm," he said, "and if we find this gold I, too, shall make a dream come true, one for which my means hitherto have not been sufficient. I know of a buried city in Babylonia, one that has not yet come to the knowledge of any other American or European, and I shall excavate it. It goes far back of the Babylonians, to the time of the Sumerians and perhaps back of them. I shall uncover archaeological discoveries of enormous importance. I shall be a benefactor of the world, and all by my own unaided efforts."

"We'll find the gold," said Charles in sanguine tones.

"It's as good as found already," said Herbert.

Chapter Seven - Among the Stars

Professor Longworth and Jedediah Simpson o' Lexin'ton, K—y, at once took their places in the little community, and Charles and Herbert rejoiced every day, because they had extended the invitation, and because it had been accepted. The Professor, despite his queer appearance, was a man of infinite wit and resource. He had been everywhere, he had seen everything, and he had done most things. Moreover, he retained a keen interest in daily life, and Jed was a perfect well of optimism. The union of the four greatly lightened the labors and vastly improved the comfort of all.

Jed took charge of the cooking, and the Professor prowled through the village, minutely examining everything. He was of the opinion that it had been abandoned many generations, and perhaps had not been visited by anyone in the last hundred years, except their own little party.

"The cliff dwellers have vanished, that's certain," he said. "The tribe that lived here is extinct, or a pitiful remnant of it may be hidden in the fastnesses of Northern Mexico, while their village in this place is protected from another invasion of Utes or Apaches by some sort of superstition. All savage tribes are greatly given to superstition, and certainly, as I have said before, there is no wilder or stranger country in the world than this."

"No," said Herbert, "I don't believe there can be. It seems to me that we're in a sort of an oasis on a mountain top."

"Probably this is a peninsula of green and fertile country," said the Professor, "running back for some distance and then dropping down into the desert, or hooked on by a narrow neck to the great Arizona pine belt. But whatever it is we might as well be on the crest of a lone peak of the Himalayas, so far as the rest of the civilized world is concerned."

"But snug and comfortable," said Herbert with enthusiasm.

"Yes, snug an' comfortable, Herb," said Jed, "with most o' the comforts an' not without some o' the luxuries o' civilization. Now there is the matter o' music. Jest listen."

He produced from under his coat a small accordion and suddenly began to play, while he sang the accompaniment, "Poor old Uncle Ned, he had no wool on top of his head."

Professor Longworth promptly drew a revolver and made an ominous gesture.

"Now, that's enough, Jed," he said. "You're a good man, a useful man and a friend of mine, but there are limits. Put up that accordion and quit singing."

Jedediah Simpson o' Lexin'ton, K—y, put the instrument back under his coat.

"Genius is always bein' squelched," he said, "an' gen'ally by those who pretend to be its best friends. Now when I git that big, red brick house o' mine in the outskirts o' Lexin'ton, K—y, I'm goin' to have an organ built into the wall, one o' the biggest in the world—I've heard tell o' sich things. I'm not goin' to play it myself, I guess it's a little late fur me to be up with the top-notchers now, but I'm goin' to hire the best D. M. thar is."

"D. M.!" interrupted Herbert. "What's that?"

"Doctor o' music. All these learned an' gifted fellers have letters before an' after their names nowaday—the Purfessor has used up all the letters o' the alphabet, an' then some more—an' every time I come into the house my D. M. will strike up, 'See the conquering hero comes, oh, see him! see him!' Now, how would that strike you, Herb, fur real bang-up style?"

"It strikes me pretty hard," said Herbert.

"An' I'd go aroun' to the best hotel in Lexin'ton, K—y," continued Jed, "an' I'd hire the best room in the place, an' I'd leave a call with the clerk for five o'clock in the mornin'. An' when the man knocked on my door at the app'int-ed time, an' called out, 'Wake up, Mr. Simpson, it's five o'clock,' I'd call right back, 'Git right out o' this, I don't have to.' I tell you, Herb, thar's nothin' like bein' rich. Then, an' only then, you can be jest as sassy as you want to."

"I'll be willing to listen to your D. M., Jed," said the Professor.

"An' you don't shoot him, neither, Purfessor, ef you don't happen to like him," said Jed. "You give me that promise right now."

"I promise, Jed," said the Professor earnestly.

Jed heaved a deep sigh of relief.

"Now," said the Professor, smiling, "I'll give you real music. I do not wish to discourage a worthy ambition, but Jedediah admits that he has begun late. Hence I have to restrain him with my revolver. Instead, I'll let you hear some great singers."

He went to one of the cliff houses and returned with a polished mahogany box from which jutted the mouth of a small brazen trumpet.

"This," he said, "is a music box on the phonograph plan but beautifully condensed. Small as it is, it sings gloriously and, well—some great prima donnas are small, you know. I have with me thirty of my favorite records, and this little box has sung splendidly for Jedediah and me in many a strange place. You will not feel jealous, will you, Jedediah, you with your accordion, if I let it play a few airs for the boys?"

"Me jealous?" said Jed. "I wouldn't think o' sech a thing. I like that box as well as you do, Purfessor, so let 'er rip."

Professor Longworth put the box down on the terrace, touched a spring, and the strains of Wolfram's Evening Song from "Tannhäuser" floated out for the first time over this wild corner of the Arizona mountains.

The great song has been heard by innumerable audiences but rarely in such a setting. It was only a mechanical box, but the wild mountains and the great gorge gave back the majestic strains in many a softened note. Applause followed and the Professor gave them several others, mostly songs from the greater operas, to all of which they listened with rapt interest that only such surroundings could furnish. Then the Professor carefully covered up the box with a cloth and put it away.

"We always take it with us on our travels," he said, "and often it proves a great solace. It shall play for you again."

It was a promise kept faithfully. Many another evening it played for them, and sometimes, when the Professor was absent, Jedediah Simpson o' Lexin'ton, K—y, pulled out a tune or two on his old accordion.

More pleasant days passed. The question of the gold still remained in abeyance. It was quite sure now that they would spend the winter in the village, and, before entering upon any elaborate quest for treasure, they meant to provide to the fullest extent against cold weather. More deer and wild turkeys were found, trout were caught in the stream, and in a way they lived luxuriously. Herbert developed rapidly both as a hunter and fisherman, and he grew wonderfully in strength, agility and knowledge of the wilderness. The Professor spent a great deal of his time prowling about the village, trying to reconstruct the past.

"It's a difficult task, one of tremendous difficulty," he said with a sigh. "In the Old World, history is practically continuous. One nation develops into another. We are Old World people ourselves, transplanted merely, but here in America the native races are all strange and new, and we do not know where to begin. About all we do know is that the cliff dwellers lived."

The Professor spoke thus when they were sitting out one evening on the terrace, which they always preferred to the close rooms. The air was quite crisp after nightfall, and they had built a fire which could be seen at a considerable distance. But danger seemed so remote now that they preferred to be comfortable, and take the chances.

The blue gulf at their feet had turned into a black abyss, but overhead arched a beautiful blue sky in which countless stars sparkled and blazed. Jed was lying on his back, his head propped on a piece of wood, a picture of content.

"I ain't botherin' much about them cliff dwellers," he said, "but I'm glad they left a house for me to live in when I want it. Did you ever see a brighter sky, Herb?"

"No, I don't think I ever did," replied Herbert, gazing up at the wonderful blue dome, shot with stars of blue and silver.

"Didn't know I was an astronomer, did you, Herb?"

"No, I shouldn't have suspected it."

His irony, if irony it was, was lost on Jedediah Simpson o' Lexin'ton, K—y.

"Well, I am," he said. "I've learned a lot o' things that are mighty cur'ous an' interestin' since I've been travelin' the last ten years with the Purfessor. See that silver dot across thar, Herb? That's old Jupe, the biggest in our bunch. He's only about a billion miles away. You wouldn't see him at all if he wasn't so big. Mercury an' Venus are a lot brighter, 'cause they're so close. People sometimes call each o' 'em the mornin' an' the evenin' star, though they ain't stars at all, but jest planets like ourselves. But they ain't much more than marbles when it comes to size compared with old Jupe."

"You do know a lot, Jed."

"Shorely I do, but I learned it all from the Purfessor. He's the fount o' wisdom. After I'd traveled around a while with him, an' had seen all the won'erful countries an' seas an' lakes an' rivers I began to feel right pert an' stuck up about this world o' ours. Then the Purfessor took it all out o' me, knocked me right into a heap by tellin' me that we didn't amount to shucks after all."

"Don't amount to shucks? Why, how is that, Jed?"

"It's the Gospel truth, Herb. He showed me that the earth is jest a poor little one-cent postage stamp sort o' a planet, an' our whole bunch, even with old Jupe hisself at the head o' it, are a purty small lot. Jest about fit fur one o' the lowest-priced seats away off in the corner o' the universe, whar nobody, likely to amount to anything, will ever see us. Thar ain't anything at all strikin' about us, 'cept Saturn with his rings, which they say ain't no rings at all, but jest strings o' little moons or somethin' o' that kind hangin' along in curves an' close together. Maybe Saturn with them bright collars around his neck might git a passin' notice, but the rest o' our bunch ain't in it, not even old Jupe hisself."

"An' do you know, Herb," continued Jed, warming to his subject, "that the sun which you saw set an hour or two ago, an' which you thought so gran' an' big an' fine, all fire an' gold, or maybe like a big diamond a million miles through, is jest a cheap little fourth-rate sun, one o' the kind all soiled an' dirty that they hand down from the back shelf an' say, 'Aw, take it along, you haven't got more'n five cents, anyway'? Why, Herb, when you come to them real big suns you're talkin'! Now there's Canopy!"

"Canopus," corrected the Professor. "How many times, Jedediah, have I given you the proper pronunciation of that name?"

"Well, Canopus. Do you know, Herb, that Canopy is ten thousand times bigger than our sun? An' thar are a heap more in the class that he trots along at the head of. Thar's Rigel, an' Aldebaran an' Sirius, that's the Dog Star, an' Antares, an' Arctury an' lots more, more than you can ever count. Why, Herb, when all them big, proud, haughty suns, Canopy at their head, go slidin' by, their noses in the air, they don't take any more notice o' our little piker o' a sun than ef it wasn't above groun' at all. Makes me think o' the time when I was in New York with the Purfessor, an' I stood on Fifth Avenue an' watched all them big, proud-lookin' women ridin' by in their carriages an' always lookin' straight ahead. They never saw Yours Truly, Jedediah Simpson o' Lexin'ton, K—y, a-standin' on the sidewalk an' not ridin' at all.

"I tell you it knocked me all in a heap, when the Purfessor showed me what a poor little peanut lot we was, an' me thinkin' all the time that I was swingin' round on a right fine planet, that most o' the stars was settin' up fur an' lookin' at an' admirin'. Why, Herb, they don't ever see us at all, or if they do it's jest to laugh. I can see one o' them fine, big, fust-class stars now, callin' out to another, 'Say, do you see that funny, teeny, weeny, little sun way down

70

thar in the corner in the dark tryin' to shine an' tryin' to pretend he's a real sun?' 'Yes,' says the other, 'I caught sight o' that thar obscure object once about a million years ago, but I thought it was only a chip off one o' them fourth-rate suns, an' that it had been dead nearly ever since. An' does that thing call itself a sun? Makes me think o' that old tale about the frog that wanted to be a bull, an' kep' puffin' an' puffin' an' swellin' itself out till it busted.' An' then they both go wheelin' on, laughin' fit to kill."

"And do you still feel that way, Jed?" asked Herbert, sympathetically.

"No. I was clean snowed under fur about two days, and then I got relief. Me an' the Purfessor was in New York at that time, an' the Purfessor took me to hear a Pole feller play the piano, knowin' that I always liked music. Don't ask me his name, but you take a big lot of x's, k's, c's and z's, put 'em in a bag, shake well before takin', an' then empty 'em out on the floor. Whatever way they fall will be his name. But, my eyes, Herb, the way he could play the piano! I didn't dream that sech things could be. He began to hit them keys slow like, then he got fast, then he stopped so suddint you fell over on your toes, then a little bit o' a key 'bout as big as the voice o' a baby two days old went whinin' off into the air, but kept gittin' a little louder an' a little stronger till it got to tearin' at your heart. Then I clean forgot all about the Pole feller with the name that used up the whole dictionary, and the Purfessor and the hall an' everybody in it, and I saw 'way back thar my father that had been dead twenty years, an' my mother, jest a young woman, with soft face an' smilin' eyes, bendin' over me, an' all the little fellers that I played with when I was a boy, an' the green grass in the medders, the greenest o' the green, and the creek that me an' the other little fellers swam in, that shore wuz the finest creek that flows on this earth, an' the red apples, hangin' on the apple trees, an' the peaches with their rosy sides to the sun, an' when I come to after a while, real tears wuz runnin' down these horny cheeks o' mine that hadn't knowed sech irrigation fur twenty years afore, an' the Purfessor he don't scold me none, cause he was a-lookin' purty solemn hisself.

"An' when we goes out I says to the Purfessor, 'Purfessor, you needn't tell me any more about Canopy an' Rigel an' all them big overbearin' suns. They don't bother me no more. I guess it ain't what you might be, but what you are, that counts. I was made to fit this here round, rollin' earth o' ours, an' she looks mighty good to me. She's got some fine big seas, and she's got some fust-class continents, North Ameriky an' Europe in partic'ler, worth all the others put together, an' a power o' smart islands, big an' little, an' lots o' things mighty cur'ous an' interestin'.

"I like that feller down in Tennessee who said he wuz fur his country ag'inst any other country, fur his state ag'inst any other state, fur his county ag'inst any other county, fur his town ag'inst any other town, an', ef it come to the pinch, he wuz fur his side o' the street ag'inst the other side. That's me. I'm fur this earth o' ours. I've had a pretty good time on it; it fits me like a kid glove, an' I expect to have more good times. Old Canopy can swell till he busts, like the frog, an' all them big fust-class stars can laugh at us, jest as much as they like as they go wheelin' by; I don't hear 'em. I'm fur this earth o' ours, she's a peach, she is, an' the center o' it is Lexin'ton, K—y, as you can see when you are thar, because the sky touches the ground at equal distances on all sides of it, an' I'm fur our bunch, too, meanin' our earth an' the five planets that I can see with my eye an' the two that I can't see, Neptune an' Urany, which are thar all the same. Yes, sir, I'm proud o' old Jupe, so big an' gran', an' Saturn with them beautiful collars on, an' Venus an' Mars so bright an' gay, an' sassy little Mercury. It's a nice friendly, little bunch, kinfolks fur a long time, an' I'm fur it ag'inst any other bunch, a thousand times bigger or ten thousand times bigger."

Jed stopped for want of breath and the Professor strolled further up the terrace, to examine the effects of the moonlight on certain strata of rock. Jed nodded toward him, and said in a loud, confidential whisper to the two boys:

"Thar's one o' your real great men. I can't say until I knowed the Purfessor an' worked with him that I had a power o' respeck fur all that old-time learnin'. But him an' the fellers like him are the real thing. They have to know. The politicians an' that kind can keep on shoutin' that a thing is as they say it is, but they don't prove it. They don't ever show their cards. They just keep on shoutin', and they shout so much an' so hard that people after a while believe 'em when they ain't real at all. But fellers like the Purfessor, with all them letters before an' after their names, parted in the middle so to speak, have got to deliver the goods. If they have the cards they must show down. When the Purfessor goes over thar to Babylon to dig up that old town, fifty thousand years old, some other pow'ful learned man will say to him, 'Purfessor Longworth have you got your town?' The Purfessor will say, 'Yes,' and then the other old Solomon will say, 'Purfessor Longworth, I'm from Missoury, you got to show me.' And then the Purfessor will have to trot out his town, temples an' stores an' baths an' dwellin's, all complete, or they'll say, 'Back to the woods with you, Purfessor Longworth, you're a fake, an' fakers don't go with us.' But don't you be worried about the Purfessor, he'll trot out his town, everythin' complete, includin' the walls."

"I'm sure he will, Jed," said Herbert. He, too, had conceived a great opinion of the Professor's learning and abilities. The Professor not only knew the heavens and ancient times, but the world about him as well. None so skillful as he to find the hidden cures of roots and herbs, none knew more about the habits of wild animals and how to track them, and catch them, none was a better judge of weather signs or the properties of soils. All looked up to him, all respected him, and the two lads no longer saw anything humorous in his little figure, his great head and his enormous pith helmet.

Two or three days later the Professor and the two boys went on a com-
bined exploring and hunting expedition, leaving Jed in charge of the village. They were a formidable little party, each carrying a rifle that he knew how to use, and also a revolver, handy in case of emergency. They waved a brief

farewell to Jed and climbed up the pole that led to the path over the cliff. When they had reached the summit they stood for a few moments resting and looking about them. It was a crisp, beautiful day of extravagantly bright sunshine, and every rock stood out with singular vividness. Both Charles and Herbert were conscious of a certain pride and a homelike sense as they looked. All this was theirs and their comrades'. No one else ever came to claim it.

"It's quite sure that we stand on a peninsula here," said the Professor. "It probably descends toward the north, but I'm thinking that it's larger than we supposed hitherto. At any rate we'll see."

It was early morning and they walked briskly forward. They passed the forest in which they had first found the wild turkeys, and then another, further away, in which these great birds still perched at night, carefully avoiding as they went along the sudden precipices, the location of which they now knew pretty well. Sometimes it was hard traveling, merely a path along a steep, with the sight of pine crests far below, and now and then the foamy flash of a mountain torrent. Far away, they saw other ridges and peaks, many with white snowy crests, all lonely and grand.

They descended rapidly now, still passing through the great pine forest, until they came into a region of poplar, birch, maple and other deciduous trees. It was singularly attractive, fresh and beautiful in its foliage. A great deer sprang up almost at their feet and fled swiftly away among the tree trunks. A brook, born in some lofty crest of snow, dashed tumultuously down the slope. Herbert knelt and drank of its waters, which he found to be ice-cold.

"We have descended pretty far," said the Professor, "and I can see the valley just below. It seems to be one of those fine nooks that are scattered throughout the Rocky Mountains all the way from Mexico to Alaska."

They advanced through the trees, the Professor leading, until they reached the valley, a noble, comparatively smooth, wooded plain, four or five miles long and about a mile broad. But before they had taken a half dozen steps into it the Professor suddenly lifted up his hand and gave a warning whisper.

The brook that they had seen on the slope had become a little river on the level and then had broadened out into a flood. At a point not far ahead it achieved a width of at least sixty yards, and, as they looked, a strange little chestnut-colored animal jumped into the water with a splash, and swam with powerful hind legs, while the small front ones were peacefully folded in front of him close to his breast, toward a queer conical construction that stood with others in the center of the flood, projecting above the water.

"A beaver dam and a beaver colony," whispered the Professor, "a big one, too. We're in luck, lads. It's one that's never been seen by the fur hunters, hidden away in these vast mountains. Wouldn't they give a pretty penny to find it! Don't move boys, and we'll see a lot that will interest us."

The boys did not move, in fact they scarcely breathed so great was their curiosity. They had stumbled upon what is now a rare sight in the United States, and, sinking down softly, the three lay long, watching. They saw more of the beavers in the water or at the edge, rather thick and clumsy-looking animals, weighing probably thirty-five or forty pounds apiece, with great oval tails, as broad as long, and bare of hair, but covered with thick hard black skin.

Some of them were gnawing at a tree that they had felled, cutting it into lengths, and the two lads noted the great incisor teeth with which they bit into the wood, as a boy's jack knife slips into pine. The lengths of wood, when cut, they floated off to the lodges in the middle of the pond that they had made, and there sunk and anchored them by some method of their own.

"That's for food in the long winter months," whispered the Professor. "Look, Herbert. See what's coming!"

The great pool itself had grass and weeds growing here and there in it, but, leading off from it, were channels or runways about a yard wide, extending perhaps a hundred yards into the forest. These were perfectly clear, and Herbert saw the reason why, when he looked at the Professor's suggestion. Two beavers were floating a large freshly-cut piece of maple down a channel into the main pool.

"More food," softly chuckled the Professor. "They've been here a long time, and they've cut away the trees immediately about them, until they have to make canals leading to the trees further on, down which they can float their food supply. Just like people! The pool is their central station, and the canals are the railroads leading to it from the grain fields. They keep 'em clear, because they've got to have unobstructed navigation."

Herbert's attention now wandered to the lodges, which were perhaps twenty in number, the longer of them at least seven feet in diameter and three feet high, every one of them with two entrances below water, as the Professor afterward told Herbert. They were built of matted mud, grass, sticks and moss, and they both looked and were very strong, sufficient to protect them from any animal invader.

The dam with which they created this pool, as a site for their city, was an even greater work of engineering. It presented a convex outline against the current of the creek, and had been raised to a height of fully five feet across the channel with a length of at least sixty yards, perhaps seventy. It was built of saplings that the beavers had cut and sunk lengthwise across the stream, stones, grass, sticks and mud, and, as the Professor afterward said, had been strengthened continually by the accumulation of floating débris.

It was all very wonderful to Charles and Herbert, and they looked and admired. It was a settlement as complete and thorough in its way as that of the cliff dwellers had been, and it probably had been there a long time. It was, perhaps, not strange that no one of the three human beings felt the slightest desire to fire upon these industrious little animals, while they worked in preparation for the coming winter, as their ancestors had done in isolation and security for generations.

Truly it was a scene of activity! More sections of logs came floating down the canals, and, even as they looked, two large beavers attacked a tree at the edge of the forest, a trunk fully three feet in circumference. Each animal stood on its hind feet and gnawed in parallel lines across the grain. When they had gone deep enough they wrenched out the chip with their teeth, and then the process was repeated, going deeper and deeper. Other beavers strengthened their lodges, and still others gave new touches to the dam, everyone working as he pleased, but all contributing to the general good. It impressed the imaginative Herbert as a singularly free, intelligent and happy life, a proper mingling of healthy work and entertainment.

"I hope the fur hunters will never run across them," whispered Herbert.

"It's too much to hope for that," replied the Professor in a similar whisper, "but it may be a long time yet. At least let us think so. Now we'd better be going, boys, and, as we go, I want to show you something."

He rose up and purposely stepped on a twig that broke with a snap. A big beaver slapped the water with his tail, making a resounding smack. In an instant all the beavers leaped into the water, and, together with those already there, sank at once from sight. There were ripples on the water which quickly died away, and then nothing. The tops of the lodges showed above the water, and all around were signs of the beaver workshop, but not a beaver.

"They are in their lodges," said the Professor. "It's wonderful how big a village they will build sometimes, though of course they may be at work at the same place for many years. I've heard that up in Northern Wisconsin or Minnesota they have built dams at least two hundred yards in length, although I have seen none of those myself."

"I'm very glad to have seen them," said Herbert. "It's added to my experience something that Jed would call mighty cur'ous an' interestin'."

It was almost twilight, when they began to climb down the ancient pole ladder. A sound of long drawn notes reached their ears, and the Professor laughed.

"Jed has taken advantage of our absence," he said, "to play his beloved accordion. We'll let him finish his tune."

They slipped quietly down the ladder and Jed did not hear. The supper cooked, he was sitting before the fire on the terrace, pulling away at his accordion, a rapt look on his face as he ground out, "Massa's in the cold, cold ground." They let him go through to the end, and then the Professor called out:

"Now having listened to your music, Jed, we'll see how you can cook."

'Jed sprang to his feet with alacrity, his face beaming.

"Welcome, fellers," he called. "Supper's ready an' I hope you've had as good a time as I have. Every time I feel a little tired o' work, an' that's right often, I sit down an' play a tune on the accordion, that is, if the Purfessor ain't aroun'. It's sweet music, an' I've had heaps o' pleasant thoughts to play. I've gone right back to Lexin'ton, K—y, an' I've seen myself in my great red brick house, with the Purfessor, an' Charlie and Herb guests o' mine, settin' aroun' in big easy chairs, drinkin' mint juleps, an' that hired man o' mine, the D. M., poundin' out gran', glorious tunes on the big organ, built in the wall. Oh, I tell you it was magnificent!"

"Let us hope that it will all come true, Jed," said the Professor.

"It shorely will! It shorely will!" said Jed with conviction. "I feel it in every bone o' me."

Then they ate and told Jed of the beaver colony, and soon afterwards all were sound asleep, wrapped in their blankets on the terrace, while Jed's stars, the size of which no longer awed him, sparkled in a sky of resplendent blue.

Chapter Eight - A Sudden Encounter

Work and interest! New discoveries! Fresh wonders every day! A keenness and zest in life that Herbert a month or two ago would have thought impossible in such a place! Such were their days. Charles, on another expedition into the canyon, found his horse and mule. They had joined the larger group, brought by the Professor and Jed, had affiliated perfectly, and were grazing in great peace and content on a little grassy meadow. Charles judged that however severe the winter might be, and however deep the snowfall, they would find grass and shelter in secluded alcoves of the canyon, and so he let them alone.

But the plateau above and behind the village and the slopes beyond furnished them with the greatest interests for the present. It was a well wooded and well watered country, abounding in game, and they found there excellent supplies for the coming winter. They also discovered a hot spring, the waters of which the Professor, after testing, announced to contain strong, healing properties. Many tracks around it showed that the wild animals took the same view.

A day or two later Charles, while hunting, killed a great stag near the hot spring. The body was too heavy for him to handle, even had he skinned and cleaned it, and, considering it safe, he left it there to return the next day with Herbert, thinking that the two would be equal to the task.

The boys went down through some thick bushes to the little open space in which the body lay.

"Here we are, Herbert," said Charles, parting the last of the bushes and pushing into the open space, Herbert close upon his heels. They were saluted by a tremendous growl, a deep, full-throated, ominous roar. The two boys shrank back appalled, a form of burnt sienna color upreared itself almost

76

directly above them. They looked into a dripping mouth, and saw above the mouth little eyes, inflamed with anger. They had run into a grizzly bear, feeding on the deer that Charles had slain.

"Jump! Jump back for your life, Herbert!" exclaimed Charles. "It's a grizzly!"

He had heard all his life that an angry grizzly was the most terrible of wild animals, and he knew that this could be none other. Instinctively he sprang back as he shouted, and escaped a sweep of the mighty paw. The same instinct caused him to jerk up his rifle and fire. The bullet struck the grizzly in the shoulder, but the big fellow, uttering a terrible roar, came straight at Charles. Herbert had stood still, as if deprived of the power of motion. He was a little on one side of the bear's path, but Charles saw him suddenly reel, struck by the grizzly's paw, and then the bear seemed to lurch against him as he fell and send him to the earth with a great thud.

Charles heard a cry. A thrill of agony shot through him because he felt sure that Herbert was killed, and the next moment the breath of old Ephraim was almost in his face again. He had the presence of mind to shove another cartridge into his rifle and fire a second shot. The bear roared, wheeled half around and tore at his breast with his paws. Charles, using the moment of grace, sprang to one side, reloaded and fired a third shot. The bear staggered, but recovered and rushed at him once more.

All happened in a daze to Charles. He never could remember the details clearly, but he knew that the woods helped him. He sprang from one tree to another, dodging the bear, and all the time firing steel bullets into him. The vitality of the great animal was amazing, but at last he uttered a kind of sobbing roar, fell down upon his fore-paws, then upon his side, and lay quite still, his mouth open and the blood coming from a half dozen wounds. Charles knew by his fixed eye that he was dead, but so tremendous had been the great bear's attack and struggle that it was his first impulse to fire two or three more bullets into his body. He put it aside and rushed to Herbert.

Herbert was lying half upon his side, half upon his back. His eyes were closed, and his face was quite white, save where the blood dripped upon it from a great red welt across his head.

Charles, with a cry of grief, dropped upon his knees beside his comrade. He felt for the pulse in the wrist; but there was none. When he let the wrist go, wrist and hand fell like a piece of wood to the earth. Herbert was surely dead and Charles was stricken by a great and terrible sorrow!

"Herbert! Herbert!" he cried, but Herbert made no answer.

Then Charles bethought himself of the hot spring, bubbling up not twenty yards away. He ran to it, and filled his hat with its hot, bitter waters. Much of it leaked out as he returned, but enough remained for him to pour a copious and powerful stimulant down Herbert's throat. A little gasping sigh came forth and filled Charles with delight. Herbert was not dead! And now he could feel a pulse in his wrist! But it was a very small, feeble and fluttering pulse, and he began to chafe vigorously Herbert's palms and temples. The fluttering little pulse grew stronger, and after a while Herbert opened his eyes.

"Who—who is it?" he said feebly.

"It's me, Charles, your comrade, and we've had a fight with a bear! Here, wait a minute, I'll bring you more of that water!"

He rushed to the spring and returned with another hatful. Herbert was in no condition to resist, and Charles making a scoop of his felt hat brim poured it into his mouth. Herbert strangled and cried out in protest, but his strength increased and he sat up.

"How my head aches," he said. "I thought that somebody hit me across it with a stick of wood, and that a moment later a house fell on me."

"That's just about what happened," said Charles. "Here, let me see that wound."

He examined it carefully. It was fully five inches long, and was swollen, but Charles saw that it had not been made by a claw. He inferred that the bear in one of his wild swings had struck Herbert a terrible blow with the side of his paw, and then had run against him as he fell, blow and shock together coming very near to killing him.

"You're all right, Herbert," said Charles cheerfully. "It's just a bruise. What did you mean anyway by running into a thousand-pound grizzly in that fashion? Didn't you know that you'd get the worst of it?"

Herbert smiled weakly.

"It was my first experience," he said.

"Never mind. The bear came out of the little end of the horn after all."

"You killed him, did you, Charlie?" said Herbert in admiration.

"Yes, because I was lucky enough not to be in the way of that sweep of his paw. But I think I must have put at least fifty pounds of metal into him. He's lying here in the bushes. Come, take a look, Herbert, old fellow."

Charles helped him to his feet, and then the two, Herbert leaning on Charles' arm, walked to the great bear, and looked down at his fallen figure.

"What a monster!" said Herbert, shuddering.

"Yes, but he'll never whack a boy with his paw again. He was a thief anyway. He was stealing our deer, and he's got what was coming to him. We can't do anything just now, Herbert, with either bear or deer. We've got to leave them to chance, and get ourselves back to the village."

It was slow progress. Herbert could not walk far without resting, and the wound continued to swell. Besides his head still ached badly, and all the strength seemed to go out of his bones. But he was full of pluck. He struggled on, and Charles was often compelled to insist upon his resting.

"Say, old fellow, sit down on that rock," he would say. "I'd have had to do it earlier, if I had been in your place."

Then, but not before Herbert would rest. At last they saw the light of "home," Jed's cooking fire, and Charles helped Herbert slowly down the pole ladder. Jed saw them and came forward in amazement.

"Why, Herb," he exclaimed, "what you been doin' to your head?"

"He's been trying to sing," Charles replied for his comrade, "and I hit him over the head with a stick. I said that only one man in our camp could sing and that was you, Jed. Two singers are entirely too many. I'm sorry, but I think I hit him a little harder than I intended."

"Quit your joshin'," said Jed. "What's Herb been really an' truly doin'? Fall-in' over one o' them thar precipices, I'll bet a nickel."

"No, I didn't fall, Jed," said Herbert, "I'll tell you the whole truth about the case. I met a grizzly bear, and I said to him: 'I don't like your looks.' 'No more do I yours,' says he, and with that he fetches me a swipe on the side of the head with a paw a yard long, a foot wide and a foot thick. Then as I went down he fell on me, and he weighed at least twenty thousand pounds. When I woke up about a month later Charlie was standing by me and he said, 'It's all right, Herbert, I challenged that bear to a duel because he insulted you and I've killed him.' Sure enough he had."

"Great snakes!" exclaimed Jed. "Have you had a run-in with a grizzly?"

"Look at my head," said Herbert.

The Professor arrived a few minutes later, and at once went to work on Herbert's head. He brought out the medicine chest, without which he never traveled, carefully washed and anointed the wound, and then covered it with strips of sticking plaster.

"I'll mix you a soothing draught, and then you'd better go to bed," he said. "When you wake up I think that headache will be gone, and a few more ap-plications of this medicine will keep the fever out of your wound. You'll be well in a week."

The Professor spoke truly, as Herbert was as sound as ever at the time appointed. But the Professor and Charles went the next day to the scene of the battle.

"You had a fortunate escape," said the Professor on the way. "You came suddenly upon the animal, when he was feeding, and a grizzly cornered at such a time is a ferocious and terrible beast."

"I did not know that grizzlies were found as far south as this," said Charles.

"They range all the way down to Northern Mexico, although I imagine that they have always been pretty scarce in this region. The black and cinnamon bears are more plentiful here."

"We're nearly to the spot," said Charles. "It's just through these bushes."

They pushed into the little opening, and as they entered it they heard a flapping of wings. They saw a huge bird with a great hooked bill rise heavily, and sail slowly away. The Professor grasped Charles' arm.

"You do not have all the luck," he exclaimed. "Look! A king vulture! It's al-most as large as a condor, the greatest of all birds. I knew that this region was its habitat, but they are very rare and I never saw one before."

"Shall I try a shot?" asked Charles.

"Not at all. Situated as we are it would be a useless slaughter. It is sufficient to have seen him."

The vulture sailed slowly on toward a lofty peak, until he was lost to view, and then the man and the boy resumed the object of their trip. The king vulture had not yet begun work. The body of the bear was untouched, and so was that of the deer save for the original attack of the grizzly.

The bear was a magnificent specimen, probably nine feet in length and weighing perhaps a thousand pounds.

"We must have that hide, my lad," said the Professor. "We will need it this winter."

He drew his knife and set about the task very skillfully, Charles aiding him. The immense weight of the bear impeded them, but the task was finally accomplished, and then they hung the great skin, truly a splendid trophy, in a tree, where no prowling animals could reach it. They cut out all the choicest portions of the bear and deer, and with much labor hung them in the tree also.

"I think it likely that grizzly steak is pretty tough," said the Professor, "but Jed can do wonders with a fire and a skillet, and he may be able to turn it into a delicacy. Deer we are sure of. Now the next thing for us to obtain is a mountain sheep or, as the Apaches say, mu-u. They are up there."

He nodded toward one of the snowy peaks.

"They are up there," he repeated, "and to get them we must have patience and endurance of both fatigue and cold. It may be that we'll take a hunt later for mountain sheep."

But they were busy the next day or two carrying the deer and bear meat to the village, and tanning the hide of the grizzly, which almost completely covered the floor of one of the cliff houses. Jed looked at it in wonder.

"Ef I happen to meet old Ephraim, when I'm goin' along through the woods," he said, "I'll take off my hat ever so polite an' I'll say to him, 'This path is yours, it's always been yours an' I know it. Excuse me while I leave.' An' that bear will stand thar in wonder, seein' me hittin' the high places an' the wind whistlin' through my coat tails."

"That might be a wise proceeding," said the Professor.

It was remarkable how little either boy thought just at this time of the hidden gold that Charles had come to find. It was true that the thought of it was always lurking at the backs of their heads, but the place of something vague and far away, of something that might or might not be realized, had been usurped by present actualities. The task of house-building and house-furnishing and of preparing for the great winter in the high mountains absorbed their minds almost completely. Charles would repeat to himself the words of Ananias Brown, and seek for them a solution in his surroundings, but he would not seek with the full and concentrated strength of his mind.

After a little, he would invariably turn to things more real, things that spoke more to the eye.

The wise old Professor noted the state of mind of both boys and he was pleased. All his life had been devoted to the acquisition of knowledge, covering a vast range, and he was deeply interested in the village of the cliff dwellers, the canyon and the great mountains. He was in no hurry to leave. Moreover, he strongly approved of the friendship of Charles and Herbert. He saw that when eastern lad and western lad were brought together and the differences of manner and early training were rubbed off, they were really the same. Not alone were they developing in strength and material resourcefulness, but in character as well. Passing through the forge the original iron was now being molded into fine wrought steel.

"They are good lads," the Professor said to his faithful Jedediah.

"Yes, them's real good boys," rejoined Jed. "Their colors hold true. They don't come out in the wash, but get brighter instead. It's funny how different they wuz in their ways at first, an' how much alike they are gittin' to be now."

It was a little colder than usual that evening, and, as they sat about the fire on the terrace, the Professor brought up a subject that he had left at rest for a long time.

"I've been thinking to-day about that man, Cruikshank," he said. "He must be somewhere in these mountains, and I've a feeling that we shall meet him again. He will be trespassing, of course."

He leaned his chin on his hand and mused.

"Strange, strange!" he said. "Strange that I do not place him! He never intimated the name of the university that he hails from, and I've never heard any of my colleagues speak of him."

"We may never see him again, Professor," said Herbert.

"No, we may not," rejoined the Professor, a sudden flash illuminating his blue eyes, "but if his degrees are false, if he is merely a sounding pretender, the man should be exposed! No such fraud should be perpetrated upon the world of learning!"

Herbert was silent. In the face of such an indignation as this he had nothing more to say.

Despite the elevation at which they lived it was often very hot in the cliff village, owing to the imprisonment of air in the great cleft, and on such occasions, which frequently lasted for some days, they passed all the time, day or night, out of doors. The Professor had a small tent, but they did not spread it, preferring to spread out their blankets and sleep outside on the terrace.

They also made an open cook-fire, the Professor showing them how, and in addition doing a large part of the work. They cut two green logs on the plateau above and with much labor rolled them down to the terrace. There they laid them side by side but not quite parallel. At one end they were not more than three inches apart, but at the other the distance was about ten inches. Then they flattened the tops of the logs until they presented a smooth surface like boards, upon which they could put their pans, kettles, skillets and other cooking utensils.

Then at either end of the space between the logs they drove a strong forked stick. They could not have done this if so much silt had not accumulated on the stone shelf, but it was sufficient to hold. They laid a slender, straight, but strong pole between the logs, and the task was really done. The fire was built between the logs, which were too green to burn, and which held in the heat like the sides of a stove. Over the coals at the broader end they would place the larger kettles and the cooking utensils that they had found, and at the narrower end they would put the coffee pot and other small vessels.

In this crude but effective place they could keep a fire burning with very little trouble. When the flames died down they covered up the coals so thickly with ashes that they would still be alive the next morning.

But they did not devote their whole time to work. Charles and Herbert found a fine bathing pool in the little river, a place at which it spread out to some width and was full twenty feet deep. It was so clear that they could see the fish, particularly the beautiful golden trout, swimming in it, and they were lucky enough, too, to find about fifteen feet above the water a niche in the cliff, from which they could dive.

Here they enjoyed many a fine swim, and the diving was particularly good. The water, even on the warmest day, was almost icy cold, flowing down as it did from the snow peaks, and it was a test of courage to leap into it. But both boys were bold and hardy. They would go down to the pool nearly every morning, climb into the niche, take off their clothing and then dare each other to jump first.

"You're afraid, Herbert," Charles said the first time they made the venture, as they sat, unclothed in the niche, looking down at the clear deep waters below—he knew very well that Herbert was not afraid, but they were boys.

"Afraid?" replied Herbert. "Not I, but do you know, Charles, while it's warm up here that water looks mighty cold down there. Is that a sheet of ice over it or is it merely an optical illusion?"

Charles laughed.

"There is no solid ice down there," he replied, "but I think that water is liquid ice. Now, which of us shall jump first? To jump first or not to jump first, that is the question."

"I propose that we jump together," said Herbert. "I'll count one, two, three, and the fellow that doesn't jump at the word three is a dyed-in-the-wool, yard-wide, top-to-toe coward, forever to be known as such, and to be despised by all men."

"Good," said Charles. "Go ahead."

"All right," said Herbert. "Make ready, one! two! three!"

Before the word "three" was clear from his lips two white bodies shot out from the niche in parallel, curving lines, struck below and far out in the pool, at the same time, and then reappeared on the surface, still at the same time, spluttering and gasping.

"There is no coward," said Charles, "nobody to be held up forever to the contempt of his fellow men. But, ugh-ugh, it is cold!"

"It certainly is," said Herbert also shivering. They could not stand the first plunge longer than ten minutes, but when they emerged and dried themselves in the sun they had a wonderful glowing feeling of exhilaration. With use they were able to stay in the pool much longer, and in two or three days they lured Jed to their niche.

"I ain't partic'lerly set on so much bathin'," said Jed, looking contemplatively at the pool. "Most any good thing can be overdone, an' you know I might ketch cold down thar."

"It's not cold at all," said Charles with a twinkle in his eye that Jed did not see. "Finest temperature I ever felt. Come, over we go."

"Me?" said Jed drawing back as far as the niche would allow. "I've heard the Purfessor say many a time, 'Look before you leap,' an' that's what I'm doin', I'm lookin' before I leap, an' I ain't so sure that I'm goin' to leap either."

"Oh yes you are," said Charles. They seized him by both arms—Jed was already undressed—and as they pulled him outward, he was compelled to leap with them, He came up, apparently in a state of great indignation, and climbed upon the stone.

"Fust thing I do, when I git warm ag'in," he said, "is to whip you two young rascals. Then I'm goin' to take all my baths in that hot spring up on the top o' the mountain."

But the anger of Jedediah was a sham. Soon he became as fond of the big pool as the boys were, and proved himself a splendid swimmer and diver. The Professor also took an occasional swim there.

Chapter Nine - New Resources

Their excursions to the plateau back of the cliff village now became numerous, and they were continually making discoveries of value and interest. In a secluded rift or narrow valley Herbert found young maize growing, shooting up stalks tender and yet small, but fresh and green. It was a plot about a quarter of an acre in extent, moistened by drainage from the surrounding slopes, and with a tiny stream flowing down the center, to be lost fifty yards further on in a mighty gulf below. The corn was growing irregularly, but it showed signs of abundant life, and Herbert brought the others to see his discovery.

"This is highly interesting and it also provides a new source of food for us," said the Professor, looking at the young stalks attentively through his great glasses. "It indicates that Indians lived here long after the cliff dwellers departed or were driven away. Perhaps it is not many years since the Indians themselves left, owing to some kind of superstitious terror, to which savage tribes are subject. It may have been a pestilence or an epidemic, which they attributed to the wrath of the gods of the cliff dwellers. Consequently this place has become, as the Hawaiians would say, tabu to them. So much the better for us, as it gives us the finest kind of protection from their raids."

"An' the corn?" said Jedediah Simpson. "How about the corn growin' here ez fine an' sassy ez ef it wuz sproutin' out o' the good soil aroun' Lexin'ton, K—y?"

"It is wild corn now. It was planted first by the Indian squaws who now and then do a little cultivation, when the soil is favorable and, when the place was abandoned, the falling grain renewed the stalks year after year. If we stay here long enough we will reap where the Apache women have sown. But we must set some dead falls and snares to protect our future grain from graminivorous and herbivorous wild animals."

"'Graminivorous an' herbivorous,'" said Jedediah Simpson in a whisper to Herbert. "Do you think anybody else could sling big words like them, jest ez smooth an' easy ez a baby drinkin' milk. Don't you think the Purfessor is the greatest man the world hez ever seed?"

"He is certainly a great man," said Herbert with the utmost sincerity. "For us in this wilderness there could be no greater."

"He knows everything in the world," continued Jedediah Simpson in an awed whisper.

They set the snares and dead falls after the usual western fashion, catching a number of wild animals, the skins and flesh of which they could use. This seemed to warn the others away, and the young cornfield was not molested. Herbert, who looked upon it as his by right of discovery, found an ancient and crude hoe in a dark corner of a little cliff house that they had not visited hitherto. It was made of sharp flat stone, with a wooden handle, rotted by age. But Herbert easily replaced the handle, and went forth to work in his corn field, hoeing carefully around each stalk, that is, turning up the fresh loose earth in a little hill. Jedediah Simpson, who knew all about raising Indian corn, helped him with instructions, but Herbert insisted upon doing the work himself. He took a pride in it, and the field soon showed the effect of his systematic care. Favored by one or two kindly rains the stalks shot up in an astonishing manner, and there was ample promise of fine roasting ears in the time to come.

Jedediah Simpson lay at the edge of the field in the shade of an oak, his long thin frame stretched out on the grass, and his broad-brimmed light felt hat covering his forehead to the eyes. He was the picture of content and ease. Herbert in the sun was wielding his stone hoe with vigor, turning up fresh loose earth about every individual stalk.

"Good boy, Herb," drawled Jedediah in long, slow tones. "Thar ain't no better occupation fur a growin' lad than hoein' corn. I done my share o' it when I wuz a boy in the neighborhood o' Lexin'ton, K—y, the fairest spot on this round rollin' earth, an' now see what I am. You keep right on, Herb, an' you'll be shore to rise to the heights that I've riz to."

Herbert laughed.

"Come on, Jed," he said. "The sun's bright an' fine."

"Not me," replied Jedediah. "I know somethin' 'bout that sun, when you're hoein' corn. No, you work right along, Herbert, an' I'll take a nap in the shade o' this tree."

They let their fire go out one night a little later, and, when the Professor examined their store of matches, he was somewhat worried to find it so small.

"We must save the matches," he said, "and I will use my fire sticks, although it's hard work I assure you."

"Fire sticks?" said Charles inquiringly.

"It's a method I learned from the civilized Apaches in the eastern part of the territory, and, as a precaution, I have had the fire sticks with me ever since I came to Arizona."

The two lads and Jedediah followed at the Professor's heels, curious to see him make fire with sticks. He produced from his stores a stick about two and a half feet long and half an inch thick.

"This," he said, "is a piece of the stem of the o-oh-kád-je, as the Apaches call it, that is, the fire stick. Now this stick has to coöperate with a piece of yucca, and the rest is hard work, as you shall soon see."

He laid a piece of dry soft yucca on the ground and planted his foot firmly upon it. He dipped the end of the fire stick in some sand, and pressed it firmly into a shallow depression of the yucca. Then he began to whirl the fire stick rapidly between his hands.

The little professor was a man of great strength. Charles and Herbert did not appreciate until now how very strong he really was. He had long arms, flexible and enduring as steel, and he twirled the stick with amazing rapidity, all the time keeping the end firmly fixed in the yucca.

A minute, two minutes. Perspiration stood out on the face of Professor Erasmus Darwin Longworth, but the speed of the revolving fire stick did not decrease. Gradually a very fine charcoal was ground from the yucca, and when the Professor thought he had enough, he spread it out on the dry grass. Then he blew a light breath or two upon it and it sprang into a flame, which was quickly communicated to small sticks of dry yucca, and then to larger wood, soon making a fine roaring fire.

Professor Longworth put away his fire stick and sat down, panting but triumphant.

"Friction, my lads, it's friction that does it, as it does many other things in this world. That is probably one of the most primitive human methods of making fire, but it works. And primitive as it is, it doubtless took savages thousands of years to evolve it."

Charles tried his hand at the fire stick a few days later, and succeeded, although the task exhausted him, but Herbert failed entirely and went in disgust to his corn field.

The Professor and Charles found at the furthest corner of the plateau remains of an Apache village which had ceased to exist probably twenty years before. Scattered about were pieces of pottery in a good state of preservation, which confirmed the Professor in his opinion that the Apaches had left in a panic.

"Superstition and terror were certainly at their heels," he said. "They had suffered a great disaster of some kind, and they thought that the god of the cliff dwellers was coming down upon them with the sword of wrath. Here are a number of their cooking utensils, quite intact. See this."

He picked up a large pot of unglazed earthenware, made from red clay, holding perhaps three gallons.

"This," said he, "in the tongue of the Apache is the a-mat, that is, the pot to cook in, and this is the haht-ki-wah or bowl to hold food."

The latter was also made of red, unglazed earthenware, and was broad and shallow, holding at least four gallons. They found other bowls and pots. Some were decorated with narrow horizontal or zigzag lines, made of lighter-colored clay. None of them had legs. When used for cooking they were, as the Professor explained, supported over the fire on three stones which were called o-kuth-ku-nu.

They discovered in a little gully, half hidden in drift, two globular water jars of red clay covered with loosely woven basketwork. Each jar would hold about four gallons, and, cleaning them out, they set them aside, resolved at some convenient time to take them down to the cliff village.

Charles found in the same gully a curious flat stone, about eighteen inches long and eight inches wide, evidently shaped by the hand of man. He held it up before the Professor.

"Now what is this?" he asked—he was curious to see if the Professor would know and he believed that he would.

"That," replied Professor Longworth promptly, "is the metate or in Apache ha-pi used by the Apache squaw in grinding corn. She sits down, holds this between her legs, lays the corn upon it, and grinds it with the rubbing stone or ha-pe-cha, one of which ought to be somewhere near us. Ah, here it is!"

He pulled from the debris a stone about six inches long and three inches thick. Like the metate it was of black lava.

"When the squaw has spread out the corn on the ha-pi," said the Professor, "she grasps the ha-pe-cha in both hands, and makes a rolling motion over the corn forward and back, for all the world like the rolling pin of our mothers. We'll take these along too some day, as we shall need them when the corn in Herbert's field matures."

Under the guidance of the Professor they discovered other supplies of food, which the ordinary man would never have noticed. They gathered the seeds of the saguara or giant cactus, called by the Indians ah-áh and considered by them a great delicacy. They also took later on the ripe pods of the mesquite, ground them on the rubbing stone, and made them into bread.

But their greatest resource was the mescal or American aloe, which the Apaches eat all the year around. They went down the lower slopes, and found it in perfection on the south side of high hills and on mesas or table lands that inclined to the south. Here it grew thickly, whole fields of it in the loose stony soil, and under the guidance of the Professor they went forth with their heavy hunting knives.

They cut down the plants, taking none that was not at least eighteen inches high, lopping off the stems close to the ground. Afterward they trimmed the projecting ends of the leaves so that every plant took a shape somewhat like a large ball. Then they carried them in the large flat baskets that they had found in the village to a good place in a ravine where they dug a pit at the bottom of which they built a fire.

They threw many loose stones on the fire, and when these were steaming hot they pitched the mescal on top of them, covering the plants afterward with grass and earth.

"We'll let the mescal stay in there forty-eight hours," said Professor Longworth. "I never did this before, but I have read the descriptions of it many times."

"O' course he knows how," said Jedediah Simpson to Herbert. "Thar ain't nothin' he don't know."

After the interval appointed by the Professor the pit was opened, and the mescal taken out. The fiber then had become tougher but the fleshy part of the plant had turned to a sweet juicy pulp. The portion not to be used soon was taken out, and spread in large cakes on sticks where it dried and was rolled up.

"If we keep this long," said the Professor, "it will become very hard and tough, and we shall have to soak it in water before we can eat it, but it will be valuable to us, as a reserve supply of food, in case of need."

"The greatest man in the world," breathed Jedediah Simpson again.

But the Professor's drafts upon his resources did not stop with the mescal.

"It is well to have studied the products of desert and semi-desert lands and their uses," he said. "I have been able to put such knowledge in practice in both Asia and Africa, and that fact will help us here."

He showed them on the slopes the opuntia or prickly pear, also called the tuna, which he said would ripen in September, now at hand, and could be used, and he pointed out the Spanish bayonet, the fruit of which resembled a banana.

"It will ripen in October and can be eaten," said Professor Longworth. "In addition to these things we shall have the camas or bulb of the wild hyacinth, which the Apaches call a-nya-ka. Then there are seeds of the ground or mock orange; acorns, in Apache i-hi-mi-a; pine nuts, in Apache, u-koh; wild garlic, wild potatoes, currants, juniper berries, and many other things which I need not describe now. Every land, no matter how inhospitable it may seem, contains food for man if you only know how to find it."

"But, Professor," said Jedediah Simpson, "you're the only man that knows how to find it."

Professor Erasmus Longworth smiled benignly. He did not mind a little spontaneous and sincere praise now and then.

"Not the only one, Jedediah," he said, "but I am glad for our sakes just now that I am one of those who do know."

A day or two after the curing of the mescal Charles wandered on a hunting expedition about a dozen miles among the hills and slopes. He had not been successful, and, seeing water shining among the trees, he went at once toward it as he was both hot and thirsty. He came to a narrow but swift and deep creek, thickly lined with a species of willow.

He pushed his way through the willows, and, kneeling, drank of the water which was cold and fresh. But when he rose again he noticed that his clothing was spangled with a whitish sugary substance. He could not understand it, until he looked at the leaves of the willows and saw that they were covered with the same substance. He touched a leaf to his lips, and found it sweet and pleasant to the taste. He did not know what he had found, but, when he returned to the village, he reported his discovery to Professor Longworth.

The Professor requested a minute description of the willows, and also of the thin, sugarish covering that he had found upon the leaves. Charles was a close observer and he gave it to him absolutely correct in every detail.

"This is unique," he said. "What you have found on those willows, Charles, is honey dew. So far only one other case of this kind is known. It is found on the leaves and young stems of a peculiar kind of willow that grows along Date Creek in Arizona. You can make a fine drink out of it, as I can very soon prove to you."

The Professor and the two boys went on the following day to the creek, and broke off a quantity of the young stems and leaves of the willows which they stirred vigorously in water. The result was a pleasant and refreshing drink of which Charles and Herbert imbibed very freely, but took no harm. They returned to the creek more than once for the stems and leaves of the willows, and usually kept one of the big three-gallon jars filled with the sugar water.

The hunting was also good. They shot the hare (ku-le), the rabbit or cotton tail (he-lo), the deer (kwa-ka) and the antelope (mu-ul). It was Professor Longworth who told them the Apache names of these animals, and the village was soon as well stored with food and drink as it probably ever had been in the time of the cliff dwellers.

"The term has often been abused," said Professor Longworth, "but we are really the heirs of the ages. The cliff dwellers dug out our houses for us a thousand years ago, maybe, and have left them for us along with many valuable utensils. The Apaches have also been in this vicinity, and, in their hasty departure, left articles which have contributed to our comfort. This is certainly a wonderful region, a most picturesque and extraordinary corner of our country, and I shall never regret my stay here."

"Me neither," said Jedediah Simpson. "The only thing we need is a little more music. Ef we could only have a brass band playin' now an' then out thar on the terrace I'd be puffickly happy."

But Herbert did not miss the brass band. They were all sitting by the fire as the evenings were always chill, and he thought how wonderful his luck had been to fall in with such good and resourceful friends. He walked to the edge of the terrace and looked down in the black gulf. Then he picked up a stone as large as his fist and dropped it into the darkness. He heard one or two sounds far below, as it rebounded from the side of the cliff, and then nothing, although he stood for a moment or two with his right ear bent forward listening.

"What are you doing, Herbert?" asked Charles.

"I know," said Professor Longworth with intuition. "He's making comparisons that please him. He's telling himself how glad he is to be up here with us instead of tumbling down the cliff a thousand feet alone and in the darkness."

"That's so," said Herbert, as he returned to the fire.

Chapter Ten - The Lost Herd

They extended their investigations further and further, Charles and Herbert usually together and ranging far and wide. These expeditions were partly for game, partly for the purpose of unveiling the country and partly to find signs corresponding to the story of Ananias Brown. The two lads departed on such a trip one morning, taking with them enough food for two days. They often stayed out a night now, and the Professor and Jed would feel no uneasiness, knowing that they were sure to come back in safety.

The two made no pause as they descended the slope that led back from the plateau, two erect, strong youths, bearing their rifles lightly and walking with easy, tireless steps. They entered the little marshy valley, where the beaver colony lived and flourished, and there they stopped for the first time. They had made no noise as they came and they remained a few moments at an undisturbing distance, watching the busy beaver people. They saw them float more sections of logs down their canals, and, as they looked, a maple at the edge of the forest fully four feet in circumference, but cut through by the sharp beaver teeth, fell with a crash.

"I suppose it's going to be a hard winter," said Charles. "Look how our beaver friends are working and accumulating supplies."

"Well, we're imitating their example, at least as best we can," rejoined Herbert.

They slipped silently away, not wishing to disturb the busy and innocent little people, and swiftly continued their journey to a point in the northwest, further than they had ever yet gone. After they had walked some distance the traveling grew easier than they had expected to find it. They were ascending again, but it was up a comparatively smooth incline, among fine forest trees, free from undergrowth.

It was about noon when they stopped to eat a little venison and rest under the shade made by a group of magnificent pines. The high peaks, crested with snow, seemed nearer now, and below them they could see the tiny valley where the beaver home lay hidden.

"It's a little world, way up here on top of the high mountains," said the imaginative Herbert, "and it's ours alone."

They resumed their march and a half hour later Herbert, who was in advance, stopped with a cry of delight. He had just reached a summit and he was looking downward. Below them like a bowl of blue set in the mountain rock was a beautiful little lake, a gem of a lake, so very blue that it flashed back a deeper tint in reply to the blue skies above. It was almost perfectly round, perhaps not more than three hundred yards across, and apparently of immeasurable depth. Cliffs nearly perpendicular rose about two hundred yards above the water's surface and they were fringed all around with fine straight pines.

There lay the little lake, a deep well of blue, glittering and basking in the sunlight and Charles and Herbert felt all the joy of the discoverer. They were sure that theirs were the first white faces ever to bend over these blue waters, and in their minds the red did not count.

Herbert threw down a stone. It sank with a plunk that told of the mighty depths below, and a flock of startled wild fowl, rising from the water's edge, winged an arrowy flight. A great eagle, too, soared up, but he sailed slowly, as if in outraged dignity, and the boys fancied that his little red eyes were looking angrily down at these impertinent intruders.

"I suppose that Mr. Eagle was fishing down there in Lake Carleton, and regards it as a piece of presumption on our part to interrupt him," said Charles. "I've a good notion to take a shot at him for his arrogance."

"Don't waste good cartridges," said Herbert, "I think we'd better push on toward Mount Wayne over there, because you know that is where we intended to go."

He was pleased because Charles had named the lake after him, and Charles, in his turn, was pleased because Herbert had bestowed the name of Wayne upon the mountain.

They looked at each other and smiled.

"Well, why not?" said Herbert. "We're the discoverers, and it's what other discoverers do."

"Right you are," replied Charles stoutly. "It's Lake Carleton, and it's Mount Wayne now and forever."

They left their blue lake reluctantly and pushed on for Mount Wayne. It was their object to see what lay behind that peak. They were far up on the shoulder of it by the middle of the afternoon, and then they curved around the side among thick groves of pines and other trees, and then dense patches of undergrowth. The sun was now going down the western heavens and touched everything with red light.

Charles parted the twining bushes in front of him with both hands and pushed his body through a cleft while Herbert stood by to see the issue. He took but a single step and then threw himself back, like a soldier who would escape a bullet, his face, now turned toward his comrade, showing a yellowish hue in the fading sunlight. He raised his hand and wiped his damp forehead, while Herbert gazed at him in silence, seeing fear, sudden and absolute, in his gaze, as if death had faced him with no warning.

They stood so for a few moments, until the terror died slowly in Charles' eyes, when he took another step back, and laughing a little in a nervous way, pointed before him with a long forefinger.

Herbert advanced, but Charles put a restraining hand upon his shoulder, and bade him take only a step. Herbert obeyed and, with his hand still on his comrade's shoulder, looked down a drop of a thousand feet, steep like the side of a house, the hard stone of the wall showing gray and bronze where the light of the setting sun fell upon it.

They saw at the bottom masses of foliage like the tops of trees, and running through them a thread of silver which they felt sure was the stream of a brook or creek. They were looking into a green valley, and now Herbert understood Charles' terror, when instinct or quickness of eye, or both, saved him from the next step which would have taken him to sure death.

The valley looked pleasant, with green trees and running water, and Charles suggested that it would furnish a good camp for the night.

Herbert pointed straight before them, and three or four miles away rose the mountain wall again, steep and bare, the hard stone gleaming in the moonlight. Charles followed his finger as he moved it around in a circle, and the wall was there, everywhere. The valley seemed to be enclosed by steep mountains as completely as the sea rings around a coral island.

Both boys gazed with the most eager curiosity. This seemed to them the most singular place that they had ever seen, more singular even than the village of the cliff dwellers when they first came upon it. Both lay down for greater security and stared over the brink into the valley, which looked like a huge bowl, sunk there by nature. The sky was clear and they could see the boughs of the trees below waving in the gentle wind. The silver thread of the brook widened, cutting across the valley like a sword blade, and they almost believed that they saw soft green turf by its banks. But on all sides of the bowl towered the stone walls, carved into fantastic figures by the action of time and mountain torrents.

The green valley below could not remove the sense of desolation which the walls, grim and hard, inspired. Their eyes turned from the foliage to the sweep of stone rising above, black where the light could not reach it, then gray and bronze and purple and green as if the sun's fading rays had been tinted by some hidden alchemy. They assisted nature with their own imaginations and carved definite shapes—impish faces and threatening armies in the solid stone of the walls. Charles felt the shiver of Herbert's hand, which was still upon his shoulder, and he felt, too, that he was chilled. He knew it to be the stony desolation of the walls, and not the cold of the night, that made him shiver, for he too felt it in his bones and he proposed that they look no more, at least not then, but build a fire for the night and rest and sleep.

"Good enough," said Herbert. "It's a rather weird-looking place down there, and I want to see into it, but I don't feel like climbing down in the night time."

They gathered fallen brushwood and built a fire, but they were rather silent about it. Each knew what was in the other's mind. The mystery of the valley was upon both, and they would wait only until the daylight to enter it and see what it held.

Charles lighted the fire, and the blaze rising above the heaps of dry sticks and boughs was twisted into coils of red ribbon by a rising wind. A thin cloud of smoke gathered and floated off over the valley, where it hung like a mist, while the wind moaned in the cleft.

Herbert complained that he was still cold and wrapping his blanket tightly around him sat close to the fire where Charles noticed that he did not cease to shiver. Then Charles spread out his own blanket and both lay down, seeking sleep.

"We'll tear its inmost secret right out of that valley to-morrow," called out Charles in a defiant tone.

"We surely will," replied Herbert in the same challenging voice.

Neither knew just what he was defying but each felt that it was something very powerful.

Then they closed their eyes and said no more.

Charles awoke far in the night. The fire had burned down, there was no moon and Herbert's figure beyond the bed of coals was almost hidden by the darkness. Damp mists had gathered on the mountain, and his hand, as he drew the corners of the blanket around his throat, shook with cold.

Not being able to sleep just then, Charles rose, and put more wood on the heap of coals. But the fire burned with a languid drooping blaze, giving out little warmth, and offering no resistance to the encroaching darkness. Herbert slept heavily, and was so still that he lay like one dead. The flickering light of the fire fell over his face sometimes and tinted it with a pale red. He was so unlike his real self that Charles felt for a moment as if some genii of the Arabian Nights had changed his comrade in his sleep.

He sat by the coals a little while looking around at the dim forest, and then the attraction of the great pit or valley drew him toward it. He knelt at the brink, holding to the scrubby bushes with each hand, and looked over, but he could no longer see the trees and brook below. The valley was filled with mists and vapors, and from some point beneath came the loud moan of the wind.

The boy stayed there a long time, gazing down at the clouds and vapors that heaped upon each other and dissolved, showing denser vapors below, and then heaping up in terraces again. The stone walls, when he caught glimpses of them, seemed wholly black in the darkness of the night, and the queer shapes, which took whatever form his fancy wished, were exaggerated and distorted by the faintness of the light.

The place put a spell upon the lad. He was eager for the morning to come that Herbert and he might enter the valley, and see what, if anything, was there, besides grass and trees and water. He felt the strange desire to throw himself from a height which sometimes lays hold of people, and at once pulling himself back from the brink he returned to the fire.

Herbert was still sleeping heavily and the flames had sunk again, flickering and nodding as they burned low. Charles lay down and slept until morning when he awoke to find that Herbert was already cooking their breakfast.

"You looked pretty tired as you lay there, old fellow," said Herbert, "and so I thought I'd let you sleep a while longer."

"Thanks," said Charles. "Then I'll do the cooking next time and you can rest. Suppose we start down in half an hour?"

"That suits me," replied Herbert.

The valley assumed a double aspect in the bright light of the morning, green and pleasant far down where the grass grew and the brook flowed, but grim and gaunt as ever in its wide expanse of rocky wall. The rising sun broke in a thousand colored lights upon the cliffs, and the stony angles and corners threw off tiny spearpoints of flame. The majesty of the place which had taken hold of them by night also held its sway by day.

"The most impressive of all our discoveries," said Charles.

"It surely is," said Herbert with emphasis.

They had no doubt that they would find a slope suitable for descent, if they sought long enough, and they pushed their way through the bushes and over the masses of sharp and broken stone along the brink, until their bones ached and their spirit was weak. But the two lads encouraged each other with the hope that they should soon reach such a place, though the circle of the valley proved to be much greater than they had expected.

After a while they were forced to rest and eat some of the cold food that they had wisely brought with them. The sun was hot on the mountains and the stone walls of the valley threw the light back in their eyes until, dazzled, they were forced to look away. But they had no thought of ceasing the quest; such a discovery was not made merely to leave the valley unexplored, and rising again, after food and rest, they resumed their task. About noon they saw a break in the wall which they thought to be a ravine or gully of sufficient slope to permit of descent into the valley, but it was late in the day when they reached the place and found their opinion was correct.

The ravine was well lined with short bushes which seemed to ensure a safe descent, even in twilight, and they began the downward climb, seeking a secure resting-place among the rocks for each footstep and holding with both hands to the bushes and vines.

The sun, setting in a sky of unbroken blue, poured a flood of red and golden light into the valley. The walls blazed with vivid colors, and the green of the trees and grass was deepened. Herbert stopped, and touching Charles on the shoulder pointed with his finger to the little plain in the center of the valley where a buffalo herd was grazing. Such they were they knew at the first glance, for one could not mistake the great forms, the humped shoulders and shaggy necks.

Neither sought to conceal his surprise, and perhaps neither would have believed what his eyes told him had it not been for the presence and confirmation of the other. They knew as everybody else knew, that the wild buffalo had been exterminated in the southwest years ago, and that even then the only known herd left in the whole United States was somewhere in the tangled mountains of Colorado, and yet here they were gazing upon another herd of these great animals, at least fifty of them, for they could count them as they moved placidly about and cropped the short turf.

"Herbert, it's me, isn't it?" asked Charles anxiously but ungrammatically. "I'm really here, am I not? I'm not dreaming?"

He touched his forehead tentatively with his finger, as if to see whether it were genuine flesh and blood.

"Yes, Charlie, it's you, I certify to it," replied Herbert in a loud whisper, "but I'm glad that you're here to certify to me, too."

"And it's no delusion? Those are buffaloes, real live buffaloes? I'm not just imagining?"

"No, I see 'em, too. And we two couldn't imagine exactly the same thing."

They remained a quarter of an hour in that notch in the wall, exulting over their second discovery, for they considered the tenants of the valley of as great importance as the valley itself, and exchanged with each other sentences of surprise and wonder. The sun hovered directly over the further brink, and poised there, a huge globe of red, shot through with orange light, it seemed to pour all its rays upon the valley.

Every object was illumined and enlarged. The buffaloes rose to a gigantic height, the trees were tipped with fire, and the brook gleamed red and yellow, where the rays of the sun struck directly upon it. Again they said to each other what a wonderful discovery was theirs and looked to the rifles that they had strapped across their backs, for seeing the great game of the valley they had it in mind to enjoy unequaled sport. Herbert lamented the speedy departure of the second day, but Charles thought the night would give them a better chance to stalk the big game, and thus talking, they resumed the descent. The sun sank behind the mountains, the red and golden lights faded, and the valley lay below them in darkness. The buffalo herd had disappeared from their sight, but feeling sure that they should find it again, they continued their descent, clinging to the bushes and vines, and wary with their footing.

The twilight was not so deep that the gray mountain walls did not show through it, and, as they painfully continued their descent, the trees and the brook rose again out of the dusk. Nearing the last steps of the slope they could see that the valley was much larger than it had looked from above, and their wonder at the presence of the herd was equaled by their wonder at the manner in which it had ever reached such a place, as there seemed to be no entrance save the perilous path by which they had come.

At last they left the bushes and stones of the ravine and, standing with feet half buried in the soft turf of the valley, looked up at the sky, as if from the bottom of a pit.

The twilight was as clear around them as it had been on the mountain above, and they could see a pleasant stretch of sward, the land rolling gently with clumps of bushes and large trees clustering here and there.

They did not pause to look about, both being filled with the ardor of the chase, and walked quickly toward the little bit of prairie in which they had seen the buffaloes, examining their rifles to be sure that they were loaded properly. Both felt that sense of unreality which strange surroundings always give.

The night, now fully come, was not dark. Stars came out, and a pale light glimmered along the edges of the cliffs, which seemed, as they looked up, to threaten them.

They reached the brook that they had seen from above, a fine stream of clear water, a foot deep and a dozen or more across. They paused there to drink and refresh themselves and found the water cool and natural to the taste.

"This must flow into some cave under the mountain," said Herbert. "It's bound to have an outlet somewhere."

But Charles did not reply, merely twitching his sleeve and urging him on to the chase. Herbert was nothing loth. The minds of both were now filled with thoughts of the buffalo herd, which each in his secret heart now began to fear was some sort of a delusion after all.

Another thing that impressed them with this sense of weirdness and unreality was the absence of life in the valley. No little burrowing animals sprang up at their feet as they passed. There were trees with foliage, but no birds flew among the boughs. All around them was silence, save for the crush of their own footsteps and their breathing, quickened by their exertions. Herbert spoke of this silence and absence of life, and they stopped and listened, but heard nothing. The night was without wind. They could not see a leaf on the trees stir, the air felt close and heavy, and each lad noticed that the other's face was without color.

Fifty yards further and they came to the open space in which they had seen the herd. They felt sure now that it was not far beyond them as the heads of the animals had been turned south and they believed that they had continued to move in that direction, while they nibbled the grass. They paused to take another look at their rifles, their ardor for the chase rising to the highest, leaving them no thought but to kill. The herd, although still out of sight, had suddenly ceased to be unreal.

"I'm going to have a big bull before many hours," said Charles.

"Me, too!" said Herbert.

It seemed a great thing to them to hunt such great game, and they felt now the thrill which leads men to risk their own lives that they may take those of the most dangerous wild beasts. The dusk had deepened somewhat, and though of a grayer tone in the valley where mists seemed to be collected and hemmed in, it was not dense enough to hinder their pursuit.

Charles stopped suddenly, and put a hand on Herbert's shoulder, although one boy had seen them as soon as the other. The herd was grazing in the edge of a little grove a few hundred yards ahead of them but within plain sight. This closer view confirmed their count from the mountainside that they were about fifty in number, and the admiration of the boys mingled with wonder, as they were magnificent in size, true monarchs of the wilderness, grazing unseen by man, while the rush of civilization passed around their mountains and pressed on to the Pacific.

The figures of the buffaloes stood out in the gray twilight, huge and somber, surpassing in size anything that either boy had imagined. They felt a joy and pride that it was their fortune to find such game, and also a glorious anticipation of the trophies that they would show. Each saw exhilaration sparkling in the other's eyes, and they spoke together of their luck.

Charles held up a wet finger and finding that the wind was blowing from the herd to them they resumed the advance, sure that they could approach near enough for a rifle shot. The herd was noiseless like the boys, the huge beasts seeming to step lightly as they cropped the grass, the scraping of the bushes, as they passed through them, not reaching the ears of Charles or Herbert.

Again the sense of silence and desolation oppressed the two. The grayness over everything, the trees, the grass, the mountains, the strangeness of the place and their situation seized them, and clung to them, though they strengthened their wills and went on, the zeal of the chase overpowering all else.

Their stalking proceeded with a success that was encouraging to novices, and a few more cautious steps would take them within good rifle shot. They marked two of the animals, the largest two of the herd standing near a clump of bushes, and they agreed that they should fire first upon these, Herbert taking the one on the right. If they failed to slay at the first shot, which was very likely, the chase would be sure to lead them directly down the valley, and they could easily slip fresh cartridges into their rifles as they ran. Nor could the game escape them within such restricted limits; and thus, feeling secure of their triumph, they slipped forward with the greatest caution, until they were within the fair range that they wished. Then they stood motionless while they secured the best aim, each selecting the target upon which they had agreed.

The herd seemed to have no suspicion of their presence. However acute might be the buffalo's sense of smell, it had brought to them no warning of danger. Their heads were half buried in the long grass, and as the boys looked along the barrels of their rifles they felt again the stillness of the valley, the utter sense of loneliness which made them creep a little closer to each other, even as they sought the vital spots in the animals at which they aimed.

"We can't miss," whispered Herbert, though his hands shook with excitement.

"No, we can't," replied Charles, whose hand shook also.

Then they pulled trigger so close together that their two rifles made one report.

Deep was their astonishment to see both buffaloes whirl about, untouched as far as they could tell, and stare at them. The entire herd followed these two leaders, and, in an instant, fifty pairs of red eyes confronted the lads. Then they charged like a troop of cavalry, heads down, their great shoulders heaving up. Charles and Herbert slipped hasty cartridges into their rifles and fired again, but the shots, like the first, seemed to have no effect, and, in frightened fancy, feeling the breath of the angry beasts already in their faces they turned and ran with all speed up the valley, in fear of their lives and praying silently for refuge.

Each boy, either in reality or imagination, felt a fiery breath behind him, and unpleasantly close, and they certainly heard the trampling roar of the mighty beasts.

It was not like the attack of the grizzly; this was weird and contained for them an overpowering awe which exceeded their fright. Neither noticed until a little later that each had unconsciously dropped his rifle in his headlong flight.

Charles looked once over his shoulder, and saw the herd pursuing not fifty feet away in solid line like the front of an attacking square. He shouted to Herbert to dart to one side among some trees, hoping that the heavy brutes would rush past them, as they could not hope to outrun them in a straight course, and Herbert obeyed with promptness. They gained a little by the trick, but the buffaloes turned again presently, and then seizing the hanging boughs of two convenient trees, they climbed hastily up and out of present danger.

The buffaloes stopped about a hundred feet away, still in unbroken phalanx, and stared at them with red eyes. Each boy was filled with fear. Neither would deny it! They felt it in every fiber. They had heard always that these beasts, however huge, were harmless, their first rush over, but the buffaloes were looking at them now with eyes of human intelligence and even more than human rage; a steady, tenacious anger that threatened them and seemed to demand their lives as the price of the attempt upon their own. Both boys felt cold to the bone, and the angry gaze of the besieging beasts held their own eyes until they turned them away, with an effort, and looked at each other. Then each saw that the other was as white and afraid as he knew himself to be.

"Here we are, Herbert!" called Charles shakily.

"Yes, here we are, Charlie!" returned Herbert with equal shakiness. "But I don't know and you don't know when we are going to get away."

While they talked, the buffaloes began to move and the boys hoped that they were going away, but the hope was idle. They formed a complete circle around the two, a ring of sentinels, each motionless after he had assumed his proper position, the red eyes shining out of the massive lowered foreheads and fixed on the intruders. Charles laughed, but it was not a laugh of mirth.

"We've got nothing to fear, Herbert," he called out. "The buffalo is not a beast of prey. They'll go away presently and begin to crop the grass again."

But his tone was not convincing. His words somehow did not express a belief. He knew it, and Herbert knew it. The night did not darken, but the curious grayness which was the prevailing quality of the atmosphere in the valley deepened, and the forms of the beasts on guard became less distinct. Yet it seemed only to increase the penetrating gaze of their eyes which flamed at the lads like a circle of watch fires. The sentinels were noiseless as well as motionless. The wind whimpered gently through the leaves of the trees, but there was nothing else to be heard in the valley, and save the two boys perched in the trees, and the watching buffaloes, nothing of human or animal life was to be seen.

The night grew cold and Herbert felt chilled to the marrow of every bone. The lone valley and their extraordinary situation filled him with the most uncanny feelings. Were the buffaloes real or unreal? Was it all an illusion. Once as he looked at them, red-eyed and threatening, his hair rose slowly on his head.

"I wish they would go away!" he called to Charles. "I feel as if I were being watched by ghosts."

"Steady, old fellow, steady!" called back Charles who recognized the quaver in his comrade's tone. "Hold on to your tree! They'll leave after a while."

98

Herbert relapsed into silence, but presently he laughed in a shrill, unnatural way.

"Stop that, Herbert!" sharply called out Charles who was alarmed for him.

"I have it," said Herbert in the same, shrill high-pitched tone. "This is the last buffalo herd, the last really wild one. All of them have been hunted from the face of the earth except this lone band which is now left here to hunt us, the first human beings who have ever come against it! See, there they are, the living proof!"

He laughed in the same uncanny way. Charles laughed, too, partly to hearten his comrade, but his laughter sounded strange even in his own ears, and, looking at the silent ring of sentinels, he, too, felt the blood chilling in the marrow of every bone. When or how he should escape he could not foresee, and he did not feel the fear of death; yet there was nothing that he had in the world which he would not have given to be out of the valley.

Herbert laughed again that shrill, acrid laugh, and when Charles asked him to stop he jeered at him and bade him notice how faithful the besiegers were to their duty.

Not one of them had moved from the circle, their forms becoming duskier as the night deepened, but growing larger in the thick atmosphere. The sky above was cloudless, and the lads seemed to see it from interminable depths; the huge cliffs rose out of the mists, shapeless walls, and the trees became gray and shadowy. An extraordinary silence now reigned. The wind had ceased to move the grass or leaves. The buffaloes were motionless. And this silence was heavy and ominous. It lay horribly upon the nerves of both boys, and they longed for something to break the stillness, the leap of a rabbit, if rabbit there was, the scamper of a deer, or the brush of a wild fowl's startled wing. But there was nothing only the silent, menacing ring, and the wan moon looking down.

Charles secured himself in the crook of a bough and tried to sleep. He thought that he fell into a kind of stupor, and he awoke from it to find the wan moon and the silent line of sentinels still there. Far off in a distant cleft of the cliffs a noise arose but it was only the moan of an imprisoned wind, and it brought no comfort.

Charles called to Herbert and was glad to hear his comrade answer in a natural tone.

"Anything to suggest?" asked Herbert.

"Only that we must get away from here."

"How are we to do it?"

"We might open fire with our revolvers. But they are rather far away for such weapons, and while we might kill one or two the rest would still be there."

"That's so," said Herbert, "and do you know, Charlie, I've lost all wish to kill any of those buffaloes."

"Same here. I wouldn't kill 'em if I could."

Neither lad knew exactly why he spoke thus, but perhaps it was the culmination of many effects, the unreality, a certain awe and a belief that this was a lost, and the last herd. But both had spoken with conviction.

"Herbert," said Charles presently, "a buffalo is a buffalo and it is not a beast of prey. I think that everything has combined to scare us half to death, and that there is nothing to keep us from climbing down these trees and going away."

"Maybe," said Herbert, "but let's wait a little before we try it."

The moon, dimmed by passing clouds, came out again, and the forms of their guards grew more distinct, ceasing to have the shadowy quality, which, at times in the last hour, had made them waver before the boys. Nevertheless, the light still served to distort them and enlarge them to gigantic size, and the imagination of Charles and Herbert gave further aid in the task.

Herbert leaned against the tree trunk and Charles thought he might be asleep, but when he looked at him he saw his eyes shining with the same unnatural light that he had marked there before, and he felt with greater force than ever that he must not long delay their attempt to leave the valley. But they remained for a while, without movement or without thought of what they should do.

The belief that they had come there to be hunted by the survivors of the millions whom man had hunted out of existence became a conviction, and he felt a reluctance to meet the eyes of the avenging beasts, eyes that he could always see with his imagination if not with his own gaze. The light of the moon struck fairly on the sides of the great cliffs and the grotesque and threatening faces which his fancy had carved there in the rock lowered at them again. He could even distort the trees into gigantic half-human shapes, leaning toward them and taunting them, but he shut his eyes and drove them away.

A little later he told Herbert that they must descend, that they could not stay forever where they were, and it was foolish for them to delay, wearing out their strength and weakening their wills with so long and heavy a vigil. Herbert said no, that he could not stir while those beasts were there watching; he could see a million red eyes all turned upon him, and he knew that as soon as he touched the earth the owners of those eyes would rush upon him and trample him to death. Charles felt some of Herbert's reluctance, but knowing that it was no time to waste words told him that they must go.

"Come, Herbert," he said. "We've been frightened by phantoms. The bigger part of what we have seen has been created by our own imaginations. I'm going down."

He felt quavers himself, but his will overcame them, and he began to descend the tree. The greatest tremor of all shook him when his foot struck the ground, but he stood there, afraid though resolute. Herbert, feeling the same fears, had followed his example and he, too, now stood on the ground. Their guards still gazed at them, but made no movement to attack, and they drew courage from the fact.

Herbert pointed to a dark line in the face of a distant cliff, where the moonlight fell clearly, and asked if it were not the ravine, by which they had come. Charles said yes, and, not giving him time to think and to hesitate about it, seized him by the arm and pulled him on, telling him that they must reach the ravine as quickly as they could and leave the valley. They advanced directly toward that segment of the watchful circle which stood between them and the point they desired to reach.

Charles retained his firm grasp upon Herbert's arm, and felt the flesh trembling under his fingers.

As they advanced the line of buffaloes parted and they passed through it. They stumbled upon their rifles, lying upon the ground where they had thrown them in their panic flight, and mechanically they picked them up again. Neither had the slightest desire to fire upon the buffaloes, but now they felt immense relief. Fear rolled away from them and they walked with buoyant steps. Charles dropped his hand from Herbert's arm and they walked on at a swift pace, their eyes fixed on the dark line in the cliff which marked the ravine, their avenue of escape from the valley.

Herbert suddenly put his hand upon Charles' shoulder and motioned him to look back. When he obeyed he saw the buffaloes following them in a long line, as regular and even as a company of soldiers. Herbert laughed in a mirthless way, and said they had an escort which would see that they did not linger in the valley. Charles could not say that he was wrong, and the effect of this silent escort was to chill his blood again.

The outline of the pass grew more distinct, the tracery of bushes and vines that lined it was revealed, and in a few minutes they would arrive at the first slope. Charles felt like a criminal, a murderer, taken in disgrace from the place of his crime, and this feeling, once having seized him, would not leave, but grew in strength and held him. Herbert was his brother in crime, and certainly his face, his nerveless manner, showed his guilt.

Charles hastened his footsteps, eager to leave the place. Herbert kept pace with him, and in silence, they reached the first slope. They did not look back until they had ascended some distance, and then Charles laughed from sheer relief. The buffalo herd was going away among the trees.

"Those animals are real, after all," said Charles.

"Yes," said Herbert, who felt the same relief, "but our imaginations have worked powerfully. I've read of such things. This extraordinary valley, the night, our finding of the wonderful lost herd and a touch of superstitious awe have made us see with magnified eyes."

"But we were really chased by the buffaloes."

"Of course, and they watched us in the trees a while."

"I wonder how they got in there."

"By some narrow cut that we did not find."

"I'm thinking," said Charles, "that perhaps the members of this herd have developed qualities that were not possessed by the ordinary buffalo of the plains. Far up in the mountains of northwestern Canada there is a rare species of buffalo called the wood buffalo, but which is larger and fiercer than the ordinary kind. It was probably the same in the beginning, but, being driven into the mountains, developed a greater size and a more ferocious temper from the necessities of a harder environment."

"You are probably right," said Herbert, "and that most likely is why they besieged us. But, although they scared us half to death, Charlie, and have made me stiff with cold and cramp, I no longer have a wish to kill a single one of them. Their secret is safe with me. I'll never tell."

"Nor I, either," said Charles with emphasis, "except to the Professor and Jed, who are as true as steel."

"Of course! I didn't mean to exclude them!" said Herbert.

They continued their ascent, and, after finishing the night on the summit, reached the village late the next day, to find the Professor and Jed, somewhat alarmed over an absence prolonged beyond the second night. But the Professor marveled when they told the reason why.

"It was a great discovery," he said, "and you were lucky to make it. But I am glad that neither of you injured any of those magnificent beasts. Let them remain lost like the beaver colony."

Jedediah Simpson o' Lexin'ton, K—y, grinned.

"'Tain't many boys nowadays that has the chance to be treed by a buffalo," he said, "an' I'll bet, Charlie, that when you an' Herb were a-settin' up thar among the boughs you'd have been glad enough to hear me playing 'Home, Sweet Home' on my accordion."

"We certainly would, Jed," said Charles. "It would have sounded mighty good just then. We thought of you more than once."

"And now," said the Professor, "after such an arduous adventure, you are entitled to a little rest."

Chapter Eleven - The Ancient Tower

But they did not rest long. The first night after their return the two boys withdrew early to their beds in the little cave houses. As the houses were small and close every one of the four now had a house of his own as a bedroom. Charles' was next to Herbert's and with a brief good night they entered, each into his own place.

Charles stood in the room a minute or two before lying down. Much sweeping and dusting and dousing with water had made it fresh, sweet and clean. All the mold and old smells of ages were gone, and he rejoiced to be in the strange but snug little place again. He looked out at the window cut in the rock, in the fashion of a rude circle seven or eight inches in diameter, and saw a patch of dark sky. No star appeared in his area of vision and he knew that all of them were now hidden by clouds. A wind began to moan in the great canyon, and the air took on a chill.

Charles knew that they were about to have one of the rare rains that fall in that region, and he was glad of it. He would feel all the finer and more comfortable in his cliff cell with a storm without. The wind rose higher, and the air poured in at the little window in a full fresh stream. He also left the low door open and another current came there. The direction of the wind showed him that the rain would not enter at the door, and the atmosphere of the room would remain fresh, vital and cool. His strength had increased greatly in the wild mountain life and his lungs, already very strong, had expanded greatly. Like a strong engine consuming quantities of fuel he demanded much air.

He watched a little longer until he saw streaks of lightning blaze across the horizon and heard the deep muttering of thunder in their own and other mighty canyons. The sound in that vast maze of high mountains and tremendous gorges was inexpressibly solemn and majestic, even terrifying. Charles, despite habit, could never hear it without awe, and he felt sure that the old cliff dwellers who passed their lives amid such surroundings must have created all their gods out of the thunder, the lightning and the storm.

He saw the lightning blaze and then strike with an incredible detonation on the black basalt of a cliff a mile away. For a moment the stone stood out in the intense light, and balls and shafts of fire seemed to leap from it. Then the darkness closed in again, but twenty seconds later the lightning was playing around the crest of a high, bald peak, crowning it with fire. Soon both lightning and thunder ceased and the rain rushed down.

Then Charles took off his clothes, and lay down on his bed. They had not neglected to provide themselves with comforts and good beds were among their early achievements. He had made a smooth layer of turkey feathers, over which he spread tanned skins upon which he lay luxuriously, drawing the blanket over his body, because the air was now very cool. He fell at once into a deep sleep, slept on through the storm, and long after it had passed. Herbert in the next room was sleeping the same way.

Professor Longworth and Jed Simpson were up early the next day, but they moved quietly about the village.

"Let them sleep," said the Professor. "Best thing for their nerves that they could do."

The whole canyon, after the storm and rain, was filled with pure air, with a touch of crispness in it. The village seemed to have come fresh from the bath, and Professor Longworth, as he strode up and down the terrace, gazed at the peaks and ridges with a kindling eye.

"What a world! What a world!" he murmured. "And how it is defended from the advance of man!"

It was the isolation and the tremendous ramparts of nature that appealed to Professor Longworth. Man could come there but little, and it was for him to find out and explore. He had with him just the comrades that he liked, friends but no rival. He would not have exchanged his position then for that of any other man in the world. But he did not spend his time in dreaming. He formed a resolution which he intended to carry out in a few days.

Charles and Herbert did not awake until past, noon, and, while they ate breakfast, Jed and the Professor ate luncheon with them. Jed had exerted his culinary skill to the utmost. He had caught trout, and they had venison, canned food and coffee. The boys ate with ravenous appetites, and the Professor regarded them approvingly.

"Your nerves are all right," he said. "I ordered this large meal for you purposely, but I take it that you do not want any buffalo steaks on your bill of fare."

"No! No!" said Charles and Herbert together.

The Professor laughed.

"I don't wonder that you were scared," he said. "This is a strange region and its principal note is weirdness. I do not know any more interesting country in the world and I mean to look further into it. You and I, Charles, are going, the day after to-morrow, on an exploring expedition across the mesa back of the peninsula. The race of people who made villages like this did not confine their houses to the sides of cliffs. They also built on the mesas, in the valleys and on the mountain tops. It was a strange old life. I can reproduce much of it, but I cannot reconstruct it as a whole."

Charles was delighted at the prospect of the trip. Jed and Herbert were to keep house, and both were content to stay. They had many things which they wished to do about the village.

Charles and the Professor started early on the appointed morning, each carrying a rifle, pistol, hatchet and knife. The hatchets were to be used in preparing camps. They also took blanket rolls, although the weather was fine and rain was highly improbable. In such a dry region it was not likely that two big rains would fall within a month of each other. As a precaution, they strapped two great bottles of water to their waists, although the Professor had a wonderful genius for finding water and he believed that it was plentiful in the mountains.

Skilled campers and travelers, their burdens were not great, and easily reaching the top of the cliff they waved farewell to Herbert and Jed. According to the Professor's calculations they would be gone about a week.

They traveled the full length of the peninsula, mostly through forest, and the size of some of the trees indicated a fine depth of soil upon that lofty ridge. There were tall pines, large oaks, aspen and cedar and low scrub and sage brush. Twice they came to little fountains, emerging at the base of low hills. The last of these, just as it came from the earth, had formed a basin for itself, worn out in the solid rock six inches deep and a foot across. After filling the pool the water flowed in a stream across the mesa and then fell down a cliff a thousand feet high where it was lost in a fine mist. The fountain itself was shaded by two massive and splendid oaks.

It was an attractive place, and they took their noon rest and food beside it. The Professor pointed out the tracks of animals in the turf on either bank of the stream.

"Bear, deer, wolves, mountain lions and other beasts come here to drink," he said. "In the old days—how many centuries ago I cannot tell—it is likely that men often came, too, but they have passed—forever, I suppose."

"But the prospect for game looks good," said the boy, "and on a trip of a week we'll need it."

"So it does," said the Professor. "We can undoubtedly find wild turkeys and mule deer."

"This plateau seems to have plenty of both wood and water," said Charles. "Then why don't the Indians roam here?"

"It's extreme isolation and the fact that it is broken up so terribly by sharp ridges and mighty gorges," replied Longworth. "Savage man is naturally lazy and the Apaches, Utes, Piutes and Navajos prefer easier country. The cliff dwellers, I presume, came here originally for protection, and now that they are gone the country is left to the winds and the wild beasts. I think the heat of the noonday sun is abating somewhat now, Charles, and we might as well be moving."

"Just one more drink before we go," said the boy.

Lying flat on his chest he took a long, cool drink. It was splendid water, coming somewhere from great cool caverns in the heart of the mountain. Longworth drank also, and then they replenished their large thermos bottles. Then they resumed the journey, although they sauntered along at their leisure, looking at the tracks of animals, and examining the country with questing eyes.

They had now left the peninsula and the mesa and were descending a great slope, covered with thin grass and with patches of pine here and there. They looked upward, as from the side of a bowl, and all around them were ranges and peaks in inextricable confusion as if they had been hurled at random by the mighty hand of the Infinite. Most of the slopes were dark far up with heavy masses of evergreen, but above the pines rose the bald and stony peaks, some crested with snow.

"It seems to me," said the boy, "that the country always grows wilder."

"At least it remains as wild," replied the man, "and I am glad that it does. I am here to see Nature's great, and not her commonplace, achievements. Our slope is descending fast now, and by night we shall be at least three-quarters of a mile below our village."

"What is that ahead of us?" asked Charles, gazing down the slope. "Is it a tall pinnacle of rock, carved by the weather?"

Professor Longworth took forth his field glasses, gazed intently, and then his face began to show traces of excitement.

"Not at all, Charlie, lad!" he exclaimed. "That is one of the things for which I have been looking, but which I scarcely hoped to find. That was done, not by nature, but by the hand of man. It is a tower built by the cliff dwellers and I can see from here that it is a magnificent specimen almost perfectly preserved."

The tower was about two miles away, but looking very much nearer in the amazingly thin and clear mountain air. The Professor, full of eagerness, now dropped his sauntering gait, and hurried toward it. Charles, his curiosity also aroused, kept by his side. He soon saw with the naked eye the truth of the Professor's words, as he could discern the lines between the stones of which the tower was made.

As they came nearer, they saw that the tower stood on a shelf overlooking a deep valley. Charles judged that it was about fifty feet in height, twenty feet square at the base and ten feet square at the top. It was built of large stones, laid one upon another without mortar, but very skillfully.

"Stop," said Professor Longworth, when they were within fifty feet of the tower. "I want to exult, Charlie, boy, just a little bit, before we touch hand or foot to the prize."

Charles understood him perfectly, and standing side by side they gloated together.

"There is another a quarter of a mile further on," said the Professor, pointing with a long forefinger, "but time and the storms have taken half its height. The one before us is probably the finest in all these mountains. It is indeed a rare triumph for us to find it."

"What was it for?" asked the boy.

"It is hard to say. Most likely it was at once a watch tower and a tower of defense. Also, it may have had some connection with the sacred rites of that ancient race. Now, having paid due respect to it, Charlie, we'll enter the tower and examine it in every part."

There was a large opening on the side facing the mountain. Evidently it had been a low door, but some of the stone about it had fallen away and the hole now exceeded the height of a man.

"I shall be very much surprised," said Longworth, "if we do not find inside a stone stairway leading to the top, although it is sure to be exceedingly narrow."

"In order that it might be held easily against enemies?"

The Professor nodded.

"Here we are now," he said, stepping boldly in at the door. Then he stopped and sniffed the air repeatedly. Charles did likewise.

"It's the odor of an animal," said the man.

"And of a big one," said the boy, "or it would not be so strong. Look, here is some of his hair that he left as he came in or went out."

He took two or three wisps of coarse brown hair from the crannies between the stones about the doorway, and held them up for the Professor to
see.

"They belong to His Majesty," said Longworth.

"His Majesty?"

"The grizzly bear, the most formidable of all our wild animals, as you and
Herbert have cause to know. The interior of the tower's base would form a
snug winter den for one of those monsters and it has certainly been used for
such a purpose. But His Majesty is not at home at present. Doubtless he has
left it, until winter comes again, and meanwhile, we will invade without fear.
Ah, here is the stairway that I expected. Follow me, Charles, and be careful of
the steps."

There was full need for care. The little winding stairway of stone was not
more than a foot broad, and there was no coping. The stones themselves, despite the mold of time and the drift from dust and vegetation, were as slippery as glass.

"They have been trodden by thousands of feet for centuries," said the Professor. "No archaeologist is skilled enough to tell how long this tower has
stood here. Keep as close to the wall as possible, Charlie. Broken bones are
best when you are in a big city near a great hospital."

Fifteen feet up and they came to the fragments of a platform. Wide, flat
stones projected from the whole circle of the tower, and there were remains
of wooden rafters long since fallen in. But there was no trace of ironwork,
nor did they ever find it in any work of the cliff dwellers.

There were two narrow windows level with the platform, one overlooking
the valley, and here they stopped a minute or two for breath. Charles saw
through the window the depths of the valley, apparently a mass of vegetation
now browning with late summer, and he understood how useful the tower
might have been to people who watched for enemies coming from below.

"There was another platform about fifteen feet above this," said the Professor, "and I can see there the light from windows also."

They climbed slowly to the second platform, and then to the roof, which
was partly open, where stones had fallen in. The Professor surmised that in
ancient times it had been closed wholly, except for a kind of trap door.

Feeling the stones carefully in order that they might see that they were
firm enough to sustain their weight, they drew themselves carefully upon the
top of the tower. Here they rested a while, looked out upon the vast expanse
of mountains, and then into the deeps of the valley.

"It is a much bigger valley than the one in which you and Herbert found
the buffaloes," said the Professor. "It is four or five miles wide and even with
my field glasses I cannot see its end. I judge by this tower and the ruined one
farther on that it was inhabited by a race unlike the cliff dwellers and hostile
to them. In its original condition, this tower was impregnable against every-

thing except hunger and thirst. I suggest that we descend now and make an examination of its base. I want to see just how it was built."

They climbed down laboriously and carefully, and when they reached the bottom, Charles was glad to rest some minutes and take long breaths. But he did not take his rest inside the tower. It seemed to him that the animal odor was stronger than ever, and he and the Professor retreated to the shade of a great oak that grew near. Here the air was pure and sweet and crisp with the mountain tang.

"It is growing late," said the Professor, "and as we are in no hurry I think we'd better camp here. Unless I'm fooled greatly we'll find a spring among the cedars over there. They look as if they had their feet in moisture, and it is also likely that the ancient people would build the tower near water."

Charles explored the cedars and found a small but good spring, with which they replenished their thermos bottles, upon which they had drawn heavily after the descent of the tower. The shade of the oak was obviously the best place for a camp and they spread their equipment under its branches.

Charles brought fallen brushwood and built a fire. The Professor made coffee in a small pot, and cooked venison over the coals. Charles was sure that they could find wild turkeys among the pines and oaks, but they decided not to hunt them yet awhile.

They ate and drank with sharp appetites, put out the fire and laid their rifles and heavy belts again the tree. They hung their knapsacks of provisions and thermos bottles on a high bough, and then, spreading their blankets on the grass, lay comfortably upon them. The Professor produced his pipe, and smoked with great content.

"In an hour it will be dark," he said, "and we can sleep here in entire safety under this tree. I do not think there is the remotest danger from Indians. It is possible that not a warrior has trodden this slope in a hundred years."

"And if they'll keep off for another hundred," said Charles, "we'll be all right. I've had one sight of Apaches, and it's enough for me."

"I'll have to-morrow morning for a good look at the tower," said the Professor, "but there is light enough left for me to do a little work now."

He drew forth his little geological hammer and, going to the base of the tower, began to pick at the stones. He soon became so absorbed in his congenial task that he wholly forgot the passage of time and the deepening of the twilight. Charles forgot them, too, because the walk of the day and the climbing of the tower had made him tired. Lying on the blanket in a state of relaxation, he fell into a pleasant doze, from which he was suddenly roused by a sound that roared in his ears, tremendous and terrific.

Undoubtedly it was his condition on the halfway road to sleep which made the sound so overwhelming, but its real volume was mighty enough. Charles sprang to his feet as if he had been touched with electricity, and he saw two enormous grizzly bears rushing down upon them.

"Run, Professor, run!" he cried impulsively, and he caught a glimpse of Longworth as he dropped his little hammer and rushed into the tower.

Charles had no chance to reach the tower, but the trunk of the great oak, under the boughs of which he was resting, was not five feet away. Fear put the wings of Mercury on his heels. One jump and he was at the tree. Another jump and he had seized the lowest bough. A mighty convulsive jerk, and, drawing himself up, he leaped for a higher bough, just as the claws of one of the grizzlies tore the bark where his heels had been. Breathless, the perspiration dropping from his brow, he climbed higher and higher, until he sat on a thick bough a full thirty feet from the ground. Then for a while he hugged the body of the tree and trembled, while he listened to the roaring and growling below.

"Stick tight, Charlie, boy!" cried a voice high up in the air. "I looked out of a window, saw that you were safe, and then came up here."

Professor Longworth was perched on the very top of the tower. He had lost his huge pith helmet in his flight, and his hair was flying wildly. He panted from his great exertion in his run up the stairway. The bears, a male and female, meanwhile rushed back and forth between tower and tree, tearing at both and growling horribly. They were joined soon by two half-grown youngsters which imitated their parents.

"Well, Charlie," called the Professor, "we've had sudden visitors. I hope you like 'em."

"I like 'em better with trees and towers between them and us. It seems that we were right, Professor, about their having had a den in the tower, but we were not right about their having abandoned it. They're at home every evening."

Professor Longworth laughed nervously.

"Do you appreciate the fact, Charles," he called, "that we have left all our weapons on the ground? Even my geological hammer is down there. I have only my penknife, and, with that, I'm not dreaming of tackling two full grown and two half-grown grizzlies, mad with rage at our invasion of their house."

"This tree and I do not part company, at least not for a while," Charles called back. "It's the finest tree I ever saw, a beautiful tree, a protecting tree, it grew here for the especial purpose of saving my life, and has been waiting for me a hundred years, maybe."

He was trying to take it lightly, but it was a hard task. He still trembled a little, but his will was resuming control of his nerves. The bears were yet running to and fro, froth on their lips. They pawed at the guns and pistols, and the boy was afraid that they would seize them in their teeth and twist them out of shape. But finding that they were mostly cold metal and not good to eat they soon let them alone, and then began to roar for the food which was suspended from one of the boughs.

The bears, stretch as they would, could not quite reach the knapsacks containing the supplies, and they roared and growled again in disappointment and anger. Finally they gave it up. Then one of the great animals crouched at the foot of the tower, and the other at the foot of the tree. The smaller two prowled about like two curious boys, looking into everything. One of them found the pith helmet and took its brim in his mouth.

The Professor's anger was aroused, and he began to shout maledictions. He valued that helmet. It had stood as a friend many a day between him and the blazing sun.

"Drop it! Drop it!" he cried. "What do you mean, you ignorant and silly bear? It's not good to eat! Drop it, I say!"

Some impish spirit of mischief possessed the young bear. He dropped back on his haunches, still holding the helmet lightly by the brim in his teeth, and looked up at the Professor. It seemed to the imagination of Charles that he closed one eye, and winked at the Professor who continued shouting at him to drop the helmet.

The noise attracted the attention of the other young bear which came up, smelled at the helmet, and patted it lightly with his paw. Professor Longworth groaned.

"The young rascals," he cried. "They will not leave a shred of my helmet, and there is not another in all these mountains."

The sportive instincts of the young bears were alive, but they were not manifested in the way that the Professor expected. The one that held it in his teeth dropped it to the ground, and the other struck it lightly with his paw. It rolled like a ball four or five feet, and the other knocked it back again.

Charles was compelled to laugh, but Professor Longworth was very angry. His pride was hurt.

"The scamps!" he said. "It makes my blood hot for two young bears to have fun with an important article of my apparel."

The helmet rolled nearer to the edge of the cliff, and one of the youngsters, giving it a harder slap than usual, it whirled over, catching in a projecting bush five or six feet below. Both bears crept cautiously to the edge, and tried to reach a paw down, and hook it back again. But they soon gave it up, and lay down under the boughs of the oak. The Professor breathed a deep sigh of relief.

"So far as I can make out in the dusk," he called, "my helmet is unhurt, and I shall rescue it later. But these demons seem prepared to stay here forever. Have you any suggestion to make, Charles?"

"I can't think of any now. I suppose that we shall have to wait."

The night had now come, but it was uncommonly bright. The sky was a clear blue, sown with brilliant stars. The boy and the man could see each other perfectly, and they talked at intervals from height to height. Any hope that the bears would go away was dissipated by the fact that the tower was their home. They remained stretched out but watching, one the tower and the other the tree.

"Let this be an important lesson to us, Charles," said the Professor. "Never again in the wilderness should we lay aside our pistols, no matter where we may be. I can see our weapons there against the trunk of the tree, but they might as well be a hundred miles away."

"Maybe my fellow here will soon leave the tree," said Charles, whose hardihood was coming back. "I think I'll go down a little and see."

"Be sure of your grip. Don't fall!" called the Professor.

Charles descended cautiously about ten feet, and then drew back in fright. Both bears instantly rushed to the trunk of the tree, and, rearing to their full height, clawed ferociously at the bark. Their eyes were shot with blood, and foam ran from their mouths. Charles climbed back into his safe seat.

"We'll just wait," said the Professor.

But the waiting was very long. The bears did not show the slightest sign of raising the siege. Even the youngsters stretched themselves on the turf and watched. The night advanced hour by hour. More stars came out, and danced in the vast light sky. The valley became a great blue gulf and beyond the bald crests nodded in the dimness to one another.

Charles grew very stiff and tired, and moved about on his bough. He went down a little again to test the bears a second time, but they became as wild as before. Resuming his original place they waited two or three hours longer. It was then past midnight and the siege was becoming intolerable. An idea occurred to the boy.

"Professor, you see how my descent arouses them," he called. "Now you go down the tower, part of the way, showing yourself at the windows. They'll go mad, rush in the tower and try to get at you. Then I'll skip down the tree, seize a rifle and belt of cartridges, skip back up again, and the rest will be easy."

But the Professor shook his head, and protested vigorously.

"You must not think of it!" he cried. "The risk is far too great. A single slip, and they would have you."

"But I won't make the slip."

"How can you tell? Anyone might fail at such a time. No, no, Charlie, we must wait!"

"But Professor, waiting does us no good. We have been on our perches seven or eight hours now, and the bears show no signs of leaving. Why should they go? Their home is here and they see breakfast, dinner and supper waiting for them up above. They're suited, if we are not."

Charles insisted so earnestly that Longworth finally consented to what he called a half trial.

"Charles," he said, "you're not to leave the tree unless the bears come wholly within the base of the tower. Then you would have a fair chance of getting back. You promise that, do you not?"

"Yes, I promise. Suppose we begin now."

"All right, I'm going down now within twelve or fifteen feet of the bottom, and you may be sure that I won't make any slip on the stone steps."

The Professor was looking over the edge of the roof. The four bears were all lying on the ground, apparently asleep. He picked up a loose piece of stone, hurled it at the old male, and then began the descent of the steps.

All four of the bears were raging in an instant, and rushed toward the tower. The Professor thrust his head out of a window at the first platform and taunted them with all the wrath of a treed man, and all the knowledge and vocabulary of a scholar. He denounced their ancestry of geological eras, millions of years back. He poured maledictions upon them by name and species to their remotest and most doubtful kin. He assailed their shape, manners and character, in English, Latin and Greek, in words of from one to ten syllables, and, descending to the lower platform, he said it all over again with additions and adornments.

As he came nearer, the bears, evidently thinking that they were about to obtain their food at last, became excited to an extraordinary degree. They dashed in at the doorway, and Charles knew that their paws were on the first steps, their mouths slavering.

The boy had already slipped down to the boughs just out of reach. Now he dropped lightly to the ground and seized his rifle and belt of cartridges, throwing both over his shoulder. Meanwhile he heard the continual crackle of Professor Longworth's vituperation. He did not know that any man had so rich a vocabulary, and he did not dream that anyone could talk so fast and so fiercely. Mingled with his voice came the terrible growling and snarling of the bears. The Professor, in fact, was only two or three feet beyond their reach, and they were perfectly mad with the desire to get at him. The boy had completely disappeared, for the moment, from the bear mind. Certainly Professor Longworth was doing his full duty.

Charles drew himself up with care to the first bough. There he paused until he could secure rifle and cartridges against the danger of dropping them. Then he went up to his old seat which was the securest in the tree, and sang out at the top of his voice to the man:

"All right, Professor. I'm safe, and I have the rifle and the cartridges. The rest is just detail."

Longworth's stream of language ceased abruptly, and he reascended to the roof. The puzzled bears came out of the tower, and began to smell at the fresh footprints of Charles under the tree. The boy, meanwhile, was examining his rifle to see that it was all right.

"Take your time, Charles," called the Professor. "Don't risk any shock and the loss of your seat after a shot."

"I won't," replied the exultant boy. "I'm not going to throw away my advantage."

Those bears knew nothing about rifles, and probably had never seen a human being before. Their rage was transferred now from the tower to the tree and as before they tore at it. Their wrath was not diminished when a steel bullet struck the old male in the throat and plowed downward through his body. The shock hurled him to the ground but he sprang up and tore at the tree more fiercely than ever. He was a truly terrible sight, wild with rage, blood pouring from his terrible wound. Charles had planned to finish one before he began on another, and picking his spot he sent a bullet into the old male's heart. Even then the tremendous vitality of the animal sustained him for some minutes, but finally he staggered and died.

It took four shots to kill the female, two finished one of the youngsters, and the other taking alarm dashed into the brush. Charles might have shot him as he ran, but he let him go.

"Well done, Charles!" shouted the Professor from his tower. "The siege is over, thanks to your daring and skill, and we can betake ourselves to solid earth again."

The two, immensely relieved, descended to the ground.

Chapter Twelve - The Community House

Professor Longworth regained his rifle and belt, before he examined the dead bears.

"How do I know that a whole herd of grizzlies will not come rushing out of the bushes after us?" he said whimsically. "Never again will I be so careless."

Then, in the bright moonlight, they contemplated the dead monsters. They reckoned that the old male would weigh at least a thousand pounds—he was larger than the one that Charles and Herbert had met—and the female but little less. Their huge claws, many inches in length, were like terrible steel barbs.

"Ursus horribilis," said the Professor. "They truly deserve the name. At close quarters nothing could withstand them. Those claws would rip up either a lion or a tiger."

"Are we to let these great skins go to waste?" asked Charles.

"No. Fortunately I have had much experience in taking pelts and we will remove them. Then we'll lug them up to the first platform and leave them there to dry until we can come again for them, when we'll add them to the one we've already got."

But skillful though Longworth was and efficient though Charles proved himself to be it was broad daylight before they finished taking the hides from the three bears. Then it was a tremendous task to get them up to the first platform, and the two were thoroughly exhausted.

But long before this was done they had visitors. Five great triangular heads were thrust from the bushes, and five pairs of burning eyes regarded them.

"Mountain wolves," said the Professor. "They are big, fierce fellows, but they won't attack us. They are waiting for a great feast here after we are gone, and they will get it. It seems a pity to leave two thousand pounds or more of bear meat for such woods rovers."

"They'll not be alone," said Charles. "Look up."

Far in the blue the forms of vultures were hovering.

"And I suppose there'll be mountain lions, too, and other guests," muttered the Professor. "Well, we'll keep 'em waiting a while. It's time for breakfast, Charles, and we'll have some breakfast ourselves before leaving."

They lighted the fire again and Longworth cut some of the tenderest steaks from the younger bear, which they cooked and found very good indeed. While this pleasant task was proceeding, a whining and growling came from the bushes. At least a dozen triangular heads appeared at the edge of the thicket. Overhead the vulture shapes had increased fivefold, and were hovering lower.

"The second table is in a hurry," said the Professor, "but it will have to bide the good time of the first table. I'm not nearly through; are you, Charles?"

"Not by any means. Young bear is wonderfully good when you have a mountain appetite. Yes, thank you, I'll take another piece. Does that whining and growling in the bushes annoy you, Professor?"

"It didn't at first, but it does now. I'm getting too much of it. Suppose you take a rifle, my lad, and smash a hole in one of those ugly, triangular heads."

Charles, nothing loath, sent a bullet at the largest of the heads. He heard a yell and saw a form leap upward and sink back into the bushes. Then came a terrific whining, barking and growling. It was such a horrible mingling of sound that Charles shivered.

"Merely a bit of cannibalism," said the Professor, calmly, going on with his own breakfast. "They are eating the fellow you slew, and they are probably thanking you for the act. Ah, they are through now. They certainly ate him in a hurry."

Noise in the bushes ceased, but no more heads were thrust out. Wolves learn fast and a single bullet had taught them the value of invisibility. The Professor rose presently and with an air of deep content stretched his arms.

"Now, Charles," he said, "we'll gather up our belongings and go, but we'll do it with calmness and deliberation. The loss of a night's sleep, a siege of seven or eight hours and much danger are not calculated to promote zeal and industry. We'll leave slowly, and further down the valley, when we find a good place, we'll take naps that we need badly."

Charles saw the Professor's mood and he shared it. He resented leaving the bodies of the bears to the wolves and vultures, and he intended to tantalize them as long as possible. They packed with great slowness, although the shadows of the hovering vultures sometimes fell on their faces, and two or three of the more reckless or more impatient wolves showed their heads again through the bushes.

114

They took with them enough tenderloin from the young bear to last two or three days, and finally departed. When they were less than a hundred feet away, they heard the rush of feet and the whirr of wings. They looked back and saw that the three bodies were covered with the black and gray of bird and beast.

"What an ignominious fate for the monarch of the mountains!" said Professor Longworth.

They kept along the edge of the shelf and then found an easy slope by which they descended into the valley. When they reached the bottom they came into a little grove of oaks. It was then about ten o'clock and the sun was growing warm. Both were becoming very weary and the Professor decided that they should spread their blankets in the heart of the grove and make up for their lost sleep.

"I think that we need not yet have any fear of Indians," he said. "Undoubtedly this valley is too much isolated for them. At any rate I'm willing to take the risk. I want sleep badly."

"I feel that I must have sleep or die," said Charles, casting himself down on his blanket.

"You will have sleep and you will not die," said the Professor, also stretching himself out on his own blanket.

The two were sound asleep in five minutes and nothing disturbed them in the grove. They were shaded by the oaks from the sun and a pleasant breeze blew, lulling them to deeper slumbers. It was the middle of the afternoon before they awoke, and when the Professor noted the time of day by the sun, his face showed satisfaction.

"Sleep not only knits up the raveled sleeve of care," he said, "but it also strengthens sinew and tissue. We are men again, refreshed and reinvigorated. Now for some more of those bear steaks."

After eating, they went further into the valley and found that a fine mountain creek flowed down its center. In places the water rippled over shallows, but at intervals it gathered in deep, still pools.

"Probably splendid trout here," said Longworth, "but we're not equipped for them now. As nearly as I can make out, Charles, this valley is about twenty miles long, and it seems to be closed, but undoubtedly we'll find at the lower end an opening or slash in the mountains. In any event we'll see."

They traveled down the valley all the rest of the day. They saw several deer which were uncommonly tame, bearing out the Professor's theory that man did not come there. They proceeded very deliberately as they had no reason for haste. In places the soil was very fertile and well wooded, but in others it was hard and rocky with signs now and then of a lava flow.

Above them they saw long mesas, thrust out like tongues, and back of these low peaks and ranges with higher mountains behind them. They also saw running back into the lower ranges little box canyons in which grew many low trees, with lofty pines scattered here and there. The cliffs, vivid red or yellow in color, were very soft, the Professor said, being composed mostly of pumice stone. Little streams flowed out of three of the canyons and emptied into the creek.

Finally they came to a huge wash which Professor Longworth entered, and from which presently came the pecking sound of his little geological hammer. But this sound was soon stopped by a wild cry of exultation. Charles, who had stopped at the edge, rushed down into the wash. The Professor had begun to peck again, but now frantically, with the hammer.

"It's a find, a bone find, a find of prehistoric animals, Charlie, lad!" he cried. "Surely on this trip into the mountains I'm the luckiest man on earth!"

Longworth's helmet which had been recovered undamaged was set on the back of his head, and he was making rock and earth fly from a huge bone that projected from the side of a gully. He had wholly forgotten the sun, which now blazed down upon him. But as Charles joined him he grew calmer.

"It's tremendous luck that I came into this wash," he said. "The bones of huge animals millions of years old are projecting everywhere. Here are the great lizard-like creatures and also crocodiles, gigantic monkeys and the Lord knows what. I've no doubt that a capable scientist could profitably spend his whole life in this valley."

But the two only passed the day there. For a range of two or three miles they saw the bones, and Professor Longworth wrote in his notebook a long and minute description of the place.

"I shall come back here later with a properly equipped force," he said. "Meanwhile we have to let them lie. Nobody else who knows anything about such things is likely to find them."

"How do you account for the presence of such great animals so high above the sea?" asked the boy.

"It wasn't high when the dinosaurus and the ichthyosaurus and the rest of them roamed about here. The vast plateau of western and southwestern North America seems to have been the greatest animal range in the world. Wyoming, which is now from 6,000 to 14,000 feet above the sea, was the heart of it, but the big game, and real big game it was, too, Charles, fairly swarmed here also. Huge animals, too huge to sustain well their own weight on land, waded in the marshes and shallow parts of the rivers, pulling down the long grass and tops of bushes for food. What a world that must have been, Charlie, lad! Think of the cave bears, by the side of which our grizzlies would have been puny, the monstrous saber-toothed tiger, two or three times as big as any that now grow, the immense mastodon and the mammoth perhaps fifty feet long. And back of them the great armored and lizard-like creatures, some of which may have grown one hundred and fifty feet in length. What a world! What a world! Charles, I would willingly take a year out of my life to be carried backward through time, and see this region as it was five million years ago!"

"Man then must have been pretty small potatoes and mighty few in a hill," observed Charles.

"Undoubtedly he was," said the Professor, whose eyes were still glowing. "Now, what was he five million years ago? We have nothing to go on, but he must have existed in some form even then. He may have run on four legs, but, whatever he was, he must have been physically a poor and inferior thing, hiding away in caves and burrows. The world belonged to the great animals. If you had no firearms, Charlie, lad, you would certainly be frightened if you met a saber-toothed tiger six feet high and fifteen feet long, wouldn't you?"

"I'd be frightened if I had all the firearms in the world."

Longworth laughed.

"So would I have been scared," he said. "Man must have had a terrible time of it in those days. No doubt, countless millions of our ancestors were devoured by wild beasts. The mammoth, the mastodon, the saber-toothed tiger and the others must have looked down upon us as a very inferior order of beings. Perhaps it's only in the last fifteen or twenty thousand years that we've been getting even."

The Professor left the wash with great reluctance, and they camped among trees about two miles farther on. Here they passed an undisturbed night, and were ready the next morning to resume their journey down the valley.

As they had expected they found the great slash in the mountains through which the creek flowed. It was not more than fifty yards wide and was not visible until they came near. The stream here was about thirty feet wide and two or three feet deep, flowing over a rough, stony bed. But there was plenty of space between it and the mountain as it ran through the gorge, and they followed it until they emerged upon a vast sun-burned plateau, which looked like the wreck of a world consumed by fire.

"We'll fill our water bottles again," said Professor Longworth, "and follow the stream, though we'll have to go high above it now. I've an idea that we are coming to a great canyon. This creek probably flows into the Colorado and goes ultimately through the Grand Canyon. It is the Grand Canyon of which all the world hears, but the west and southwest contain many other deep and beautiful canyons. There are dozens of great lateral canyons opening into those of the Colorado."

They filled their water bottles, and took a long rest also. Then they began the passage of the great, volcanic plain, although the volcanic forces which had thrown up these mountains had been dead for ages. They soon left all timber behind them. The soil was stony and rough, and the sun blazing hot. They took occasional sips of water, but the evaporation was so great that they were as thirsty as ever five minutes later.

But thirst and heat did not dim Longworth's enthusiasm. He looked upon every phase of this vast, dead region with the most eager interest.

"Perhaps nowhere else can anyone see the world in the making so well," he said. "Here we behold in layer upon layer the processes of youth, maturity and decay. Have you observed, Charles, how this plain is rising?"

"I have. I have noticed it in several ways. I can see it with my eyes, and I can tell it by the strain upon my muscles. Moreover, Professor, I'm hot—awful hot."

"But you can be and you are likely to be a great deal hotter," said the Professor cheerfully. "We have left our little river, Charlie, lad, but it's somewhere there on our right. In another mile we shall reach the crest of this plain, and then I want to turn in and see the stream."

It was a long mile, with hard and sharp lava under foot and a ferocious sun overhead, but they made it and then turned in to the right, until they came to the stream, or rather its channel. Here they lay flat on their stomachs and gazed into the mighty depths below. The little river, eating away for untold centuries, had cut a tremendous slash across the vast plateau, on its way to the Colorado, and the two looked down upon a spectacle at once beautiful and appalling. They saw the thinnest thread of white water more than three thousand feet below. On both sides rose the cliffs, red and yellow, as the sun shone upon them, and carved by weather and time into fantastic shapes. The chasm did not seem to be more than two hundred feet across at the bottom, but at the top it was a thousand feet from edge to edge. Longworth examined it for more than hour through his glasses.

"Wonderful! Wonderful!" he said. "Ah, my boy, think what patience and industry allied can accomplish! See what a mighty chasm this little river has cut through solid stone in a few millions of years! And what a lesson it teaches us! Charlie, lad, it is one of the regrets of my life that I cannot live a thousand years. In a millennium I could learn something. I could make a fairly comprehensive study of earth and man. But as I cannot get the thousand, I'll do the best I can in the seventy or eighty allotted to me."

Charles was interested, too, on his own account and also because the enthusiasm of the Professor was contagious. All the singular phases of this strange, south-western world appealed to him, and he had also the taste for knowledge.

"Professor," he said, "the plateau seems to descend now. I can see mountains on the far side."

"So can I," said Longworth, and then he studied them through his glasses.

"They are at least forty miles away," he said, "and they seem to be bare. But we'll keep on until we reach them."

"Suppose we turn back into one of the little box canyons," said Charles, "and stay there until night. Then we can travel in the cool dark."

"A good idea," said Longworth. "These box canyons are hot, but sometimes you can find something at the head of them that will keep you cool."

They turned at once from the stream toward the mountain on their left, and passed up one of the box canyons. It was hotter there than on the plateau, but when they came to its end, they found a deep hollow opening in the stone. Charles was surprised to find how far back it ran, and how cool it was under the shade of the stone.

"Our cliff-dwelling friends have been here," said Longworth, "although they probably have been gone also for some centuries. It is likely that we'd find just such a house as this at the head of every one of these canyons. But one is enough for our purpose. We'll sleep here in the shade."

They slept in the dark, cool shade until the night was more than two hours old. Then they awoke and started again, refreshed greatly. They walked all night, cooked bear steaks at dawn, and finding another cliff house in a canyon, remained there throughout the day, sleeping most of the time. Before dawn on the following morning they reached the end of the plain and entered bare and sterile mountains. But they were fortunate enough to find a spring containing an abundance of cool, fresh water, and they slept beside it in the partial shade of some stunted piñons.

They did not resume their exploration until late in the afternoon and then they found their little river flowing between desolate banks of black basalt. It seemed to have lost some of its water by evaporation, but it was now not more than three or four hundred feet below the level of the earth, and after much hunting they found a descent to its waters where they replenished their own supply.

The Professor with his glasses saw a valley ahead, which they expected to enter on the following day.

"It seems to be sterile, except in spots," he said, "but there is bound to be water, since our river flows through it somewhere. I can make out patches of vegetation here and there, but I should say that on the whole it is decidedly inferior to the valley that we have just left."

Charles shot a mule deer that day, a fine fat young buck, and they were very glad to get such a good supply of game. Having used the best of the flesh for two meals, they took a good supply with them, and entered the valley which had steep slopes and but scanty vegetation.

"The cliff dwellers have been here, too," said Professor Longworth, whose keen eyes nothing escaped. "See how they have irrigated wherever possible on these barren slopes. Now here are the remains of a little dam, which could not have watered more than twenty square feet of ground, and there is another dam, one of stone, almost as good as it was when it was built."

They found one section of soft cliff that looked like a huge beehive. The little people had scooped innumerable holes in the rock, none of them running back very far, but all quite livable, according to the cliff dweller standard. They spent some time in examining a number and found them mostly blackened with smoke. There were places cut out in the walls as depositories for tools or weapons. Much broken pottery was scattered about the floors.

"More mystery. More mystery," said Professor Longworth, musingly. "Why did these people disappear so entirely before the white man came? It surely could not have been wholly due to the ravages of Apaches, Utes and other Indians."

119

They left the slopes, found their little river again and followed it down the valley. They again saw evidence of much big game, bear, deer and mountain lion, but no sign of human life. Toward night they saw to the left of the river a large structure in a fair state of preservation, which the Professor welcomed with a shout of delight.

"It is one of the communal dwellings of the little people," he said. "Good fortune is still with us. But as we are tired we'll let our prize wait until morning. It is something wonderful to which we have come, Charles, and we ought to approach it with fresh minds and fresh bodies."

But they were up at earliest dawn and entered the great communal dwelling. It was built of heavy stones, and across the front was a row of twenty rooms, of uniform size, that is, about six feet wide and about ten feet long. All these rooms opened to the south.

This row sent off a short wing of rooms at each end toward the north. Each wing contained six rooms, the same in size as those in the front row. The row and the wings enclosed a great estufa or central court and back of the court was an immense burial mound.

"This and others like it probably represent the highest architectural achievement of the cliff dwellers and their kindred of the mesa and the plain," said Professor Longworth. "Thirty or forty families dwelt here, with a complete tribal and communal life. The workmanship of these rooms is good, too."

The outer walls of the building were about a foot and a half thick, made of two layers of stone placed six or eight inches apart. The face of the outer row was dressed, and the space between the two was filled with bowlders and adobe. The partitions between the rooms were made of a single row of stones about eight inches thick.

The estufa was choked with pottery, fallen stones and other remains. In the opinion of the Professor it was originally sunk below the surface of the surrounding ground. Back of it loomed the great burial mound, now partly covered with vegetation. Charles would have passed it by as merely a hill, but the Professor knew better.

"Enough people," he said, "lie inside that hill to make a great tribe, if they could rise from the dead. It may have been used as a burial mound for a thousand years, and, if we were to dig into it, we'd probably find skeletons within three feet of the surface. They lie there, hundreds and hundreds, heaped upon one another, layer after layer. Pottery and other household articles are also buried with them. But they'll lie untouched by us. This, too, must wait another day. But doesn't it awe you a little, Charles, to look upon all this ruin and think how completely its people have vanished?"

"It does give me a queer feeling," replied the boy, "standing as it does in all this loneliness and desolation out here in these wild mountains. Let's go in, Professor, and examine some of the rooms."

"That will be profitable work," replied Longworth eagerly, "but we'll keep our weapons with us, Charles. We'll not make such a mistake as we did back at the tower."

They spent a long time prowling from room to room, and examining the relics, which consisted chiefly of pottery, stone weapons and stone implements for cooking. Longworth saw much that he would have liked to take away, but he knew that they could not burden themselves for the return trip.

They were so interested that it was noon before they realized it. The day was uncommonly hot and the rays of the sun blazed vertically overhead.

"I propose that we take our luncheon in one of the houses that still has a roof on it," suggested the boy. "It will be dark and cool in there."

"A good idea," said Longworth, "we must not over-exert or overheat ourselves in our zeal."

They selected a house in the center of the first row, over which the roof, partly of stone and partly of wood, was almost perfect. Its temperature was good, and as they sat on stones they ate their luncheon and enjoyed the grateful coolness. The cold water in the thermos bottles was exceedingly refreshing, and they drank freely, knowing that an abundant supply was near at hand.

The Professor closed his eyes and dreamed a little. Charles thought at first that he was asleep. But he was not. He opened his eyes presently and seemed to be looking at something far away.

"Charlie, lad," he said, "my mind had gone back hundreds of years. I was reproducing this great communal dwelling, as it must have been, maybe a thousand years ago. I saw the people at work with their stone implements along the slopes, irrigating and hoeing their little fields of maize and beans, and other grains and vegetables. They were a dark race, perhaps not more than five feet high, but they were thick and strong, and wonderfully sure of foot. Men and women worked together in the fields, and now and then they sang strange old songs, which are lost forever.

"The girls were bringing water from the river in low, wide jars which they balanced on their heads. They were very smooth of face, with a glow in their dusky cheeks. Their long black hair probably fell in loose coils. They, too, sang those strange old songs which are lost to all the world, and I've no doubt that the young men, as they looked up from their work in the fields, thought the girls very fair.

"Here, just in front of the row of houses, the old men sat in the cool of the evening. They were the village elders or heads. They took tallies of the work, they saw that plenty of water had been brought, and they heard reports from the scouts who had gone far down into the lower valley to watch for their enemies. They must have been watching always, and I've no doubt that the bold, skillful and strong among the young men took turns at it. They probably cooked their evening meal on the ground in front of the building, and perhaps they had no fires or lights of any kind in the houses. So they probably went to sleep as soon as dark came, and were up with the first bars of dawn. It was a perfectly organized little community, working hard and always on guard against those unknown enemies in the valley below."

"What did they do in winter?" asked Charlie. "All these mountains fill up with snow then?"

"Winter must have been their resting time. When they got in all their vegetables and grain and their supplies of meat, which they must have obtained mostly by traps and pitfalls, they stayed snugly in this great house, and let the snow heap up about them. Then the men hammered out their stone tools and dishes and tanned deer and bear skins. The women plaited baskets and made robes and mantles of turkey feathers. There were feasts and celebrations, courting and marrying and giving in marriage. Don't you think, Charlie, lad, that knowing nothing of the world without, and hence having nothing finer to envy, they could have been pretty warm and comfortable here?"

"It certainly seems so to me, especially when a blizzard was yelling along the slopes and through the passes."

They resumed the work of examination, but did not carry it on more than two or three hours, as the afternoon was very hot. Then they retreated again to the dark, cool shade of the house, and owing to the heat, decided to light no fire, making their supper of cold food.

"We'll lie here until the night comes," said Longworth, "but for the sake of air we'll sleep outside."

Charles was content, and, spreading out his blanket for the sake of softness, he lay down upon it. His exertions and the heat threw him into a deep languor, and gradually his eyes closed. Professor Longworth did not disturb him, and soon he was asleep. But the boy came back to wakefulness with the Professor's hand upon his shoulder.

"Open your eyes, Charles," whispered the man, "but don't speak. Above all, make no noise of any kind."

The man's words were tense, thrilling, and Charles knew instinctively that some great danger had come. He rose to a sitting position. It was full night now, but they could discern objects at fifty yards. The boy's eyes followed the man's pointing finger, and he saw six dusky figures standing, almost in a row, and looking at the old building.

They were Indians, tall, built powerfully, long of hair and naked, except for the breech cloth and moccasins. All of them carried rifles and there were knives in their belts. They stood there staring, but the man and boy were well hidden in the low room.

"What are they?" whispered Charles.

"Utes, I think," replied Longworth in a similar whisper. "Probably a hunting party that has wandered far south. The Utes are formidable Indians and this band would be too much for us in a fight, but we are not in as much danger as we seem, Charles. The Indians from further north regard these ruins with awe. They think they are haunted by the ghosts of those who once dwelled here. All savage peoples, as I have remarked before, are naturally superstitious. I think we'd better lie flat on the floor, Charles, while we are peeping at them. Then they cannot possibly see us, and I want to watch everything they do."

The Utes came forward three or four paces, and then stopped again. They never ceased to regard the great communal dwelling. The Professor laughed low.

"They are divided between curiosity and superstition," he said. "Considering their early training and what they are they are certainly brave men. Now superstition is holding them, for they remain in their tracks. Now courage has overcome superstition as they advance another step, but only one. See, they stop, and I would wager that they are trembling with awe. Bravo! How the mind triumphs over cowardly flesh! They have come forward another step!"

"But what if they keep on coming?" whispered Charles.

"Then it would be a very dark night for us. But we are in no danger. Not the slightest. Did you ever hear me groan?"

"What do you mean by that, Professor?"

"You'll soon see that I'm one of the finest groaners you ever heard, and, on occasion, fine groaning is an exceedingly valuable accomplishment. Listen!"

Charles' blood ran cold as a most awful sound, like the cry of a lost soul, rose by his side. It began in a sigh, turned to a moan, then swelled to a shrill, weird pitch, and died away in an agonized sob, which the valley gave back in echoes, scarcely less poignant than the original. The whole atmosphere of the place was changed. The dead had come back and the skeletons walked in rows, arm in arm.

Charles saw the Utes jump into the air and retreat a dozen steps. Then they paused, evidently trying to gather up their courage, but that awful cry arose again and then a third time. They were brave men, but they could stand no more. Uttering six simultaneous howls of terror they dashed down the valley.

Far in their northern villages the returning hunters told how they had found a great ruined building, haunted and guarded by its own dead.

Professor Longworth rose to his feet and laughed in a satisfied way.

"As a groaner you must lead the world," said Charles admiringly, "and it certainly came in handy. We have won a splendid victory without firing a shot."

"We can now go outside and sleep," said the Professor. "They will never come back. To-morrow I think we'd better start for home."

They slept peacefully, and began their return journey.

They camped one evening, in a stony little valley, enclosed with a rim of pines and cedars. As the nights were always chilly, and fallen wood was plentiful, they built a fire where the largest of the pines would protect them from the wind, and made ready for supper.

"We'll gather some of the loose stones so plentiful about here," said Professor Longworth, "and do our cooking upon them."

Charles walked down toward a small basin, about twenty feet in circumference, in the center of which detached stones lay in abundance. He picked up two, but deciding that one would not suit his purpose, dropped it when he was about five feet away from the center. When he reached the edge of the basin he happened to look back, and he uttered a cry of amazement.

The stone he had dropped was moving along the ground. It was a slow motion, but it was perceptible. Charles stared in astonishment. The twilight was coming and he thought at first that he must be suffering from some optical illusion. He shook his head. His brain was certainly all right, and so were his eyes. There was the stone creeping along the earth toward the huddled group at the center, in which it had lain. It was one of the most uncanny things that he had ever seen, and he felt a chill run along his spine. Then he laughed at himself. It could not possibly signify any kind of danger.

He put down at his feet the second stone which he had retained in his hands and watched it. It was about four inches in diameter and would have weighed several pounds. Again that chill ran down his spine. The second stone gathered itself up, as it were, and began to creep toward the common center. He went down to the group of stones, took two more and put them down on the ground at a distance of about five feet. The same extraordinary thing happened. These stones, like their predecessors, began to return toward the common center.

The curiosity of Charles was aroused intensely and he tried the experiment with others, and yet others. Not one of them failed. All began their slow return to the common center. The basin was filled with creeping stones.

"Charlie, lad," called the Professor, "why don't you come with the stones? The fire is ready!"

"These stones are unwilling to come, Professor. Whenever I put one down it makes at once for its old home."

"What are you talking about?"

"I'm not joking. Just you come and see."

The Professor stepped to the edge of the basin, and he uttered a cry of pleasure.

"What do you make of it?" the boy asked. "I never saw such a curious thing before."

"But I have," said Longworth. "I've seen the walking stones in shallow basins in Nevada, but I did not know that there were any down here. Their behavior will impress and even terrify the unlearned in such matters, but the explanation is scientific and simple. All of these stones are powerfully charged with lodestone or magnetic iron ore. See how they are gathered together in a cluster like a basket of fruit. But while I say the explanation is simple, Charlie, it is also impressive. We're only beginning to explore the hidden forces of nature. Just think what man will know ten thousand years from now!"

But Charles did not bother himself much about ten thousand years hence. After supper he experimented again and again with the stones, and they never failed to "walk."

They started once more the next morning, and on the way they gathered the bear skins which they had left in the tower, and which were now quite dry. They made a safe return and their comrades received them with joy, listening with wonder to the tale of their adventures.

Chapter Thirteen - The Grip of The Shaman

Charles, true to his nature, which was extremely bold and enterprising, became the most skillful and daring hunter of the little colony of four, and his range gradually grew further and wider. Sometimes he went with the others, oftenest with Herbert, but frequently alone.

Now in the search for deer he followed for the second time their mountain stream far down toward the desert, noticing with interest the path by which they had come, recalling the old landmarks, a rock here, an upthrust of black lava there.

The deer were still evasive, as he approached the outlet of the stream from the hills into the plains and, as the twilight was approaching, he decided to spend the night there by the bank of the little river. He was often gone forty-eight hours at least, and he knew that his absence would occasion no alarm at the village. Hence he made his camp with a clear conscience.

It was the kind of camp that a strong active boy could make in ten minutes, merely a heap of dry leaves, raked up under the shelter of some bushes. Rain fell rarely there and the pure air bore only the scented odors of mountain forests. Charles ate venison from his knapsack, drank at the stream yet cold from its mountain run, and then lay down on his bed of leaves beneath the bushes.

Twilight was at hand. Far off in the southwest where the plains and the desert lay he saw the sun setting like an immense red shield. Behind him the hills and the mountains were already black with night. A light wind blew gently among the oaks and the cedars and the piñons.

Charles lay outstretched on the leaves, his rifle by his side. He was relaxed mentally and physically. Without any will of his own, his mind wandered back to the little station in the desert. He had no regrets for it, but he felt all the old pity for Ananias Brown, the man with the hideous marks in his palms, the man who had died, but who might be no Ananias at all. Yes, Charles was very sorry for him, but he was glad that he had refused to stay any longer in the telegraph office.

It had been perhaps a wild venture of his, but it was turning out well. He had found good comrades and they would yet find the gold. What more could he ask? His deep sense of peace and satisfaction grew deeper still, and permeated all his being. How wonderfully soft was his bed of leaves! And the air that he breathed was like some great tonic.

The wind still blew gently. The light drone of an insect came to his ears, and a lizard near by pattered over the dry leaves. But Charles did not stir. He saw the great red shield of the sun sink behind the swells and pass swiftly out of sight. He saw the night drop down on the plains and darkness cover everything. His eyes drooped and the boughs of the trees, that had shown dimly, floated away. He stirred slightly. He was conscious that he was very happy, and then he fell asleep.

The lad awoke in some unknown hour of the night, and he did not at first know where he was, but the feeling in his mind, instead of being happiness, was alarm, a vague, mysterious apprehension that seemed to have come in his sleep. He did not move his body, but his right hand crept a little from his side, and then lay across the stock of his rifle. The cold wood and metal were good to the touch, and brought reassurance.

The night was somewhat lighter than it had been when he fell asleep. A good moon rode high in the sky and its light fell on trees and bushes. Charles did not see anything, but he believed that he had received a warning. Still he did not move. His right ear was close to the earth and he listened a full two minutes. Then he heard a sound that was not of the wind, nor a lizard scuttling over the leaves. It was the tread of human footsteps and it was very near. Moreover, it was made by more than one.

It might have been prospectors or wandering hunters straying far, but it never occurred to Charles that it could be either. His mind leaped at once to the conclusion that savage Apaches were near enough for him to hear them walking.

He was glad now that he had chosen the shelter of low-lying bushes and that he was sunk deep in his bed of dry leaves.

The footsteps came closer. He was only a boy and his muscles began to quiver, but with a powerful effort of the will he kept them still. His breathing seemed painfully loud to him, a sound that must be heard, but mind again came to his relief, telling him that it was not so.

The footsteps still approached and from his leafy covert the boy saw four men step into a little opening.

His instinct had been right. They were Apaches, the most cruel of all Indians, tall, slender men about five feet ten inches in height, dark mahogany in color, their coarse black hair cut straight around in front and hanging almost to the eyes, as a shade against the sun, but long behind, and tied up with garters or pieces of red flannel, in which was fastened a slender stick about eight inches long, used as a comb. Tied to a central lock in the head of every one was a feather, hanging at the end of a string, two or three inches long and fluttering in the wind. In one case it was a quail feather, in another that of a hawk, the third was that of the eagle, and the fourth came from that of the wild turkey. Three of the feathers were tinted red, and one white.

The men had no beards or mustaches, although they were of mature age, only a few scattered hairs on chin and lip. Their foreheads were low and narrow, receding from prominent brows. Their eyes were far apart with heavy lids painted black to brighten the eyes. The iris of their eyes was dark mahogany like their skins, but the rest of the ball was yellowish. Two of the men had Roman noses, but those of the others were broad and flat with conspicuous nostrils. Two of them had pierced nostrils with beads hanging from them.

Their ears were small and well shaped, but were disfigured by cuts. The lobes were slit, and strings of small beads, mixed with mother of pearl or stone pendants, hung from them. Their mouths were large, with long thin lips and small, closely set teeth.

The hidden boy staring with fascinated eyes took in every detail of these terrible visitors. They wore no clothing except moccasins and breech clouts. The latter were made of buckskin with the hair on, and hung down behind nearly to the ground, resembling a tail.

Although clothed but little they were armed amply. Every man carried a rifle which Charles could see was a breech loader of the finest pattern. At the belt that held the breech clout were revolver and knife. The boy surmised from their manner and the fineness of their arms that they were chiefs. He could hear them talking in clicking tones, but, of course, he did not understand a word they said.

They were not more than fifteen feet from him and they stopped there in the opening, gesticulating now and then toward the mountains. The boy had a horrible fear that they had learned of the presence there of his friends and himself, and he felt that he must return quickly with a warning. But for the present he was occupied with the task of keeping himself immovable and still.

The Apaches talked for three or four minutes, then turned and went back down the stream. Charles watched them, until their figures blended with the darkness, and he did not stir for at least a quarter of an hour afterward. Then he rose very cautiously, holding tight to his precious rifle, and feeling of the pistol in his belt. He followed the stream forty or fifty yards, and then halted in a cluster of piñons.

The boy was divided between two opinions. He knew that he ought to warn his friends, but if he were to go back now he would have little to tell them, except that he had seen four Apaches at the entrance of the pass. Ought he not to continue with the stream and learn more before he returned to the cliff village? The latter opinion conquered, and he continued to follow the stream, stopping at intervals to look and listen.

But he neither saw nor heard the Apaches again and his confidence began to increase. It was not such a dark night, and the trail could lead only one way—by the side of the river. If any other Apaches were near he would discover their presence in the course of time. Charles knew that he must be exceedingly wary. Apaches were cunning and their cruelty was beyond description. A sudden lifting of the wind or the light sound of a rabbit leaping through the brush would cause him to pause and watch a long while before he resumed his slow advance.

He tried to guess the time and concluded that it was about halfway between midnight and day, finding that he was right, as in about three hours he saw a faint gray appearing in the east. The gray turned to silver, and then that enormous red shield came up again out of the desert plains.

Charles was at the mouth of the pass. Before him, as he looked southward, the gray swells stretched, and, now and then, one of the dancing "dust devils" that had mocked him of old would rise up and whirl away out of sight. He murmured,

"O'er the measureless range where rarely change
The swart gray plains, so weird and strange,
Treeless and streamless and wondrous still."

He saw nothing but the desert before him and the mountains behind him. What had become of the Apaches, those dreadful figures of the night? They had vanished, melted away, dissolved into the ether. It must have been a bad dream, born of the wilderness and solitude!

He heard a light step behind him and whirled quickly, but not quickly enough. Strong arms seized him and pinned him face down to the earth. His wrists and ankles were bound with rawhide, and then somebody turned him over with contemptuous foot.

Charles lay on his back and looked up into the eyes of the four Apaches whom he had seen in the night. Cruel their countenances seemed then, but far more cruel now, and in the eyes of every one was savage and derisive laughter that cut him to the bone. While he had been trying to stalk them, they had deftly turned and had stalked him, capturing him with consummate ease and dispatch.

One of the Apaches took his rifle, examined it, and then, with an air of satisfaction and possession, put it upon his own shoulder, another helped himself to his revolver, and a third deftly ran through his pockets, taking any valuables that might be left.

"Me Big Elk," said the oldest and evidently the most important of the four. "Who you? Where you come from?"

Charles was a boy of spirit. He regarded himself as lost anyhow, and he did not see any reason why he should involve his comrades in his own fate.

"So you understand English then," he said contemptuously. "Well, it doesn't matter to you who I am or where I come from. It's unpleasant enough to be here in your dirty hands, without having to talk about it."

Big Elk frowned and contracted his eyes. His glance was very savage indeed.

"You talk when we want you to talk," he said. "How you like to have nice little fire built on your chest, nice little fire that will burn all day? How do you like to be buried in the sand up to the chin and left there?"

"I shouldn't like any of those things," said Charles, as he closed his eyes and shuddered. But he was resolved nevertheless not to tell of his friends in the cliff village.

The four Apaches talked together again a little while, and then Big Elk turned once more to the captive.

"You walk," he said, "you go to our village."

He unbound the boy's ankles, and Charles rose gladly to his feet—he did not like lying there, all trussed up like a dressed chicken.

"I'm ready to walk," he said more cheerfully. "Which way do I go?"

Big Elk pointed toward the desert.

"Off there," he said, "and you no run. If run we all shoot at once."

"Don't be afraid that I'll try it," said the boy. His hands bound and four Apaches close behind him, he had not the remotest idea of making such an attempt.

He followed the line of Big Elk's pointing finger, and walked toward the desert, which was now but a little distance away. They were yet beside the river which had ceased to boil and eddy and which was spreading out into a smooth and shallow stream, preparatory to its entrance into the desert, where it would, at last, be lost.

But just before they reached the sands Big Elk took him by the shoulder and turned him toward the right. Charles without a word walked on, passed among some dwarfed trees and scrub bushes, and entered a shallow but cozy valley.

He stopped in surprise at the edge of the valley. It contained a considerable Indian village, evidently pitched there within the last few months, but showing all the signs of active savage life.

The village contained about a hundred circular brush huts, called in the Apache language a-wah, every one about five feet high and ranging from six to eight feet in diameter. They were thatched with grass and soap weed, and had an opening on one side which served alike as a door and an escape for smoke. By the side of many of these huts seeds, meat, buckskins and extra clothing hung on upright frames.

When the four men descended into the valley with Charles a cry was raised and the population of the village, men, women and children, poured forward to see the captive. The boy regarded them with as much interest as they looked at him, though not with the same degree of triumph.

The women were not beautiful. They were all tattooed. The married women were distinguished by seven narrow blue lines, running from the lower lip down the chin, the outer one starting from the corner of the mouth and frequently having a row of arrow-shaped points turned outward. Sometimes two zigzag lines ran from each corner of the mouth, while the three between were straight. The men were not tattooed, but most of the young warriors had small fringed and beaded buckskin pockets suspended from the bead necklaces that they wore. These pockets contained little mirrors, which the young dandies often took out, and in which they admired themselves prodigiously.

Both men and women were heavily painted with a red mixture made chiefly from clay, which they used in summer to keep themselves cool, and in winter to keep themselves warm. The faces of the men were also smeared with a paint of galena, which denoted war, although Charles did not then know it. The women were almost as lightly clad as the men, their costumes consisting of a deerskin kilt hanging from the waist.

They showed the greatest curiosity concerning Charles, crowding around him and touching him. One old squaw plucked at the hair on his neck, but all shrank back when a formidable figure appeared from one of the brush huts, even the chiefs giving way with deference.

It was the figure of a very old man, tall and erect. Flaming eyes looked out from deep hollows, showing the savage spirit within. He was wrapped in a beautiful Navajo blanket and as he came forward the people opened in a wide lane before him. It was the chief shaman or medicine man of the village, Ka-jú, who might be a hundred years old, who was on familiar terms with the spirits and whose authority was unbounded, because he was a favorite with Se-má-che, the Sun God, the Manitou of the Apaches.

Ka-jú stopped directly before Charles and regarded him intently. The boy gave back his look and thought that he had never seen a more hideous face. The dark mahogany skin was seamed and lined with countless wrinkles. The lips were pressed closely together, showing that the gums were toothless, and the yellowish eyes were filled with fathomless cunning and cruelty. It seemed to Charles that he was in the presence of a wicked spirit out of an older and more savage world. He shuddered but he still returned the gaze of the shaman.

Ka-jú turned away and spoke to Big Elk, who listened respectfully and then conducted Charles to one of the brush huts, into which he was thrust and left alone.

The boy's arms were still bound, but the cords had loosened somewhat, and they did not hurt him. He lay down on a bed of dry grass in the dark little place, and, for a while, gave himself up to the most bitter thoughts. He was mortified that he had been taken so easily, and he was filled with apprehension for the future. The Apaches would torture him to death, then they would go up the pass, find his friends and slay them.

Big Elk a few hours later brought him a gourd of water and some balls of dried maize meal, both of which were very welcome, because he was hungry and thirsty. The Apache remained with him while he ate and drank, and when he had finished he said:

"You come out, you see the shamans make great medicine for the Apache village."

"Gladly," said Charles springing to his feet. He was eager for the fresh air and he wanted, with all a boy's curiosity, to see what was going on. Big Elk led the way, and he stepped out into the sunlight, which was dazzling after so much darkness.

Charles looked up and saw the great mountains that had sheltered his comrades and himself. Would he ever again behold that friendly village on the cliff?

He was closely guarded by Big Elk and others who stood about him, and there was not the remotest chance for a dash, but he was no longer the center of attention. The eyes of everybody were directed toward a large brush hut in the most conspicuous part of the village, and Charles, too, was soon an absorbed witness of a singular scene.

The samada or brush hut was about ten feet in diameter, much larger than the others, and its sides were open next to the ground. Under it their chief shaman and his assistants had illustrated their heaven or spirit land, in a picture about eight feet square, made by sprinkling red clay, charcoal, ashes, powdered leaves and grass on the smooth sand.

In the center of this space was a round, red spot a foot in diameter, and circling about it were several successive rings, alternately red and green, each about an inch and a half in width. From the outermost ring radiated four triangular-shaped figures, each corresponding to one of the cardinal points of the compass, giving to the whole the look of a Maltese cross.

All about the cross and between its arms were figures of men, every one with its feet toward the center. Some were made of charcoal with ashes for eyes and hair, and others were made of red clay. These figures were about eight inches in length and it was a curious fact that nearly every one of them lacked an arm or a leg or even a head.

Charles was witnessing the casting of a spell to protect the Apaches from disease and disaster, and to bring them victory and plenty. Even then he guessed its import.

While all the population of the village was gathered about the samada, but at a respectful distance, the shamans, led by their venerable chief, Ka-jú, seated themselves in a circle around the great picture. Then the other Indians made a close ring about them, the old man sitting down Turkish fashion just behind the shamans, the young men standing just behind the latter, and back of these the women and children also standing.

A curious heavy silence followed. The whole painted throng look intently at the picture and the figures of the little men. Charles could not keep from sharing their interest, although he did not know what was to follow.

The silence was broken by the shamans who began a slow, monotonous chant, in which they invoked the aid of the spirits for their tribe. Presently the chant ceased and Ka-jú, gray, ancient and toothless, arose. Poising himself a moment he stepped carefully between the figures of the men, dropping upon every one, except three, a pinch of yellow powder, which he took from a small buckskin bag, handed to him by the next oldest shaman. He did this very deliberately and the crowd watched him, breathing heavily with excitement, but uttering no other sound.

When the last pinch of powder was dropped he handed the buckskin bag to the shaman who had given it to him, and then retraced all his steps. As he did so he took back from every figure a little of the powder that he had placed upon it, almost filling his palm, when he had finished. The other shamans did the same, succeeding one another in the task, in order of seniority. All the while the people watched them eagerly, because the powder was now consecrated, and when sprinkled upon the body was a protection against wounds and disease.

When the last shaman had taken his share some powder was yet left upon the images and the people made a wild rush for it. Those who were strong enough or fortunate enough to obtain it rubbed it over their bodies and went away, considering themselves safe now from evil spirits. But the shamans carried away their own powder, reserving it for future use.

Charles was permitted to remain outside for some time. He sat on a rock near one of the huts and he was despondent, but he tried not to show it. Curious eyes were always upon him, and he never saw pity or mercy in any of them. How foolish he had been to follow the Apaches, instead of retreating at once to his comrades!

As night came on he received another gourd of water and more balls of maize meal, and then Big Elk escorted him back to his hut. There his ankles were rebound and, lying upon his bed of dry grass, he found sleep after long seeking.

Chapter Fourteen - The Witless Dance

Charles was suffering alike from physical exhaustion and excess of his emotions, and his sleep resembled stupor. He did not awake until the sun was far up over the Arizona mountains and plains, and he might not have awakened even then, but the presence of four men in his hut impinged upon his consciousness.

He opened his eyes, writhed into a half-sitting position on his bed of leaves and saw the ancient shaman, Ka-jú, Big Elk and two others. The door of the hut was open and the bright light of the morning fell upon their mahogany faces. But it was old Ka-jú at whom Charles looked. His face seemed more cruel and horrible than ever. The boy had never seen such a type before. The

132

impression that it was a survival from a cruel old world of long ago clung to him. As the toothless mouth was drawn up to compress the lips together the sharp pointed chin and the great hooked nose, pointed also, almost met. The eyes with their yellowish pupils were full of cruelty like those of the tiger. It seemed to Charles that Ka-jú was at least a hundred years old, and perhaps he was—a hundred years crowded with cruelty, the practice of savage rites and the reliance upon superstition. Charles could see in those saffron eyes a consuming hatred of himself and all of his race! It was his instant impression that his fate rested only with Ka-jú. Big Elk and the others, however important they might be elsewhere, were only pawns in the presence of the shaman.

Now Ka-jú disclosed that he could speak English.

"You sleep late," he said. "Se-má-che (the Sun God) rose over the mountains three hours ago."

"It is true," replied Charles with some spirit, "but you have furnished me such a magnificent room here and such a nice bed that I could not keep from oversleeping myself. Blame your excessive hospitality, my ancient friend."

Ka-jú looked at him and frowned. Charles' words were too large for him, but he gathered from the tone that he was being derided, and the head shaman of the Apache-Yumas was a mighty man among his people, the close friend of Se-má-che himself and well-nigh the lord of life and death. It was not for a boy, a prisoner, to mock at him and as the lips were pressed more tightly together over the toothless gums a pebble could have been held between the pointed chin and the pointed nose. The yellowish eyes might have been a century old, but they were not too old to be full of baleful fire.

"You sleep late," repeated Ka-jú in an ominous tone, "but a longer sleep may be coming for you."

Charles shivered a little, despite all his pride and will—he understood the threat of Ka-jú.

The shaman said some words in Apache and the other three unbound the boy's wrists and ankles. He sat up and stretched arms and legs luxuriously. The circulation had not been impeded, but it was pleasant to have one's body free, even if it were only within the narrow space of an Apache hut. The feeling brought courage back with it.

"Why have you four come to see me here?" Charles asked, addressing himself as usual directly to the shaman.

"To ask you questions," said Ka-jú, "questions that may help you, that may save you from the torture."

"What are they?" asked Charles, although he could guess their nature.

"You came down the pass out of the deep mountains," replied the shaman, waving his withered hand toward the north. "Far up the pass on the cliffs is a village where an old, old race dwelled long ago. They were driven away by my people who afterward lived on top of the cliff, not in the side of it as these people had done. By and by a great pestilence came upon us. The little people who lived in the cliffs had prayed to their gods to avenge them, and many of us died. It was in my time but before the time of these who are with us. We fled away and we have never been back. But we may go again. The face of Semá-che is not now turned from us. We have the sacred dust. You saw, yesterday."

"How does all this concern me?" asked Charles.

Old Ka-jú leaned forward, his fierce eyes holding the gaze of the boy.

"You came from the pass," he said, "but you have not been alone there. Others are with you, four, five, six, maybe ten, perhaps men who hunt in our mountains for gold. You lead us there, you show us the way to take them, when they think nobody coming and we let you live."

It seemed to Charles that the face of Ka-jú was that of a genuine fiend, fresh from the infernal regions, as he made this horrible proposition. The soul of the boy revolted, and giving himself no time to think of the consequences he exclaimed:

"Help you to ambush my friends! I'd rather die a dozen times than do such a thing!"

"You will die at least a dozen times before you really die," said the shaman, grinning horribly.

Charles shuddered from head to foot. He could not help it. The recoil came from his first high emotion, and he foresaw all that they would do to him. He might give them his promise, lead them on a false trail, and escape somehow in the bush! Such a thing would be pardonable in the face of torture and death. But his courage came again. He would not do it.

"I can't help you," he said; "I don't even say that I have friends anywhere in the mountains."

"We may find a way to make you serve us," said the shaman. "The flesh is brave, before it feels the touch of steel and fire."

Charles lay back upon his bed of grass. He did not wish to hear any more threats—the sound of them was too unpleasant—and he was anxious above all that the horrible old shaman should go away. His face was enough to call up the most cruel of realities.

Seeing that he would not talk, the four left, but Big Elk came back presently with some food and water, which the boy could scarcely touch.

"Eat, drink," said Big Elk, "you need strength." He spoke in the most matter-of-fact way, without a touch of sympathy in his voice, but Charles, reflecting that the advice might be good, forced himself to finish the breakfast.

"Now you come," said Big Elk, leading the way, and Charles followed him into the sunshine. The shaman was close by the door, outside, regarding him with malignant triumph, and the entire population was assembled again as if to witness some rite. Charles had a sudden horrible fear that he was to be the chief figure in this rite.

A great cry went up when he appeared in the sunshine, but it was stilled in a moment, when old Ka-jú raised his withered right hand. Big Elk took the boy by the right arm, another strong warrior took him by the left, and as the shaman led the way out of the valley toward the edge of the desert they followed close behind. But Charles made no resistance. He knew that it would be futile and even in this terrible moment he had his pride. But the insistent question, what were they going to do with him, pricked him continually like the red hot point of a needle.

They emerged upon the sands. Charles saw the brown swells, stretching away until they met the horizon, and a whirling "dust devil" passed for a moment against the lowest belt of sky and was lost. Behind him he heard muttered words, the low breathing of hundreds of savages and the shuffling of impatient feet. The sky was a burning blue, and he saw that the desert sands would be hot to the touch.

He turned half around. Warriors, women and children were gathered in a great semicircle about him, and every savage face showed eagerness and delight, never sympathy.

Ka-jú came close to the boy and stood before him. Charles was the taller and the old man had to look up into his eyes.

"Once again," said the shaman, "I make you the offer. Will you take us to your friends in the mountains, take us there when they sleep?"

"No, I will not," replied Charles, making a supreme effort of his will.

The shaman stepped back and made a gesture. Four men, with stone-headed hoes and spades, began to dig a hole in the ground. They went down rapidly in the loose hot sand, and Charles saw that the pit they dug, although not very wide, would be deep. The horrible shudder ran through every nerve again. They were going to bury him standing, up to the chin, press the sand about him and leave him there, with the brazen sun blazing upon him, and the vultures awaiting their prey. He looked up and saw two of them already wheeling in the blue, drawn by some hideous instinct.

The eyes of the boy wandered back to the hole that the warriors were digging. It was down three feet, and then four feet. It would soon be five feet and then they would put him in it. He had heard of this form of torture among the Apaches and it seemed to him the most horrible that human cruelty could devise. He turned half around once more, and looked at the semi-circle of Apaches. Not a ray of human sympathy appeared in the eye of warrior, woman or child, only an eager interest and delight. He wondered that beings fashioned like himself could do such things.

He watched the workers and saw how the perspiration rolled off their mahogany-colored bodies. He himself, although he stood idle, felt the brazen glare of the sun that seemed to be burning into his brain. His fate was very near, apparently it was inescapable, and yet he had a feeling that it could not be real, it was a phantasm, not a thing that could happen to him, and this blessed feeling upheld him in his moment of greatest need, enabling him to stand erect and present a stoical face to those who watched hopefully for signs of flinching. But his heart beat heavily, and little black specks in myriads began to dance before his eyes.

He heard behind him a cry, not loud, but coming from many throats. It was a cry of surprise and he whirled to see. The savage eyes were turned from him, and were gazing at something that had appeared upon one of the swells of the desert though far away. He saw it, too, but at first thought it might be one of the black specks that danced in such myriads before his eyes. Then he was sure that it was not a black speck. It was larger, it came on toward the Apaches, growing larger still, and it took the shape of a man.

An Apache, probably a runner returning to his tribe, Charles thought, and then when the exclamation of surprise came again from the people about him, he knew that he was mistaken. It was no Apache; then it must be a white man!

Charles gazed with all his eyes. His heart had taken a sudden upward leap. Help might be coming, though the advance of a lone man promised but little. But at least it would cause a wait and he was glad now even for a delay of a few minutes. That pit and the perspiring Apaches who dug were real after all.

The advancing figure rose upon the plain and Charles winked his eyes rapidly, lest he had been deceived by some mist. The outlines grew familiar. It was unbelievable. He winked his eyes again to clear away a deceitful mist, but no mist was there. They had not yet bound his hands and feet for the pit, and he rubbed his eyes with his fingers, but he did not rub the advancing figure away, nor its familiar appearance.

It was a white man who came, and, as he rose now on the crest of a swell, an enormous pith helmet came into view, then a round, red face, the eyes shaded by huge glasses, and a small, trim figure in neat khaki, carrying a box under one arm.

It was Professor Erasmus Darwin Longworth. No one who ever knew him could mistake him, and the amazed boy would have shouted a warning, he would have cried to him that he was coming straight among cruel and merciless Apaches, but the actions of the professor were so strange that his tongue lay dry in his mouth, and he was silent with astonishment.

Perhaps it was the blazing sun of the Arizona desert, perhaps it was delving too much and too deep into the world of knowledge, but Charles had never seen the Professor behave in such a frivolous and extraordinary manner. He came on with a light, dancing step, swaying rhythmically from side to side, and now and then holding his free hand above his head in the manner of a Spanish dancer. Occasionally he sang snatches of song in a not unmusical voice. Charles thought that he recognized more than once a strain of plantation melody.

The Apaches were silent. The shaman, old Ka-jú, was a little ahead of the others, and his shrunken figure was bent forward. But the yellowish eyes that had seen so much in nearly a century of life were regarding the stranger with an intent, suspicious gaze. Charles never knew why he did not call out to the Professor and greet him as the friend that he was—perhaps it was due to his amazement and the fact that the Professor did not appear to know him.

There was a rapt look on the Professor's face, and he did not seem to see the Apaches until he was within twenty feet of them. Then he began to sing incessantly, and to dance back and forth with all the agility of an acrobat. He danced forward to old Ka-jú, made imaginary crosses in front of his face, and sang with renewed vigor. The shaman shrank visibly, and a look of fear came into the old eyes that feared so little. The Professor danced away and made similar crosses before the face of Big Elk. The chief turned away in unconcealed fright, and the Professor, advancing into a little open space, continued to sing and dance. Murmurs of pity arose, and now Charles understood why. This strange little man under the enormous pith helmet, who sang and danced, had been bewitched, and he was protected by Se-má-che. None might harm him.

The Professor still sang and danced. Once he danced near Charles and under the words of the song came to the boy's ears: "Don't be afraid, I'll save you." Hope leaped up in the boy's heart. How could he ever have despaired while Professor Longworth lived! That brain filled with the wisdom of ages would save him. He did not know how, but he knew it.

The Professor presently stopped dancing and singing, took the box from under his arm, and laid it upon the sand. Then he knelt before it and said cabalistic words in a low tone. The Apaches silent, save for their heavy breathing, regarded him with awe. His prayer finished he turned a wheel and out of the box, mellow and clear, came the strains of "Dixie."

A gasp of astonishment burst from the Apaches. This singular being was certainly bewitched and without mind, but it was equally certain that Se-má-che, the Sun God, the master of the universe, spoke through him, and no one might lay a hostile hand upon him without danger of being smitten dead by Se-má-che himself. Did he not achieve the greatest of all wonders! He put a little box upon the ground, and forth from it came beautiful sounds, such as Se-má-che alone could produce.

The shaman stroked his beardless chin, and doubt and terror struggled in his soul. For full two generations he had ruled this band of Apaches and never before had he encountered anything like this. Great as his authority might be, he could not exert it against one protected by Se-má-che, and he, too, was almost convinced by the singular box that sent forth such wonderful strains of music.

The air was finished, the Professor bent over the box and another was begun. Over the yellow sands rose the solemn notes of the Tomb Song from "Lucia di Lammermoor," and now the professor's head, under his enormous pith helmet, was bowed with grief as he danced slowly and solemnly.

When the song was over he bowed his head above the magic box and wept. Then he lifted it in his arms and approached Big Elk as if to give it to him. But that valiant warrior, uttering a cry of terror, fled. It was refused also by a second and a third and then he approached the shaman.

Old Ka-jú stood his ground, as the Professor, with mincing step, approached, but Charles saw that the wrinkled, ancient face was ghastly, and that perspiration stood upon the mahogany brow and cheek. The Professor came closer, dancing more wildly than ever, and holding out the magic box in his hands. The shaman raised his own hands, but only halfway. Then his courage broke. He dropped his hands, and, as he shrank back, a deep sigh came from the crowd. Now that the great shaman had shown fear nothing on earth could convince them that Se-má-che himself was not acting in the person of the stranger.

When the shaman gave way, the Professor, still dancing and now singing, also approached Charles. He held out the box to the boy and said under his song, "Take it; it is set for the 'Donna e Mobile.'" Charles took the box boldly and touched the spring. Out came the strains of the famous old air from "Rigoletto," and, as Charles held the magic box in his hand, the Professor danced and bowed before him. Another gasp went up from the Apaches. Was the prisoner, too, a favorite of Se-má-che? If not, why did the witless one worship before him?

The song ended, and the Professor remained perfectly still, with head bowed before the captive youth. He was fixed in that position for a full minute, and not a soul among the Apaches dared to disturb him. The only sound they made was that of their heavy breathing. Then the Professor slowly raised his face until he looked directly into the eye of the sun through his great glasses.

The Apaches uttered another cry. He was returning, without flinching, the gaze of their own great God, Se-má-che. The Professor raised both arms and made gestures with them toward the sun. Then he turned to the prisoner again and took the box from his hand.

Ka-jú, the shaman, was watching it all with those keen old eyes of his. Suspicion and terror were still fighting in his mind, but suspicion was getting the better of terror. He had seen white men before, and he knew that they were full of guile and cunning. What was this magic box? He would renew his courage, take it in his own hands and let it play for his people. He would show them that his medicine was as good as any in the world.

The aged, the bold shaman, Ka-jú, had done many bold things in his life, but never before one so bold as that, when he stepped forward and held out his hands for the magic box. Perspiration stood again on brow and chin but he made the offer, nevertheless. Professor Longworth stared fixedly into his eyes and he saw there fear, but a will controlled by fear, and he felt a momentary thrill of respect for the old savage. Then he handed him the box, and began to dance before it.

Ka-jú held the box in hands that trembled, and listened for the song, but no song came. A low but swelling cry of horror rose from the throats of the

Apaches. The magic box would not play for the greatest shaman of them all, but it would play for the prisoner and the stranger. Then they were under the protection of Se-má-che and Ka-jú was committing sacrilege. The cry of horror turned to something else and, for the first time in half a century the shaman heard the rebuke of his tribe. He felt himself that he had done wrong, and a guilty conscience added to his terror. He dropped the box on the sand as if it had been a poisonous snake and shrank back among the warriors.

The Professor picked up the box, pressed the spring and forth came the flowing strains of "The Beautiful Blue Danube." Here certainty was piled upon belief, and surprise deepened when the strange, little man turning to them addressed them in their own tongue.

"He is mine," he said, nodding toward the prisoner, "I have come for him. Give him to me."

The Apaches did not expect so great a request and they looked blankly at their shaman. But he trembled. He alone had committed sacrilege and he alone had the punishment of Se-má-che to fear. He could not say no, much as it tore his soul to let a captive go, and he merely nodded and waved his hand, so much as to say, "Take him, he is yours."

Charles stepped forward and no hand was raised to stay him, but the anger of the witless one rose and he said in a stern voice to the Apaches:

"I wish him as he came to you. 'Tis Se-má-che who speaks through me. The Sun God may need him for the sacrifice, and I take him into the deep mountains."

Frightened hands brought the boy his rifle, pistol and knife, his ammunition and the other articles that had been stripped from him when he was captured, and the Apaches seemed relieved when he received them.

"Follow me," said the Professor in English to Charles.

He pressed the spring, the music box began to play a swift military march, and holding it, tucked under his arm, he danced away along the edge of the plain, where it merged into the scrub and the foothills. Charles, his head erect, his eyes on the Professor, followed as if he were held by the spell of the witless one.

Chapter Fifteen - The Shot of Shots

"Don't speak yet," said the Professor in a low tone when they had gone about fifty yards. "My power over them cannot last long. An influence of this kind goes away with the one who creates it."

But Charles could not be restrained wholly.

"You are the bravest man in the world, Professor, and the wisest," he breathed in tones of the deepest gratitude.

But the Professor merely danced on for another fifty yards. Then he said:

"I don't think I can keep this up much longer. I was never a dancing man, and if I were I should not choose such a blazing sun as this under which to make my exhibition. But another fifty yards and I'll turn into the bushes. The fright of old Ka-jú will last just about so far."

Charles longed to look back. He wanted to see what the Apaches were doing, but he did not dare. It was his part to follow with eyes fixed upon the one whom Se-má-che had chosen as his messenger.

The fifty yards that the Professor had named were passed. Then the little man turned abruptly into the scrub, and Charles as quickly followed. The Professor stooped down and picked up a rifle from the place where it lay hidden in grass and leaves. The music box he strapped upon his back. "We cannot part from so good a friend as this," he said. "But come, Charles, we must run for it. My spell has now just about worn out. These things are psychological, and with our disappearance from sight that shrewd old medicine man will realize that we have no more to do with Se-má-che, the Sun God, than he has."

The Professor dashed forward into the mouth of the pass that led toward the village and Charles closely followed him. All sorts of joyous thoughts surged up into the boy's mind. He was free again! Rescued in the most extraordinary manner by this wonderful man! He was armed, too, and he had all his strength. He did not believe that he could be taken again.

Behind them rose a great cry.

"There!" said the Professor. "The spell has broken. The courage of the old shaman has come back, and he will urge the others to follow us. It's quickness and skill now that will save us, Charles, my lad."

"I owe you my life, Professor," said the boy, as they ran together. "It was a wonderful thing to do. How did you know I was there?"

"I missed you, came down the pass and saw you in the hands of the rascals. The rest—well I think I may say it was an inspiration."

"I heard you speaking in their own tongue. I didn't think you knew Apache."

"I make it a point to learn languages. It's a part of my business. It's a very simple matter, after you learn the first twelve or fifteen. The others are merely derivations and the ordinary linguist can pick one up in a week or two. Of course, I have studied the Apaches and their tongue. I would not think of coming to their country without first doing so. Those behind us are Apache-Yumas. They call themselves in their own language Tulkepaias or Natchous. They live north of the Gila between the Verde and the Colorado. There is another branch of the Apaches, the Apache-Mojaves, who call themselves in their own language the Yavapais or Kokenins, who claim as their country the region from the valley of the Verde and Black Mesa to Bill Williams Mountain. I might mention also a third branch, the Apache-Tontos who live in the Tonto Basin and around Pinal Mountains."

The Professor spoke in a matter-of-fact tone. It came from him naturally and not as learning that might be displayed.

"All Apaches look alike to me," said Charles.

"That is, equally bad," said the Professor. "Well, we won't discuss it, but I think, my boy, that we are running too fast. If we keep up this pace we shall exhaust ourselves at the start. The Apaches are good trailers, but this is hard rough ground, and they will have great difficulty in following us. If they do overtake us, I wish I could get a shot at that old shaman. A sure bullet now might save many a white man from torture and death."

The Professor ferociously tapped the barrel of his rifle. Charles could not see the eyes behind the glasses, but he believed that the little man was in earnest. They were his own sentiments, too.

"They will certainly follow us up the pass," he said.

"Beyond doubt," said the Professor, "and the desire to overtake us may make them follow us to the cliff village. But if so, the four of us can probably hold them off there. It's a place of great strength."

They ran rapidly up the stream. There was practically only one path to choose, that is, to ascend by the side of the stream, as the mountains on either side were too steep for flight. The Professor, though small, was compact, and he seemed to be made of woven wire, while Charles was full of youthful strength and life. They did not stop their steady trot for about three hours, when they drank from the stream which was now cold in its rush down from the snowy mountains. They rested a little at the brink, always looking toward the south, whence the foe would come, if he came.

"Perhaps they've turned back," said Charles hopefully.

"I think not," said the Professor. "The shaman has probably convinced them that we are impostors and they must be raging. They are likely now to rush to the other extreme, and, under the impulse of it, they will overcome, for the time at least, all the superstitious fears that they may have had of the cliff village."

"Which means that we must make a fight?"

"I fear so."

The day was now far advanced and they were deep in the hills among the ash, the piñon, the oak and the cedar. The way had grown rough and they were compelled to rest, sitting in the deep shade on the crest of a precipice, full two hundred feet above the stream. Professor Longworth produced some venison from his pocket, and they chewed it hungrily. Charles was not a demonstrative boy, but he could not keep from saying again:

"Professor, I can never thank you enough for coming as you did. They were going to bury me alive, and leave me to the snakes and the vultures."

"Don't bother about the thanks, my lad," said Professor Longworth, "I was glad of the chance to save you and, moreover, it has given me one of the most interesting experiences of my life. Perhaps never again shall I have the opportunity to test the power of superstition over a shaman so old and cunning

141

as the one they call Ka-jú. It was a chance that can come only once in a life-time, and even then to but a few men. After all, I am more in your debt than you are in mine."

Charles gazed in astonishment at the Professor, but the little man was obviously in earnest. To his inquisitive mind it was a wonderful, a surpassing experience, and the danger of it was a matter of small moment.

"The human mind can be crushed for the time being by a blow," he said. "Ka-jú, although before alive with suspicion, was overwhelmed with terror when the music box would not go for him, while it went freely for you and me. But his mind was too strong to remain under the influence of that blow. It came back like a bent sapling rising again, when we disappeared in the bush. Then disbelief and rage of pursuit rose in him. It is certainly he who is urging on the chase."

"I wish I could get a shot at him with this good rifle of mine," said Charles vengefully. "I don't think I'm bloodthirsty, but if my bullet hit true I'd get rid of a monster."

"That is so," said the Professor with emphasis, "your bullet would certainly strike in both senses at the heart of our danger, and as I remarked just now would be a great benefit to the country. I wonder if I could not get a chance myself. The pursuit may be drawing near."

He crept from the bushes, thrusting forward his fine breech-loader, and looking with the eye of a hunter down the pass. Charles had noticed before what a splendid rifle the Professor carried, and he had noticed too, on more than one occasion, with what skill he could use it. Now this strange, apparently awkward man, the flower of schools and old learning, showed all the craft and knowledge of those who are born in the wilderness, the lives of whom depend daily upon their courage and caution.

He did not move bough or leaf, as he crept forward. He made no more noise than the crawling scorpion, and the piercing eyes behind the great glasses sought out every object in the pass. Charles felt, as he looked, a deep and overwhelming sense of power, of the knowledge that is power, and of the indomitable soul that is power also. The figure of Professor Erasmus Darwin Longworth swelled and grew gigantic. If only one man was to be with him in the wilderness in this moment of danger it was best that it should be he. He saw now that there was full reason for the worship given to him by Jedediah Simpson o' Lexin'ton, K—y.

The Professor, after a scrutiny of at least five minutes, announced that he saw nothing moving in the pass.

"We might escape them easily," he said, "by taking to the slopes behind us, and climbing deeper into the higher mountains, but we cannot think of such a thing, and leave Jedediah and Herbert unwarned at the village."

"No," said Charles, "we couldn't think of it."

The Professor took another look down the pass, and then rose to his feet.

"They are coming now, my lad," he said, "which means that it's time for us to go. They must feel sure that we will run straight ahead and they will press on on the same course."

He led the way, and they resumed their frontier trot. An hour, two hours passed. It was very warm in the cleft between the high mountains, but the afternoon was advancing, and shortly the twilight would touch them with its cool wing. Charles looked down the pass and saw bushes moving.

"They have gained," he said. "They cannot be much more than a mile away."

"Yes, you are right," said the Professor calmly, "and they will presently emerge into the bare stretch in the gorge that you see below. I have been thinking of an experiment ever since I saw that bare place. Charles, what is your opinion of that old shaman, Ka-jú?"

"I think him the cruelest and most wicked man I ever saw," replied the boy, wondering at such a question at such a time.

"You are undoubtedly right. Now what do you think he would do to us if he caught us, and to Jedediah and Herbert if he caught them?"

"Beyond a doubt, he would put us all to death with the most horrible tortures."

"You are surely correct, and as he must have lived nearly a hundred years already, you would not have any very harsh thoughts concerning the man who put an end to such a wicked life?"

"I would not!"

"And that ending, moreover, would be conducive, in your opinion, to the safety of our comrades and ourselves?"

"It would."

"Then it must be done," said Professor Longworth. "We'll sit down here behind these rocks and wait a bit."

They crouched behind an upshoot of black lava and waited while the blazing sun beat down upon their heads. But they thought little of the sun. They never took their eyes from that bare place in the pass, into which it was likely that the Apaches would soon emerge.

A long minute of waiting followed and another minute twice as long. Then a brown figure came from the brush into the little open place at the bottom of the gorge. It was followed by two more, and then a half dozen.

"Do you see Ka-jú among them?" asked the Professor.

"Yes; I am sure of it," replied Charles. "I'd know that manner and figure as far as I could see it. He's the stooped man in front."

"Then I'm afraid that the days of Ka-jú are numbered," said Professor Longworth calmly. "The great shaman of the Apache-Yumas is about to depart upon the long journey."

He rested his rifle upon the rock in front of him, and looked down the sights.

"How far away would you say he is?" he asked.

"It must be nearly a mile."

"A long distance, Charles, my lad, but if there's anything I can do of which I'm particularly proud it's my sharpshooting, and this rifle of mine, as you will observe, has telescopic sights."

He took another look down the sights, elevated them and called sharply: "Watch, Charles!"

He pulled the trigger, there was a flash, a crack, a little puff of white smoke, and the greatest shot ever known in the southwest had been made. The wicked old shaman lay stretched upon his back, a bullet hole through his head, from side to side, his dead face staring up at the sun, while his followers were fleeing in terror back down the pass.

"Come, Charles, my lad," said the Professor quietly, reloading his rifle, "the pursuit is over."

The boy, awed somewhat by this man who could slay with a rifle bullet at nearly a mile, resumed with him the flight which now became deliberate.

"The Apaches have received another shock," said the Professor a half hour later, "but they will recover from that, too. We may yet have to deal with them some time or other."

But there were no further signs of pursuit, and they reached the cliff village in safety, where Herbert and Jed listened in deep surprise to their amazing experience.

"It was wonderful the way you were rescued, Charlie, old fellow," said Herbert. "The Professor came just in time. You'll never have a narrower escape in all your life."

"That's so," said Charles.

The Professor strolled to the edge of the terrace and looked down into the gulf. The eyes of Jedediah Simpson o' Lexin'ton, K—y, filled with affection and overwhelming admiration, followed him.

"Didn't I tell you he was the greatest man in the world?" he said to the two boys. "Don't he prove it every day?"

"I'm beginning to believe that you're right, Jed," said Charles gravely.

They scouted carefully up and down the pass at intervals for the next two or three weeks, but the Apaches were gone.

"The death of the shaman coming on top of their superstitious fears will keep them away for a long time," said the Professor, "but some time or other a bold spirit will rise up to lead them again into these mountains. All human experience tells me so."

Chapter Sixteen - "Behind the Veil"

They accomplished a few days later another object that they had in mind and that was the slaying of mountain sheep, the Apache mu-u. The Professor accompanied Charles and Herbert on this expedition which led them high up on a snowy peak, and they secured three splendid specimens, one an old ram weighing about three hundred and fifty pounds and with horns eighteen inches in basal circumference. They brought in the skins and horns and put them as trophies in their cliff houses.

They were comfortable now, amply prepared for the winter and Charles' mind reverted with great force to the original cause of his journey. It seem to him a duty to prosecute the search for which he had come. He said over to himself again and again the vague words of the dying man, and compared the proof.

"Up and down! up and down!" he had no doubt, as he originally thought, referred to the irregular floor of the first canyon through which he had come, and the highest white peak standing alone must be Old Thundergust—at least, he had named it so. But "behind the veil! behind the veil!"—what did that mean? He repeated the words to himself often, and then the meaning came to him suddenly, like a flash of intuition. At least he believed that he had solved it.

All at once he was eager for the gold, in a flame, in fact, to find it. The treasure, after being in abeyance, had reasserted its power to lure him. He approached the Professor who was standing on the shelf, and said:

"Professor, I feel that I have solved the secret of Ananias Brown's words. It has come to me all at once. Will you and the others go with me?"

"Of course," said the Professor, and he called to Herbert and Jed.

"I don't think the trip will take us far," said Charles. "It leads just through the street of our city here."

They did not question his intuition, but went with him without a word. The terrace in front of the village seemed to stop abruptly at either end, but Charles had noticed at the north a rude trace on the side of the cliff, and he believed that it had been made originally by man, though almost wholly covered up by nature.

"I've a theory that this path or at least what used to be a path leads some distance further," he said. "Just wait here a minute, will you?"

He returned to the first cliff dwelling, and, securing the miner's pick that had been in his pack, broke a way through some dense undergrowth, clustering at the head of the trace. It had grown so thick and strong, and the slope at that point was so steep that it took him, with the help of the others, half an hour to do the work, and they had, too, to practice the greatest caution to prevent a fall that would have been fatal.

When they had cut a path through the thick bushes in the crevices of the cliff, and Charles had come out on the other side, he uttered a joyous "Ah!"

"Have you found what you expected to find?" asked the Professor.

"So far, Professor," he replied.

"This is surely mighty cur'ous an' interestin'," said Jed.

Herbert was silent, but no detail escaped him.

145

They entered upon a clearly defined trail or trace, hidden from notice before by the rocks and trailing bushes, but affording a comparatively easy footing. Charles, usually so contained, began to show excitement, and the others shared it with him. They, too, suddenly felt the spell of gold, and their blood sparkled into a flame.

The path now led along the slope in a parallel line, a slope itself and scarce a foot in width. No eye, from either below or above, could have noticed it there. It led straight on, a long distance toward the waterfall where the canyon stopped, and Charles noticed the fact exultantly. Again were his hopes confirmed.

"Will this path take us to the top of the mountain or to the floor of the canyon?" asked Herbert.

"Neither, I think."

Straight the path went on, not veering from its horizontal course, and leading directly toward the waterfall.

"It shorely is mighty cur'ous an' interestin'," repeated Jedediah Simpson o' Lexin'ton, K—y.

They had started late under the impulse of the moment, and the day was somber and dim. A strange new influence, the sudden spell of the old lost gold, now overpowered the four.

A pale sun looked over the vast mountain and shed faint rays on each face, turning it to gray, and leaving the features dim. They seemed so shadowy in the pallid light that Charles feared to reach out his hand and touch any one of them, lest the fingers meet no resistance. Yet they had been too long together now for him to doubt the reality of the misty forms, or to believe that they were not his tried comrades.

Their figures wavered, swaying easily, as if they yielded to the lightest breath of the wind, and would mark, moreover, by their own motions the uncertain state of their minds. They heard no noise, save the wail of the wind among the cliffs and peaks, and the rustle of the withered leaf as it fell. They looked up again at the sun, but it was pallid, and was yielding still further to the advance of clouds. The light faded, and the tops of the trees and cliffs were lost in the mists and vapors.

Charles felt a moment of terror lest he had missed the way, and the gold should elude them forever, continuing its long centuries of hiding from the hands of man. The word swam around them, a mystic globe without a pathway. A sense of guilt began to mingle with his feeling of fear, as if he were seeking a treasure to which he had no right. He was a thief, creeping forward, trying to find out what the earth would conceal. Then his reason told him that he did no wrong. The men who heaped up the treasure were dead hundreds of years without a rightful successor, and they should disturb the possession of no one; yet the feeling of guilt remained and troubled him; he believed that unknown eyes were watching him, he trembled when the scant foliage rustled before the wind; there was a noise at his feet, and he sprang into the air to escape the fangs of a rattlesnake, but it was only the tiniest of lizards scuttling over the dry leaves. Herbert trembled and turned paler and grayer than ever in the wan light. He, too, was in the grasp of superstitious fear. Over them loomed the vast desolation of the Arizona mountains, somber and wan, and the four were alone in the world.

They advanced a few steps, choosing their way with care, and came to the edge of a mountain pool, made by rare, but recent, rains, whose waters were jet black, save where the scanty sunbeams made gray spots upon its surface. There they sat upon the stones, and gazed at the inky gulf. The sigh among the peaks told that a light breeze was blowing, but they saw no motion on the surface in front of them. Not a wave was raised, and the water failed to quiver in the dim light; all was dull, stagnant and dead. Charles cast a stone into the middle of the pool. It sank with a murmur, but there was no echo. The mountain rose up beyond it, bare and sombre. The pale light of the sun fell upon its rough sides, distorting the crags into fantastic shapes.

Herbert looked down into the pool, and spoke of the evil chance that a slip would bring. It never occurred to any of them that a fall into those waters could be other than mortal, and when the boy spoke they crept away from the bank, the black depths filling them with a curious fear.

Although knowing that he sought to commit no sin, Charles felt again the sense of guilt and his eyes wavered like those of a thief, when Herbert looked at him. They had no right, a vague instinct told him, to seek the treasure, guarded unnumbered years by a dead hand, and yet there was no living being who had a claim upon it, perhaps none but themselves who knew of its existence. He spoke aloud, asserting their title to it, then waited in fear lest someone should have heard him and deny their right.

They passed around the pool, looking fearfully into its black depths, and went deeper into the maze of a vast, lonely mountain.

Once they heard a rustle and a sound, like a faint pressure upon the earth, on the slope above them, but looking again they saw nothing. Then, after the momentary pause, they went on with cautious footsteps. Yet two fiery eyes were regarding them from a crevice in the rocks where the tawny body of the dispossessed mountain lion lay, blending with the tawny earth and stone, and watching again with angry and jealous eyes these formidable strangers in his domain. Doubtless some far-away ancestor of his had seen far-away ancestors of theirs, but no knowledge of it had come down through the generations to the mountain lion.

He had heard them coming, and he had crawled among the rocks where he might see them pass, and yet they might not see him. His soul was filled once more with curiosity, hatred and anger. He could have struck down any of the four with his great tawny paw, but their aspect and the strange human odor that came to him filled him as always with dread. He would have fled back up the mountain, and far from these extraordinary creatures, but the path would lie across the bare rock where the light lay with dreadful brightness, and their terrible straight gaze might fall upon his tawny body.

He crouched lower and lower and with burning red eyes watched them as they crept along the mountain slope. Their strength was absurd in comparison with his. He could see that they kept close together, that they tottered, that they might fall of their own weight and unsteadiness into the dark gulf below—all these things he saw, but fear of them ruled him nevertheless, and he shrank against the hard stone, trembling lest a single stray glance of theirs might light upon him. They passed on and a turning of the cliff hid them from his sight, but as long as the faint human odor that bore upon it the breath of terror came to him he clung to his crevice in the cliffs. Then when it reached him no longer and the pure air blew over the mountains, he sprang from his place of hiding, rushed up the slope, not stopping until he was far from the place that bore the dreadful taint that made him afraid.

The four went ahead, knowing nothing of the lion and his watchful fears. They, too, stole on, still dwelling in the heart of fear. The peaks about them were now alive and personified. Far to the north a monster, with his head among the snows, gazed at them in hoary disapproval, and to the east and west other white heads nodded in confirmation of their leader. Gigantic and age-old they looked down in contempt upon the brief and tiny human creatures that crawled along the shoulder of one of their number. A wind, too, arose and moaned among the gorges, singing the same song, majestic and weird, to which the solemn mountains had listened for æons. But it fell upon the human motes, and they shivered, and kept close together.

Soon it grew darker. The twilight had come and then quick upon it the dark, but there was a faint bluish light which permeated the night and showed the way, though it threw all the objects around them—trees, rocks and gullies—out of proportion.

The mountain grew wilder and more difficult, and Charles did not wonder that the secret of the lost treasure had remained hidden so long. Their progress was slow, the intricate character of the slopes delaying their steps, and the imperfect light compelling them often to feel the way, lest they break their limbs on the sharp stones or end their lives at the bottom of the cliff. They had never before noticed such strange shapes in rocks and mountain slopes; the crest of the ridge in front of them looked like the upturned edge of a saber, the projecting stones in the sides of a cliff formed a sneering and gigantic face. The path wound between huge rocks along the edge of fathomless dark gulfs. Long, sharp briars and the stubby arms of bushes grasped at their clothing. Heavy vines, gray and coiling, hung down from either cliff above them, and when they trailed across their faces they started as if they had been touched by a serpent. Never before had they been in such a desolate and lonely world, and now and then they dragged their feet over the stones that they might reassure themselves with a friendly noise. But the echo increased the sound manyfold.

After many windings they approached the waterfall and they were so close now that it conveyed a new sense of beauty and size, the waters showing fleeting colors in the sunshine, and their roar growing loud in the ear. Once Charles stooped in the path and picked up a rusty iron implement, something like his own miner's pick that he carried, but of an antique make.

"That is shorely mighty cur'ous an' interestin'," said Jed.

"It is at least significant," said the Professor.

The path now led directly to the edge of the fall, and they saw that the water, after rushing down a steep incline, leaped far out when it came to the precipice, leaving, as at Niagara, though on a much smaller scale, a space between the fall and the rock behind it.

"The path will have to stop here," said Herbert.

"It will go behind the fall," said Charles, and after a sharp turn around a great stone it led straight in between the water and the cliff, as he had predicted. Again Charles did not hesitate. He advanced boldly, the others following through a light spray, and they passed behind the fall, picking their way over slippery stones, until they came out on the other side, where the path as before led on ahead.

"Behind the veil," said Charles to himself, and then:

"O'er the measureless range where rarely change
The swart gray plains, so weird and strange,
Treeless and streamless and wondrous still."

All felt instinctively that they were now near the end of their search. In truth Charles believed it to be so close at hand that he was seized with a sudden fear, lest someone was watching and following them, and would demand a share of the gold, a profit in their work. He resented the suspicion, and was filled with anger against the unknown. All the treasure was theirs, there was not a dollar which they did not want. The story had come to him as an inheritance, they had done all the work and taken all the risk, and they did not propose to be robbed on the eve of the harvest by an intruder. His hand slipped to the butt of the pistol, which he carried in his coat pocket. He was ready to use his weapon like a castaway at sea, fighting for the last drop of water, and his face grew damp with the continued dread that somebody was at hand to force a partnership in their discovery.

Once a stick broke under Charles' feet with a snap, and they paused in fear, lest the noise had given warning of their movements. They were crouching then behind the bushes and they remained there, quite still for five minutes, when, hearing nothing, they resumed their search.

The wind soon ceased and its moan was succeeded by complete stillness. Long black weeds grew in the ravine that they now entered, and their slender stems were outlined like threatening spears against the sky. They paused for a few moments at the exit of the ravine, and looked at the tangled mass of vegetation that covered the hollow, seeking to see a way through it. Charles' eye alighted at last upon a line which seemed to cleave a path among the somber weeds and trailing vines, and when he called the Professor's attention to it, he responded at once, saying that he was sure they were following in the footsteps of the old Spaniards. His surmise seemed correct to Charles and, the magnetic power of the gold increasing as they approached it, they entered the path which was not a path at all, merely a streak of bushes and briars lighter and less stubborn than the rest, as if used for a way long since, but grown up again, and pressed on, determined now to reach the treasure and anxious to put their hands upon it.

When they were nearly across the new dip which seemed to narrow at the far side into another ravine, Charles' foot struck a hard object, and stooping to see what it was, his eyes caught a bright gleam. He lifted a stone about the size of his fist and held it where the moonbeams, falling upon it, disclosed fine light streaks running through the mass. He believed these to be threads of gold, and all surmised at once that the fragment had been dropped in the path by those who worked the mine in old times.

This was the last proof that their course was leading them directly to the treasure, and Charles could not repress a cry of triumph. The visions of wealth which had wavered dimly at a distance before him were so close now, so warm, so palpable, that he felt the treasure, untold sums of it, in his hands. There were many shining and brilliant things that he would do; money would give him the power. But he kept these thoughts to himself for the present and still led on.

The ravine seemed to run far back into the mountain, but it was not so rough as the path over which they had passed. At points the cliffs overhung it and at other points receded; in the narrow places they were in the shadow, in the wider the moonbeams fell upon them, and thus they advanced across bars of light and darkness, their regular sequence reminding them strangely of the rising and falling of their hopes, their sanguine feeling that they should find the treasure, their despair and then hope again. The cliffs around them were of reddish stone with innumerable streaks shining through them, and to their excited fancy everything was impregnated with gold. They felt that now they were face to face with the treasure, and they were oppressed by a kind of awe as if the heaps of gold that lay beyond had a superhuman authority, and forbade them to speak in their presence. They were approaching the master, and unconsciously they showed reverence for the power to which most kneel. Nor did they have any shame at the time.

Presently the ravine ended, seeming to die out against blank wall, but when they looked more closely they saw an opening in the dark stone.

The mouth of the cavern seemed high enough for entrance, without their stooping, and they paused in front of it before taking the last steps in their search. Dark as it was in the ravine the cave itself showed nothing but blackness. It seemed to be a pit of mysterious depth, and all its aspects were repellent, as if it would still preserve the secret that it had kept so long.

Yet, the feeling of apprehension, inspired by the blackness of the cave mouth, was but momentary. They now permitted neither fear nor exultation to rule them, and believed it fitting to preserve a dignity equal to their fortune. They sought to dismiss expression from their faces, and to affect an air of careless humor.

They took a step or two into the opening and Charles, after a strong attack of nervous hesitation, drew out his little match case and struck a match. It was with the most extraordinary feelings that he watched the tiny flame flicker and sputter, and then grow stronger. It seemed to him that all he hoped for depended upon that feeble sputter.

The light became steady, and he uttered an irrepressible cry of joy. They stood in a low-roofed cave, partly natural and partly dug out by the hand of man, and at the far side, leaning against the wall were many objects resembling sacks of provisions. He lighted another match, crossed the cave floor and touched one of the sacks. It was made of the hide of some animal, and as it crumbled away at his touch, its contents poured out with a dull metallic sound on the stone of the floor. Charles stooped, plunged his hand in the yellowish flood, and lifted it up, palmful, just as the match went out. But he struck another match with his free hand, and held its light over that which lay in the palm.

The Professor, who stood beside him, bent down and looked at the light that shone on Charles' face.

"Gold!" he said. "Hundreds of pounds of it! Ours! Spaniards washed it out two or three centuries ago; this was their storehouse!"

His voice trembled slightly as he spoke. None of them worshiped money, but they were not so foolish as to despise it.

"This is shorely mighty cur'ous an' interestin'," said Jedediah Simpson o' Lexin'ton, K—y, in an awed whisper.

"Why was it left here?" Herbert asked.

"This was their storehouse," said the Professor. "All were killed by Apaches and the secret was lost. It has been waiting here these many generations for us. We are the heirs."

Then Charles murmured under his breath:

"Poor Ananias Brown! How ill he deserved his first name!"

They went outside, and, after much hunting, secured sticks that would burn. Then they returned to the cave, where they examined the treasure with minute care, thirty bags in all, chiefly in grains and scales of gold, and the Professor calculated that there were approximately two tons of it, worth about a million dollars.

"It was washed out of a river bed somewhere," he said. "Probably our own little river above the fall, and the Spaniards may have been working here a year, or two years."

The cave was a dark little place, not too dry, but it was a true golden chamber for them. Charles, searching amid the débris on the floor, found two or three ancient implements, resembling those used for the washing out of gold, and he was confirmed in his opinion that the treasure had come from a river, although it was not important now to know where, and they had no intention of searching.

After more than an hour spent in the cave, they tore themselves away from the golden heap, and returned to the cliff dwelling.

Jedediah Simpson o' Lexin'ton, K—y, had been silent throughout the return journey "home," but he was full of something, and upon their arrival it burst forth.

"See here, Charlie," he said, "I ain't got no share in this! That gold belongs to you an' Herb there. Me an' the Purfessor jest lighted down on you by accident."

"He speaks the exact truth," said Professor Longworth quietly.

"And I ain't no butt-in," continued Jed. "I was jest talkin' through my hat, when I was paintin' all them gorgeous pictures about the big organ in the wall, the D. M., and the red cart with the yellow wheels. I don't come in on this."

"You come in exactly to the extent of one quarter," said Charles firmly. "I am the original depository of the secret. The chance was left to me by Ananias Brown, but I never could have done the task alone. You and the Professor have already saved my life three times, and it's not going to be any easy task to get this gold away from here and put it safely in bank. Herbert and I need you now worse than ever. We've made the agreement, and it's your duty as well as ours to stand by it."

"Of course it is," said Herbert.

The Professor bowed his head in assent. In his heart he thought that their greatest tasks and dangers were yet to come, and that he and Jed would be needed badly.

"Now don't you be a fool again, Jed," said Herbert reproachfully. "I've been looking forward to riding in that yellow cart of yours, with the red wheels, and I certainly want to hear the D. M. play the big organ."

Jed's face beamed.

"You boys are shorely white," he said. "But I hope somebody will try to take that gold from us, an' in the big fight I can prove I'm worth my share."

"You may have the chance, Jed," said the Professor.

Chapter Seventeen - Winter in The Canyon

They would have departed now, but at least a week was required to make new skin bags for the gold, and other preparations, and meanwhile winter suddenly rushed down upon them. All had foreseen it in a way. The nights, always chill on the mountains, had shown an increasing coldness. The hot sunshine of the day was tempered by a sharp, raw breath; the foliage, save that of the evergreens, visibly turned browner, and the Professor thought of the day when great storms of snow and sleet would rage through the canyons and over the peaks and ridges.

About this time the dispossessed mountain lion began to grow angry. He had been in an unhappy humor all the autumn, and when the chillier breath came into the air he thought often of his snug winter home in the cliff village. For months he had nursed his rage, because he was driven forth from what had been his by long prescription, and if anywhere in his animal brain he could feel revenge he cultivated it as a precious flower, and watched it grow. He would have gone long since to claim his own, but the deadly human odor repelled him and made him afraid.

He would come sometimes to the edge of the plateau, resolved to right his wrongs, but then, when he smelled the trail, where those terrible human beings had passed, his legs would totter and his heart become weak. Yet the desire grew within him in the same ratio that the air grew colder, and he longed for the lost flesh pots of the cliff village which he had regarded as his own. It may be that his winter life there in a place, made so tight and so warm, had unfitted him for the selection of a den of his own on the mountain, but his instinctive knowledge that winter and bitter cold would soon come began to fill him with a certain mingled rage and need that perhaps took the place of courage.

He slipped through the pine trees one day to the edge of the plateau, where he sniffed at the path leading down to the cliff village. He smelt the human odor, but he knew that only one of the terrible human beings had passed there, and, though he shivered with dread, he did not turn as usual and go back. He crawled down the slope, going a few feet at a time, feeling often the desire to run, but always inciting himself to go on with the mingling of rage and need that was his substitute for courage.

He stopped at last where he could get a good view of the shelf, and lay back against the rocks, his tawny coat blending with the tawny tints that had come lately into the scanty foliage. Thence he peered with red eyes at the shelf, where he saw the boy. Herbert's back was turned to him. If he approached carefully he might spring upon him, slaying him and ridding the place forever of his presence. Then the other beings would perhaps go away of their own accord, and the lion once more would be sole lord of the village. The mingling of rage and need swelled, and now it became something really like courage. Intent on his purpose and resolved, the dangers became less, just as they do with men.

The lion resumed his careful creeping down the path, seeking to keep his own colors blended with those of rock and shrub, nor to send a single pebble rolling from its place. He was nearing the shelf when he saw the boy turn, glance about him, down at the gorge, up at the slope and afar at the peaks. Then he walked toward a cliff house, near to the one in which he had often sheltered, and the lion was assailed again with a dreadful fear; every nerve in him quivered and he was wild with a desire to rush away and hide. But he conquered it, and when he saw the boy emerge from the house he reached the shelf with one bound, and then sprang at him.

In the last moment of the lion's life he saw the boy raise to his face something which to his dim mind may have resembled a club. But a club it was not, because a dazzling burst of flame leaped from the end of it, hot lightning flashed through his brain, and when his leap ended he lay upon the shelf, dead, a mountain lion who had paid for his rage, want and curiosity with his life.

When the others came home Herbert pointed out to them with very little concern the body of the lion.

"I caught a glimpse of him crawling down the slope," he said, "and I was just in time to get the rifle."

"Lucky the gun was handy," said Jed. "He must have been hard pressed to come down here an' attack a human bein'. See how lank he is. I guess the old fellow was hungry, an' perhaps, too, he wanted a winter home. Thar are signs that he has used this place fur a den."

They had put their food supplies in one of the cliff houses, where they made it secure from any interloping wild animal that might not be awed by the fate of the lion, and meanwhile they devoted attention to other needs of housekeeping. The Professor, patterning after the cliff dwellers, made rude needles, punches and awls of the smaller bones of the wild turkey, and of the larger, knives, chisels, scrapers and even rude spoons. With such crude needles and the tendons of the deer and other animals, and coarse cords, made from dry yucca leaves, they were able to achieve great progress in the construction of clothing.

While they were working the tint of brown on the mountain was deepening fast and the chill in the air remained long after the dawn. It might be hot in the gray loom of the south where the desert lay, but here at their great elevation they were in another world. The fire, kept burning all the time now, they had lighted in a large round chamber, one of the best preserved of all the older houses. A narrow stone bench ran around the wall, and in the center was a pit in which the fire burned. The dome-shaped roof was made of logs hard and black with time, the ends resting upon stone piers which projected into the room. A flue of good size built into the wall led to the open air. All was in a fine state of preservation, and, considering the rudeness of the materials, showed an ingenuity which the modern man might do well to imitate.

Near the pit and on the earth outside they found fire-sticks, their charred ends still showing, and once or twice they picked up bunches of cedar-bark strips, bound about with the threads of the yucca. These the Professor used as tinder.

"Our predecessors were forced to resort to many clever devices," said he, "but so long as we have the matches left we can risk our fire going out once or twice."

But all were so sedulous that the fire never died a single time, and now as the mornings grew colder they began to cook in the house at the fire-pit. The Professor, four or five days after the discovery of the gold, looking up the canyon toward the row of white peaks in the north, predicted that they would have winter in a week, but he reckoned without the spirit of the wilderness which is capricious at best and which decided to send the great cold upon the four in the canyon much ahead of time. When they arose the very next morning thereafter, they looked upon a changed world. The sun had come, but there was no sunlight, only a dull, sodden, gray veil that hung between earth and sky; the white peaks, that usually looked down upon them in silent majesty, were hidden now, but from their crests a raw wind moaned through the canyons and gorges. While they watched, the brown clouds thickened, and spread from horizon to horizon. The gray loom of the desert to the south was hidden as well as the peaks to the north, and the wind grew damp. Charles, who was looking, was conscious of a step beside him, and he saw Herbert, wrapped in a new skin cloak.

"Winter is coming down upon us," said Charles, "and its edge is snow. See, Herbert, it is here now."

A large brown cloud opened a little, and dropped down a small white flake that settled upon his pointing finger. Then came its fellows, at first slow, then fast, and they lay where they fell, unmelting. Crests and cliffs sank away behind the floating veil, and the earth turned white.

"Winter is here," said the Professor solemnly, "and we are snowed in. No one can come until spring."

"All of which is mighty cur'ous an' interestin'," said Jedediah Simpson o' Lexin'ton, K—y, "but we can stand it."

"Yes, we'll go into winter quarters," said the Professor.

All walked back together to the common room—estufa it is called—and built up the fire in the pit, until it glowed red. Jed had been able to improve the flue somewhat, and they were troubled little by smoke. The fire was very cheerful and very glorious on that first morning of winter. Jed cooked their breakfast, and he chose the choicest of the venison steaks, filling the room with a pleasant aroma. They no longer had any bread, and they missed it greatly at times, but they had gathered a store of nuts on the mountain slopes, on which they would draw whenever they celebrated what they called one of their little festivals. This was such a time, and they added a small supply to the venison and turkey.

"I'm sorry I can't give you fellows coffee any longer," said Jed.

"So am I," said Herbert, "I'd be willing to pay a doubloon for a cup, and I'd do it every morning—if I remember right a doubloon is about sixteen dollars, but I'd think it cheap at that price. Look how the snow thickens."

From the tiny window, not much more than a peep hole, they could glance down upon the canyon, and now they saw but little, except an almost solid fall of white. The heavens had certainly opened and they knew what it portended. The snow would lie many feet deep in every canyon, gulch and crevice, undisturbed until the spring. There was no possibility, the cliff trails being gone, that any wandering footstep would come their way through the long winter months. Yet all turned cheerful faces back to the cheerful fire. In the whole time that they had been in the canyon they had not eaten a gayer breakfast than the one that followed, and they sat a long while after appetite was satisfied.

"It is still coming down," said Herbert, going once to the door, "and it comes as if it intended to fill up our canyon, and that you know is a matter of two thousand feet anyway."

"I think we're safe on the shelf," said the Professor, "but even here we shall have to make roads."

"No doubt of it," said Charles, and after a while they went forth upon this important task. They used now the bone scrapers that the cliff dwellers had left behind, as well as their own shovels, cleaning paths between the houses that they used. The snow poured down and covered up the paths again, but at any rate it was much thinner there, and their task would be easier when the fall ceased. They were light of heart at the work, now and then casting a little snow upon one another, the two boys throwing an occasional snowball.

When they were tired they rested, going back to the estufa, and there they again watched the snow coming down. All that day it fell and all the following night, and the next morning it ceased abruptly. The clouds suddenly fled away, leaving the skies a solid sheet of dazzling blue. A wintry sunlight, silver rather than gold, came out, and tinted the mountains which now lay under a deep robe of white. No wind blew, all around were the peaks and slopes, still and pure. The white cover extended down to the edge of the gray desert, but in the mountains it lay very deep.

They cleared the paths on the shelf again, and it was not a light task, but the labor gave them an interest, and made their thoughts flow in healthful channels. Now and then they shoved great masses of it over the edge of the shelf, and watched it go thundering into the canyon below, where it was received into the bosom of other and greater white masses.

Long days followed. There was little to do. Food they had in plenty, enough to last the winter through, no matter how long it might be, and the snow was too deep to allow of hunting expeditions or any other kind of journeys on the mountains.

Three or four days later, the mountains rocked in a sleet storm, far more terrible than the snow, and far more dangerous. The wind blew fiercely down the canyon and the air was dark with the driven hail. It beat upon the cliff houses like the bullets of a myriad riflemen. Well for them that these houses were of stone upon which many another storm had lashed in vain!

They were in the estufa when the storm began and they watched it for hours. It was without beauty, only grand and terrible in its manifestations. The wind shrieked and roared in the canyon, and now and then a pine tree, beaten or blown down, fell with a crash into the abyss below. Great masses of snow, set in motion by the wind, at first rolled off the slopes, but by and by when the surface began to freeze they held fast.

Night came with the wind still blowing and the hail driving. The world the next morning seemed to be sheathed in glass. The hail and the surface of the snow had frozen hard and fast in the night, and the whole earth lay before them polished and glittering like a huge mirror. Everyone drew back at first in alarm. A single slip might send him thundering far down into the canyon below.

Charles' miner's pick was in the estufa, and with it they broke paths. It was very cold, but the air was life-giving, and the boys never before had seen anything like the sight which they now beheld. The sun had risen in overwhelming splendor of red and gold in a perfectly blue sky, and the mountains flashed in a light that was dazzling. The reflection was so brilliant that, at first, they were compelled to shade their eyes, but when they grew used to it they often stopped in their tasks to look at the peaks and ridges which gleamed in every shade of opalescent light, as the sun crept on up the concave arch of blue. Everything seemed to be made of glass and crystal, and the passage of anyone through the mountains was now a sheer impossibility. The wonderful glittering world before him brought to Herbert's mind old, dim Arab tales of enchanted mountains, raised by genii, which the hero must scale.

That which Herbert in no spirit of jest called "The Ice Age" endured long. It was one of the coldest winters ever known on the mountains, but a winter now of clear skies and of the cold sunshine, that is silver rather than golden. Day after day they saw the mountains sheathed in the strange glittering coat of mail, and night after night they looked forth on peaks and ridges that showed wanly through the dusk. If the ice melted a little in the day it froze again at night, and outside the paths they had cut, no footstep was ever safe.

It was warm and cheerful in the estufa but they began to chafe, they felt the need of exercise, and of some change from their narrow quarters. They decided at last to cut away the ice from the path to the plateau, and using deerskin cords, with which to tie themselves to rocks and trees at the most critical places, they succeeded after much labor and some danger in making a safe road. It was laborious walking on the ice above, but they enjoyed the freedom, and every day now they climbed the cliff to the ice-field and spent an hour or two there.

Winter waned and then came great rains, ice and snow melted and the water poured in mighty torrents down the cliffs and through the canyons. Peaks and ridges were lost in a smoky haze. The black rock and the gray earth showed again. By night and by day they heard the deep sighing sound of snow and ice, as loosened from its hold, it plunged down the slopes into the gulf below. The air was growing less chill, and warm breaths came up from the gray desert that lay to the southward. Now the four grew restless, and fate, timing itself to their mood, was preparing a great change.

All had been greatly worried about the horses and mules during the winter. The snow and cold were so much greater than anyone expected that they began to fear that they had perished, an event that would prove well-nigh fatal to their plans. As soon as possible Charles and the Professor went down into the canyon. The little river was a swollen torrent of ice-cold water from the melting snows, and farther up the slope they saw masses of snow, loosened by the new warmth, come crashing into the gorges below.

"We'd better turn south," said the Professor. "It would be the natural instinct of the animals to go in that direction, as the great cold approached, that is, they would move steadily toward the lowlands."

They traveled southward and downward for many miles, and the main aspect about them was yet that of winter. Patches of snow were on all the cliffs, and the river still ran an ice-cold torrent.

"There is plenty of water now in the beds of streams that are usually dry in the desert," said the Professor.

"Then maybe the animals have wandered out there, and are lost to us forever."

"It is not at all probable," said the Professor encouragingly. "There was no grass then on the desert, but there has been plenty of it in the canyon."

At last they reached a region, low enough to be entirely free from snow, with young grass already growing along the stream, and in the alcoves of the cliffs. Suddenly Charles uttered a shout of joy.

"Look, Professor, look!" he cried. "Here's our band!"

In a snug little valley with arching cliffs all about, eight horses and mules were grazing. They were thin, as if they had gone through hardships, but they looked strong and healthy.

"That's settled," said the Professor in a tone of relief. "We have not lost a single animal, and we'll leave them there for the present. We can get them with ease when we want them."

They returned with the good news and now great thoughts began to surge in Jedediah Simpson's mind.

"I'm thinkin' about my responsibilities," he said one evening to the others. "Bein' a rich man now, I've got to conduct myself accordin'. I've got to put a restrainin' hand on the temptations o' the mind, an' put down all foolishness. Jest now, Herb, the question is about that D. M. I think I want a rather oldish man who ain't disposed to be flighty, an' he must know a power o' tunes. I heard the Purfessor say once that a king o' Spain had the same great tenor to sing him to sleep with the same song every night for twenty years, but I ain't got any great confidence in the jedgment o' Spaniards. They 'pear to me to be a queer sort o' foreign folk, an' besides, I won't be no imitator, even ef the man was a king. No, my D.M. will have to give me variety, or he'll lose his job."

"Are you going to live a high life, Jed?" asked Herbert.

"No," replied Jed gravely, "I ain't goin' to devote all my money to the temptations o' the flesh, eatin' an' drinkin' an' sech like. My appeal is goin' to be to the intelleck, an' the sense o' lib'ty. The things that I get will satisfy the eye an' the mind; that's the real power o' money, to give you freedom, independence, an' the right kind o' man ain't goin' to abuse it. But, Herb, thar ain't nothin' like lib'ty. When I buy my house, I'm goin' to name it Arizony Place, after the territory in which I've found my wealth. Then I'm goin' to the best tailor store in Lexin'ton, K—y, an' ask for the best goods in the place. The head man will show me four or five bolts o' mighty fine cloth. 'Which do you think will suit my style o' beauty best?' I'll ask, kinder careless like. Then he'll sorter hum an' hesitate, not likin' to play a favorite among his own goods, an' I'll cut in with, 'Never mind, jest measure me a suit off every one o' them five bolts. I like change.' Then after he gets over his surprise an' pleasure he'll begin to mention the price, but again I cut in with, 'Don't bother about that, I never ask prices. When the suits are ready jest send 'em an' the bill along with 'em to Jedediah Simpson, Esquire, at Arizony Place, the big red brick house with all them huge grounds about it. The check will come to you by the first mail.'

"Say, Herb, that's what I call real true blue, genuine, dyed-in-the-wool, blowed-in-the-bottle happiness, to walk right in, buy a thing you want, say you don't care what the price is, an' mean it, too. After I buy the suits I'll drive about the city in my red cart with the yellow wheels, an' people will look at me respeckfully as I pass an' will say to one another: 'That's Mr. Jedediah Simpson. He an' three others made their money in Arizony after many trials an' dangers, an' now he's handlin' it like a gentleman. He's a pillar an' an ornyment to our town.' An' I'll drive on, an', after all my business is finished, I'll drive back to Arizony Place, an' have the D.M. play me a tune, somethin' upliftin'. Say, Herb, would you have the D.M. wear a uniform? I ain't made up my mind about that."

"No, Jed, I wouldn't. Only bandmasters wear uniforms. Organists usually dress in black clothes."

"Then it's black clothes for my D.M. Another thing, Herb, that I've made up my mind about, is to have a big fountain always playin' on my front lawn. Bein' around in all them dry countries o' the East with the Purfessor has made me powerful fond o' fallin' water."

"Did the Professor," asked Herbert slyly, "ever tell you of an old Eastern tale about a man who bought a basket of glassware for sale, and as he was sitting dreaming of all the wonderful things he would do when he had turned over that glassware about a thousand times, suddenly kicked all of it to pieces, while still in his dream?"

"Yes, I've heard that tale from the Purfessor," replied Jed stoutly, "an' it don't scare me none, because I'm not goin' to fall to sleepin' an' dreamin'. I've got my hands on that gold an' I'd like to see the feller that can take it away from me."

"That's the spirit, Jed," said the Professor.

Chapter Eighteen - Gray Wolf's Coming

While young spring was touching the mountains with green, the desert also was waking from sleep and putting on its scanty signs of new life. In a valley to the eastward of the canyon, a band of Apaches had spent the cold months, although a few of the warriors now and then roamed far in the hope of finding game or perhaps a wandering prospector who might be picked off with the aid of a happy bullet and never be missed by his own people.

This was the band that had taken Charles, and that had lost the great shaman, old Ka-jú, slain by a rifle bullet, fired from a great distance, perhaps by Se-má-che himself, and it retained for a long time its respect for the terrible pass and the inviolate home of the cliff dwellers. But with the months the influence of these events waned, and the Professor's prediction came true.

One spirit more daring than all the rest wandered, just as the snow was melting, into the mass of mighty cliffs and peaks about the great canyon. This warrior entered tentatively upon the first fringe of the cold mountains. Then, as the snow melted, he went on up the great canyon to behold at last a sight that stirred in his primeval blood the desire for action. Upon the very shelf where cliff dwellers had been slaughtered long, long ago, he saw two lads going to and fro. They were well tanned, but undeniably they belonged to the white race, and they were far, very far from their people. They might disappear here and no one of their race ever know the secret of their disappearance. All the cunning cruelty and hate in the warrior's nature blazed up at this happy chance. He remembered the face of one of the boys, and he began to believe now that his release had been secured by some one of the white man's cunning tricks.

He crouched in the bushes, where he lay motionless more than an hour, his body apparently a part of the earth, but his burning black eyes intently watching the two white beings on the shelf above him. He saw a third white face also much tanned, but undeniably white, and then a fourth. The last was a little man, but with a great head covered by an enormous pith helmet, and the warrior with fierce anger remembered him too. The four attended to various duties and talked together now and then. They seemed to be wholly oblivious of danger, and the cunning Apache judged from what he saw that they had been there a long time.

The soul of the savage leaped within him at the great opportunity. There were human beings like himself. They were not protected by Se-má-che. He might have waited around until he could pick off one or two himself, but the Apache takes no needless risks, and he stole away from the canyon, and then across the desert to his comrades. The tale that he told—he was a bold and convincing orator—filled them, too, with the same desire, and they entered the mountains to achieve their triumph.

No warning came as yet to the four. They had enjoyed immunity so long since the slaying of old Ka-jú that the thought of the savage seldom entered their minds, and they were occupied now with preparations for the departure with the gold. Meanwhile the Apaches were in the canyon, encouraged by the fact that Se-má-che seemed to take no notice of their entrance, and were now cautiously approaching the path that led to the shelf.

Spring had made progress. A green robe lay over the lower slopes of the mountains, and above shone a sky of peaceful, unbroken blue. A little wind played among the grass stems, and the new-blown flowers. The four were having their breakfast again in the open air, and all were in the finest of humors. Then Herbert took a notion to wander on the shelf.

The boy was silent and abstracted. He could not have told why he was sad, but for the first time in days he was thinking of Mr. Carleton, who had perished so miserably, and he was blaming himself because he did not think of him oftener and grieve more. But from this tragedy his thoughts turned to something vague and intangible that suddenly oppressed him. The sixth sense, which perhaps belonged to the caveman, was registering an alarm; he had a feeling that danger was near; the feeling was unaccountable, but it grew in power, and he looked out at the canyon, the mountains and the lofty row of white peaks to the north. This was "home," peaceful and protecting, with green on the slopes and golden sunlight above, but this air, seemingly so pure, was surcharged with an unknown quality that made his nerves quiver as he breathed it.

Without saying a word to the others, and almost forgetting for the moment their presence, he rose and stood at the edge of the shelf, gazing into the blue abyss. Here his sense of danger increased, as if he were coming nearer to that which brought the danger. Why he felt that way, at that particular moment, he could never tell. Nothing stirred but the little wind that played among the grass stems and leaves. No sound came to his ears, but the unknown warning was repeated.

A pebble rattled on the slope, and he looked down with eyes that had grown far more acute than those of the ordinary lad. A weed by the path moved more than it should have done in the wind, and he glanced at it twice. The second time he saw behind the bush a pair of fierce black eyes, gazing intently upward, and then he saw the coarse black hair and low brown forehead of the head to which the eyes belonged. In an instant he knew and, every nerve attuned, he was ready for what he had to do.

He stepped back from the edge, shouting to the others that they were attacked, and then he sprang forward again. At that moment the black hair and the brown face appeared over the terrace and Herbert promptly fired at it with the revolver that he always carried more from a sense of duty lately than from any fear of danger. A cry followed, and then the sound of a body falling until the echo died far away. After that there was silence in the great canyon, save for the little wind that played among the grass stems.

In an instant the other three were running toward him.

"Apaches!" shouted Herbert.

"Ah," said the Professor, "I am not surprised!"

Charles and Jed ran for the rifles, and in a few seconds every one of the four was provided with his powerful breech-loader. The boys learned in their long stay in the mountains presence of mind, great resource and the use of but few words.

"They're on the slope," said Herbert.

"We can beat 'em," said Charles.

"Here, things favor the defense," said the Professor.

"This is mighty cur'ous an' interestin'," said Jed, "but I think we can handle it."

It is truth to say that they were not afraid. They were the primeval men now, defending their home. But they had the best of modern arms, and they awaited the contest with the joyous thrill that the strong feel. The attack, for the present, did not come.

Now courage and patience were matched against courage and cunning. The most terrible of human tests was at hand, long waiting in the face of mortal danger. Hour after hour passed, the morning waned, the sun reached the zenith, pouring down floods of golden rays, then the afternoon, too, waned and long black shadows began to creep over the mountains, but the two men and the two boys, rifle in hand, still knelt on the terrace, watching the head of the path, hearing every sound, and seeing every weed or bush that quivered. They felt able to stand on guard, until the end, whatever it might be. The Apaches had not gone—instinct alone would have told them that—and they knew that, sooner or later, the attack would be made. The twilight deepened into the night, and after a while the moon came out.

While the four waited on the shelf, watchful and listening, a group far down in the canyon were also watchful and listening. They belonged to a far-off, more primitive age, and they belonged to it wholly; it was not for moments, it was no psychic revulsion; they dwelt all the time in that fierce old past, and now they were at war with the present.

They sought foes who in their minds were typical of that present with which they fought, and they saw a chance for at least a partial vengeance. All their natural instincts were awake. They were akin now to the animal, and were moved largely by the same impulses. Se-má-che had given them no warning and now he must favor their attempt. The blood-red sun, dropping suddenly behind the mountains, added a new fire to their passion, the weird, ghost-like darkness that crept up the canyon conveyed to them no sense of awe or fear; it was merely the coming of the night which might help them, and they rejoiced in accordance.

As the swift twilight went and black night covered the mountains, the darkness, like the red light of the sun, served to give a new touch of flame to the blood of the besiegers. One, leaner, gaunter, and uglier than all the rest, stalked now and then among them. It was their leader, Gray Wolf, and he urged them always to persistence.

The night advanced, the faint wind died in the canyon, the sickle of a pale moon was blotted out by clouds, and darkness, heavy and brooding, lay over all the great mountains. Nature was silent and waiting, as if she expected a black and ugly deed; the air in the deep canyon became close and heavy, and then, when the somber skies, unlighted by a single star, lay close to the earth, Gray Wolf and his men, fierce for blood, began to creep slowly upward. They were in no hurry; if there was any quality that the Apache possessed in surpassing degree it was patience; he was ready to wait through any measure of time if the taking of a life were only at the end of it. Perhaps no other human beings ever bore a greater semblance to serpents, as they went on, always upward. Had the eyes of men been able to pierce the blackness they would have seen only sinuous brown forms blending against the brown of the slopes.

Gray Wolf, as became him, was always in the front, and he never doubted that they would succeed in their attempt; the defenders would be taken by surprise and the rest would be easy. All the omens were propitious; not a single ray of light came through the clouds, and every voice was dead in the canyon; his savage heart thrilled already with the joys of the coming triumph. Yet he lost no particle of his caution. Now and then, with a soft warning hiss, which redoubled his likeness to a serpent, he would cause all the band to stop, and they would lie there for minutes against the slope, absolutely motionless and scarcely breathing.

Up, up they went, and still no noise reached the listening ear of Gray Wolf. A laugh rose in his throat, but went no further than his lips. They were but whites on the shelf, and, with only the dulled senses of the whites. A more chivalrous enemy might have wished a harder prey, but not so the Apache; courage he had when it was needed, but it gave him the keenest joy to win the greatest prize without cost; he loved to find a sleeping foe.

Gray Wolf presently stopped again, and measured the distance to the shelf, which he could not see, but whose location he knew well. Two hundred yards! He resumed his advance, but stopped again at the last hundred. Still no sound, nothing whatever to indicate that his coming victims suspected their fate to be so near. Gray Wolf brought his rifle well forward, and loosened the knife in his belt. Big Elk, second in command and just behind him, did the same.

Gray Wolf and his band passed the last hundred yards more slowly than any of the others, because they now had the utmost need of caution if they would win the easy victory that the Apache loved. But there was yet nothing to indicate that the victims suspected; the black night and the quiet mountains remained favorable. Now he could see the edge of the shelf in the darkness, and no watchful form stood upon it.

The yards melted slowly to nothing, and then Gray Wolf, with all the caution that the Apache learns on his swart, gray plains, drew a little to one side, and beckoned to the stoutest of his band to go up first. They went forward without a word, eager for the triumph, and two straightened up, ready to climb upon the shelf.

Gray Wolf at that moment saw dark figures rise from the ground, made gigantic and terrible by the dusk, and flame shot down almost directly in the face of the leading Apaches, who uttered groans and crashed away down the mountainside, rolling like bowlders. The great canyon took up the sounds, and sent them echoing away toward the white peaks.

Gray Wolf was a brave man, but his brow grew cold with sweat, and red terror plucked at his heart. It was not the white men, but he and his own warriors, who had been surprised. The band fled far more swiftly than they had come to the comparative safety of the canyon-bed below. The four on the shelf could not see the dim, retreating figures in the dusk, but they heard the groans, the rattling sounds, the fall of bowlders and the scraping of bodies, and they knew that the Apaches were in wild retreat. Exultation lifted up the souls of everyone, but most of all that of Jedediah Simpson o' Lexin'ton, K—y.

"Swing low, old chariot, swing low," he chanted. "Can't you come again, you purty brown men! That was jest a military salute we fixed for you an' now you have run away! It was so sudden! So impolite! Come again, we're waitin'! 'I'm waitin', only waitin' for thee.' 'Oh come, won't you come?'"

"Jed," said the Professor, "you bloodthirsty creature, stop that noise!"

"It ain't a noise, Purfessor," said Jed. "It's a song o' action. I come o' fightin' stock. I've got pioneer blood in me, an' I feel that blood risin' to the top right now. Settin' here we can lick the whole Apache nation, ef they are a nation, an' I'm close to cryin' fur fear they won't come again."

He threw himself flat down on the slope and began to creep over the very edge. His eyes were two coals in the dark, and the song of battle was undoubtedly singing a fierce tune in the ears of Jedediah Simpson.

"Jed, you fool, come back!" exclaimed the Professor, seizing him by the hair and giving it a jerk.

"Leggo, Professor, leggo!" exclaimed Jed. "That's my hair you're pullin'."

"I know it," said the Professor, retaining his firm grasp, "and I'm keeping you from making a fool of yourself. If you go crashing down there we'll lose a valuable man whom we need in the defense."

Jed stopped and the Professor let go of his hair. But Jed remained crouched at the very edge of the terrace, his rifle well forward, his eyes still like coals, seeking to pierce the depths below.

Savages do not like a headlong attack, and the Apache is the wariest of them all. Moreover, he had already had his lesson. All looked now for a long period of terrible waiting, which would oppress nerve and brain alike, and wear down more than real strife. It was this that they dreaded, to sit there in the dark, not knowing what was planned against them, with nothing to show when the blow would be struck, nor where.

"Herbert, you and I will bring food and water, while Charles and Jed continue the watch," said the Professor. "They aren't likely to attack again just now."

The skies had become clear, a vast dome of dusky blue velvet in which the placid stars held on their way. The whole gorge glowed in the moonlight, and on the slope across it Charles saw the stunted bushes move. Then there was a tiny spurt of fire, the echo of a gunshot traveled up the gorge, and a bullet pattered upon the terrace.

"Don't be troubled by sech a thing as that," said Jed scornfully, "the shot was fired practically at random, as they can't see us from the other side o' the canyon."

Three more shots were fired presently, but like the first, they pattered vainly upon the black basaltic cliff.

"They will soon grow tired o' that," Jed said with increased scorn; and he was right, as the distant bombardment was not renewed.

All of the next day passed without attack or interruption of any kind, but the defenders never relaxed their vigilance. Then the second night came.

Professor Longworth, the two boys and Jedediah Simpson sat on the shelf by the side of one of the cliff houses and talked in whispers. The Professor, although in a state of siege with the probabilities inclining to torture and death, was uncommonly cheerful. Charles made a mental remark that the Professor in such situation was at his very best. Danger, instead of depressing him, seemed instead to arouse some extraordinary intellectual quality that exhilarated him. It was apparently a pleasure that necessity should draw upon his resources, hidden resources, perhaps, of which no one dreamed.

"They can climb the slopes elsewhere and reach the plateau above us," said Herbert.

"Undoubtedly," replied the Professor.

"And we may be attacked in the dark both from below and above," continued Herbert.

"That's so," broke in Jedediah Simpson, "an' then we'll be caught between two fires. An' I hear that them Apache fires can be terrible warm. Leastways, they'll do it, ef the Professor here don't stop 'em."

His tone, even in the low whisper in which he spoke, expressed a confidence in the Professor that was at once touching and encouraging. Both the boys felt cheered by it.

"Yes, Jedediah, you are quite right," said Professor Longworth calmly. "We should be caught as you say between two fires—that is if we sat still. But there is a way to escape such things. You can move from the space between the fires, or you can put out one fire or both. It is a scientific problem, capable of demonstration; if you sit still in the path of a steam roller you are likely to get hurt, but if you will move out of its way it will pass on without touching you. In addition you can disable the man who runs the steam roller, or you can damage the machinery of the roller itself. In either event it cannot start. There are plenty of alternatives for a resourceful man."

"Ain't he a wonder?" breathed Jed, in tones of admiration, tinged with awe, into the ear of Herbert. "Them Apaches are as good as beat off already. I ain't afeard, a-tall, a-tall!"

"I feel, too, that the Professor will pull us out somehow," Herbert whispered back.

"The night is dark," continued Professor Longworth, casting a glance up at the black heavens, "which favors the besiegers, a fact patent even to those who have made no study of the military art. Therefore the Apaches will come, trusting that they will be face to face with us before they are discovered. They will not come up the path from the gorges, because that path is narrow, difficult to ascend, and they have had terrible proof that it will be well guarded. Hence they will try to drop from the cliff above upon us. It is a perfectly simple matter, clear, logical and easily capable of demonstration, as we shall see to-night."

"Since you have fathomed the offense, what is your plan for the defense?" asked Charles.

"The plan was formed a half hour ago," replied the Professor in a tone of calm confidence, "and I think it a good one. To-night, my boys, we shall draw upon resources that we have not yet put into play. Herbert will watch at the head of the path from the ravine. You and I, Charles, will go upon the plateau, and await the coming of these foolish Apaches, who in their sanguine desire for our scalps know little how well fitted we are to keep them on our heads. I'll be back with you in a moment, my lads."

He slipped into the cliff house, and returned bearing in one hand a small object round and relatively long, and in the other a package. Then he and Charles mounted the primitive ladder to the head of the plateau, and Herbert and Jed, rifles in hand, moved to the head of the path leading up from the gorge.

*****

Meanwhile a great impulse was stirring the souls of the warriors in the Apache camp. Gray Wolf was one of those bold spirits who defied precedents. His inquiring mind persisted in ascribing things to natural causes. Se-má-che

166

might have his favorites, those whom he loved and protected, but, if such there were, it must be the Apaches themselves, and not white men or white boys.

Gray Wolf talked to Big Elk and he talked to the others. Never had he been more fervent, never more logical, and they were convinced. He laid his plan before them, he would take the lead and the chief danger himself and success must crown such worthy efforts. His, too, was a reasoning, scientific mind like that of Professor Longworth. It was easier to come down upon an enemy than to climb up to him. Hence they would reach the plateau and descend on the cliff village.

Taking a dozen of the best warriors and seconded by Big Elk, Gray Wolf and his band circled about the side of the mountain and reached the plateau above the village. It continued to be just such a night as suited their noble purpose. The heavens were an unbroken dome of black. The light of not a single star was able to pierce through the dark covering, but the Apaches, used to it, moved easily without falls or noise.

The confidence of Gray Wolf was communicated to Big Elk and all the members of his redoubtable band. They would break the spell which had hung so long over this place. Even if Se-má-che had once turned his face away from them there was nothing to prove that he had not now turned it back upon them. They dreamed already of an easy conquest. They might find the white defenders asleep and scalp them without resistance.

Gray Wolf was a little in advance, Big Elk was next to him and the others came just behind, a silent and shadowy file. There was, for the moment, peace on the plateau. The trees and grass stirred faintly, and out from the black depths of the gorge came a moaning, but the Apaches knew very well that it was the wind drawn between the high, basaltic walls. Nothing occurred to show them that the enemy was on guard.

Gray Wolf, from his position in advance, could see shadowy black depths and he knew that it was the gorge not more than thirty yards away. There was no sign whatever that the enemy was watching for this approach from the rear, and his Apache heart throbbed with the thought of a speedy triumph of the kind that the Apache heart loves. The greatest need for caution came now, and, obedient to a low signal from him, all sank down until their mahogany bodies were blent with the black basalt of the cliff.

Gray Wolf uttered another low word, the signal for the creeping advance, and then occurred an extraordinary thing, something for which neither he nor his comrades could account in either Apache life or Apache mythology. A brilliant beam of light suddenly came from nowhere, piercing the darkness like a flaming arrow and struck full upon the face of Gray Wolf, dazzling and blinding him for the moment.

It was such a bright light, of such an intense burning white, that, despite one of the blackest nights ever known in the Arizona mountains, every feature of Gray Wolf stood revealed in all its Apache ferocity. There were the mahogany skin, roughened by wind and weather, the coarse, straight black hair, the hooked nose, the yellowish eyes, the small even teeth and the slight projection of the countenance into a canine shape that had given him his name, Gray Wolf.

The face of Gray Wolf was more clearly seen in that burning glare than if in sunlight, and a low gasp of astonishment and terror came from the warriors. Then the light went out, not sinking like the light of a torch, but vanishing utterly and instantly into space, leaving the warriors staring blindly into the darkness.

Gray Wolf, despite his courage and logical mind, was taken aback. He did not deny it even to himself. No such thing had ever before occurred in his experience. It might be a bolt from Se-má-che, but if so it was a bolt that had not struck him down. He was alive, unharmed and the phantom light was gone.

He gave the low signal and resumed the advance, but before he had gone a foot the phantom light came again, shooting down in the darkness like a beam from a falling star, only far more vivid. It struck now not upon the face of Gray Wolf, but upon that of Big Elk, his lieutenant, who stood just a little behind him. Gray Wolf turned and stared at his comrade. The face of Big Elk seemed to be a luminous projection in the darkness, resting upon nothing. All the rest of his body was hidden.

Big Elk himself uttered a cry of terror, not a gasp, but a distinct exclamation of fright, of the kind not often drawn from an Apache. It was more than he could stand. This must be Se-má-che himself giving his frightful warning to those who would commit sacrilege. His heart filled with terror, and mahogany beads of perspiration gathered on his mahogany face. Then the light shifted from him as suddenly as it had come. But it did not go away. It struck once more upon the face of Gray Wolf, remained there only an instant, and then played in successive flashes upon every member of the crouching band.

The Apaches shivered, Gray Wolf not excepted, but still they did not run. They were brave warriors, driven on by a great impulse, and they were loath to yield. But while they did not go back, neither did they go forward.

Gray Wolf tried to follow that brilliant beam which now played about them with such dazzling speed that the eye could scarcely follow it, but he grew more dazed and terror steadily mounted in his soul.

"It is the eye of Se-má-che," someone groaned, and immediately others repeated the groan. The terrible gaze of the Sun God, coming forth from the blackness of night, was upon them, because they were about to commit sacrilege. But they yet held fast, and in a few more seconds the light vanished. The Apaches still crouched on the black basalt, listening to the hard breathing of one another, and the groaning of the wind in the gorge, which their fancy now magnified tenfold.

Then came a third sound, a sharp buzz like that of the rattlesnake and, as the mahogany flesh of the Apaches crept on their bones, a bright light, hissing as it came, shot up from the very pit of the earth, rising in terrible reds and yellows and blues above the trees, and cleaving the sky in a long shining lane.

Apache human nature could stand no more. There was a simultaneous yell of terror, to which the redoubtable Gray Wolf was not the least contributor, and presently the sound of pattering moccasins was lost in the far beyond.

Professor Erasmus Darwin Longworth and Charles descended the pole ladder to the terrace, very well satisfied with themselves.

"We routed them without danger to ourselves and we did not fire a shot," said the Professor. "It was simple. A good hiding-place for ourselves behind the rocks, that powerful electric torch of mine, one that I hold in reserve for the most urgent cases, and a handful of powder for colored fire, such as boys use on the night of the Fourth of July, only far stronger, but which I had brought along to use for signaling to Jedediah. Simple, most simple indeed! Just as all great results are achieved by the simplest methods! Have you noticed that, Charles, my lad? Telegraph, telephone, electricity, wireless, all are the simplest of processes, when you understand them."

"Yes, when you understand them," said Charles behind his teeth, and he added in the same place, almost using the words of Jedediah Simpson o' Lexin'ton, K—y, "What a wonderful man! What infinite resource!"

The Professor could not hear him, and in a minute or two more they were on the terrace, relating the event to two delighted hearers.

Chapter Nineteen - The Mighty Defender

Professor Erasmus Darwin Longworth was very grave. He felt that three lives besides his own were in his keeping, and he was resolved to protect them. None knew better than he the cunning and cruelty of the Apaches. Already he had once saved Charles at great risk to himself, and he was willing to undergo such risks again for any one of the three or for them all.

But the Professor was a wise man, learned, as few are, not alone in theory, but in action as well, and, telling the other three to watch closely, he withdrew in the morning to one of the cliff houses, in which some of his most precious possessions were stored. This house was comparatively well lighted, with a long narrow window, a slit between the stones, and drawing his materials close to the window the Professor began a work which he prosecuted with great care. He took from a case six small metal shells, not as large as a hen's egg.

These little eggs were hollow and empty with a small hole at the end. The Professor filled every egg carefully with a composition into which picric acid entered. Then he closed up the apertures with fuses, and gingerly placed the six eggs in various pockets of his Norfolk jacket.

"I thought to use these for blowing out stone," he said grimly to himself, "but I may need them more for other purposes. One must prepare for every contingency."

He returned to the terrace, making no explanation concerning his absence in the stone hut, and they resumed the watch. Another hour passed, and then they heard a dull, rumbling noise on the plateau.

"What under the sun can that be?" exclaimed Jedediah Simpson.

The rumble increased to a roar, and then something struck upon the terrace with a crash. They had a glimpse of a great stone bounding by them, they felt a rush of air past their faces and then the stone shot into the gulf, from the bottom of which came the far echo of its fall.

In a minute or two another struck upon the terrace with great force, and then rebounded into the gulf. The boys looked at each other with blanched faces. This was a form of attack that they did not know how to meet.

"Great Jupiter!" exclaimed Jed, "I hope none o' them stones will hit me!"

But Professor Longworth never lost his composure.

"I thought they would come to that," he said. "Of course they've recovered their courage by daylight, and perhaps suspect a trick, when I frightened them with the electric light. It's a wonder they did not use those bowlders sooner."

"But how are we to get back at them, Professor?" asked Charles. "If they keep on some of these things are bound to hit unless we withdraw to the shelter of the stone huts. And if we do withdraw the pass is left undefended."

"All that you say is true," replied Professor Longworth. "But I think I have a method of meeting them. You three remain here, shelter yourselves as well as you can from the stones and watch the pass."

They obeyed in silence, and the Professor went back toward the cliff house, nearest to the pole ladder stairway. A stone almost grazed him before he reached it, but he did not turn aside. When he was under the shelter of its walls he rested a moment. Then finding a foothold on the rough stones he climbed up to the flat roof. There he lay extended, not moving at all for at least three minutes. Then he slowly raised himself until he stood erect and close to the face of the cliff. The three at the head of the pass could see him, but the Apaches on the plateau could not.

The three, despite their urgent duty to guard the pass, could not keep from watching the Professor, standing on the flat roof of the stone cliff house. His face was almost entirely hidden by the enormous pith helmet. A shaft of sunshine struck fairly upon his great glasses and gave back a golden gleam. His figure remained rigidly erect upon his toes and then his right hand slipped into a pocket of his Norfolk jacket.

A great stone crashed down, and the Professor seemed to mark the point from which it came. The three saw his hand come swiftly from his pocket. In his hand he held something small, shaped like an egg, that gave back a metallic gleam when the sun struck upon it. The Professor's arm curved back like that of a baseball player, and then shot forward with amazing swiftness.

The little metal egg left his fingers like a stone from a sling. It flew upward and inward, struck well back upon the plateau, and its impact was followed by a terrific report. Earth and stone flew into the air, and there were cries of pain and rage.

"He has thrown a bomb," said Charles, "and it has hit among the Apaches!"

"They might have known he'd a-done it," said Jed. "Ain't I said all the time that he's the greatest man in the world. It ain't only the fact that he's read all the books ever printed, but he can do everything, too."

The Apaches waited a long time before they rolled another stone, but the moment it fell the Professor threw a second bomb in the direction from which it came, and, after that, the bombardment ceased entirely.

Professor Longworth waited a long time, descended the roof and returning to the stone hut, in which he had charged them, carefully removed the four remaining bombs from his pockets.

"I don't think they'll try that trick again," he said to himself.

The remainder of the day passed in silence. Then came the long night. But it, too, finally passed, the darkness fled, the red sun shot up from the deep, and vapors rose from the earth. Once again the waves of hot air from the desert met the waves of cold air from the peaks, and over the mountains the clouds began to grow. Mists gathered, and close suffocating banks of air floated down the canyon. The four saw, but, save the Professor, scarcely noticed, the change in the heavens, and the Apaches below, so intent for blood and revenge, took no notice either.

But the clouds presently covered all the heavens and began to give forth flashes of fire. Then the peaks grumbled to one another in low thunder.

The four still watched. Two or three shots were fired from below, but they whistled above their heads, and the four paid no attention save to infer that all the Apaches had returned to the bottom of the canyon. Then followed a long silence and they still waited. After a while the storm came. The flashes of lightning were so fast and intense that all the mountains swam in the red glare, peaks and ridges stood back against an ashen sky, and every canyon and gorge rumbled with the continuous thunder. Then the rain rushed down, the lightning and the thunder ceased and nothing was heard, save the beat of the water upon the thirsty ground, which drank it up and asked incessantly for more. From the door of a cave house, to which they had retreated, the four watched it.

There was a noise from the canyon and all started. The Professor sprang from the entrance, and the rain dashed in a torrent into his face, but he heard a crash far down the slope, repeated four or five times, and then a thunderous echo that came through the rain.

"It was only a bowlder loosed from the mountainside by the wind and water," Herbert said. "Those old cliff dwellers must have grown used to the grandeur of nature."

The Professor shook his head.

"See," he said.

All were by his side now, and they looked down. The mighty sweep of the rain had driven away the mists and vapors, and they could see through it as through a veil darkly. The other side of the ravine showed dimly like the black wall of a well, but the little river had suddenly increased many times in volume, and, with a joyful roar, leaped forward in a whirl of foam.

"There must have been a cloudburst further up," said the Professor, "and if the Apaches were down there on the floor of the canyon when this came, they are not likely to do any hunting of man or beast again. The stream is running now, a great flooded river."

They stood there a while, secure in this little fortress, and looked out at the wildest world that any of them had ever beheld. The thunder and the lightning had ceased entirely, but they heard plainly the rush and sweep of the torrent, as it rolled down the canyon, bearing bushes and trees upon its muddy surface.

"I'd rather be here than thar," said Jed Simpson, and the others gave him silent but hearty assent.

The rain died away and ceased, the clouds fled, and the sun came out, shedding a flood of golden light over the ravine and the slopes, the muddy torrent sank fast, until it became again the thin, sprawling creek of every day, and only the dripping trees and bushes told of the storm that had passed.

"One thing is sure," said the Professor, "if the Apaches were in the canyon they were washed away, but if they got out in time they are not likely to come back again soon. They will be convinced that all the gods in every mythology are against them."

"You never spoke truer words, Purfessor," said Jed. "It's all been mighty cur'ous an' interestin', but it seems to me that Natur' took a hand in our favor."

"She certainly did, Jed," said the Professor sincerely, "and now I think we'd better scout a little below, using all due caution."

They crept down the slope, muddy and slippery from the passing water, seeing no signs of the Apaches. But the appearance of everything, the torn nature of the valley, the bowlders overturned, and the débris caught high in clefts, convinced them that the warriors had been overtaken by the mighty flood. They reached the bottom, and still saw no signs of the besiegers. Charles wandered away from the others, and his eye was caught presently by something brown, a new object lodged in a crevice almost at the base of the far slope. He could not make it out clearly, but he had his belief about it, and he resolved to investigate.

He soon reached high-water mark, and he was surprised to find that it had come so far up the slope. It was evident that a tremendous volume of water had swept down the canyon, and the belief, formed an hour since in his mind and shared by the others, was strengthened. Everything about him now showed the fierce path of the waters, the pines had been ripped away, bowlders had been swept from the slope, and over all was a covering of thin, yellowish mud left by the ebb.

Charles crossed the shallow, listless creek, and reached that brown object which proved to be what he had suspected, the dead body of an Apache.

It seemed to Charles that every bone in the body of the warrior had been broken, and it required no wilderness lore to tell him that the man had been caught in the cloudburst. Continuing his search down the canyon, he found four other bodies, all mangled and crushed in a frightful manner. It was his belief that they had been so intent upon the siege, so eager to secure their victims, that they had failed to take warning from the clouds and vapors, and hence had been destroyed as a punishment.

But had all the Apaches perished? That was the vital question. A single survivor, hidden among the undergrowth or the rocks, could do destruction, and Charles, resolved to make sure as nearly as he could, scouted for a long time, as the others also were doing. He might have continued the search yet longer had he not heard near the mouth of a narrower canyon, entering into a main one, a groaning that seemed to him to have a human note. The sound came from a slight depression in the floor of the canyon, and, advancing with the greatest caution, he looked down upon an Apache pinned into the mud by the stem of a tree across his legs.

Charles' first impulse was to shoot the savage, as he would have dispatched a wounded rattlesnake, and, in the light of Arizona experience, that was the wisest thing to do. He leveled his rifle at the Apache, who was as evil-looking as the rest of his kind, but he could not fire; it was not in him to shoot even a savage, who nevertheless hungered for his life while pinned to the earth.

The Indian had heard Charles' footsteps, and turned upon him eyes that did not plead for mercy. He expected his enemy to do what he, in his place, would certainly have done. Neither did his look change when the gun was lowered.

Charles hesitated, he felt that he was doing a foolish thing, not because of himself but because it might imperil the lives of his comrades. But the impulse of humanity conquered, and he rolled the tree from the Indian.

The Apache said something in his own tongue, whether to express surprise or relief Charles did not know, and tried to rise, but failed. Charles ran his hand along his legs, and could feel no fracture, although he had suffered severe bruises, the soft mud having saved his bones.

The Apache made several more efforts, and finally succeeded in sitting up, and then in standing. He spoke once more in his own tongue, and the note of it was undoubted satisfaction. Charles stood several yards away, and leveled his rifle at the mahogany body again.

"Sit down on that log, Mr. Apache," he said. "This is a court now, and I am the judge, jury, and counsel for the prosecution. You are the criminal. Take the chair as I tell you."

The Indian may not have understood the words, but Charles' gesture was sufficient, and he sat upon the log, turning an immobile mahogany face upon his captor.

"Can you talk English?"

"Some."

"Then you know what I am saying?"

The Apache nodded.

"What is your name?"

"Gray Wolf."

"Well, my friend, you are a very ugly and a very muddy wolf at present, and you have been upon a very wicked work, but you have been punished. All your comrades, I think, are dead."

There was a sudden look in the yellowish eyes of the Apache, perhaps of grief, perhaps of disappointment.

"The flood came when we were getting ready to go against you again, and it has taken all except Gray Wolf?"

"That is so, and now, Mr. Apache, I am going to do a very foolish thing. Don't you think that, after a little exercise, you could walk pretty well?"

"Walk all right soon."

"You have lost all your arms; they are swept away down the canyon, and if you were to find them you would have no ammunition for them. Isn't that so?"

The Apache bowed in confirmation.

"And you probably have near here a camp above high-water mark. Show the way to it."

The Apache, without hesitating, led to a rude camp in an alcove of the rocks, where venison and water bottles were stored. Charles did not waste time. He bade the Gray Wolf take as much of the venison as he wanted, and two of the full water-bottles, and then, at the muzzle of his rifle, he escorted him far down the canyon.

"Now, Mr. Apache," he said, "keep going to the south, and, if you look back before you are out of sight, you will meet a bullet. And the same bullet will be reserved for you if you ever come here again. March!"

Gray Wolf never uttered a word, nor allowed a single change of expression, but kept his face to the south, and stalked solemnly off at a steady gait. Charles, rifle in hand and standing on an elevation, watched the brown figure grow less and less, never veering from the direction, until it became a mere speck, and then passed out of sight.

"That, I hope, is the last I may ever see of you, Mr. Gray Wolf," he said aloud. "I have had Apache enough to last me the rest of my life."

Then he went back thoughtfully, his mind turned now to matters other than the fight for mere life. He did not doubt that Gray Wolf was the only survivor of the band. He walked slowly toward the cliff house. Now that the deed was done he had a great fear that he had been too impulsive. Perhaps he should have asked his comrades what to do with the Apache, but the feeling that had created the original impulse returned at last. The others could only have done what he did. They could not put a wounded man to death in cold blood. His spirits rose. Afar he saw Jed bending over something, and as he approached he began to sing the song of Ananias Brown:

"O'er the measureless range where rarely change
The swart gray plains, so weird and strange,
Treeless and streamless and wondrous still."

Jed looked up.

"Natur', or what is bigger than Natur'—God—was shorely with us, Charlie," he said. "Here's a dead Apache, half buried in the mud. The flood swooped right down on him jest as it did on them wicked people in Noah's time, an' another in the same fix is a little further back."

"Yes," said Charles, "and I've seen several also."

They joined the Professor and Herbert presently, and the four continued the search together. They found sixteen bodies in all and no sign of a living Indian.

"These Apache war bands are usually small," said the Professor, "and it not likely that a single warrior has escaped, but if so, let him go; we do not want him."

Charles' heart gave a bound of joy. The Professor, without knowing it, had commended his deed. But the boy remained silent.

"This is a warning to us," said the Professor, "that we should go as soon as possible. We were far safer in the canyon in the winter than we shall be in the spring or summer."

All knew the truth of his words. They felt some alarm again lest their animals had suffered in the flood, but the instinct of horse and mule had held good. They were far down the canyon and on an upper slope when the storm had burst, and the subsiding flood passed them by, leaving them unharmed. There the comrades found them and after some difficulty succeeded in catching them and reducing them all to the service of man once more.

The skin bags were completed, the gold was put in them, and loading them upon the animals they said farewell to the cliff houses that had given them a comfortable home so long, and started down the canyon. But when the time came to go they found that they had regrets.

"I hope that nobody will ever harm the place," said Herbert.

"It's all mighty cur'ous an' interestin'," said Jed. "Now, who'd have ever thought that when I come up here with the Purfessor, huntin' the oldest rock above water, that I was goin' to find my fortune and become one o' the leadin' citizens o' Lexin'ton, K—y?"

They started early in the morning and when night came they were far down the canyon.

Chapter Twenty - The Departure

They made their camp in a grove of pines, by the side of the little river which had now grown wider but much more shallow.

"I think it is like our life," said the Professor, as they sat by the supper fire. "It comes down a turbulent stream from the mountains in which it had its birth, to grow broader and more placid as it emerges into the low and level lands, at last to sink out of sight far beyond the desert sands, but after its long subterranean journey to reappear somewhere else, a bright, brilliant and laughing stream. Who knows?"

"Yes, who knows?" said Herbert, upon whose mind this imagery struck with great force.

But their spirits were too high to permit more than a moment's reflection upon such serious questions. Even Professor Longworth, a man well into middle age, was gay and jovial. Jed had taken the fishing tackle and caught some trout in the stream. These he was now frying on the coals and the appetizing aroma arose. Charles gave Herbert a shove and sent him down among the pine needles. Herbert jumped up, caught his assailant, and in a moment the two were rolling over and over in a wrestle.

"Look at them kids!" said Jed admiringly. "This wild life certainly does give a boy muscle an' spirit. Jest pumps him full o' rich blood. Now, stop that, you two young grizzly bears. The trout'll burn in the next minute an' ef you ain't here in time me an' the Purfessor will eat 'em all."

"I believe that's what you want to happen, Jed," said Herbert. "You are full of tricks, and I tell you right now that if you don't give us the right kind of hotel service I'm going to kick. I want a cup of coffee for my supper, and I don't pay the bill if I don't get it."

"Now, don't you be too fasteejous," replied Jedediah Simpson o' Lexin'ton, K—y, in high good humor. "You must be like them old Roman fellers the Purfessor told me about, always huntin' fur hummin'-birds' tongues to eat. Thar ain't no pleasin' you. You might bring me a thousand dollars in gold out o' one o' them bags that are all ours an' say to me: 'Mr. Jed, good Jed, nice Jed, intellectooal Jed, Jed, the lover o' music, here are one thousand dollars in gold, all o' which I offer to you fur one little cup o' brown coffee.' I'd say to you: 'Mr. Herbert Carleton, you do be most temptin' with your offers, but they ain't good enough. You ain't got gold enough to buy a cup o' coffee from me. River water will do you.'"

"That's so, Jed," said Herbert. "I suppose there isn't a cup of coffee within a hundred miles of us, but I do wish I had one. Money will buy nothing here."

"No, but it will when you get back to the big towns," replied Jed, "and when I reach Chicago or New York I'm goin' to the finest restaurant in the place. Ever hear that story of the feller who made a whole pile o' money in the mines in the West, got elected senator, an' went with his daughters to Washington? They goes right into the big swell restaurant, where the band is playin' an' flowers are standin' in all the windows. People all about, waiters with black clothes an' shinin' shirt fronts flyin' here an' thar, mostly thar. Senator an' fambly lookin' hard at one o' them meynoos on which everthing is writ in French. Can't make out a thing. Important waiter standin' by, an' grinnin' a little. At last the Senator gits mad an' he says sharp to that grinnin' waiter, 'Never min' about all them French things, jest bring us forty dollars' worth o' ham an' eggs.' Mebbe that'll be the way with Jedediah Simpson, Esquire, but I ain't goin' to take no chance. I'm goin' to practice in them silverplated restaurants in them big cities before I settle down in little old Lexin'ton, K—y, among the real people."

The Professor smiled.

"I see, Jed," he said, "that the responsibilities of wealth are going to make you a very stern and solemn character. I've no doubt that when I come to visit you in Lexington you will have your D.M. to play the saddest sort of music, and all your talk will be about the degeneracy of the age and the folly of the common people."

Jed shook his head energetically.

"Not me, Purfessor! Not me!" he said. "I ain't goin' to have all the juices o' life dried up in me, jest because I'm a millionaire. That D.M. is goin' to play some purty gay tunes I can tell you, an' at fittin' times there are goin' to be lively times around Arizony Place. Young people will be thar, laughin' an' makin' merry, an' me lookin' on an' smilin,' an' thinkin' myself most as young as any o' 'em."

"That's the proper spirit, Jed," said the Professor approvingly. "Keep up your interests in things and you won't grow old."

"That's right, Purfessor," said Jed admiringly. "I'm always tellin' Charlie an' Herb here that you're one o' the great men o' the world with the right to put thirteen letters o' the alphabet in capitals before your name, an' the other thirteen after it, also in capitals. An' about them young people when they are havin' a good time at Arizony Place I'll gradually draw 'em all together in the biggest an' finest parlor, right under them glitterin' chandeliers, made a-purpose fur me in Paris, an' then when I gits the eyes an' attention o' all fixed on me, an' they hardly dare to draw a breath they're so interested I'll tell 'em the tale o' how I found my wealth in the wild mountains o' Arizony with the best three pards any man ever had in a big adventure. Thar was one Purfessor Longworth, who knowed pretty nigh everything, an' what he didn't know nobody had no business knowin' anyway, an' then thar wuz two boys, one wuz Charlie who come out o' the west an' t'other was Herb who come out o' the east, jest about the finest pair o' lads in the world, all wool an' a yard

177

wide, lined with copper, riveted with steel, double-distilled, true blue, half hoss, half alligator, white all over, an' fit to fight their weight in wildcats, an' I'll say to all them nice young people, 'Boys an' gals, you're fine, you're the real stuff, the state o' Kentucky is proud o' you, the Union is proud o' you, the world is proud o' you, an' so am I, but you ain't the Purfessor an' Charlie an' Herb, an' I wish them three wuz here right now, the Purfessor sittin' in front o' me an' higher up, an' Charlie an' Herb, one on my right hand an' t'other on my left hand.'"

Water rose in the eyes of the impressionable Herbert.

"You mean that, Jed," he said, "and we feel the same way about you."

The Professor and Charles were silent, but they were deeply moved.

"Here, take your fish, Charlie," said Jed, after his burst of emotion. "An' you too, Herb, here's your'n."

Besides the fish they had venison and bear meat, and they fell to with great zest. They had heaped up the gold by the camp fire and the horses and mules were grazing near. The fallen wood of last year burned brightly, and they felt easy and cheerful. To the north of them showed the loom of the great mountains from which they had come, but the white heads of the peaks were lost now in the coming dusk. In the west tints of purple and orange and gold lingered for a few moments to mark whence the sun had gone and then, with the suddenness of the southwest, the great cloud of the dark came down enfolding all the earth. But the fire was a tiny core of light in all that vast silence, and the four cheerful figures sat beside it talking.

"We must keep a watch," said the Professor. "In a wild country and with such a great treasure as ours, some alert eye must be open all the time."

He took the first watch himself, and the other three, wrapping themselves in their blankets, were sound asleep in five minutes, their feet to the fire, their heads pillowed on their arms. The Professor sat a long time in silence. He heard nothing but a stray wind among the pines, and now and then the stamp of a horse's restless foot. He took off his pith helmet and rubbed his forehead. Then he looked up at the vast, beautiful sky, sown with brilliant stars, and the wise old eyes expressed admiration and devotion. Prodigious learning had not made him a cynic, it merely made him more humble, more appreciative of the tremendous power that had called the universe into being, and silently the Professor adored the Master of that universe. Then he glanced with sympathy at the recumbent figures. Trusty comrades they were, and if he had had sons he would have liked them to be like Charles and Herbert. They were almost sons to him, as it was, and he was happy in their presence.

A horse stamped louder than usual. Something stirred in the bushes. Was it a wild animal drawn by the fire? The Professor half rose, and he held his rifle in his hand. The keen eyes were gleaming through the huge glasses. Was danger at hand? He merely wished to know. No throb of fear stirred the little man of the lion heart.

He listened again. A horse snorted, not loudly, but as if disturbed, and the Professor rose to his full height, the rifle held well forward and ready for instant use. He slipped softly through some thorny undergrowth, until he entered the grassy circle in which the horses slept or grazed. They were at rest now. The Professor remained hidden in the shadow, but no horse stamped or snorted again. He was a man who knew not only books but the wilderness and he stayed long in the deepest shadow, watching. Then he advanced into the circle and looked about with minute care. Presently his eye was caught by a trace in a soft place of the earth, and drawing from his pocket a hand glass of power he knelt beside it, examined it with care. It was not the footstep of a horse or a mule, nor yet that of any of his comrades, but it was undeniably the footstep of a man. All the four wore moccasins that they had made for themselves, but this was the imprint of a boot, where the stiff heel and the stiff leather sole had crushed down. A white man! Obviously so! He found two or three more of the imprints in the bright moonlight, and they led toward the far edge of the thorn thicket, but there he lost them, and could discover nothing more.

The Professor walked slowly back to the fire. His comrades were still sleeping soundly, but he was no longer at ease. A footstep, the footstep of a white man, and that man had come like a thief in the night! And he had slipped away like the same thief! The Professor cast a glance at the mound of gold. Some old words of his about the difficulty of finding it and the equal difficulty of retaining it recurred to him and he was sorely troubled in mind.

Time passed on. Moonlight flooded the camp with silver, and the Professor, rifle across his knee, still watched. He was to have called Charles at one o'clock for the second watch, but he let the hour go by. It was past two when he awoke the lad and told him what he had seen.

"I don't think that any attack is likely to be made upon us, at least not tonight," he said, "but be vigilant, Charles, be vigilant!"

"I certainly will be, Professor," replied the boy confidently, as he took his seat on a fallen log, rifle in hand and ready.

Charles felt no fear. Naturally strong and brave, a native of the border west, where he had always been thrown upon his own physical resources, he was accustomed now to wild life and danger. It had been nearly a year since he left the little telegraph station at Jefferson, but in that time he had grown wonderfully in all respects. Now he sat upon the log, eyes wary and every nerve attuned. There was still a flood of silver moonlight in the glen, and a myriad of beautiful stars wheeled and danced in the shining blue. Charles listened but heard nothing and then glanced at the recumbent forms of his comrades. The Professor had stretched himself near by, feet to the fire and now he looked the smallest of the three, his head on his arm and his face in the dark.

But Professor Erasmus Darwin Longworth, who could rightfully put all the letters of the alphabet in capitals after his name, was not asleep, although he pretended to be. The situation, the presence of the gold and the unknown footsteps in the earth preyed upon him. He had a heavy sense of responsibility, but it was not for the gold; it was for these two boys, brave true lads to whom the tendrils of a heart hitherto lonely were strongly attached. It was his duty to get them back to civilization, to see that they had the chance in life due to everyone, and the Professor felt in his inmost heart that the barriers were not yet passed. Prescience, or the sixth sense, warned him that dangers were about them as thick as fallen leaves in an autumn forest.

But in spite of the omens and his desire to continue a sentinel, the Professor, who had watched long and hard, was very tired and very sleepy. His lids shut down, he opened them angrily, but they shut down again and stayed shut. Despite his great will, Professor Erasmus Darwin Longworth, with the right to use twenty-six letters after his name, all in capitals, was sound asleep.

But Charles continued his alert watch. He had enjoyed a good sleep and no weights were pulling at his eyelids. He felt no warnings of the sixth sense, but he was quite as sure as the Professor had been that the strange footsteps in the turf meant something. It was a concrete fact that needed no power of the imagination to increase its importance.

He lay down once and put his ear to the ground, that great conductor of sound, but he heard only the rustling of the wind and the slight movement of the horses. Then he resumed his seat on the fallen log, leaning against an upthrust bough, silent and attentive. Floating mists and vapors came up and dimmed the starshine. The last coals of the fire died down and went out, the recumbent figures of his comrades blurred with the darkness, and then suddenly a horse neighed loud and shrill. The neigh was followed by the trampling of feet and Charles rushed into the grassy opening. A dark form glided away from the far side of one of the horses and Charles fired at it as it passed out of sight. Then he ran forward in pursuit, but there was nothing, and he turned back, because the animals were rearing and trampling behind him, and his aroused comrades were among them rifle in hand.

"What is it, Charlie, what is it?" cried Herbert.

"I don't know, but a horse neighed and when I came a man was among them. He ran into the thicket there, and I fired at him but missed."

"Our earlier friend of the footprints, I have no doubt," said the Professor. "It's well that you watched so closely, Charlie."

"Now, this is mighty cur'ous an' interestin'," said Jed. "'Pears to me that feller or fellers wants our horses and mules."

"That's just it," said the Professor, "and without them where would we be? Ah, look here!"

He had been prowling at the edge of the thicket and suddenly he took out his hand glass. The starshine had returned, and the glass distinctly revealed a red stain on the grass.

"Your aim was not as bad as you thought, Charlie," he said. "You hit him, but the wound must have been a slight one, as this is the only stain that I can find."

They searched in the thicket for footsteps, but found none. Then they built up the fire again, and slept no more that night. All felt oppressed. There was something weird and uncanny in the attempt upon the animals, and, for the first time in days, they felt the desolation of the wilderness.

Dawn came shooting up like a bright star, and the mists and vapors that clogged their minds fled away with the darkness.

"Now for the next march to wood and water," said the Professor cheerfully, "and we'll shake off this prowler, whoever he may be. It was probably some prospector of the worst type, who was trying to steal one of our horses. At any rate, Charlie, you stung him, and that is a punishment."

"Whatever it is, it is shorely mighty cur'ous an' interestin'," said Jed, shaking his head.

They ate breakfast quickly and started. The four walked in order to keep the gold-laden horses and mules as fresh as possible, and thus they passed down the canyon. It was a long journey and they did not intend to exhaust themselves by excessive haste. They kept near the edge of the river, that in fact being the best path, and marched steadily on for hours. The stream was yet fresh and sparkling from the melting snows, and behind them the line of white peaks still stared solemnly down at them.

They had made many miles, when they stopped for the noonday meal and rest, still beside the flowing stream. Vegetation was becoming less abundant as they proceeded further away from the high mountains, but there was yet plenty of grass for the animals, and an abundance of sparkling water to refresh the eye as well as the taste. The heavens were a sheet of gold and blue, and a pleasant wind came from the peaks to temper the heat.

"This is somethin' like," said Jed, lolling on the grass, not a single weird tremor of the night before left to him. "I've never got over the feelin' I had when I was a boy, rollin' 'roun' an' kickin' on the grass. The touch o' it seemed to make me stronger an' livelier then, an' it's the same now. How I do love green grass, an' up thar at Lexin'ton, K—y, it don't ever die much, even in the winter. I intend to have mighty big grounds 'roun' Arizony Place, grass, thick, green an' long, almost as fur as you can see, with whoppin' big shade trees, beech an' oak an' ellum. I do like trees mighty well, too, Herb, they look so gran' an' fine, an' when a wind comes along they bow their heads to it, ever so polite and graceful, an' say, 'How do you do, Miss Wind, you are blowin' mighty beautiful to-day.' A big tree is shorely a gentleman, Herb."

"It surely is," said Herbert

"An' I've been thinkin' that I'd have marble statoos about among the grass an' trees, an' then ag'in I'm thinkin' I wouldn't. I don't know, Herb, I don't know."

"I shouldn't if I were you, Jed," said Herbert. "I think that style has largely passed out."

"Well, I am mighty glad to hear you say so," said Jed with a deep sigh of relief. "I want to do the right thing, but I ain't particularly in love with them marble statoos. The Purfessor took me to see some right famous ones when we wuz in Europe, an' I found out that the fewer clothes they have on the more famous they be. The real top-notchers, them that they make the fuss about, ain't got on any clothes a-tall, a-tall. As I told you, Herb, I want to do the right thing, but how'd I feel if I wuz takin' a lot o' them nice young people in Lexin'ton, K—y, 'roun' Arizony Place, an' we wuz to butt all at once into a marble lady that didn't even have on a veil, an' me a modest man, too? I'm obleeged to you, Herb, fur givin' me this good advice. It's got me out o' a tight place."

Another beautiful day was finished and they camped in the open about twenty yards from the stream. This time, on the Professor's advice, they tethered all the horses and mules, and made their own beds almost at the feet of the animals.

"It will be pretty hard to steal one now without our knowing it," said the Professor.

After cooking supper they put out the fire in order that it might not serve as a beacon to anyone whom they did not want to see, and then Herbert took the first watch. The Professor was awake throughout the lad's turn, but he concealed the fact, not wishing to hurt Herbert's feelings. Jed relieved him at midnight, and Herbert was asleep in five minutes. The Professor, too, soon fell asleep and Jedediah Simpson o' Lexin'ton, K—y, was alone on watch.

Jed lay on his side, propped upon his elbow, his rifle slanted across his body in such manner that he could use it at a moment's notice. It was another brilliant night, but it was peaceful and still, while the hours passed. Jed fell to star-gazing. His excursions into the firmament with the Professor had interested him deeply, and now he was seeking his old friends. There they were wheeling and dancing in the blue, Canopus and the mighty Sirius, the magnificent Rigel, Aldebaran, Betelgeuse, Arcturus and all the mighty hosts, suns on suns, and other myriads of suns behind them.

Deep down in the heart of Jedediah Simpson was a strain of real poetry. He was no longer afraid of the stars, as he was when he took that first flight with the Professor. They were friends now, though not as near and dear to him as the members of "his own bunch," old Jupe, Saturn with his bright collars, Neptune and Uranus and Venus and "sassy little Mercury." They were all up there, in their old places or orbits, solid, reliable fellows, perhaps the scene of future lives, and Jed took a lively interest in them all.

But his gaze came back from the heavens—Jed was no slothful sentinel— and wandered around the circle of his own familiar earth, or at least that part of it immediately surrounding his camp in northern Arizona.

They were still in the canyon, though the walls were much lower here, and Jed's gaze rested a moment on the black basaltic cliff to the right about two hundred yards away. The moonlight fell on the rock where bushes clustered in a cleft, and, as Jed's gaze passed the cluster, he had a distinct impression that he saw something moving there. In an instant the gaze came back and he was sure. The eye at the same time caught an intense brilliant beam of light that blazed out, burst and vanished. A bullet sang past the ear of Jedediah Simpson and buried itself in the earth beyond. He leaped to his feet and fired at the distant cluster of bushes, but now nothing was there but silence and darkness.

The others were on their feet, aroused by the two shots, so close together, and were full of questions. Jed quickly explained.

"Come on!" he exclaimed, "and we'll search the side of that cliff."

"No," said the Professor in a restraining tone. "If an attacking force is there we'd only be going into an ambush. We'd give them every possible advantage. We must move out of range. I've no doubt that it's our friend or friends of last night."

The camp was transferred to a point much further from the basaltic cliff, and all of them watched through the remainder of the night. It was a very long and trying vigil and it got terribly upon their nerves. Even the silence seemed to make it all the harder. Gladly they welcomed the first shimmer of the dawn, and as soon as possible were up and away.

They were silent and depressed throughout the morning. There was no doubt now that some sort of a terrible foe hung upon them, and that they were in constant danger. An invisible menace chilled the blood, and, added to the Professor's alarm, was his intense disquiet, because he could not fathom it.

"I don't feel like playin' no cheerful tunes on that little accordion o' mine," said Jed.

"I'll be glad when we get to the desert," said Charles, "it offers fewer opportunities for ambush. I'd like to see its gray loom now."

When they encamped at noon in broken ground a bullet was fired at them from a little canyon two or three hundred yards away. When they rushed into the canyon they found nobody there, but, by much diligent searching, the Professor discovered two footprints. After a long examination through his magnifying glass he said that a man's boots had made the impression, and he had no doubt it was the same man that Charles had seen on the first night.

"Whew!" said Jed rubbing his forehead. "This is gittin' a heap too warm to suit me. Ef we can't smoke that fellow out, whoever he may be, this ain't goin' to be no trip in a parlor car."

"Yes, but we cannot stop to search," said the Professor. "Our chief object is to get to Phoenix as quickly as possible with all our gold."

That night they encamped in the open and kept the closest kind of a watch. For hours all was quiet and they thought they had shaken off their enemy, but far toward morning a daring attempt was made to stampede the animals. When the four rushed to the rescue two forms, not one, slid away in the darkness, and when they fired at these fleeting phantoms two shots were fired back. Luckily no one was hit, but again they found nothing save a footprint here and there, always of a booted heel, and they gathered once more by the camp fire, more anxious and more disturbed than ever.

"We at least know," said the Professor, "that we have more than one man with whom to deal, and I think we are pursued for a purpose."

He looked significantly at the gold. The others understood his meaning and agreed with him.

"So long as we can keep 'em off, whoever they may be," said Jed, "we're all right."

Thus the march and the invisible pursuit continued. Other attempts to stampede the animals were made, more bullets from ambush were fired at them though nobody was hurt, and they secured no target in return.

The Professor read the hideous ingenuity in it all. The incessant series of ambushes and nocturnal attacks would wear out anybody. Human nerves could not stand it; already both Charles and Herbert showed the effect, and if he himself did not show it, he certainly felt it. But the problem of identity, who these besiegers were, troubled him most of all.

The pines now began to dwindle in size and frequency, and then to disappear, the river was losing volume in the sands, up from the swells shot the thorny and malformed cactus and off under the horizon they saw the dancing "dust devils" once more. Seldom have people welcomed the sight of the desert as did these four. "Now to shake off our enemies," said Herbert.

Chapter Twenty-One - On the Hot Sand

They marched two more days through sand and cactus, but were not troubled again by the mysterious pursuers, and their supplies of water sank rather lower than the Professor liked.

"There is plenty for the four of us who are human beings," he said, "but eight horses and mules require a great deal of water. We would not want to abandon the animals under any circumstances, and certainly we cannot dream of it, now that they alone can take our gold to civilization."

"Camels could take us across the desert without water, I suppose," said Herbert. "I've heard that they can go eight or ten days without a drink. Now if we only had some camels! Why have they never been introduced in the southwest, Professor?"

"It may be because our genuine desert area is too small, and that consequently they have not received the attention necessary in breeding," replied the Professor. "We have no really great deserts on the scale of those of Africa,

Asia and Australia. It may be, too, that our cold winter climate does not suit them. The camel has been transplanted to Australia, and has improved there. Already the Australian camel is superior to his Asiatic and African brethren. Before our great Civil War Jefferson Davis, then Secretary of War, imported a herd of camels, and sent them into the southwest for the use of the army on the desert. But they were not a success, and they were turned loose to roam as they pleased."

"What became of them?" asked Herbert with much interest.

"Members of the herd were seen now and then for a long time afterward, but I don't suppose they had a fair chance. They offered too tempting a bait for hunters, and most of the camels were shot by them. A few descendants may be roaming yet about the foothills. There are stories now and then that one is seen, but I cannot vouch for their truth."

"I think the stories are true," said Herbert, always anxious to believe in the romantic and remarkable.

But the conversation ceased there. It was too hot, and they were too tired and dusty to waste energy in talk.

"Our deserts may not be as big as them that deface the maps o' Afriky, Asia an' Australier," said Jedediah Simpson, "but they're big enough to hold a heap o' onpleasantness. See that vulture flyin' aroun' up thar. He thinks I'm to be his in the course o' time, an' he worries me."

"He won't get you, Jedediah," said the Professor, comfortingly. "I can't spare you; I'll need you for a long time yet."

"I hope so," said Jed, and then he added with energy:

"Now, what under the sun is that?"

He pointed to a distant sand hill where two dark figures could be seen against the horizon.

"It may be one o' them mirages," he said, "or may be I'm just seein' one o' them grains o' sand which are so thick in my eye, but anyway it's mighty cur'ous an' interestin'."

The Professor's glance followed Jed's long pointing finger, and instantly his little figure became taut with excitement.

"Animals!" he exclaimed, "and large ones. They can't be buffalo, because the buffalo is extinct save for the few in the mountains. The elk and deer do not roam on these sand plains, and they are too big for antelope. Having eliminated all these possibilities only one conclusion is left, and I must prove that to be true. Jed, my field glasses at once!"

Jed promptly brought the powerful glasses and the Professor took a long look through them. Then he leaped up and down in his joy.

"It is true! It is true!" he exclaimed. "They are camels, a pair of them, descendants, perhaps the sole surviving descendants of the herd that Jefferson Davis imported. What a lucky discovery, a fact that I must report to our geographical and faunal societies. I can see them distinctly, hoofs, body, head, tail and all, evidently a male and female. So, survivors do exist down here

185

after all. What a stir this will create among the learned men when I get back to civilization. But I must have trustworthy witnesses. Here, Charles, take the glasses and look!"

Charles distinctly saw the camels. It was not possible to mistake such shapes as theirs, which those of no other beasts resemble. They stood there, motionless, side by side, apparently looking out over the desert sands. Charles wondered if they felt themselves the last of a lost race, or if, by some dim intuition, they knew that their brethren swarmed on other continents beyond their reach.

Herbert and Jed also took long looks, and the three witnesses were ready for the Professor, should any presumptuous learned body ever choose to dispute his word.

"I wish I had time to follow them up, and perhaps to lasso one," said the Professor, "I might discover a number of vastly interesting details, such as the effect of a new climate and region upon the camel. Now, I wonder if an important variation from the original type could have occurred here. But we must go on. This troublesome gold claims our attention."

"Yes, we must get our Spanish gold safe to civilization," said Charles.

"Spanish gold it may have been once," said Professor Longworth, "but a better name for it now is Apache gold. It is the Apaches that we have had to fight for it, and if the Apaches had not caused you two boys to flee into the canyon, and then up to the cliff village it probably never would have been found."

"That's right. Apache gold it is and Apache gold it shall be," said the other three in unison.

And so they always spoke of it as Apache gold, despite what came after.

The Professor sighing deeply after another look at the camels gave the word to resume the advance, and they marched on through the deep sand. But everyone looked back and the camels still stood motionless on the sand hills, until they passed out of sight under the horizon.

It was late afternoon now, and it seemed to the two boys that it was hotter than ever. The sun, apparently, was only a mile or two away and it was bent upon burning them up. Puffs of wind arose and the whirling "dust devils" trod the plain, a swift procession. The sand, when it was blown in their faces, scorched like coals. The boys looked longingly at the water bags. The animals neighed and became uneasy.

The Professor, walking now, marched at the head and, as the afternoon waned and they came into rougher country, a look of relief appeared in the shrewd eyes behind the great glasses. Here were hills rather high, but like all the rest of that country bare and hideous.

"It will be three hours or more until darkness," said Professor Longworth, "but we will stop here and renew our supplies of fresh water."

"Renew our water!" exclaimed Charles. "Why, there cannot be any within at least twenty miles of us."

"I don't believe thar's any within a million," said Jed.

"As I said, we'll stop here and renew our supplies of fresh water," said the Professor quietly. "It is not a hundred yards away and there is plenty of it. Will all of you help me to take the packs off the animals as quickly as possible? They've had a long, hot march, and they need rest."

The Professor spoke with decision, and they did not think of questioning his statement any further. The packs, including the bags of gold, were removed and several of the animals neighed with relief. At the Professor's order a shovel and two spades were taken from the packs.

"Now follow me," he said.

He led them between two of the bare hills into a little valley or dip, which was as dry and bare as the hills.

"Now dig, Jed," he said, pointing to the center of the dip.

Jed, without a word, dug—his faith in the Professor was sublime—and the two boys helped with all their power. They threw up sand and dirt very fast, forming a conical pit, so the walls would not fall in on them, and when they had gone about ten feet Charles suddenly felt his feet grow wet.

"Why, there is water here!" he exclaimed.

"Certainly," replied Professor Longworth. "What else did you suppose we were digging for?"

They threw out dirt and sand for four or five minutes more, and then the water, fairly cool, ran in quite freely. The diggers ceased their labors and climbed out, Jed murmuring on the way:

"He is shorely the greatest man in the world. Thar can't be a doubt o' it. He looks down at the san', an' the livin' water comes up at his call."

"It is perfectly simple," said Professor Longworth. "Science accounts for everything. Man does not create something out of nothing. He merely discovers something that has existed always, and now and then by uniting several of these somethings he creates a new effect or at least one that he had not observed before. All our inventions are really discoveries. This matter of the water, however useful it may be to us, was a mere trifle in observation. All desert countries contain much water, though it may lie underground. Having that initial knowledge the question is how to reach it. That also is simple. I had observed that we were proceeding into a low part of the plain, despite the presence of hills. This dip seemed to me to be the lowest spot in all the country about, and naturally it would be a focus for underground water. As soon as we dug down far enough it began to soak and seep in in abundance. It is mere child's play, provided you have the tools with which to dig. Many a man has died of thirst, when he could have easily reached water in an hour."

"We certainly do live and learn," said Charles.

"Learn," said the Professor with emphasis. "Why the wisest of men are but in the infancy of knowledge. Ah, if I could only get a glimpse of the things that men will know ten thousand years from now!"

They filled their camp kettles, and gave the horses and mules an abundance. Then they replenished their own supply, and stayed by the "soak" until morning. But they resumed the march at earliest dawn, greatly refreshed and strengthened. Three at least had renewed confidence, knowing now that if one could not find water on the desert he might find it beneath it.

Their journey that day led into country not quite so bad. The giant cactus was abundant, and now and then they passed one or two little marshy pools, with a spear or two of grass growing about the margins. But the water was invariably alkaline, too bitter for the taste, and Jedediah Simpson expressed great disgust.

"'Pears to me," he said, "that the right place for salt water is right in the middle o' the ocean. Thar's enough out thar to last the whole world always, without sprinklin' a lot o' it 'round on the land, whar it ain't needed an' whar fresh water is needed."

Late in the afternoon they camped for the night by a sand hill, and Herbert strolled forward a little to explore. He passed around the sand hill, leaving his comrades and the animals out of sight and then, in the first faint shades of the twilight, he saw a beautiful lake surrounded by green grass and green trees, the clearest and most silvery water and the greenest grass and trees that he had ever seen, the most welcome of all sights to eyes seared with days of hot sand.

Herbert knew very well that it was a mirage, but it pleased him to look at this mystic creation as long as it would endure. Only about three minutes were allowed him, and then it floated away. There were the sand and cactus again, and, in addition, a marsh that sent forth a misty exhalation.

Herbert wondered if this marsh might not be an exception to the others, and contain fresh water instead of salt. Inspired by such a hope he walked rapidly toward it, but it proved to be further away than he had expected. It was almost a quarter of a mile across the sand before he reached the edge of the marsh and then, when he stepped forward, his feet sank suddenly. He started to turn back but his feet went down deeper.

It was not until he had made two or three efforts to leave this dismal place that looked like a marsh that Herbert realized what had happened to him. He was imbedded in a quicksand, and the more he struggled the deeper he sank. Even then fear did not strike him until he had gone far beyond his knees. But when fear did come it turned his heart as cold as ice. The twilight was spreading over the lonely world. A blood red streak in the west marked where the sun was setting. The east was already in darkness and the desolate night wind was beginning to moan. His comrades were hidden from him by the hill and the terrible sand was pulling at his legs like some subterranean monster that wished to devour him whole.

Herbert had good lungs, but at first he had been so nearly paralyzed by the suddenness and imminence of his danger that he forgot the use of his tongue. When the memory of it returned to him he shouted as few boys have ever shouted. He tried the white man's shout and then the long whining Indian cry, uncertain which would carry the further. No response came to either.

He was now down almost to the hips, and he felt as if he were held in a vise. The last strip of blood red sun was gone, and darkness was sweeping fast from east to west. He must die there in the night and alone by the most horrible of deaths. An icy perspiration broke out all over him. Then raising his voice, in one last despairing effort, he uttered a tremendous, piercing cry.

In the twilight he dimly saw a figure appear on the sand hill, and hope fluttered, but it was gone in an instant, and then hope was still. Some one of his comrades had heard vaguely, but, believing it a mere echo, had turned back.

The boy could not keep down a great groan, and then hope that had seemed dead forever fluttered once more. The dim figure reappeared upon the hill and ran rapidly toward him. Herbert began to shout again, and never ceased shouting. The figure came on swiftly, running with extraordinary speed, but would it arrive in time? Could it possibly be in time? Could anything drag him out of that terrible grasp?

The twilight was deepening, but as it came nearer Herbert saw that the running figure was that of the Professor who held in his hand some strange object that he whirled now and then about his head.

The Professor came to the edge of the marsh and stopped abruptly about twenty feet away from Herbert. Despair seized the boy again. The Professor could not reach him and save him!

"Throw up your arms!" shouted Professor Longworth in a tone so sharp that it had to be obeyed. Up went Herbert's arms until they were thrust up straight on either side of his head.

Professor Longworth's own right arm shot back, and then shot forward. Something black uncoiled itself and hissed through the air. A loop fell over Herbert's head and arms, slipped down his body and lay upon the quicksand.

"Now drop your arms!" shouted the Professor in the same tone.

Herbert involuntarily did so, and felt his waist suddenly compressed. The Professor, a little man of tempered steel, set his feet in the sand and pulled with mighty force on the lariat. Herbert ceased to sink, but he did not begin to rise. The underground dragon was still fighting for him. He felt as if he were about to be pulled into two halves, but his body still held itself together in one piece.

Another figure came running out of the dark, seized the lariat also, and, as the two made a mighty pull together, Herbert was dragged out of the dragon's mouth, across the quicksand and then upon firm ground. There he fainted.

Professor Longworth raised up the boy gently and poured some whiskey between his teeth from a little flask that he carried.

"Poor lad!" he said, "that was a terrible experience. If I hadn't heard his cry, divined the trouble at the first glimpse from the hill and gone back for the lariat he never could have been saved. Nor would he have been saved

189

then, Jedediah, if you had not come so quickly. I don't think I could have pulled him out alone."

"This is mighty cur'ous an' interestin'," said Jed, "but I don't want it to happen to any of us ag'in."

Charles also came running up at this moment, and, at the same time, Herbert opened his eyes once more. He sat up and rubbed his waist.

"Am I all in one piece?" he asked weakly.

"Safe and sound," said the Professor cheerily. "You'll have a sore body for several days, but it won't interfere with your eating and sleeping. But I would advise you not to walk into a quicksand again."

"Not if I can help it," said Herbert with so much emphasis that the others were compelled to laugh.

In a quarter of an hour he was able to limp back to camp, and Jed, on the way, said in a low tone to Charles:

"Never get into danger until you are sure the Purfessor is somewhar near. He saves us all, every time."

"Your advice is the best in the world," Charles whispered back in deep conviction.

Herbert was much shaken by his adventure. He had passed through many dangers, but none like this, which was so mysterious, almost invisible, merely the silent, deadly sucking of the sand, from which he had been rescued only by the promptness and skill of Professor Longworth, the man of infinite resource. He was also so sore around the waist that he could scarcely walk.

He was helped back to the little camp by Charles and there he sank down exhausted against a saddle.

"About done up for the time, I suppose, Herbert," said the Professor sympathetically. "It was certainly an experience that nobody would ever want to undergo a second time, and I suppose that lariat of mine nearly cut you in two. But we had to pull, Herbert, we had to pull! If we couldn't save all of you we meant to save the top half."

"An', ef it wuz me," said Jed, "I'd rather have the top half o' me saved than no half at all. Then I could eat an' talk an' cuss, an' enjoy the beauties o' the landscape, an' maybe I could hire somebody to haul me 'roun'."

Herbert smiled wanly. He knew that their jokes were intended to cheer him up, and he did feel a great joy and relief, after having achieved such a narrow escape, but his body was very tired and sore.

"You must excuse me, fellows," he said, "for making such a sour face, but I haven't had the habit yet of going down quicksands. Perhaps after I've had a lot of practice I can take it easy."

Professor Longworth smiled sympathetically.

"That was an experience sufficient to shake the strongest man that ever lived," he said. "What you need, Herbert, is complete rest to-night and you shall have it."

All the horses and mules had been tethered for the sake of safety. It was not likely that they would wander away in such a country, but, in view of the double stake of the gold and their own lives, they took no chances.

The night, as usual, after a day in the burning desert, came on dark and chill. There was but little twilight, the sun sinking suddenly followed by complete darkness, and a rising wind that was edged with cold. The abrupt transition made them all shiver, and the Professor looked rather apprehensively at Herbert.

"In his weakened state this cold may strike into his system," he said in a whisper to Charles, not wishing Herbert to hear.

"Then we must build a fire," said Charles; "I saw a lot of the dried stalks of the cactus lying about not far away, and you know how they burn."

The Professor, after a little hesitation that Charles did not notice, said:

"You are right. We must have that fire, it will save Herbert from an attack which he cannot afford at this moment to have and it will comfort and cheer all of us."

Out on the desert the chill winds moaned, as if to prove the truth of the Professor's words, and Charles and Jed hurried away for the cactus. But Professor Longworth murmured to himself, and this was the cause of that little hesitation: "I would rather not build the fire if we could do without it. It will tell where we are to those who follow us—and I am sure that we are followed."

With all this sand, darkness and moaning wind it was like a haunted desert, even to the stout soul of Professor Longworth. But Charles and Jed came quickly with an abundance of cactus stalks, light and dry. They piled them in a heap, and the Professor set fire to them with one of the precious matches. "I don't feel like working with the fire stick to-night," he said.

The blaze leaped up. Fire on the desert, where the darkness and the cold and the loneliness have been before its lighting, is a wonderful thing. It brings not heat and light alone but life itself. The four, dark and depressed before, became at once bright and joyous. Herbert, who had been resting his sore body against a saddle, rose up and spread out his fingers to the blaze.

"It's splendid," he said. "It's like a great tonic."

"I've seen many a good fire," said Jed, who hovered very near, "but I believe this beats 'em all. Jest look at the color o' them blazes, Herb! I kin see yeller an' red an' blue an' white, an' green an' purple an' some eighty or a hundred more mixed colors, the names o' which I don't know."

"So can I, Jed, every one of them," said Herbert with emphasis.

Professor Longworth laughed cheerily.

"It's your fancy," he said, "fancy induced by your feelings, but sometimes fancy is more real than fact. Did you ever hear of the great English painter of misty sunsets? A countess looking at one of the greatest of them all in his studio said, 'I never saw a sunset like that,' and he promptly replied, 'No, Madame, but don't you wish you could.' Some of us, my boys, have eyes to see and some of us have not, some of us see the colors and the brightness, but others see only the ugliness. All of which is apropos only of a little fire in the desert, and I have preached enough."

The cactus burned with a light flame, and fast, but Charles and Jed brought plenty more, and for a long time the joyous blaze of many colors was not suffered to diminish. The four human beings were not the only ones who appreciated it. The horses and mules neighed or brayed their appreciation, and drew as near as their lariats would allow, staring with great, mild, sleepy eyes at the red and yellow of the flames. The dismal wind still blew across the desert, varying its note, but always dismal, as it dipped down in the hollows or rose on the sandy crests. Now it troubled three of them not at all. Only Professor Longworth listened to its note.

They let the fire sink after a while, although a flaming bed remained much longer, and then wrapping themselves closely in their blankets they fell asleep—all save one.

Charles stretched himself at length on the sand with his elbow under his head as a pillow, and, as he slept, he dreamed. He dreamed that he saw some strange animal which was nevertheless very gentle and which came close to him, and he reached out his hand to stroke it. But the touch of its body was cold, sending a deadly chill to the heart, and he awoke as an ominous hiss sounded in his ears.

His head was still raised by the supporting elbow and coiled at his side was the cold body that he had touched, the great rattlesnake of the desert, the venomous head uplifted and ready to strike.

The paralysis of the sudden awakening, and of the terror that came with it, kept Charles still. For a few moments he could not have moved if he had wished to do so. The coals had not yet gone entirely out, and there was light enough for him to see the rattlesnake, coil on coil, and the swaying head.

Reason followed paralysis. He knew that if he moved the snake would strike and he saw no way to escape. He glanced about him in a wild, but voiceless, appeal for help, and there on the other side of the fire Professor Erasmus Darwin Longworth was propped upon his left elbow, while his right hand slowly raised a revolver to a level. It seemed to Charles that he could see the eyes speaking behind the great glasses, and they said to him so plainly that anyone might hear, "Lie still! I will save you!"

Not a nerve in Charles' body moved as he lay upon the sand. Then a pistol cracked across the fire, and the swaying head of the serpent, shot off as cleanly as if it had been cut with a knife, flew entirely over the boy, and fell three feet beyond. The coils relaxed and lay still.

Charles did not yet move. Although he knew that he was now safe the tension had been so great that he collapsed completely, body and mind.

The Professor leaped across the fire, raised his head higher and poured into his mouth fiery liquid from a little flask that he always carried in a pocket of his Norfolk jacket.

"It's all right, Charles, my lad," he said. "Mr. Rattler is in two pieces now, and cannot possibly do harm to anything. Undoubtedly he crept here for warmth, lay by your side and would not have harmed you had you not touched him as you slept. But on the whole it was well that I was awake, and that I am a good shot."

"It certainly was!" said Charles now coughing from the liquor, but revived, "but, Professor, you've saved both Herbert and me within the space of a few hours."

"Didn't I tell you," said Jedediah Simpson o' Lexin'ton, K—y, in the tone of admiration and awe that he so often used when he spoke of Professor Long-worth. "He saves us all every time."

They beat up the sand about them for more rattlesnakes, but found none, and all gradually went to sleep again, all save one.

Professor Longworth was still uneasy, but it was not about quicksands or rattlesnakes. He had liked little those attempts upon them, as they left the mountains, and he did not believe that they were immune, merely because they were now in the desert. He had always the sense of being followed. The mystery of these attacks would be explained some time or other, and per-haps it would be an explanation little to their taste.

Professor Longworth did not sleep all that night. The darkness decreased after a while before a late moon and stars. It was about three hours after midnight, when he saw what he took to be a light on the desert. But it was so faint that he was not sure. It was merely a pin point under the dusky north-ern horizon, but he had eyes of uncommon keenness, and he believed that it was a light.

He rose to his feet and gently took his powerful glasses from their place in a pack. He was careful not to disturb any of the sleepers. This was a worry that he alone must carry for the present. The glasses by the moonlight, now brilliant, distinctly showed that the bright pin point was a light. It was being moved back and forth, and, searching the horizon with the glasses, the Pro-fessor found further to the west and further away from their camp another light being moved back and forth in the same manner.

"Men signaling with torches," said he to himself, "and I believe that those who swing them are those who follow us."

Both lights went out presently, and the Professor, watching until daylight, saw nothing more. He did not speak of them to the others, nor did they know that he had not slept at all that night.

Chapter Twenty-Two - The Desert Battle

"Last stretch," said Jed, as they resumed the march over the gray sand. "I see Arizony Place comin' nearer an' nearer, but when I git thar, boys, I'm goin' to take a long rest on the grass under the shade trees. This thing o' bein' sniped at by fellers that you can't see and then plowin' 'roun' in red hot san' is gittin' to be like a man I knowed once that hired out to a stingy farmer. The farmer give him corn bread an' molasses to eat every meal. At the end o' about six months Jake, that hired man, said, 'Corn bread an' molasses are mighty fillin' but ef I was to git somethin' else to-morrow you wouldn't hear me makin' any kick.'"

When they had gone scarcely a mile after this speech the figure of a man hove in sight, a man walking, a strange figure on the desert.

"Now who under the sun can that be!" exclaimed Jed. "This is shorely mighty cur'ous an' interestin'!"

The Professor took his field glasses from a pack and looked long and earnestly at the advancing figure. When he put it down his eyes snapped.

"There is something familiar about the man who is approaching us," he said, "but I am not sure. I will say nothing until he reaches us."

The man came directly toward the party, but they saw as he came near that he was a forlorn enough figure. The remains of a pith helmet, resembling that worn by the Professor, were jammed down upon his head, his clothing was unkempt and in rags, and his shoes were almost soleless. He was tall and thin with a hawk nose.

"Professor Cruikshank!" said Professor Longworth in no welcoming tones.

"Yes, it is I, Professor Longworth," said Cruikshank, "and necessity compels me to come to you for help. I assure you that it is as bitter to me as it is unpleasant to you. But my guide and servant deserted me in the mountains, taking my horses with them, and leaving me to starve. I have lived on roots, nuts and a few stores that they did not take. I had expected to die alone on the desert, until I caught sight of your party to-day, and have managed to reach you, as you see. Surely, Professor Longworth, you will help a brother scholar!"

"Certainly," said Professor Longworth, although his voice was still cold. "Jed, food and water at once."

Cruikshank ate and drank eagerly, and the two boys were touched with pity. He carried neither baggage nor rifle, saying that his treacherous servants had stripped him of both, and he bore all the appearance of a man who had known the last stages of despair.

"You will let me go with you?" he said.

"Of course," replied Professor Longworth, but still coldly. "We could not repel any man under such conditions. We are on the way to Phoenix."

"That will serve me well enough," said Cruikshank with a deep, satisfied sigh. "Professor Longworth, we have been rivals but not, I hope, enemies. Now we are not even rivals. I confess that I have failed completely in my expedition, while you to all appearances have been highly successful. I see your train is loaded down with specimens."

"Yes," said Professor Longworth dryly, "I have all these bags filled with valuable Arizona rock, but I cannot describe it to you. We are scientific men,

Professor Cruikshank, and you understand. It is a secret that I must keep, until I surprise the world with it."

Professor Cruikshank laughed gayly.

"I understand thoroughly," he said. "It is your discovery, Professor Long-worth, and I have no right to the remotest share in it. Beaten as I am and owing my life to you as I do, I should be a pretty poor specimen indeed if I tried to pry into your secret."

Professor Longworth regarded him with more approval. Yet the situation remained embarrassing. Here was a fifth man, whom they could not drop, but who could have no share whatever in their success. He would be with them but not of them. They must make the best of it, and Jed and the two lads, taking the Professor's hint, spoke of the bags as containing Arizona rock.

They resumed their march southward. The desert deepened again. Its glare burned their eyes and hot winds swept across it, scorching their faces. But Professor Cruikshank was cheerful, even joyous. He showed all the exhilaration natural to a man rescued from imminent death, and his flow of spirits pleased the two lads.

"It is obvious that the Professor doesn't like him," thought Charles, "but that may be due to scientific rivalry."

Their progress now was much slower. The coppery sun was just overhead and the sand shimmered in the heat waves.

Back to Charles came once more the chant of Ananias Brown:

"O'er the measureless range where rarely change
The swart gray plains, so weird and strange,
Treeless and streamless and wondrous still."

They stopped at noon and hovered in the lee of the animals for a little shade, but wandering breezes blew the sand in their faces and it scorched like hot ashes.

"I think we can reach a bit of an oasis by night," said the Professor meditatively. "I made notes on my journey northward and I do not think I am mistaken in the spot. There is a little water, a few yuccas and some grass for the animals."

"Then that's the place for me," said Herbert. "Oh, weren't those beautiful mountains that we left behind? And wasn't that a beautiful river? And the trees and the grass on the plateau, was ever anything finer?"

The others laughed despite themselves at Herbert's heartfelt words.

"These lads were foolish enough to venture on a prospecting tour and I picked them up last autumn," said Professor Longworth to Professor Cruikshank.

"Fine fellows," said Professor Cruikshank.

Toward night they reached the oasis, merely a valley or depression, sheltered by high hills of rock jutting like bare ribs from the desert. The sand had blown in ridges against the rock, but in the center of the valley was a pool of water thirty or forty feet across and nearly a foot deep formed by a little stream which flowed out of the rock at one end and into it again at the other. It was surrounded by thin but succulent grass and a few trees grew here and there.

It was a glorious sight to the scorched and thirsty travelers as they entered it. The horses, scenting water, quickened their pace. The mules lifted up their heads, emitting raucous but triumphant brays and all rushed forward. Herbert threw up his battered old hat and with a cry of joy followed horses and mules. The others came on more sedately

"Now shorely this is temptin'," said Jed. "We've got springs all over Kentucky an' they're pure an' cold, but I don't know when I ever saw water that looks better than this."

Flocks of wild fowl whirred away as the intruders dashed to the water, and Charles and Jed shot a pair of fat fellows, a species of duck, which they roasted and found very good. The water was comparatively cool and fresh, and they felt as if they had reached a very pleasant haven.

"Ours is really a very small desert as I told you boys the other day," said the Professor, while Jed was cooking over a fire of sticks, "and in quality it is by no means so bad as those mighty deserts of the Old World, but a man can die in it of heat and thirst."

"Which might have been my fate had I continued the attempt to cross it alone," said Professor Cruikshank, looking afar at the sands and shuddering.

"You are familiar with the deserts of Asia and Africa, are you not, Professor Cruikshank?" said Professor Longworth.

"I have traveled in them somewhat," replied Professor Cruikshank modestly.

"You represented some university, I suppose? I believe you told me the name, did you not?"

Professor Cruikshank shook his head and smiled.

"Let my poor little university and my modest degrees rest in obscurity," he said. "A beaten man will say little about himself. I've failed so utterly, Professor Longworth, that I feel like hiding permanently somewhere here in the west."

Professor Longworth turned away with an impatient little movement to the roast duck that Jed was handing to him. He ate with a good appetite, but for some time he had less to say than any of the others. Not so, Professor Cruikshank, who chatted agreeably about the west with which he seemed to be well acquainted.

"A wonderful country! A wonderful country!" he said. "It's bold and picturesque in its features and infinite in its variety!"

"That's so," said Charles. "I was born in it, and I love it."

"I wasn't born in it," said Herbert, "but I've learned to love it, too."

"Youth is adaptable," said Professor Cruikshank benevolently, stretching his long, thin figure comfortably on the grass. Herbert at that moment rather liked him. "Adaptable" seemed to be the very word for Professor Cruikshank himself. Certainly he had fallen in easily with their ways, and already he had been helpful in many details. He assisted Jed in collecting sticks for the fire, showed considerable knowledge also of cooking and behaved on the whole like an experienced desert traveler.

"Isn't this a pretty pickle for a scientist," he said with a faint laugh. "I started into northern Arizona with the intention of making wonderful discoveries. I was going to surpass everybody, even so experienced and famous a man as Professor Longworth here, and lo! here I am, worse stripped than the man who fell among thieves, although in one respect I am luckier than he, as he was picked up by only one good Samaritan, while four have taken me in charge."

He smiled very agreeably, and Herbert's heart warmed again toward him. The situation was one to promote good feeling. After the dust, heat and glare of day in the desert the little oasis was a haven, and the sight of water, real fresh water, a trickling stream of which you could drink and a wide pool in which you could bathe, was refreshing to soul and sense alike. Herbert understood now what was meant by the "shadow of a great rock in a weary land."

All had taken a dip in the pool after supper, and now they were lying comfortably by the dying coals of the fire on which Jed had cooked their supper. The animals cropped the grass at the water's edge and the sacks of "specimens" were heaped up only four or five feet away. The night was cool, even crisp, and Jed's stars flamed in the blue. It was a time of rest for man and beast, a time of peace and soothing quiet.

Professor Erasmus Darwin Longworth lay near the fire, his enormous pith helmet on his head, his eyes concealed behind his great glasses. The Professor did not move or speak, but he was neither asleep nor dreaming. He was still examining his beaten rival, Professor Cruikshank, with minute care. Had he ever seen him before at any meeting of any learned society? What was his reputation? What his specialty? What letters in capitals did he have a right to write after his name? He could not recall, and he was sorely vexed and troubled in spirit. His eyes wandered again to the two lads, so like the sons, whom he did not have, but whom he could wish to have. His weight of responsibility grew heavier, because the Professor did not forget the mysterious foes who had come on nights before and who might come again.

The talk died down. The night grew colder. The Milky Way streamed a brilliant banner across the immeasurable heavens, and Jed's stars wheeled and danced in their old places, vast cores of infinite light. Some of the wild fowl, defying man and forgetful of the slaughtered two, came back to the pool and were swimming peacefully near the farther shore.

"To bed! To bed!" said the Professor. "To-morrow's march is likelier to be hotter and dustier than to-day's, and we shall need all the rest that we can get."

Professor Longworth arranged the places in a row before the bed of coals, and that of Professor Cruikshank was in the center. It was Jed's time to take the first watch and the others, rolling themselves in their blankets and using saddles for pillows, closed their eyes. Shortly after midnight, the usual turn of the watch, Charles relieved Jed, and, in order that he might get a better view, he took a seat on the rock outcrop above the camp. There he could see everything in the glen, and also far upon the desert.

Charles had his blanket draped about his shoulders, as the chill was sharp in the night air, and he felt more lonely here than in the mountains. There were no wise white peaks to nod to him in a gossipy way, no great forest to give back a pleasant song under the touch of the wind. Only the vast rolling gray desert lay before him, still and dead. He looked down at the little oasis, and he could count the recumbent forms—his three comrades, good and true, and the stranger who had come to them for help.

Then he looked from the oasis and up at the stars. Now he shared Jed's admiration. The skies were of an exquisite, even poignant, beauty. Constellation after constellation leaped forth and he tried to make out the fanciful figures by which astronomers called them.

The boy sat motionless on the rock. Nothing stirred in the glen below. He could not see that any of the recumbent forms had moved a single inch. Far out a coyote, the mean, slinking wolf of the desert, howled. It was a lone, weird sound, a single note breaking all the vast voiceless void, and Charles gathered himself a little closer together. He felt cold, but as if his nerves rather than his body were chilled. He glanced again at the recumbent forms. They were still motionless, and the fire had gone completely out, like a spark of life departing.

The coyote howled again, and now his note was much nearer, inexpressibly mournful, and coming back in plaintive echoes from the desert. Charles saw a dark form skulking between two swells and he would have taken a shot at that miserable, haunting creature had it not been for the fear of alarming his comrades.

He glanced once more at the glen and the sleepers. Then he started and looked more closely. One of the recumbent forms had certainly moved! It was moving now! It was long, thin, sinuous, like a crawling serpent, and that hideous simile came to Charles as it slid over the ground, bending its form to fit every undulation. He stared like the bird, fascinated, and as he stared the mournful howl of the coyote came again, and yet nearer. The figure sprang noiselessly to its feet and made a rush for the animals. At that moment there was a shout and a shot and Professor Longworth leaped up, smoking rifle in hand. The shout and shot were followed almost instantly by another shot, from a revolver, hitherto hidden, and a bullet whistled by Charles' head.

Professor Cruikshank darted away from the animals, ran swiftly among the pines and was lost to view just as Charles fired at him in return. The coyote howled no more, but there was a patter of rifle shots from the swell, as Charles leaped down into the glen and rejoined his comrades.

Professor Longworth was in a rage. His pith helmet had fallen off, and his great, shining bald dome was revealed. It seemed to Charles that even the top of his head was flushed in the moonlight.

"The scoundrel! The unutterable scoundrel! The fraud!" cried the Professor. "I always believed he was a fraud, and he pretending to be a learned man with university degrees! Ah, Charles, while you were watching for enemies without I was watching for treachery here in our own camp and I saw it! I believe I missed him, but now we know where we stand! It's somebody wanting our gold! I don't know who they are, but that's what they're after!"

"Down, Professor! Down!" suddenly exclaimed Charles, dragging him from his feet. He was just in time. The bullet passed where the Professor's body had been, but Jed firing from behind his saddle at the flash, avenged the Professor's dignity. A cry answered the shot and there was the sound of a fall. Shots replied to shots, and the desert battle was on.

"Keep down, everybody!" cried Charles.

His advice was full of wisdom, and they obeyed it, flattening themselves upon the earth and pulling the saddles in front of them, as Jed had already done. Here they had an advantage. They were in the darkness, while their enemies, whoever they might be, would be in silhouette, the moment they appeared on the stone outcrop at the brink of the oasis.

The shots ceased and silence, tense and painful, followed.

"Is anybody hurt?" whispered the Professor.

"All right," responded everyone.

Suddenly a shot was fired, and a fierce, wild scream of pain arose. A horse stamped, reared, and breaking its tether, ran to the other side of the oasis and then back again.

"Poor brute," said the Professor. "I wish I could avenge that shot for him!"

"Mebbe you'll git the chance," said Jed. "All this is mighty cur'ous an' interestin', an' I'm a long ways from seein' to the bottom o' it, but it 'pears to me that things have come to a head. Did you git him, Charlie?"

Charles had fired suddenly at a head that appeared on the stony rim.

"I don't know," he replied, "but I hope so"—the fury of battle was in him.

"Beyond a doubt they are after our gold," said the Professor. "Therefore we will use it as a defense against them. Here, lads, help me."

With much labor they formed a circle of the thirty bags of gold, piecing it out with the saddles, and then lay close to the earth inside. It was a fair sort of fortification, and the Professor smiled in the dark.

"We're pretty comfortable here," he said. "Water and food are at hand and we can stand a siege better than can the besiegers who lie on the thirsty desert."

They lay perfectly still for a long time. The wounded horse ceased to complain, and the others sank to rest again. The heavens remained as brilliant as ever, the stars dancing, as if looking down with intent interest at the desert combat. A figure appeared in a crevice of the rocky outcrop, but the sharp eyes of Jed were upon it and he fired. The body rolled down into the oasis and lay still. Herbert shuddered, but in a moment recovered himself. Here in the lone desert there could be no other way.

"One's accounted for," said the Professor. "One enemy the less."

Then came the heavy silence again. The waiting and watching got terribly upon Herbert's nerves. He wished they would make a rush, do anything that would force action, but he must lie still, cramped and painful, and see what was not. He created phantoms. He saw figures that he knew were mere fancy climbing down the stony outcrop, and he heard sounds where he knew sound there was none.

Presently all heard the faint report of a distant shot, and this Herbert knew was real.

"Now what under the sun can be that?" exclaimed Jed. "Can they be fightin' among theirselves. It is shorely mighty cur'ous an' interestin'!"

The Professor was stirred by the same wonder, but he said nothing.

"Professor," said Charles, "I'm going to creep into that little bunch of pines. I think it likely that they'll make a rush soon and if I can sting 'em on the flank, that is from an unexpected quarter, it will help greatly."

"Yes," said the Professor, "it's good military tactics."

Charles slipped away into the bunch of pines, and as he reached their deep shade, he heard that faint rifle shot again, and this time it was followed by a cry from above. Charles' wonder increased. Could these unknown men be really at war with one another?

But he lay close now in the shelter of the clustering pines, and watched the stony outcrop at every point of the circle. He, too, like Herbert, felt the influence of fancy. The rough stony ribs took on strange fantastic shapes. He heard many uncanny sounds, and his blood was continually in a quiver, but his nerves remained steady, and he waited, motionless.

Far toward morning Charles saw sinuous forms slip over the outcrop. At the same instant, one of the figures threw up its hand and rolled down with the groan. Over the plain came for the third time the echo of the distant rifle shot. But Charles had no time to think of it now, because the rush had come. He fired at the first of the invaders and three shots also flashed from the ring of gold. Two men fell and the three who were left hesitated. As they hesitated Jed's fatal bullet cut one of them down and the other two ran.

Charles leaped to his feet, and one of the fugitives came directly upon him. It was Cruikshank, pistol in hand, and they stood eye to eye a moment. The man's face was no longer smiling. It was streaked by rage, despair and every evil passion. Charles' rifle was unloaded now, and the man raised his pistol. The boy was at his mercy, but a rifle cracked at the rim of the oasis, the pistol dropped from the man's hand, and his tall, thin figure, swaying first, fell to the earth. Over the stony rim appeared the dark face of Gray Wolf, the

Apache, the distant marksman. He had paid his debt when the price was needed most, and Charles understood.

Gray Wolf lingered there only a few moments, making a significant gesture, and then he was gone. Out on the desert, the last survivor of the invading band, was galloping his pony for life.

Charles turned back to the oasis. His comrades, unhurt, were looking down at Cruikshank, whose face was dark with pain, and a feeling that was a compound of rage and despair. The others who had fallen in the rush lay quite still and would never move again. The man raised himself slowly, and but a little on his elbow.

"You win, Professor," he said, looking up at Professor Longworth. "I never fooled you for a minute, and I know it. I might have made others think that I was a great scientist, but not you. Yet I am or was an educated man."

"Who are you?" asked the Professor. There was a certain pity in his eyes as he looked down, because he knew that the man would not live five minutes longer.

"I? I'm Stephen Earp, leader of the Earp gang, bully boys in their time, but wiped out now by you and some sneaking enemy we didn't see."

The man's face contracted and they waited for him to speak again, and he spoke, but more slowly and with greater effort.

"I suppose—a man had best tell—when he's about to take the long trip— We were after your gold. It was I—who tried to tear his secret from Ananias Brown—you remember the black marks in his palms. I'd been spying on you a long time in the canyon—and—we waited for you to bring it out—for us— but we lose."

He closed his eyes and, when they waited for him to say more, they saw that he was dead. They buried him there, and the desert hid him and his real identity forever.

On the march the next day Charles told of Gray Wolf.

"It was a curious deed," said the Professor thoughtfully. "They say that the Apache has no gratitude, but this would prove to the contrary. Still he may have been spurred on by the love of battle, and his ability to lie in comparative safety and shoot the Earps while they were besieging us. But it would be a poor business on our part to question his motives."

Chapter Twenty-Three - The Last Fight

As they marched Professor Longworth reverted to the subject of Gray Wolf and the Apaches.

"As I said before," he remarked, "Gray Wolf is sure to leave us alone, nor is it likely that we will suffer anything from the warriors of his band. As I take it, he will lead them further north deep into the mountains, but, unfortunately, there are different divisions or tribes of the Apaches. Young as you boys are, you are veterans in danger now, and I need not conceal from you that all of the Apaches are in a highly disturbed and restless state. I wish that we were entirely clear of their country."

"An' we can't march so fast, havin' our gold," said Jed, "nor could we leave it ef we was in danger."

"That is so," said the Professor. "Riches bring responsibilities in the desert as well as in the city."

Charles saw very clearly that their leader was troubled, but he did not share the Professor's anxiety. It seemed to him that they had triumphed over so much that they could not fail now. They had escaped the first attack of the Apaches, they had found a home in the canyon, they had discovered the lost gold, they had beaten off the Indian invasion, and finally they had repelled and annihilated Earp and his band.

Charles did not now believe failure possible, and he hummed happily to himself as they rode on over the plain. He was building castles in the air and Herbert, his comrade, was doing the same. They had left the oasis and were upon the sand once more, but all their water bottles were filled and animals and human beings alike felt strong and fresh.

It was remarkable how quickly the oasis disappeared from sight. After riding a half hour they could not see a trace. The swells shut it out and on all sides of them waved the desert, bleak and bare, save for a lonesome cactus now and then. No wind blew that morning and the sand was at rest, but the sun grew very hot, and tongues and throats became parched again. The still close air enveloped them like a steaming blanket, but Charles was not anxious for the wind to rise as he knew that it would cut with a burning edge.

They saw some piñons in a little hollow shortly after the noon hour and they camped in their partial shade. The trees were of fairly good growth, but there was not a drop of water in the hollow.

"We could probably get water by digging," said Professor Longworth. "It seeps into this depression and nourishes the roots of the trees. It is amazing how far trees will send down their roots in the desert in search of the fluid which is life to all things. I confess that I should like to see water myself, but we do not have time to dig for it."

They gave a part of the precious store of water to the horses and mules, and they would have spent all the remainder of the day among the piñons, traveling in the coolness of the night, but Professor Longworth was uneasy. He was anxious to be once more on the road to Phoenix, and he hurried them away.

They were aided in the afternoon by faint, drifting clouds, not clouds that promised rain, but clouds that mitigated somewhat the fierceness of the sun. It was a wonderful thing to have a sky which by a stretch of the imagination could be called gray, and the spirits of the boys rose again.

"I know it isn't going to rain," said Charles, "but I like to imagine it raining. It just couldn't rain too hard for me. I'd like to turn my face up to it and let it beat on it with forty horsepower. I'd like to feel it going right through my clothes and wetting every inch of me."

"What's the use of thinkin' of things that ain't goin' to happen?" said Jed. "It makes you like the feller in the old story who was burnin' up with thirst, who always saw water just before him, but who could never quite reach it."

"Guess you're right, Jed," said Charles with a laugh, "and I won't think any more about rain."

The Professor took out his powerful glasses and examined the whole circle of the horizon with minute care. He saw nothing but the ridges of sand, the lonesome cactus, and now and then the ragged and ugly yucca. He felt relief, but his apprehension would not disappear wholly, and he still urged forward the little troop. When night came on they were in the open desert, and they traveled over two hours after dark before they made camp.

The night was cold and after eating supper they wrapped themselves in their blankets. The horses and mules were tied together, and the sacks of treasure lay on the ground in the center of the group. They did not arrange any watch as they were sure that the animals would give an alarm if the enemy attempted to approach.

Charles was very tired from the long hours of riding over the monotonous desert, but he did not go to sleep. He was lying on the southern edge of the little camp. The night was very still. The weary horses and mules did not stir. The boy was warm and snug in his blankets, but the anxiety of the Professor, so obvious in the day, had been communicated to him now. He told himself that he was foolish, but after all the others were asleep he saw a faint light in the south.

The light was so tiny that he lost it two or three times, and only by following the line of the horizon could he find it again. Then he thought it was some manifestation of nature, something with which man had nothing to do, but the light increased and glowed. He gently awoke the Professor and the two watched the light.

It seemed to be two or three miles away, and while at first it was apparently level with the earth it gradually rose and stood out clear of the desert, burning now with a steady radiance. Then Charles knew that human hands were at work.

"Apaches?" he said in a whisper.

"I fear so," said Professor Longworth.

"Look!" said Charles.

The light suddenly began to whirl swiftly. Charles and the Professor watched it intently for a full minute, and then when the boy's eyes shifted away he uttered a deep:

"Ah!"

He saw on the western horizon another light whirling in a manner exactly like that of the first. The Professor also looked.

"Apaches!" he said. "There cannot be any doubt of it. They are signaling to one another, and it is safe to say that their signals are about us. I feared this, my lad, I feared it!"

"It seems that they are across our path," said Charles.

"Yes, they are between us and Phoenix. We might try to steal past them in the night, but in the morning they would surely see us on the open plain. It is likely, too, that their numbers are too great for us to face. It is some band or division of the tribe to which Gray Wolf does not belong."

"Then what are we to do?"

"We must go north again. I have not seen all of Arizona, but I have studied it thoroughly from maps, and we ought to find low mountains or at least hills, about fifty miles due north. We might get away from the Apaches there, or if we were cornered we should have a far better chance for a successful defense."

"Then it would be wise to start at once?"

"Undoubtedly. Neither we nor our animals have had the rest that we need, but we cannot linger here with the Apaches advancing upon us. It is likely that some wandering warrior has seen us or our trail, and has taken the word to the bands."

They awoke Herbert and Jed, saddled or loaded their animals and started due north. They saw the signals once more from the crest of a swell, but after that came complete darkness and silence. All four were anxious. They recognized the full danger to be expected from a band of mounted Apaches, and they urged on the tired animals in every possible way. For a long time no one spoke, and then it was Jed giving utterance to his woe.

"I can't see what fun it is to the Apaches to drive us back toward the mountains," he said.

"That is not what they seek," said the Professor grimly. "It's scalps that they are after and they enjoy the taking of them."

Jed took off his hat and felt uneasily of the top of his head.

"An' my hair is long an' thick, too," he said. "I used to be proud of it."

"Just think what a fine scalp you can furnish, Jed," said Herbert.

But it was rather grim jesting, and they went no further. The horses were beginning to stumble through weariness and they stopped a while. The wind had risen and was sending the fine sand in their faces. But they did not mind it. Rather they rejoiced. The wind would blow their trail away, and the Apaches must depend upon their sight. Their chance of escape increased with the rising of the wind.

They rested an hour. Then the cold began to have an effect upon their relaxed frames and they started anew. They did not stop again before dawn, which came on swiftly, bright and hot.

As the clear light poured down, the boys saw the loom of the hills in the north and it was a grateful sight, but when they reached the crest of a swell, the Professor took forth his glasses and turned his whole attention to the south. Finally he closed the glasses and uttered an impatient little exclamation. The boy understood.

"They are there?" he said.

"Yes," replied the Professor. "I had hoped that we had shaken them off in the darkness, but I can make out indistinctly the figures of a group, twenty-five or thirty in number and yet many miles away. Nevertheless they are coming toward us."

The four looked anxiously at one another. The blown sand had hid their trail, but the Apaches, the most cruel of all Indians, had followed nevertheless. The four did not now have their strong cliff dwelling, from which they could fight as from a fort. They stood only in an open plain among the shifting sands and under a merciless sun. Yet there was one possible avenue. They still saw the faint outline of hills in the north, and there they might find shelter. Professor Longworth had reckoned well, when he changed their course in the night.

"We must continue our flight toward the north," said the Professor earnestly. "We have a long lead and although our animals are tired we may reach a refuge, some vantage point that will reduce the odds against us."

Jedediah Simpson said nothing. Without the aid of the powerful glasses he could not see the Apaches, but he knew well enough from what the Professor had said that they were there, and a great rage mounted in his brain. A patient and enduring man, his limit had been reached. He wanted to be let alone. He could not see why so many men sought his life. At last it had flicked his nerves on the raw and he was growing very dangerous. He ran his hand along the steel barrel of his rifle and felt lovingly of the trigger. Since these Apaches were so anxious to overtake them let them do it. He and his comrades would make them regret it. He stared back at the horizon of sand and saw nothing there, but his anger continued to mount just as if he had seen.

They sought to urge the animals to greater speed, but the mules rebelled so vigorously that they dropped into a walk again. Charles thought it was just as well, as they were bound in any event to save their strength, and perhaps they would need it most for a final spurt.

The two boys looked anxiously toward the hills. They wished to see them come nearer. They wished to see their outlines appear. They were like shipwrecked sailors pulling desperately in an open boat for land. But the hills seemed to be as far away as ever. Only the experienced eye could have told them from banks of clouds lying low. The fugitive four fell now into silence. Again the sun poured down dazzling beams, every one tipped with fire. The earth swam in a red glare, and they pulled their hats low to protect their eyes from the blaze. Some of the horses began to pant, and, at times, the riders leaped down and ran by the side of them. The light wind powdered them all, human beings and animals alike, with the dust of the desert.

Charles looked back again and again, but saw nothing. An ordinary traveler would have said that there was no danger, he would have said that the desert was empty of everything save themselves, but Charles knew better. Professor Longworth was not one who would make a mistake. His mind always worked with scientific accuracy, and when he said that he saw the Apaches, he saw them.

They toiled on for an hour. Higher and higher went the sun and deeper and deeper grew the glare. They were wet with perspiration, and the flame seemed to burn into their brains. Their pace sank to a walk. The animals could do no more. At last when they reached the summit of a swell higher than the rest they perceived tiny figures like jumping-jacks on the southern horizon. These figures—and they now saw that the Professor's higher estimate of thirty was none too great—moved ludicrously, like manikins directed by a human hand. But it was only the effect of the great distance. They were Apaches, and they were coming with their minds full of the most terrible purpose that can animate human beings. The four looked at one another and every one read the minds of all the rest.

"They will overtake us before we can reach the hills," said Charles.

"They will," said Professor Longworth, who was feeling in the breast pocket of his Norfolk jacket, "but if my memory is right something else will serve us. As I have told you before I have very complete small-scale maps of Arizona, and I always carry them next to me in an inside pocket."

He drew forth a map, looked at it, and cried aloud exultingly.

"My memory was right," he said. "Pardon me if I claim that it always is. Directly ahead of us and about five miles away is a most remarkable waterhole, one that has been used from time immemorial by Indians, and later also by settlers and gold hunters. Its formation is peculiar, and it may make a better fort for us than any that we could find in the hills. It is queer that I did not recall it earlier."

"About five miles did you say?" asked Charles.

"Well," replied the Professor, speaking with scientific caution, "it might be near six or just a little over four, but I think that five is a better and, in fact, a just approximation."

"Then," said Charles, "the Apaches cannot possibly overtake us before we get there."

"No, they are yet several miles behind. We will even have time to make certain useful dispositions before they come up."

"An' then," said Jedediah Simpson, a triumphant note appearing in his voice, "we'll give 'em Hail Columby, happy lan'. Let 'em come on. I'm tired of bein' chased, Purfessor! I tell you I'm tired of it, an' I feel as if I could lay down on the sand in some snug, sheltered place, an' be jest as happy as a mockin' bird, shootin' at Apaches all day long."

"Jedediah," reproved the Professor, "I'm sorry to see you showing such sanguinary instincts. Have I been teaching you the beauties of science and learning all these years to see you show under pressure only the instincts of a man-killer? To fight well in self-defense is a good and great thing, but to revel in battle merely for its own sake is a reversal to the primeval. I fear greatly, Jedediah, that in spite of all my teaching you are a throw-back."

"But these Apaches have made me mad, Purfessor," said Jed in a tone of apology. "How can you love them that chase you, hot fur your scalps?"

"I will overlook it this time, Jedediah," said Professor Longworth forgivingly. "I will admit that the Apaches act in a most irritating manner, and perhaps you also suffered from a touch of the sun. But do not make another such sanguinary display."

Jedediah made no further protest, but his blood nevertheless was yet hot. Once more he lovingly stroked the steel barrel of his rifle, which was hot also from that touch of sun, and meditated over what he would do when the chance came. The Professor consulted his map a second time, put it back in his pocket with a sigh of satisfaction, and they quickened their pace. When they mounted the next crest he used his glasses again, but now he looked toward the north instead of the south. When he returned them to their case, he uttered a second sigh of satisfaction.

"I see the water-hole," he said. "I can mark it by the trees about it. It is not more than three miles ahead, and now we shall have time to take the precautions that I had in mind before the Apaches arrive."

A mile further and they saw with the naked eye the clump of trees standing out like a dot on the plain, but in a slight hollow. Charles inferred that the upshoot of water there was seepage from the distant hills or mountains.

The animals presently scented the water, neighed with pleasure and hastened their pace. Jedediah Simpson also felt pleasure, but his martial instincts were yet strong. He hoped that the Apaches would not cease coming, and that they would attack. He looked back to see if he might not get a shot at long range. But the distance was far too great. He, too, sighed. But the emotion was far different from that which had caused the sigh of Professor Longworth.

Charles was carefully examining the oasis as they rode up. It was unlike the one from which they had fought the Earps. He saw a circular valley or dip, several hundred yards across. Here the sands of the desert gave way to rocks, and in the center of the valley grew a close ring of oaks and aspens, perhaps thirty yards across. The boy knew that the water was within the ring of trees, and the animals knew it, too, as despite their weariness they broke into a trot, headed straight for the oaks and aspens.

The riders sprang down and halted the animals at the trees. Charles, pressing forward, passed among the trees and looked down at the water-hole. The ground dropped away gradually for a descent of eight or ten feet to a tiny circular plain covered with deep, rich and very green grass. In the very center of this was a well-like, conical opening a dozen feet deep, at the bottom of which flowed a strong stream of clear, cold water.

"It is all that I had heard," said Professor Longworth with deep satisfaction. "Here we have water, grass for our horses, breastworks of solid rock, and it will be strange if four good shots like ourselves, armed with such improved rifles as ours cannot hold back thirty Apaches."

They quickly led the horses among the trees which grew so closely that they were compelled to push through, and then down the incline upon the grass where they turned them loose, having previously unloaded the sacks of treasure and put them near the well. All this did not consume five minutes, and then the Professor and Jed turned back to the trees, rifle in hand.

"Charles," called back Professor Longworth, "you go down to the water, but be sure you do not drink much at first. Just a little for yourself and Herbert. Then take the two tin pails from the pack and bring it up for the horses and mules, just the same. Don't give them much for a while. No matter how strong the temptation, do exactly what I say."

Charles promised faithfully, but already he was feeling the temptation. He and his comrade were looking over the edge of the natural well at the flowing water below. The trees, of unusual height and size for that region, made a deep shade within the little green glen. The water, ten feet below, gurgled a cool invitation and dancing shadows from the trees fell across its surface.

Charles took a tin cup and climbed down. The sloping walls were of solid rock with many projections and it was an easy task. The nearer he came to it the better the water looked. It was absolutely clear and he knew that it was cold. He dipped with the cup, and his hand went under at the same time. The water, so cool after the burning heat of the desert, sent a delicious thrill through every vein. He would take a little drink, and then hand another up to his waiting comrade.

But he put away that temptation also. He did not touch the water to his lips, but climbing a little way up the side, extended the cup to Herbert.

"No, you drink first," said the younger boy who was lying down with his head over the edge of the well.

"Your time, Herbert! No foolishness! Hurry up or I'll drop it, and we can't afford to waste time!" said Charles.

Herbert drank, draining the cup to the last drop, and sighing because there was no more. When he passed the cup back to Charles he said:

"A little more of that, old fellow, after you've had your drink. It's certainly the finest water that ever flowed."

"Not another drop do you get for a long time," said Charles sternly. "It's not good for you, young man, and I'm going to teach you self-control."

He drank his own cup of water slowly, and then had a fierce desire for more. The first seemed only a taste, and it would be so easy to take a second cup. But with a fierce effort he triumphed over self, and calling loudly for a pail, began to pass water to the animals which were now crowding so closely to the well that it was all Herbert could do to keep one or another of them from falling in. They allowed a pail for each, and then taking another small drink for themselves hurried with a filled pail to the oaks, where the Professor and Jed sat watching, rifles across their knees.

"Have you obeyed my instructions?" asked Professor Longworth severely.

"I have," replied Charles. "We have not had much more than a taste. I could drink every drop in that pail without stopping."

"But you have been tempted?"

"Terribly."

The Professor laughed.

"I believe you," he said, "and, after Jedediah and I have each taken a drink, you and Herbert can have another. Now, Jedediah, you drink first and I will tell you when to stop."

Jed took the pail and drank eagerly. As the cold fluid trickled deliciously down his throat and sent a pleasant thrill through every nerve and sinew much of his sanguinary impulse departed. He had a more kindly feeling toward the whole human race, and he would have been glad for the sake of peace and good will if the Apaches had gone away. It was wonderful water, and the more he drank of it the better he liked it. He lifted the pail higher and higher.

"Jedediah, how dare you! And you a man of mature age! After the years of careful training that I have given you to show so little self-restraint! If you drink more of that water you will swell up and die miserably!"

He snatched the pail from the man's hand and faced him sternly. Jed quailed before those flashing eyes.

"I did fergit, Purfessor," he said humbly. "I was tempted an' I was fallin'."

"I will forgive you this time," said Professor Longworth, "but see that you are always a man hereafter. Look at me and imitate my example."

He drank moderately and allowed Charles and Herbert another small drink apiece. Then he set the pail, still half full, between two trees and said sternly:

"It will remain there until I say when it can be touched again. Now we will devote our attention to the Apaches, a factor with whom we must reckon."

The Indians were now within a mile of the water-hole, although they looked much nearer in the clear sunlight. They were coming on rather slowly, in a loose line that extended for a hundred yards or more across the plain. Professor Longworth handed his glasses to Charles, and when the boy studied the Apaches through them, he shuddered.

The powerful glasses brought the Indians close up to him. He saw their horribly painted cheeks, their cruel eyes, their long, coarse, black hair, and their naked bodies, covered with strange designs. He knew that they would be absolutely merciless. There was no Gray Wolf among them. He thanked God for the natural fortification of the water hole, and for the improved weapons they carried.

"Not a pretty sight," said Professor Longworth dryly, as the boy handed back the glasses. "Now I think, Master Charles and Master Herbert, and you, Jedediah, that we shall have a trial of patience. The Apaches regard us as trapped, and, having nothing but time at their disposal, they will play with the rat in their trap, but at a safe distance."

The Professor made no mistake. The Apaches halted presently and dismounted. Most of them stood in the apology for shade offered by some yuccas and mesquite, but Charles judged that the sun annoyed them but little. Children of the heat, sand and cactus, it was only a pleasant summer day for them.

"I wish they'd come on an' make a clean stand-up fight of it like men," said Jed, whose martial ardor was rising again, "'stead o' fooling about, trying to wear out a body's patience."

"I am afraid, Jedediah, that they will have little respect for your wishes," said Professor Longworth. "They probably know exactly what you want, and that is just exactly what they will not do."

"Guess you're right, but say, Purfessor, ain't it time fur me to take another drink?"

"A little one, Jedediah, only a little one, and beware! My eye will be upon you."

Jed drank, but this time restrained himself, and put the pail back at the proper time. The Apaches, after lolling a while, detached themselves into three bodies. One remained under the yuccas and mesquite and the other two filed off, one to the right and the other to the left. Each body contained about ten warriors. Professor Longworth rapidly formed his plan of defense.

"I will watch the division on the right," he said. "Jedediah will take the one on the left and you two boys will devote your attention to the center, which remains there under the bushes. We have every advantage except numbers. We can stand in excellent shelter behind the trees and the slope. The Apaches can approach us only on the open plain, where they will have no shelter at all. We hold the water and the grass for our horses, while they have neither. If we use the utmost caution and patience I think we shall succeed. At least, if I may make a scientific and mathematical calculation and reduce it to the basis of percentage, I should say that out of a hundred chances we have fifty-five to their forty-five."

"And we also have a little inner circle of defense," said Charles. "We can unite in half a minute at any place of attack, while they are scattered widely."

"Quite so, quite so," said Professor Longworth, approvingly. "You make an excellent military point, not the least in our favor by any means. I judge that there will be no attack at present, and in a half hour or so, if I am right, Herbert, you might leave your station and water the stock again. There is nothing like keeping ourselves comfortable, while the Apaches are in the sun without water."

The Indians remained in three bodies about three-quarters of a mile away, and did nothing but make some derisive gestures. Those opposite to Professor Longworth were especially offensive in their manner.

"Jedediah," he said, "it may show a lack of poise in me, unworthy of a man of science, but the actions of those Apaches annoy me."

They were all so close in the little circle that they could see everything and could converse with one another in an ordinary tone.

"I think they're trying to make fun of us," said Jed.

"I'm quite sure they are," said Professor Longworth. "Such people as these are a strange compound of the savage and the child. If I may again use the scientific basis of mathematics I would say that they are sixty per cent savage and forty per cent child. Now, I wish that brute would stop making those horrible and offensive gestures! Nay, since you will not stop them, my brown friend, I must even stop you!"

He raised his rifle with the telescopic sights, the same with which he had made the wonderful shot down the valley slaying the shaman.

"I may not be as successful as I was before," he said. "That happens only once in a lifetime, but it is likely I can give our Apache friend a hint that his performances are disagreeable and must be stopped."

He sighted long and carefully, and pulled the trigger. The dancing Apache suddenly stopped dancing, clapped his hand to his shoulder, then sprang up-on his pony and galloped out of range, the other Apaches doing likewise. The Professor, after pulling the trigger, had dropped his rifle instantly, and picked up his glasses.

"I barked him in the shoulder," he said. "It was not a serious wound, but it stung and he has lost blood. You were foolish, my friend, to come within range of a rifle carrying telescopic sights, and you have paid the price."

The other two parties of Apaches also drew off at least a half mile more, and sat down on the sand. The Professor smiled, and his smile was that of a contented man.

"As they are at a good distance now," he said, "there is no reason why we should not enjoy all the comforts of home. Herbert, bring us food from the packs, and I think it is safe at last to drink as much of that fine cool water as we want."

Herbert obeyed with alacrity, and they ate and drank under the shade of the oaks and aspens. Strength flowed into their bodies and courage rose in their hearts. It seemed to the two boys that they could stand a siege there forever, and that they had little to fear, save an attack in the darkness.

"Is the night likely to be dark?" asked Charles of the Professor—he, too, had fallen into the habit of regarding this man as the possessor of all knowledge.

"Quite the contrary," replied Professor Longworth. "We are sure to have a clear blue sky, studded with a full moon and a myriad of brilliant stars."

"Then they cannot approach us unseen over the desert?"

"I think not. Not against eyes like ours, sharpened by danger and expectation. Now, Herbert, put away those scraps of food. We are well supplied, but as we may have a long siege here we must husband everything. After that both you and Charles can take a nap. Jedediah and I will watch."

Neither boy believed that it was possible to go to sleep, but both did so in a very short time. While they slept in the shade, the two men continually examined the plain. The Apaches remained in three groups, evidently meditating nothing for the present. Professor Longworth, even through his glasses, could not see any movement among them. Relaxed, they were waiting with invincible patience.

The sun declined. Cool shadows began to touch the sand, lately burning hot, and the loom of the distant mountains melted quite away. The three dots on the plain that marked where the Apaches rested disappeared, but the men could see clearly for a long distance on every side of the water-hole. The night came suddenly, and the stars sprang out, many and bright, as the Professor had predicted. He awoke the two boys, thinking it best that all should now be on guard, and taking their places, they watched.

Herbert and Charles were refreshed greatly, and having a sublime confidence in Professor Longworth, they awaited the issue without doubt.

The four took their stations at equal distances about the circle. Professor Longworth would have put the two boys together had it been possible, knowing that it would lend confidence to each other, but the whole plain must be covered and they stood, or rather sat, at different points.

Charles faced the north. He, like the others, waited in comfort. He sat on the edge of the slope, just behind great twin oaks, where he could see between them, and yet remain sheltered from the keenest eye. There was no strain at all about his position. He leaned easily again the grassy bank, and his rifle rested before him. All the heat of the day was gone, and a light, cool breeze blew among the trees. The horses and mules, having grazed in the deep grass until they could graze no more, were at rest and made no noise. From the well came the faint gurgle of the cold, swift stream. Overhead the great stars of the south wheeled and danced in a vast dome of silky blue.

It might have been a wilderness idyll. Those lying within the luxuriant green of the oasis saw only peace and beauty, all the greater by contrast with the desert without. But Charles had seen too much to be deceived by the quiet. He never ceased to watch that expanse of gray desert. The moon and great stars gave a good light, and he could see several hundred yards.

A long time passed. The four watchers exchanged occasional words across the tiny valley, and now and then Professor Longworth, leaving his post, stood a while in turn with the others, and gave them encouragement.

"The night will remain clear to the end," he said to Charles, "and it is in very truth a most lucky thing for us. The Apaches, knowing that we will watch, may consider the attack too dangerous, and go away. At least I hope so, but I do not expect it."

"Nor do I," said Charles. "I think they will try to stalk us."

"Very likely."

The Professor went on, spoke to Herbert also, and then returned to his own post. Charles continued to gaze out upon the plain, where nothing moved. More hours passed, but the brightness of the heavens was un-dimmed. The moon and stars yet shone with their full fire, and Charles, look-ing with all his eyes, could see nothing pass within his range of four or five hundred yards.

He heard once or twice a whirring in the trees above him. It was nesting birds returning to their homes in the tiny oasis. Out of the north came a faint, lonesome howl. It was the coyote lamenting his hunger.

Charles judged that it was now midnight, and his eyes were weary with straining over the gray plain. Now he fancied that he saw objects there, and then he knew that it was fancy only. The objects that he had seen were gone like moonshine. Came a time when one of them did not vanish. It was only a black spot on the desert's face, thin and impalpable like a shadow, but it re-mained. It interested Charles. He concentrated his gaze upon it, and he saw that it was moving toward the oasis.

In order to be sure that fancy was playing him no tricks he looked away and then looked back again. The shadow was still there, although a little nearer. It seemed to lie perfectly flat upon the face of the desert and to have no thickness at all. The word "shadow" fitted it perfectly. Then he saw behind it another shadow precisely similar and another and another.

Charles raised himself a little higher. He had seen so much now that imag-ination was forgotten. He reasoned like the Professor, with scientific and mathematical accuracy. Everything was reduced to the basis of percentage, and feeling that a certificate of no reasonable doubt could be issued he called gently to Professor Longworth, who came across the valley and joined him.

"See the line of shadows coming toward us?" said the boy.

"I do," said the man, "and that line of shadows is a line of Apaches. You have done well, Charles. You have seen in time their silent approach and we are forewarned. Bring Jedediah and Herbert, and, unless I reckon very badly indeed, a terrible surprise is awaiting somebody."

Charles called softly to the others, who joined them at the threatened point, and the four watched the line of shadows come nearer and nearer. The silent approach seemed ominous to Charles and he felt his blood grow cold. But the impulse to battle was rising higher in Jedediah Simpson than ever before. He was continually thrusting forward the muzzle of his rifle, but he would not pull the trigger except at the word of Professor Longworth, at whom he looked anxiously more than once.

"Not yet, Jedediah," whispered the Professor soothingly, "but it won't be long now. Charles, are those extra rifles ready?"

"Here they are, Professor."

"Very good. Now all of you can take aim. Herbert, you choose the first shadow, Charles you take the second, the third is for you, Jedediah, and I will

213

aim at the fourth. I will not count or say any words, but when I cough lightly, fire."

Charles lifted his rifle and aimed at the second shadow which was still slowly creeping forward. Then he waited. The deep silence was unbroken. The crawling Apaches made no noise, and it seemed that the Professor would never give the signal. But suddenly he coughed, and four rifles crashed as one.

Two of the Apaches still lay upon the ground, but they were not creeping forward any more. The other two who had been selected as targets leaped to their feet with cries of pain. The warriors behind them also sprang up, and uttering their war cry, rushed toward the oasis. But the four defenders snatched up the extra rifles and sent in more deadly bullets. Then their pistols flashed, and the Apaches flinched at the formidable barrier. Gathering up their fallen they swiftly disappeared again over the plain.

The complete silence came again, and it seemed that scarcely a minute had passed. There was nothing visible to remind the defenders of it but wisps of smoke floating among the trees. The startled animals, after a brief tumult, had also relapsed into stillness. They reloaded their weapons, and then they examined the plain from every side of the oasis. They saw no sign of the Apaches.

"They relied wholly upon surprise," said Professor Longworth, "and since they failed to achieve it they are not likely to attack again soon. The Apaches are not fond of storming a strong position held by desperate defenders. We will watch well, of course, but I think that we can take things easy for the rest of the night. I shall trust my judgment and you lads so far that I will take a nap myself."

He was as good as his word, rolling himself in his blankets and falling asleep very soon. But none of the others slept, although two were sufficient for the watch. Their nerves were not under as complete control as those of the great scientist and philosopher who was their leader. But Charlie and Herbert now sat together, while Jed watched from the other side.

"I'm glad the Apaches took their fallen away with them," said Herbert. "I should not like to see anybody lying out there."

"I'm glad, too," said Charles, and then after a moment's thought he added, "We're mighty lucky, Herbert, or Providence watches over us. In all our life in the wilderness something seems to happen in our favor whenever a great crisis comes. We wouldn't have had a chance against the Apaches if we hadn't found this water-hole just in time."

Herbert nodded.

"Even the skies remain bright at night in order that we may see the advance of the Indians," he said.

They watched until the coming of the dawn, when the brilliant sun sprang up and the hot glare of the day replaced the coolness of the night. They saw the Apaches far off, evidently taking their ease also. Professor Longworth awoke, and bustled about cheerfully.

"A happy morning to you, boys," he said. "It seems to me that we have indeed fared well. We yet hold our house, that is, this water-hole, and the fine bit of green surrounding it. We have an ideal place for both beauty and comfort while our besiegers must abide in the hot sand."

He examined them through his glasses. They were in only two parties now, and they were eating their breakfast. Apparently the taking of white lives was the last thing of which they were thinking.

"They are taking their food," said Professor Longworth to the others, "and it is a reminder to us that we, too, need breakfast. But we must first water the horses and mules, and I delegate that task to you two boys. Meanwhile I admire more and more the beauty of our combined nest and fort."

He looked with approval at the trees, the grass and the fountain. Herbert and Charles obeyed zealously, and gave the animals all the water they wanted. Then they brought up a supply for the two men and themselves and now they drank freely. They followed with a breakfast of good solid food from their packs. Jed went so far as to boil some coffee on a fire, made of fallen brushwood, and they found great solace in it. Then Professor Longworth surveyed the situation once more, and it gave him great satisfaction.

"Our besiegers," he said, "will have to send part of their force away to the hills after water, and they may also have to obtain a food supply. I think that in the language of the day it is the part of wisdom for us to sit tight. What we have to dread most is a dark night, but at this time of the year we are not likely to have it here in Arizona."

They spent a luxurious day. It was easy enough for one to watch while the others lay at ease or went about such tasks as they thought were needed. The second night came on, clear and bright like the first, with all the great stars out in their full glory. The Apaches, about midnight, crept within three or four hundred yards of the water-hole, and fired several shots at random. The defenders did not deign a reply, and another morning came, just as bright and hot as any of its predecessors.

The sunlight revealed the Apaches yet there at a safe distance. But their numbers seemed to be fewer than on the day before.

"They have sent the others for water," said the Professor. "They mean to hold us here indefinitely, trusting to some lucky chance that will put us in their power. Well, be it so. I know of no pleasanter place than this fragment of a green acre in which to pass a few days."

Professor Longworth was right. The long siege had begun. With infinite time at their disposal the Apaches had infinite patience. Days and nights passed. They stalked the water-hole in some fashion nearly every night, and once Jed was scratched by a bullet. One Apache fell before the return fire, but as he was carried away by his comrades they did not know if his wound was mortal. By day, the warriors sometimes indulged in sports on the sand, racing their horses and at times gambling. They seemed perfectly content with life, and prepared to stay a year.

The defenders were comfortable in body and mind the first four or five days, but then the boys began to grow nervous and restless. The eternal siege weighed upon their minds. They longed for movement. They wanted to be once more on the way to Phoenix with their gold. They also noted with alarm that their food supply had diminished greatly. But Professor Longworth was cheerful.

"Don't worry about starvation, boys," he said. "We have a number of excellent horses here to eat, not to mention the mules. Oh, you need not make wry faces. I know that horse meat is not a dish to set before a king, but in a pinch it will serve admirably. It has saved my life twice, once in South America and once in the deserts of Central Asia."

More days and nights passed. The last of the food supply was in sight, and Professor Longworth began to look seriously at the youngest of the horses. All of the animals were fat now, but they had eaten away most of the grass about the oasis, and, since they could not feed themselves much longer, it was evident that they must now feed their masters.

The next was the first dark night and the Apaches came very near, but they were driven off with a few good shots. All remained awake and at dawn Professor Longworth, who was examining the horizon with his glasses, broke through his usual calm and uttered a cry of joy.

"More horsemen are coming," he said, "and they are not Apaches. They are our own gallant cavalry, at least fifty in number. Look to the north there and you can soon see them with the naked eye. Lads, the long siege is raised!"

Soon the line of men in blue, riding hard, appeared above the horizon. They galloped straight toward the Apaches, who were obviously taken by surprise, and the rifles began to crack. It was an unequal combat. In a few moments the warriors, who had not fallen, were scurrying over the desert on their ponies. The four defenders, in their joy and enthusiasm, rushed from the trees and sent bullets after them.

Then the cavalry came up, led by a young captain named Collins, who smiled at the warmth of the greeting that was given to him.

"It seems that we have come in time," he said. "A wandering hunter who had seen some of them in the hills after water told us that the Apaches were down here somewhere on the warpath. So, we have come."

"Never were men more welcome," said Professor Longworth earnestly.

They reached Phoenix in due time and their treasure, divided into four exactly equal portions, was disposed of in safety. It created a great stir in the southwest, and many went into the mountains to search for more hidden treasure, but they found nothing.

*****

Two young men were in the graduating class at Harvard four years later. They were remarkable for size, strength and self-control. They had won honors alike in the classroom and on the athletic field. Herbert intended to be a lawyer and Charles a railroad builder in the west. Herbert's sorrow for the tragic death of his cousin had been abated considerably by the discovery on his return from Arizona that George Carleton had been converting his ward's money to his own use.

When the graduation exercises were over the two went to New York, and there, when a great liner came in, they gave a joyous welcome to a little man clad in khaki, wearing an enormous pith helmet and huge green glasses.

The newspapers had been saying a great deal lately about Professor Erasmus Darwin Longworth, who had discovered and exhumed the great, buried city in the southern part of Babylonia, thereby carrying back recorded history at least a thousand years. In fact, the entire learned world rang with the fame of this wonderful man. He had returned to his native land by the way of Europe, and his march was the triumphal progress of a king. A bitter rivalry arose among the famous universities. Every one was anxious to confer a degree upon him first. He could have used all the letters of the alphabet, in capitals, after his name, a dozen times over, had he chosen, but Professor Erasmus Darwin Longworth was a modest man, as all truly great men are.

Now, the Professor was thinking little of his degrees, but only of his two boys who were yet boys to him.

"Ah, Charles and Herbert, how good it is to see you again!" he exclaimed as he wrung a hand of each.

Tears were actually starting in his eyes, but fortunately they were hidden by the green glasses.

They stayed a few days in New York, and then took the train for Lexin'ton, K—y. A tall man, in a magnificent plaid suit, received them at the station. He drove them himself, behind two glorious bays in a high vehicle, painted red, not a shy, retreating red, but a daring, brilliant red, that could look the whole world in the face without shame, to the outskirts of the city, where they walked through wide, green grounds to a great, red brick mansion.

Jedediah Simpson o' Lexin'ton, K—y, preceded the others, and when he stood in his own doorway facing them, he said:

"Welcome. Welcome, pardners, to Arizony Place!"

Charles and Herbert jumped up the steps, but when Professor Erasmus Darwin Longworth, coming more sedately, put his foot upon the door sill, the D. M., at his seat high up in the hall, began to thunder forth upon the great organ the triumphal strain, "See the Conquering Hero Comes."

The End